DAYS LIKE THESE

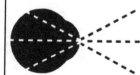

DAYS LIKE THESE

SUE MARGOLIS

KENNEBEC LARGE PRINT
A part of Gale, Cengage Learning

GALE
CENGAGE Learning·

Farmington Hills, Mich • San Francisco • New York • Waterville, Maine
Meriden, Conn • Mason, Ohio • Chicago

GALE
CENGAGE Learning®

LIBRARY OF CONGRESS CATALOGING-IN-PUBLICATION DATA

Names: Margolis, Sue, author.
Title: Days like these / by Sue Margolis.
Description: Large print edition. | Waterville, Maine : Kennebec Large Print, a part of Gale, Cengage Learning, 2017. | Series: Kennebec Large Print superior collection
Identifiers: LCCN 2017008480| ISBN 9781432839000 (softcover) | ISBN 1432839004 (softcover)
Subjects: LCSH: Domestic fiction. | Large type books. | BISAC: FICTION / Contemporary Women. | FICTION / Humorous. | FICTION / Family Life.
Classification: LCC PR6063.A635 D39 2017 | DDC 823/.914—dc23
LC record available at https://lccn.loc.gov/2017008480

Published in 2017 by arrangement with The Berkley Publishing Group, an imprint of Penguin Publishing Group, a division of Penguin Random House LLC

Printed in Mexico
1 2 3 4 5 6 7 21 20 19 18 17

I want to have children
while my parents are still young enough
to take care of them.

— Rita Rudner

CHAPTER ONE

"Gran'ma, did you know that a shrimp's heart is in its head?"

"I did not know that," I say, noting that my grandson's upside-down face has turned a worrying shade of red. He's doing a headstand on the sofa, his body leaning against the back cushions.

"It's true. I read it in my *Amazing Facts* book. And butterflies taste things with their feet."

"They don't. That's stupid," Rosie pipes up. "Now shut up. I'm trying to watch the movie."

"Yes, they do. And you shut up." Sam pokes his tongue out at his sister.

"Sam, don't do that. Rosie's right. You're spoiling the film. And I wish you'd get down off your head. Your face looks like a tomato. It can't be good for you."

"Gran'ma. Now you're talking, too," Rosie pleads. "I can't hear."

I whisper an apology.

"I like standing on my head," Sam says. "And Mum and Dad say it's OK."

His parents are both doctors, so — assuming he's telling the truth — who am I to argue?

"Well, I think you look stupid," says Rosie.

"You look stupid."

Rosie has had enough. She reaches onto the coffee table, picks up the remote and hits the off button. "There." She's sitting with her arms folded, her face defiant and cross.

"Hey, that's not fair," Sam says. "I was watching that."

"No, you weren't. You were talking and standing on your head."

"I can multitask." He sounds just like his father.

"And Gran'ma was talking, too."

"You're right," I say to Rosie. "We were both being rude." I shoot Sam a stern look, which I'm not sure he can see from his upside-down position. "We'll be quiet from now on . . . won't we, Sam?"

He offers a reluctant OK and then tells his sister to put the movie back on.

"No. You've both ruined it."

I've apologized. I'm not about to beg

forgiveness from an uppity five-year-old.

We've been attempting to watch *Wallace and Gromit* — the kids on one sofa, me stretched out on the other. Rosie had been campaigning to watch *Frozen.* Sam, who understandably loathes girlie princess films, was pretty vocal about not wanting to watch it. He was campaigning for *Spider-Man.* I was with Sam on this. Not only has Rosie forced me to watch *Frozen* so many times that every time I set the table I find myself singing "who knew we owned eight thousand salad plates?" — I also happen to think it's sexist twaddle. But *I let it go.* I've refrained from telling her that if she makes me watch it again, I will be forced to eat my own head. I have also resisted the urge — as has her mother — to spoil the magic by telling her that there's more to life than being in possession of a hand-span waist, strange steroidal eyes and a handsome prince.

Since Rosie refused to watch *Spider-Man,* I suggested a few gender-neutral films and in the end we agreed on *Wallace and Gromit: A Matter of Loaf and Death.*

"OK," Rosie says, partially emerging from her funk. "You can put the movie back on. But you both have to promise to be quiet."

"Duh. We already did." Her brother is roll-

9

ing his eyes. Since he's still standing on his head, this looks particularly amusing.

I pick up the remote and hit "play" — only it doesn't. The film starts speeding back.

"Grandma, what on erf are you doing?" Rosie cries. "Quick, press 'pause.' "

"I am pressing 'pause,' but it won't stop."

Rosie leaps off the sofa. "Look. You're pressing 'select.' My granddaughter can barely read, but she recognizes every word on the TV remote. She grabs it, hits "stop" and "fast forward" and in a few seconds we're where we're meant to be. She pats me on the head. "It's all right, Gran'ma. It's complicated for old peoples."

"Er, excuse me," I say, grabbing the remote again and with complete accuracy hitting "pause." "I'm not quite in my dotage. I only pressed the wrong button because I'm not wearing my glasses."

"What's 'dotage'?" Rosie says.

I explain.

"Nana Frieda's really old. So is she in her dotage?"

I want to say that my mother has been predicting her imminent decline and demise ever since I've known her. So you could argue that she's been in her dotage for the last fifty-seven years. But this isn't the time

10

for a discussion about how my mum has spent her entire adult life enjoying bad health. So instead I go for a more diplomatic response.

"Well, Nana's in her eighties, so technically speaking, I guess she is in her dotage. But I wouldn't say that when she's around. Plus she's pretty strong and still gets about so maybe she isn't quite there yet."

"Then why does she say she's ill all the time and that her kit-kas will be the end of her?" I'm laughing to myself. Hearing my grandchildren struggle to speak Yiddish always amuses me.

"And what are kit-kas?"

"It's pronounced 'kish-kas.' And it means guts."

"Yuck."

"Nana Frieda says things like that when she gets a bit tired. Don't take any notice. She's fine, honestly."

In fact, right now — despite her numerous ailments — my mother is shopping in the West End. She's gone with her best friend, Estelle Silverfish, to look at spring coats. I offered to drive them into town. But they said — quite rightly — that even on a Saturday the traffic would be murder. So they schlepped on the tube.

As the film gets under way for the third

time, the washing machine beeps from across the hall to tell me the laundry's done. If I don't transfer it to the dryer right away, I'll forget. Then everything will end up smelling of mildew and I'll need to put it through again. I tell the kids to carry on watching without me. Then I head into the downstairs loo-cum-laundry-room.

I try to ignore the bulging refuse sack sitting on top of the dryer. It's been there for months, stuffed with Brian's clothes. Not the decent stuff: the suits, jackets and lamb's wool sweaters. I haven't got the heart to bag them up — let alone get rid of them. This is just old jeans, shirts, boxers and the like. Every time I go to the supermarket, I mean to take the bag with me and drop it in the textiles recycling bin in the car park. But somehow it hasn't happened.

I transfer the laundry to the dryer, set the timer and hit "start." The whirring of the drum sets up a vibration. A thick navy sock with a yellow toe end falls out of the black sack, onto the floor. It's one of Brian's GoldToe socks. He used to say they were the most comfortable socks on the planet. He was evangelical about them. "Gold-Toe . . . now, there's a proper sock," he'd say to any male companion prepared to have his ear chewed. "It's like walking on a

12

cushion. The bugger of it is you can't get them over here, or even on Amazon. I order them from Macy's in New York. Even with the import duty, it's worth it."

He even gave Sam and Rosie's dad, Tom, a pair to try. Our son-in-law — who shops in American Apparel, wears edgy thick-rimmed glasses and has one of those short-back-and-sides, heavy-on-top hipster hair-cuts — accepted the seriously uncool socks with admirable good grace.

A few days later Brian wanted to know how he was getting on with them.

"Yeah. Great. Very comfortable."

Rosie, who was sitting on my lap, whispered in my ear: "Daddy's fibbing. Mummy won't let him wear them 'cos she says they're for old mens. But let's not tell Granddad 'cos he'll get upset."

I gave her a squeeze and said that might be for the best. Not that Brian would have been remotely offended if Tom or Abby had handed back the socks. Brian was many things, but thin-skinned wasn't one of them.

I pick up the sock and hold it to my cheek. Pretty soon I'm blubbing. It's been eighteen months since I last saw him. Touched him. Heard his voice. I'm still raw. Memories still lacerate.

For months, Abby has been nagging me

to get rid of the sack of clothes. Last weekend when she stopped by for a cup of tea, she was on me again.

"Mum, why is all that stuff still in the loo?"

"Come on. You have to admit I've made progress. The bag's been in my bedroom for months. At least now I've moved it downstairs."

"You have . . . into another holding area," she said, leaning against the kitchen worktop and taking another sip of tea. "How long do you intend to keep it there?"

"I don't know. Until I'm ready to part with it, I guess."

"But it's just old underpants and socks."

"I know, but your dad's clothes help me stay connected to him. Imagine if they were Tom's."

She took the point but she didn't back off. "Why don't you let me deal with it? There are recycling bins at the end of my street."

"Darling, I know you're trying to help, but you have to stop putting pressure on me. I'll know when the time is right."

"Somebody has to put pressure on you. It's been well over a year since Dad died and you still haven't cleared out his things. How many times have I offered to come and help? You need to do this."

"Why?"

"To move on."

"Why does the whole world want me to move on? Suppose I don't want to?"

"So instead of getting on with your life, you're going to stay like this . . . in some weird limbo. I don't understand."

"Of course you don't," I said, aware that my words sounded sharper than I had intended. "Because you've never had your husband of nearly forty years die on you."

"I know, but . . ."

"You have no idea what I'm going through. How much I'm still grieving. Every day I decide that this will be the day I'll get rid of the bag and then I find an excuse not to do it. I procrastinate because it feels like I would be abandoning him, casting him adrift."

Abby put an arm around my shoulders. "Oh, Mum . . . that's daft. You wouldn't be abandoning him. It's your memories that are important. Nothing could destroy those — certainly not getting rid of some clothes."

"You're right. I know I'm being ridiculous. . . ."

"And you know that Dad would have wanted you to get on with your life. It's time to start. It really is."

"And I will, soon. I just need a bit more time."

Abby sighed but didn't push it any further. We stood there, not saying anything for a few moments. Then, by way of lightening the atmosphere, she asked after her grandmother. "So, which bit of her body is Nana Frieda complaining about now?"

"Her kishkes seem to have gone quiet for the time being. Right now it's her legs and her back."

"I honestly don't know how you cope. I love Nana to bits, but she's so bloody needy."

When she was a young woman, my mother's ailments were imaginary. In her old age they are real, although — much to her disappointment — not particularly serious. These days my mother doesn't so much suffer from hypochondria as from hyperbole. The touch of arthritis, acid reflux and slightly raised blood pressure are real. The problem is the drama. Mum never has a bit of an ache or a pain. She is always in agony. When she catches a cold it's "an acute chest infection." A headache is a migraine. A stomach pain is gastric flu. You can bet your life that if my mother ever gets pneumonia, it won't be double — it'll be triple.

Her GP, the endlessly tolerant Dr. Moore,

whom she's been seeing for a decade or more, might send her for the occasional test. Mum gets straight on the phone to her friends from her seniors' day center: "The doctors" — note the plural — "have no idea what's wrong, so they're sending me for a battery of tests."

My mother uses illness to get love.

Time and again when I was a kid, I would come home from school to find her reclining on the sofa, forearm draped over her brow. "Judy . . . darlink . . . my back is in two." Only she pronounced "back" as "bek." She'd been in this country since she was seven years old and she'd never lost her German accent. "And maybe you could make me a hot water bottle." Or she would have one of her "migraines" and be in bed with the curtains drawn. In the summer her ankles would swell up so I would be the one schlepping bowls of cold water into the lounge so that she could soak her feet. "You're a goot girl," she would say. "Come here for a kiss." She would make room for me on the couch and cuddle me in her bony arms. Then she would start singing — softly, wearily as if she weren't long for this world: "You are my sunshine, my only sunshine. . . ."

I knew that people didn't die of backache

or swollen ankles, but even so I worried about my mother. It didn't help that she was so tiny and birdlike. Even without her symptoms, she gave off an air of vulnerability. I remember taking my fears to my father. I don't know how old I was — six or seven maybe.

"Daddy, is Mummy going to die?"

He started laughing. "Not unless she gets run over by a bus. I know there's not much of her and she doesn't look very strong, but your mother manages to cart huge bags of groceries back from the store every day. She cooks. She keeps the house spotless. Take it from me, the woman is as strong as an ox. Stop worrying."

"But she's ill all the time and I get scared."

"She's not ill exactly. She gets a bit under the weather sometimes. And then she needs to lie down. That's all it is. So just be kind."

"I am kind."

"I know you are, sweetheart," he said, cupping my chin. "It's hard for both of us. But we have to remember what she went through."

Those words have been the sound track to my life.

As I fill the kettle, I can hear squabbling coming from the living room.

Rosie: "You always get to choose what to watch. Now it's my turn. I want the remote."

Sam: "No. I'm the oldest. I'm choosing."

Rosie: "That's not fair. You're a big fat bully and I hate you."

It would appear that *Wallace and Gromit* has finished. Rosie starts wailing. I leave the kettle on the drainer and head into the living room. Abby says I make life hard for myself, wading in every time the kids squabble. She says she only goes to Sam and Rosie: "In the event of a heavy thud, loud crash, bloodcurdling screams that last longer than a minute . . . or they've been quiet for more than half an hour and have access to matches."

I've told Abby that if she's happy to ignore her kids when they start squabbling, that's fine by me. But she mustn't expect me to follow her example. Sam and Rosie aren't my children. I have an obligation to hand them back without dents, scuffs or missing body parts.

In the living room the kids are squaring up to each other. Rosie lands the first blow. She kicks her brother in the shin. "I hate you!"

Sam slaps her arm. Soon they're on the floor, arms and legs flailing. Since I would rather not get hurt, I decide against wading in to try to separate them. Instead I yell, "Right, that's enough! This ends now or there's no chocolate cake."

My mother's homemade chocolate cake — moist, thick, with buttercream filling and frosting — is one of their favorite treats. But they don't react to the threat.

"OK . . . If you stop right now you can have ice cream with it."

They're crimson-faced and scowling but standing still.

"Right . . . that's better."

"Gran'ma," Sam pipes up. "You just bribed us." His smarty-pants grin exposes his new teeth, which are too big for his nine-year-old face.

"Did I?"

"Yes. Plus you're rewarding our bad behavior. Mum tells Dad off when he does that. She says that if you bribe children or reward bad behavior, they turn into monsters."

"I don't want to turn into a monster," Rosie said.

"Shut up, Rosie. It doesn't mean actual monsters. It means you get to be horrible and spoiled."

I want to tell them that I bribed their mother from the moment she could grasp the concept and she hadn't turned into a monster. Back in the day — before the sanctimonious child experts put in their two pence' worth — besieged, dog-tired mothers like me may have thought twice about bribing their kids. But when they were out of options, they rarely thought a third time.

"Put your damn seat belt on! I said, put it on . . . OK, put it on and I'll take you to the park later. . . . Eat your cauliflower, and I'll let you watch *The Flintstones*."

When Abby refused to get dressed for school, I'd bribe her with sweets. I lost count of the times she left the house and the only thing in her stomach was a handful of red Skittles — she didn't like the other colors. As she got older and smarter, she demanded cash.

Abby didn't turn into a monster. She turned into a doctor — not that doctors can't be monsters. My mother insists she knows several: the ones who dare to tell her there's not much wrong with her.

People say that with a nurse for a mother, it's not surprising Abby decided to study medicine. But she could have followed her dad into teaching. I think there was more to her decision. Growing up, she worried to the point of obsession about any kind of suffering, be it animal or human. If she wasn't fretting about the badgers and the moles being left out in the winter cold, it was the starving children in Africa. Abby's need to bring aid to the afflicted seemed to be hardwired into her DNA. She was fifteen when she started reading books about Mother Teresa. When she decided to become a doctor, her father and I were delighted. "Thank the Lord for that," Brian said. "For a few years there I thought the kid was going to become a nun and bugger off to a leper colony."

After Abby qualified, she went into general practice. She also volunteered with the medical aid charity MediGlobal. Somehow she managed to sweet-talk the practice partners into allowing her six weeks' unpaid leave each year to do this.

Even as a medical student, when she couldn't work as a doctor, she would spend her vacations in the Congo or Malawi, going from one impoverished village to another giving talks about HIV or breastfeeding.

She met Tom shortly after she became a GP. She was doing a stint in Bangladesh after floods had devastated crops, destroyed homes and left thousands starving and injured. Abby was helping out at the maternity hospital. After a complicated delivery, a

22

baby boy had been left with a broken arm. Tom was a fellow volunteer and the young orthopedic surgeon who mended him.

I tell the kids that one bribe probably won't turn them into monsters. "Right, I think that in order to keep the peace, I should choose what you watch next."

" 'K." Neither of them seems overjoyed at the prospect.

But *Kung Fu Panda* seems to do the trick. I head off to the kitchen, telling them I'll give them a shout when the ice cream has defrosted.

It's almost four. Abby will be back from the hairdresser's anytime now. Mum shouldn't be far behind. She rarely stays out past teatime. I put the kettle on and take a tub of Ben & Jerry's out of the deep freeze. While I'm pottering I switch on the radio and catch the end of a heated debate about fracking. This segues into the news. After four days, they're still leading with the earthquake in Nicaragua. I turn up the volume.

"The quake, which has devastated several suburban areas around the country's capital, Managua, is being compared to the one that hit Haiti in 2010. So far it is thought to have claimed hundreds of lives. The number of injured hasn't been confirmed but is expected to be in the thousands. As they wait for aid to arrive, those who have lost their homes will be spending another night on the streets amid the destruction and devastation. . . ."

I can still remember the TV images from Haiti — frantic parents, their clothes ripped apart in searching for children in the rubble. Bewildered kids, some little more than toddlers, wandering the streets. But the news is always full of tragedy and catastrophe. People become immune. We shut off. Others, like Abby and Tom, don't do that. They find it impossible. Tom went to Haiti. Abby wanted to go, but Sam was only two and she couldn't bear to leave him. In fact, she hasn't been on an assignment for Medi-Global since well before the children were born.

Abby told me the other day that Tom wanted to go to Nicaragua. But it depended on whether the hospital was prepared to release him. Right now they're short of doctors. I would have asked her for an update when she dropped off the kids, but she was running late and didn't get out of the car.

Sam interrupts my thoughts. "Gran'ma, please, can me and Rosie have some OJ or apple juice?" My grandson likes to try his luck. Abby and Tom only allow the kids to have fruit juice as a special treat.

"No. It has to be water. Fruit juice rots your teeth. You know that." I start running the tap.

"Did you know that Dad's going to the earthquake place to help all the hurt people?"

"I didn't. But your mum said he might be going. How do you feel about that?"

"Good. He's making people better. If he didn't go they might die."

"That's right. You should be very proud of him."

"I am. I'll miss him, but me and Mum and Rosie can manage without him for a bit. Other people need him more."

I tell my grandson what a generous, kind and very grown-up young man he is. He blushes.

I know that Abby is more than capable of managing without Tom. But when she told me that he was hoping to go to Nicaragua, she didn't seem too happy about it. She looked weary and preoccupied. It occurred to me that she was angry about being left alone to cope with her job and the kids. It wasn't like Abby, but maybe she'd accused him of abandoning her and they'd had a fight.

I hand my grandson two glasses of water.

"Please try not to spill it."

" 'K."

He disappears into the living room. When the doorbell rings, I'm in the middle of trying to get my mother's chocolate cake out of the storage container. I've been clumsy and my fingers are covered in frosting. "Can one of you get that?" I call out to the kids. "It'll be your mum."

A moment later Abby appears. "OK, be honest," she says, putting her keys and handbag down on the kitchen table. "Have I had too much taken off? Is it a total disaster?"

My daughter's straight fair hair, which used to come halfway down her back, now skims her collarbone. The heavy, blunt fringe touches her eyebrows. With her thick black eyeliner that flicks at the corners, she looks like an Egyptian princess — only more Aryan.

"It's fab. Honestly. Makes you look more sophisticated — more grown-up."

"You mean old."

"No. I mean sophisticated. I love it."

"Really?"

"Really. Now stop being so needy and go and get some plates and lay the table."

She's about to hang her coat on the back of the chair and she stops. "Is that really how you see me? As needy?"

I'm caught off guard. "What? No. Of course not. It was an off-the-cuff comment. Why are you being so sensitive?"

She hangs up her coat. "Sorry. I didn't mean to jump down your throat. Things are a bit fraught, that's all."

"I can imagine. Sam just told me Tom was going to Nicaragua."

"Yeah, the hospital just gave the OK."

"When does he leave?"

"Day after tomorrow. They're flying him out on a military transport." She asks me to make an extra cup of tea, since Tom's on his way over to say cheerio.

"Are you worried about him going?"

"They're talking about the possibility of aftershocks. Then there's the usual danger of typhoid and cholera. But Tom's had all his vaccinations. He doesn't drink the water. There's not much else you can do."

The bell goes again. Thundering child hooves down the hall. "Hey, Dad. I've been telling Gran'ma how shrimps have their hearts in their heads and butterflies smell with their feet."

"Wow. I bet she found that fascinating."

"We're in the kitchen," Abby calls out.

Tom is wearing a puffer jacket and beanie hat. He's blowing on his hands, which are

27

red from the cold. I ask why he's not wearing gloves.

"Lost them."

"Again?" Abby says. "You're worse than the kids. I'm going to buy you a pair of mittens on a string."

"OK, but they have to be SpongeBob."

"You got it."

As Tom takes off his hat and coat, he notices Abby's hair. "Wow."

"You hate it."

"Since when did 'wow' mean 'I hate it'? I love it shorter. Makes you look older."

"Older?"

"Sophisticated," I hiss. "Tell her it's sophisticated."

"I heard that," Abby says, doing her best to look offended.

"Yeah, very sophisticated," Tom parrots. He sits himself down at the table. Under his breath he's singing "You're So Vain."

Abby slaps his arm. "I hate you."

"No, you don't. You adore me." He's looking up at her, grinning.

Abby snorts and fetches the mugs of tea, which I've left next to the kettle. As I sit down, I find myself wondering what's going on between these two. They're joking around, but Abby's being touchy. She's definitely got something on her mind. I get

28

the feeling there's more to it than her being worried about Tom going to Nicaragua.

"By the way," I say, handing Tom a slice of cake, "Sam just told me how proud of you he is."

"Yeah, he told me, too. But he's making the most of it. He's made me promise to give a talk to the school when I get back, so he can show off."

Abby pulls out a chair. I catch her and Tom exchanging what I can only describe as a "purposeful" look.

"What?" I say.

They look at each other again — clearly trying to decide which of them is going to explain whatever it is that needs explaining.

"Oh, for heaven's sake," I say, handing Abby some cake. "You're like a couple of kids. Will one of you please tell me what's going on?" I hold Abby's plate of cake in midair, refusing to hand it over until somebody speaks.

Abby takes a breath. "Right . . . So, here's the thing. I've been doing a lot of mulling over the last few days. In fact, I've hardly slept . . ."

"Why? What's the matter?"

"I think I want to go to Nicaragua with Tom." She relieves me of the plate, but my hand stays where it is.

29

"Wow . . . OK . . . So, when you say think . . ."

"I mean I want to go. I'm needed. You've seen the pictures on TV. The place has been practically reduced to rubble. They're crying out for doctors. I can't just sit here —"

"But what about the kids?"

"OK . . . I know I've said I'd never leave them, but I've been thinking about it. . . . I'm pretty sure they could cope . . ." She pauses. "So . . . how would you feel about having them?"

She doesn't let me answer.

"I know it's a huge favor to ask . . ." Another glance at Tom. ". . . particularly right now with everything you're going through. You absolutely have to tell me if you're not up to it."

"How long would you be gone?"

"Six weeks is the minimum commitment MediGlobal will accept. Tom plans to stay longer."

"We thought about asking my mum and dad to come down from Scotland," Tom says. "But they're not fit enough. Mum's in constant pain from her arthritis. Dad's back is playing up again. It would be too much for them."

Sam and Rosie have been coming to stay since they were babies. This house is their

30

second home. Even now, without Brian around to help, I'm keeping up the tradition of having the kids for the occasional weekend to give their mum and dad a break. But six weeks . . . Abby's right. It is a huge thing to ask. I'm just not sure I'll be able to cope.

"Wow. You've certainly put me on the spot."

Abby turns on Tom. "See? I told you it would be too much for her."

"Don't have a go at me. It was your idea to ask her."

"Er, hello. I am here, you know. You don't have to talk about me in the third person." I wrap my hands around my mug of tea and turn to Abby. "So you've arranged time off from the practice?"

"Mum, honestly. It doesn't matter. Please . . . forget I said anything."

"Just answer my question."

"Yes . . . I've arranged time off. The practice partners are happy to give me unpaid leave. They'll get in a locum to cover for me."

"Right . . . So, the new school term starts next week, which means the kids would be off my hands during the day."

"Mum, leave it. I don't want you talking yourself into this."

"I agree," Tom says. "Don't worry. There will be other disasters." He finishes with a quiet, poignant laugh.

"How long do I have to think about it?"

"That's the thing," Abby says. "I need an answer pretty much right away. I called Medi-Global. There's a spare seat on Tom's transport. They're putting pressure on me to let them know if I'm taking it. Otherwise they'll give it to somebody else."

If Abby goes to Nicaragua she will save lives. Without wishing to sound too noble, I believe that I have a moral duty to support her. But I say nothing. Instead I sit staring into my tea, thoughts careering around my head. Abby breaks the silence.

"Look, it's fine. It was just a whim on my part. I'm sorry."

"Don't be sorry." I ask her if she remembers the conversation we had the other day. "You told me it was time I started living again."

"And you told me you're not ready."

"Nana thinks I'm ready. She's even been at me to start dating."

"And what did you tell her?"

"I told her she's crazy."

"Exactly."

"But that doesn't mean she doesn't have a point. I dunno . . . perhaps I've become ad-

32

dicted to grief."

"Will you listen to yourself? I've made a mistake. This is all way too fast. You can't just snap out of grief."

"Who's talking about snapping out of it? All I'm suggesting is that the children might give me a new focus and help me reconnect with the world a bit quicker."

"Sounds good in theory," Tom says. "But what if you can't cope?"

"So one of you would get on a plane and come home. It wouldn't be the end of the world."

Abby shrugs. "I guess not."

It's fast becoming a no-brainer. "I want to give this a go. Please let me."

"But what about Nana? I didn't even think about her. You've got her to worry about, too. The kids would just be adding to your stress."

"Maybe not. Your nana might be a moaner, but she's also a feeder. She's not going to miss out on a catering opportunity. Believe me, she'll be in her element. I'm thinking that having the kids here could do her a power of good, too."

"You could always stay at our house if that would be easier," Abby says.

I remind her that their house — although bigger — is on four levels. Nana couldn't begin to manage the stairs.

Abby looks at me, still unsure. "So you're really up for this?"

"I'll give it my best shot. . . . To be honest, I'm more worried about you. Are you sure you're OK about leaving the kids?"

"Not really. Just thinking about leaving them makes me feel like a terrible mother. But if I don't go — if I stay here and do nothing — I might feel worse. Not now maybe, but in years to come."

Abby says they will speak to the children as soon as they get home. "If they give the OK, I'll get on the phone to MediGlobal to confirm that I'll be on the flight. If the kids object, I won't go."

I start gathering up empty mugs.

"Rosie's the one I'm really worried about," Abby says. "She's barely out of kindergarten. I can't leave her to pine for me and cry herself to sleep every night."

Tom reminds her that this is the child who went camping for a week last summer with her best friend, Cybil, and Cybil's parents. Tom proceeds to give a high-pitched impersonation of his daughter: " 'I had a whole new mummy and daddy. It was great. They let us stay up late every night and we could have Coke whenever we wanted.' "

We're still laughing when, right on cue,

Sam and Rosie come bursting in. "Gran'ma, we're hungry," Rosie says, climbing up to the table. "Is the ice cream ready yet?"

"I'm sure it is."

"Er, excuse me," Abby says. "What's the magic word?"

"Abracadabra," the kids bellow in unison. It's an old family joke. Abby waits for the correct response. Having received the obligatory "please," I cut them each a slice of cake while Abby fetches the ice cream.

"Tell you what," she says. "You can have two scoops as a special treat."

"Why are we having a special treat?" Rosie asks.

"I thought you deserved it."

"Why?"

Sam tells his sister to be quiet. He's clearly worried that Rosie is about to spill the beans about their fight over the TV remote. In which case, their mother might well rescind her ice-cream offer.

There's the sound of a key in the door. Mum calls out to say she's home. I ask if she fancies a cup of tea.

"Does the Pope do his business in the woods?"

"Nana's got it wrong," Sam says. "It's either 'Is the Pope Catholic?' or 'Does a bear shit in the woods?'"

35

His mother tells him off for swearing.

"But that's the saying: Does a bear shit in the woods? And why can't I say 'shit'? You and Dad say it all the time."

"That's because we're grown-ups," Tom says. "We get special privileges. People don't like to hear kids swear."

"That's not fair."

"I agree. But do your mum and me a favor and suck it up. One day you'll be allowed to swear."

"OK, so can I say shit when I'm twelve?"

"Maybe."

"What about fuck?" Rosie pipes up.

Abby looks wide-eyed at her daughter. "Shit, Rosie . . . I mean, good Lord. Where did you learn that?"

"Cybil's mummy and daddy say it all the time."

"Oh, great."

"And so do you and Dad."

"We do not."

"Yes, you do. You whisper it, but me and Sam still hear."

Mum comes shuffling and puffing into the kitchen. Sometimes when she goes out I stand at the window and watch her disappear down the street. She doesn't stride out exactly, but she plods with attitude. Right now, though, she's being her needy self and wants to emphasize her leg, back and bunion pain.

"My God, it's bitter out there," she says by way of a general greeting. "I can't believe it. The sun was shining when I left. The only thing keeping me warm in town was my heartburn."

Mum is minus carrier bags. I'm assuming she failed to find a new spring coat. She kisses Abby and Tom and tells them how well they're looking. "Still, you're young. Why wouldn't you?" She moves round the table to Sam and Rosie. "And how are my favorite great-grand-children?" She pinches Sam's cheek and then Rosie's. They both squirm. But they've come to appreciate that it's the price they have to pay for the occasional five-pound note.

"So, you didn't find a coat?" I say as the kettle starts boiling.

She waves a hand in front of her.

"Bloomin' waste of time that was. There's nothing to be had for love nor money. When you reach my age, you want something comfortable and serviceable. Do you think I could find it?"

These days my mother favors practicality over elegance: elasticized waists, sneakers with Velcro fasteners and polyester slacks that barely get wet when you wash them.

She tugs at the buttons on her long quilted parka. She bought it for the fur-lined hood. "All I want is a simple car coat. Is that too much to ask?" She sits down and starts rubbing the small of her back.

Tom suggests she might benefit from seeing an osteopath.

"I've seen dozens. Judy. Haven't I seen dozens?"

"You have." I place a mug of tea on the table in front of her.

"They know nothing. They click you here. They click you there. All they do is click. Waste of time."

"What about taking some ibuprofen?"

"Upsets my stomach." She winces before taking a hearty slurp of hot tea.

Tom is clearly at a loss. I decide to change the subject. "So, how's Estelle Silverfish?"

Everybody — apart from her nearest and dearest and my mother — refers to Estelle as Estelle Silverfish. None of us seems to tire of the joke — that this Jewish-sounding surname is also a small bathroom parasite.

"Her granddaughter — you know, the one that's gay — well, she's getting married next year. I've been invited, which is kind of them. Not that I'll go. I don't have the energy these days. But it's nice to be asked."

Rosie, who has been quietly stuffing

herself with ice cream, pauses between mouthfuls. "Gay is when womens love womens and men love men, right?"

"Yeah," Sam says. "And girls who are gay . . . they're called lesbinans."

Rosie nods. "So, if a woman is getting married to another woman, do they both get to wear bride dresses with veils, and crowns with jewels?"

"If they want to," Abby says.

"Would they wear dresses that matched or different ones?"

"Probably different."

"That means that after the wedding they can swap dresses and play princesses." She takes a bite of chocolate cake and thinks for a bit. "Nana Frieda, are you in your dotage?"

"In my what?"

"Dotage. Grandma said you were."

"And Grandma," I whisper-shout, "also told you to keep quiet."

"Sorry. I forgot," Rosie says, scratching at the glitter sea horse tattoo on the back of her hand. She turns back to Nana Frieda. "So, are you in it?"

"What can I tell you? When you get to my age, you don't make plans like you used to."

Abby shoots me a pleading look. I turn to my mother.

39

"Mum, do you have to be so maudlin in front of the kids?"

"Well, they need to know that I'm not going to be around forever." She pauses. "Oh, changing the subject, I've got something to show you."

My mother reaches into her oversize handbag and pulls out a MacBook Air.

"Mum," I say, "you appear to have bought a laptop."

"Wow, Gran'ma . . . cool."

Tom starts laughing. "Good for you, Nana."

"I didn't buy it. Estelle was given it by one of her rich nephews who's upgrading. If you look you can see it's a bit scratched."

I ask her why Estelle Silverfish doesn't want it.

"She's got nobody to show her how it works. She wants me to ask Tom to set it up. She's obsessed with getting on the Web." She pauses and lowers her voice. "Of course you know why. She wants to start dating. . . . At her age. I've told her she's crazy wanting to meet strangers she's never met."

"As opposed to strangers she has met," I say.

"You know what I mean. I've told her it's not safe. What if she gets attacked — or worse?" She turns to Tom. "So if you could

40

help, that would be wonderful. But only if you've got time." She doesn't know that Tom is leaving for Nicaragua.

"I can come over tomorrow," he says.

"No, you can't," Abby says under her breath. "We've got way too much on."

"I can multitask."

Abby rolls her eyes. "No, you can't. What you'll do is delegate. To me."

"The thing is," Nana says, "I'm not sure that at my age I'm up to learning about computers."

"It's easy," Sam says. "You wait. Soon you'll be able to Google and Skype and I'll help you download *Minecraft.*"

My mother is staring at Sam. "I didn't understand a single word you just said."

Rosie asks if she can have another piece of cake.

Before Abby can say "No, you won't eat your supper," Mum is sinking a knife into frosting.

"When I'm big and I've got my ears pierced and I'm allowed to say fuck," Rosie says, "I'm going to get married to a girl. How do you know if you're a lesbinan?"

CHAPTER TWO

That morning — the morning it occurred to me that Brian might be seriously ill — I'd brought him tea in bed. Of the two of us, I was the lark. Once I was awake I had to be up and doing. Brian would remain horizontal until the last possible minute. I brought him tea most days.

I placed the mug on the nightstand and opened the bedroom curtains. The sky was blue and cloudless. Sunlight streamed into the bedroom.

Brian grumbled about it being too bright and pulled the duvet over his head like a teenager. "What time is it?"

"Late."

"How late?"

"Gone seven."

"Shit. I've got a staff meeting before school." Brian was head of Parsoles Academy in Peckham. Known universally as Arseholes Academy, it was one of the toughest inner-city schools in the country. Brian had been there three years. He didn't think he'd achieved much in that time. But he had. By then none of the kids came to school with knives, they stood up when a member of staff came into a room and most of them referred to Brian — to his face, at least — as Mr. Devlin rather than Number One Arsehole.

As he chugged down his hot tea — Brian had been blessed with kishkes hewn from cast iron — I noticed that his face looked a bit yellow. Lately he'd also been complaining of backache and stomach pains. When I remarked on his skin color, he said he'd noticed it last night when he was in the shower. "I thought it was just the bad light."

He took my advice and made an appointment with the doctor. She sent him for tests. I suspected and dreaded what the results might be. As a nurse I knew too much. I said nothing to Brian. Instead I prayed that I'd got it wrong.

One night while we were still waiting for the test results, I discovered him Googling his symptoms. He was on the NHS Web site, reading about pancreatic cancer.

"For Chrissake, Brian, that's the worst thing you could be doing. You're just scaring yourself. It could be nothing."

He told me to stop patronizing him and said he wasn't one of my dimwit patients who were happy to have the wool pulled over their eyes.

Brian and I decided not to say anything to Abby and Tom until we had the test results. We knew that being doctors, they would be angry with us for holding back. But Abby was also our daughter. We didn't have the heart to tell her until it was necessary.

The oncologist sat us down and said he wished he had better news. As we suspected, it was pancreatic cancer. What was more, it had spread to the liver. It was inoperable. Brian may have winced as he received his death sentence, but apart from that he showed no emotion. He didn't even look at me. I suspect he couldn't bear to see the anguish on my face. When I reached out and touched him, he flinched and batted me away. For the next few minutes he sat there listening to the oncologist talking to him about palliative care. He nodded and interrupted to ask the odd question. Once or twice he even smiled. He could have been in a meeting with his accountant. "How long?"

"We try not to talk about time frames. People vary so much."

"I won't hold you to it. Are we talking

years or months?"

"Months."

"I see." Again not a shred of emotion. "How many?"

"It's hard to say, but probably less than a year."

"And you're absolutely sure there's nothing to be done?"

"I'm sorry. . . ."

"Please don't be. It's hardly your fault." Only then did Brian turn to me. "Well, at least we know where we stand."

I couldn't bear his stoicism, his resignation. He wasn't even sixty. He couldn't go without a fight. I demanded a second opinion, insisted that there had to be something medical science could do.

"Mrs. Devlin . . . I know this is hard. . . ."

"What about medical trials? . . . New drugs?"

"I'm sorry. At the moment there's nothing."

I wanted to get a taxi home, but Brian insisted we take the tube because it felt more normal. As we set off toward the station, I asked him if he was all right — which was stupid. The man had just been told he was dying. Despite the stoicism, there was no way he was all right.

"Do you mind if we don't talk for a bit?"

he said. So I left him alone. He picked up an *Evening Standard* at the entrance to Regent's Park Station and spent the journey with his head behind it. I had no idea if he was actually reading it. The moment we got home he said he needed to go to his study and check his e-mail.

"Can't you leave it?" I said, taking off my coat. But he was already halfway down the hall. I went after him. "We've both had a terrible shock. Let's sit down and have a cup of tea."

"I can't. There might be something urgent. Why don't you bring me a cup?"

"Brian, please don't shut me out. Stay and talk to me."

"What about?" he barked, striding back toward me. His emotions had finally caught up with him and he was scaring me. "The fact that I'm dying? That I'm petrified? That I'm so fucking angry I want to punch somebody in the face?"

"Yes."

His features contorted. I opened my arms and he came to me. He let me wrap him up and rock him as he sobbed and railed against the world and told me again and again that he didn't want to die.

That night neither of us slept. We stayed up talking. "Why you? You of all people?

You're such a good man."

"I don't think goodness has much to do with it. Pol Pot lived into his seventies."

The next day was Saturday. Brian spent most of it wandering around the house in his pajamas. I made cups of tea that we forgot to drink. On Sunday night he announced that he was going back to work. I begged him not to. "You're still in shock. You need some time to adjust, to take it all in."

But he insisted he needed to get back to normal and that burying himself in his job was the only way to take his mind off the cancer.

Abby and Tom started e-mailing medical colleagues in the US and Europe to double-check that there weren't any drug trials that Brian could take part in. But the oncologist had been right. There was nothing.

Meanwhile I spent hours on the Internet, searching for new treatments. All I found was page after page of cancer quackery. Brian was deteriorating so fast that sometimes I found myself suggesting to Abby that we give some of it a try. "It says here that sharks don't get cancer. What's the harm in giving your dad some shark's fin preparation?"

Abby would give me a look. "Mum, you

did graduate from nursing college, didn't you?"

After weeks of my nonsense, Brian got cross. He said I was turning into an obsessed crazy woman. "Step away from the Internet and let's just make the best of whatever time we have left."

There was one last family Christmas. What do you give a dying man? Answer: box sets. I bought *Fawlty Towers*. Amy and Tom got him *Blackadder* and *The Office*.

On Christmas Day, the kids tore through the house, high on sugar and excitement. I cooked lunch with Abby as my sous-chef. Afterward we watched the Queen's Speech and made fun of it. What did the royals know about anything? Brian said — as he said every year — that the whole lot of them should be made to live in the projects. Later on we played charades and Jenga. It was a perfect family day and it practically ripped Brian's heart from his chest. "I can't believe I'm not going to see Sam and Rosie grow up."

By New Year's the weight was starting to fall off him. We weren't expecting him to last more than a few weeks. But somehow he hung on for eight months. During that time, he even made plans. "Sod it. Let's have a few days in the South of France. I'm buggered if I'm about to go gentle into that good night." The South of France never happened. He tried to kid himself that he was up to it. But he was too weak. Brian took to his bed in late summer, just as the leaves were starting to turn brown and fall. The symbolism wasn't lost on him.

I took time off from hospital nursing to nurse my husband. Our family doctor had suggested he go into a hospice. Brian's response was unambiguous. "Death among the dying? Fuck that for a game of soldiers!"

In those final weeks, I spent hours lying next to him — even when he slept. I didn't want to miss a second of the time I had left with him. When he was awake, we watched episodes from one of his box sets, looked through photograph albums, maybe with Paul Simon or Dire Straits playing in the background. Mainly we lay in each other's arms and talked. By now we'd stopped crying and the anger was gone. Time was too precious. By the time Brian died, we'd said everything there was to say.

Abby stopped by most evenings. She would sit with him for a few hours — whole days on the weekend — to give me a break. I was exhausted — particularly as Brian got restless at night and found it hard to sleep. He wasn't in pain — the morphine saw to that. I think he was simply terrified of dying and the darkness made it worse. But after a while the strain started to show on Abby, too. She had her job and the children to look after. She needed a break as much as I did. I called her the night that would turn out to be Brian's last. I told her that she was wearing herself out and that she needed some downtime with Tom and the kids. "Have an early night. Maybe pop in tomorrow on your way to work."

As usual, I lay with him on the bed. It was a warm September evening. The windows were open. The scent of honeysuckle wafted in from the garden. Thanks to the morphine, he was sleeping most of the time. When he woke, it was for no more than a few minutes. He would sip some water — me holding the glass — but he had no interest in food. We didn't chat anymore. He didn't have the strength. When he tried to speak — mostly to ask for something — his sentences trailed off, leaving me to finish them. Instead of talking, we held hands.

I decided to put a *Fawlty Towers* episode on the player. As the signature tune started up, Brian smiled in his sleep. I'd chosen his favorite episode — the one in which Basil beats his ancient car with a branch because it refuses to start. After ten minutes or so, I was aware that Brian's breathing had changed. The gap between one breath and the next was getting longer. This was how people died. I'd seen it dozens of times. He wouldn't come round again. But he did. "I adore you," he said, gazing at me, eyes wide-open. I leaned in and kissed his chapped lips. "I adore you, too, my darling." I held his hand against my face and kissed it. His eyes closed. I found myself willing him to take one more breath and then another. He managed a few. Then he stopped.

Fawlty Towers was still playing in the background.

I called Abby straightaway. It was only when she arrived that the tears came — hers and mine. We stood by the bed and held each other, bodies heaving, sobbing for all the world to hear.

When there were no more tears left, I said I would make some tea. "You stay with your dad. I'll bring it up."

We sat on the bed, on either side of Brian's body, sipping tea and dunking fingers of Kit Kats.

"Remember how Dad used to dip a Kit Kat finger in his tea and suck on it as if it was a straw?"

I felt myself smile. "And he made such a horrible noise. I hated it."

"He was a great dad." She took his limp hand and kissed it.

"He was. And he thought the world of you."

"I know. It was mutual."

Abby offered to sleep over.

"No, it's OK. You go home. I'll be fine." I sensed that she didn't really want to stay, that she wanted to be in her own bed with Tom's arms around her. And if I was honest, I wanted to be on my own with Brian.

I lay down beside him for the last time. It didn't feel macabre. It felt natural. I told him again how much I loved him. I stroked his face. It was covered in thick gray stubble. I hadn't shaved him for over a week. I ran my fingers over his nose, stroked the familiar small bump just below the bridge. I felt the ridges on his nails, the lines on his palms. I kissed the dark freckles on his arms. I wanted to remember every bit of him. "You need a haircut," I said. "But I don't suppose anybody will mind."

Brian had no time for funerals and especially not for eulogies. "The moment people die, they become bloody saints. If you want to say anything at my funeral, just get up there and tell them how I snored and farted."

He chose to be cremated. Cremation was cheaper than burial and Brian could see no sense in his bones taking up valuable space. My mother didn't approve. Cremation was against Jewish law. "Mum, what are you on about? Brian was a Catholic atheist — just like Dad. And when Dad died, you had no qualms about cremating him."

She said she knew all that, but she'd lived to regret it. "I can't help thinking there's something so cold about cremation."

I said I'd get the crematorium to turn up the heat. She asked how I could make jokes at a time like this.

Arseholes Academy was closed for the day so that the staff could attend the funeral. A selection of pupils from each year group came, too. Just looking at the kids, immaculate for once in their blazers and ties, made me cry.

I managed to say a few words during the service. I couldn't bring myself to make wisecracks — and certainly not the ones Brian had suggested. Instead I quoted W. H. Auden: "He was my North, my South, my East and West . . ." Abby read the Dylan Thomas poem "Do Not Go Gentle into That Good Night."

People meant well when they told me that Brian had gone to a better place. What? I thought — better than here with me?

At the wake, the deputy head's wife went all Facebook affirmation on me: "You'll get through this. God never gives you more than you can handle." Having spent the day struggling to hold myself together, I was lost for words. All I could do was stare at the woman. It turned out that my mother had overheard the remark. "Somebody should have mentioned that to the people on their way to being gassed in the concentration camps," she said. "Particularly the children." Then she got hold of my arm and pulled me away.

During those early weeks, the first thing I thought about on waking and the last thing I thought about at night was that Brian was dead.

For months I hated going to the supermarket. I couldn't bear watching smug, loved-up couples doing their weekly shopping. I would watch as they cruised the aisles, clutching their TV chef recipes, searching for sumac and nigella seeds. I imagined them in their apartments, unpacking another kitchen gadget they'd just bought from Amazon. More than once I caught myself blubbing at the checkout and wondering why I wasn't doing my food shopping online.

When I tell people that it's the intimacy I miss, they think I mean sex. But it's not that. It's the emotional intimacy — being loved and known. They say you can never really know a person. But I think Brian and I came close.

Mum was helping me load the dishwasher after Brian's wake when she suggested moving in with me. "These first few weeks are going to be hard. I know. I've been there. You shouldn't be on your own."

I couldn't believe what I was hearing. My shocked expression clearly alarmed her.

"I'm sorry," she said. "I've upset you."

"No, of course you haven't. Quite the opposite."

For once my endlessly needy mother was putting me first. She wanted to take care of me instead of it being the other way around.

Taken aback and grateful as I was, I turned her offer down. I was determined to manage on my own. Mum shrugged and said it was my life. It was up to me. "But pick up the phone if you need me. Promise?" I promised.

Two weeks after Brian died I went back to work. I reasoned that staying at home moping would only make me more miserable. Work would be the best therapy — just as it was for Brian in the days following his diagnosis.

I'd worked on the same surgical ward for two decades and I counted many members of staff as friends. Several had come to the funeral. That first day back, I was greeted with an outpouring of kindness and condolences. I was instructed to ease myself in, to pace myself. But surgical wards are hectic. The truth is that no allowances could be made for a struggling, newly bereaved widow. Overnight, I went from the quiet comfort blanket of home to setting up IVs, giving shots, handing out medication and taking blood. The ward was full of people recovering from serious surgeries. I couldn't take my eye off the ball. Mistakes weren't an option.

The pressure meant I had no time to think about myself.

While I was working, I felt lighter of spirit. Then I would return home to a dark, empty house. Even though I'd been rushing around all day, burning off calories, I was never hungry. I lived on cheese and pickle sandwiches. I would eat while I watched the TV news. Not that I was remotely interested in current affairs. I didn't give a damn about anything other than my own grief. But I knew it would be unhealthy to retreat and lose touch with what was going on in the world. So I forced myself to pay attention to the latest interest rate rises and government spending cuts. Watching a TV drama or film was out of the question, though. I couldn't concentrate.

After the news, I would potter about, doing chores. Around ten, I'd take a shower and fall into bed, done in. Back then I still kept one of Brian's sweaters under my pillow. Every night since his death I'd fallen asleep holding it, breathing in his smell. But it was beginning to wear off. It felt as if I was losing him all over again. That was when I stopped sleeping.

In the morning I would drag myself out of bed and go downstairs to make a mug of strong black coffee. On the table to greet me was my plate from the night before — still covered in bread crumbs. Sometimes I didn't even bother to wash it. I'd just leave it on the drainer and reuse it when I got home. The plate of crumbs became the symbol of my grief and loneliness.

Friends — couples mainly — whom Brian and I had known for years invited me to dinner. I thanked them but declined. I couldn't bear to be the only singleton at the table — to be around all that self-satisfied first-person plural. "Oh, we loved *True De-*

tective slash *Better Call Saul* slash *Justified* . . . No pasta for us. We're cutting down on carbs."

As well as inviting me to dinner, people popped in to see how I was doing. But I could tell that my low spirits brought them down. A few remained steadfast and carried on coming. The rest switched to texts or e-mails.

It didn't help that my girlfriends had started retiring — and so had their husbands. Suddenly aware that the time they had left was finite, they started doing more together: traveling mainly. A few migrated for months on end to second homes. Portugal was very popular. Excellent golf. They invited me to stay, but I didn't go. I wasn't ready for jolly holidays. The upshot was that relationships I had once held so dear petered out. At the time, it didn't bother me. I was too busy grieving. I wanted to be alone. But looking back, I should have made more of an effort.

Now that I wasn't sleeping, I knew that workwise I wasn't fit for it. I spent the whole time petrified that I was about to slip up. On top of that I was still drowning in sorrow. One night — in the early hours — I found myself sitting on the stairs in my nightdress, sobbing down the phone to my mother. "It's happened. I can't cope. I'm so lonely. Can you come?"

Without murmur or complaint, she got in a cab. That night as we sat on the sofa, me with my head in her lap, she gave me some advice, which I have never forgotten. "You will get better and you will find your way back into the world. It has a way of claiming you. But don't expect to get over a loss like this. What you have to do is learn to walk alongside it."

"Is that what you do? Walk alongside the grief of losing Dad?"

"Even now. After all these years. There's no other way."

"Dad was a good man. Like Brian."

"He was. Your father was a mensch."

My goyishe father loved Mum's Yiddishisms. Like his great-grandchildren, he struggled to pronounce the words. It took him years to get the hang of words like "chutzpah." He insisted on pronouncing it as you would: "chutney." That back-of-the-throat, phlegm-clearing sound didn't come easily to him. Then there was his confusion with schlemiel (a clumsy person) and shlimazel (somebody who always has bad luck).

"Jack — all you have to remember is that if a schlemiel spills his soup, it's likely to be into the lap of the shlimazel." But he always got mixed up. And the more he got it wrong, the more Mum laughed and teased him.

My mother's laughter was a rare thing. But it taught me she was capable — however briefly — of casting out her demons. Watching Mum lost in herself as she ribbed my dad, I caught a glimpse of who she really was — or might have been.

"Tell me to mind my own business," Mum said that night as we sat together on the sofa, "but I think you went back to work way too soon. Look at you. You've lost weight. You're white with exhaustion."

I didn't attempt to argue.

"You nursed Brian all those months. You need a break. Now you need looking after."

This time when Mum offered to move in, I said yes. I also wrote to the hospital requesting compassionate leave. I was told to take as long as I needed. They couldn't pay me beyond a certain point, but they would keep my job open for as long as possible.

Moneywise, I was fortunate. Brian and I had some savings and I'd received a decent lump sum from his life insurance. I could manage without my salary.

My Jewish mother set about putting some

flesh on my bones. I still didn't have much appetite, but it didn't stop her producing vats of barley soup and trays of schnitzel and fried fish. When I couldn't get it down, she didn't complain. The next day she would tempt me with something else. When I was having a particularly bad day, she would produce something sweet — cheesecake or strudel. And always coffee. Mum ground the beans with the ancient hand grinder she'd brought in her suitcase. Then she would make coffee the old-fashioned European way, in a saucepan.

Over cake and coffee, she would reminisce about the past — hers, not mine. I'd been listening to these stories since childhood. Heartbreaking as they were, I found comfort in their familiarity. Meanwhile I was trying and failing to discover the trick of walking alongside my grief.

Mum has been living with me for over a year. She keeps telling me that I don't need to be polite and that I only have to say the word and she'll pack her bags and be off. "I won't be offended. I have a perfectly nice flat that's sitting collecting cobwebs. And you have your life to lead." Then she rubs her knees or her back and lets out a soft "Oy."

She doesn't want to leave. She enjoys having company — somebody to listen to her moaning about her acid reflux or how she's in agony from this joint or that muscle.

For my part, I've got used to having her around. We hardly argue and when we do, it's only because she keeps on at me to "get out of the house and see people." I think I've got much better lately at accepting dinner invitations. But she's not talking about dinner invitations. She wants me to start dating. I keep telling her I'm not ready.

"But you're still young."

"I'm fifty-bloody-seven."

"These days that's not old. And you look after yourself. You're well preserved. You're a good catch for somebody." She makes me feel like a rather spry herring.

The worst part is that she's been threatening to set me up on dates. She comes home from the day center and tells me how she got talking to so-and-so, who has a son or a nephew who's a "top" lawyer/doctor/entrepreneur — who's just got divorced.

"Huh, so what line of business is the entrepreneur in?" I'll say just for fun.

"I don't know. I think he sells men's slacks."

"Awesome."

I tell her that she can set me up on dates

all she likes, but there's no way I'm showing up.

Mum sighs — as if her interfering is my fault. But mostly we rub along.

CHAPTER THREE

"I can't work out," Abby is saying, "if my children are supremely well adjusted or if I gave birth to Vulcans."

"Vulcans, definitely," I tell her. "You only have to look at their ears."

Sam and Rosie agreed to Abby going to Nicaragua with their father. But it was unfair of us to joke about them being Klingons. Of course they'd had feelings and qualms about their mother leaving them to go halfway around the world for six weeks. Abby said that Rosie had cried and clung to her and said she wasn't sure how she was going to manage without "mummy cuddles." Sam probably felt the same, but at nine he was far too grown-up to admit it. Instead he said he was worried about the plane crashing. But none of their fears turned out to be a deal breaker. Young as they are, both children have a well-developed sense of altruism. Some — me included — might say it's too well developed. But with their being raised by Abby and Tom, it was bound to happen. They were used to their father disappearing to disaster zones. Now the earthquake people needed their mum, too. She had to go and they were proud of her and they were going to tell everybody at school. They did, however, demand a trip to Disneyland Paris in the summer holidays by way of compensation. Sam drew up a formal printed agreement, which his parents signed. At Rosie's insistence they did this in purple glitter pen.

"I don't get you," Tom says to Abby. "You'd be miserable if the kids had refused to let you go. Now you're fretting because they said you can."

"I know. But they might have had the decency to protest a bit more — just to make me feel wanted."

"Stop it. They did protest. But they love your mum and feel safe with her. She's like a third parent. You should be grateful for that."

"I am grateful." Abby looks at me. "You do know that, don't you?"

"Of course I do. But you mustn't think the kids aren't going to miss you. Right now they're on a high. You two are like a couple of superheroes jetting off to save lives. They want to show off to their friends. Give it a couple of days and they'll come down."

"You think so? But I don't want them to be miserable."

Tom tells her to make up her bloody mind.

"Sorry. It's just nerves." She announces that she's going to go upstairs and check on the kids one last time.

It's past midnight. The three of us are standing in the hallway in my house, waiting for the taxi, which is going to take them to the Royal Air Force Base in Northolt, a dozen or so miles away. Sam and Rosie are asleep upstairs — having fought for an hour or more over who was going to have which bedroom. They both wanted the one with the double bed. I thought I could settle the argument by telling them they could swap rooms at the end of each week. But no. Cue major rumpus about who should be first to get the double bed. In the end I made them draw straws. Sam lost and sulked. He's since decided that he prefers the smaller room because it's cozier and he is happy to remain there.

"You've already checked on them three times," Tom says. "They're fine." But Abby is halfway up the stairs.

Tom opens the front door and says that to save time he's going to wheel the suitcases into the street. I offer to help, but he says he can manage. "It's starting to snow. Stay in the warm."

I watch him maneuver the two hefty cases down the step and onto the path.

Abby comes downstairs, looking forlorn. "I can't bear to leave them."

"Oh, sweetheart."

She weeps into my shoulder while I rub her back.

"I know it's hard," I say. "But you'll feel better once you're on the plane. And the kids are going to be fine. I will cope. I promise."

"Thank you for having them. I'm so grateful."

"My pleasure. And in case I haven't said it often enough, I'm very proud of you. You're a very brave young woman."

"I don't feel very brave." She sniffs and wipes her eyes again. "So Nana's really OK about the kids staying here?"

"Nana's fine. You know what she's like — she's worried about all the noise and mess, but I've told her if it gets too much, she can always go home for a bit of peace."

"But I don't want the kids to force her out. . . ."

"It's not going to happen. Today she went out and bought kosher brisket and a boiling chicken to make soup. Believe me, your grandmother is already in her element."

Tom is hovering at the front door, saying the taxi has arrived.

"I need to pee," Abby says.

Her husband rolls his eyes. While Abby dashes to the loo, I follow Tom down the front path. The air is raw. Snow is falling in chunks and starting to settle. I pull my big cardigan tight around me. "Now, you're sure you've got everything . . . passports, visas, currency . . ."

He pats his knapsack and reminds me that it's the third time I've asked. Then he tells me I'm going to freeze if I stay out here.

"I'm fine. Don't fuss. I want to wave you off."

He's looking at his watch. "For God's sake, how long does it take to have a pee?"

Finally Abby appears. "Right. I guess we're off." Her eyes are welling up again and so are mine. I put my arms around my daughter and hold her so tight she's telling me she can't breathe.

"Phone me when you land."

"Will do."

"And you two take care. Promise me."

"Don't worry. I'll look after her," Tom says. He plants a quick kiss on my cheek. "And thanks again for everything. We couldn't have done this without you."

"No problem . . . Now go . . . before I change my mind."

I watch them get into the taxi. Abby rolls down the window and leans out: "Love you!"

"Love you, too." I wave and send kisses. Abby does the same. The taxi pulls away and almost immediately disappears around the corner. Despite the cold, I don't move. Instead I stand in the snowy silence, watching the flakes dance and eddy under the streetlamp. "Brian, it's me. If you're up there, please keep Abby and Tom safe. And if you could see your way clear to helping me survive the next six weeks with Sam and Rosie, that would be good, too."

I'm suddenly aware that behind me, a tiny voice is singing: "Grandma . . . do you want to build a snowman?"

It takes me a while to persuade Rosie that people tend not to build snowmen in the middle of the night. I promise we'll build one tomorrow. She accepts my offer and agrees to go to bed, so long as I read to her. I manage a couple of pages of *Aliens in Underpants Save the World* before my eyelids start to droop.

"When I grow up, I want to be an alien.

Or maybe a witch. But if I was a witch I would be a friendly one — not a horrible, bad one. I'm going to be a lesbinan witch with a broom."

"That sounds like fun."

"Do witches earn a good celery?"

I am far too tired to explain the difference between celery and salary. "I'm sure they do," I say. "Now lie down and get some sleep. You've got school in the morning."

" 'K. But first will you check for burglars under my bed?"

Again exhaustion stops me from arguing. I bend down and poke my head under the bed. Plenty of dust bunnies, but no burglars. "All clear."

"I can't find Denise."

Denise is Rosie's comfort object. She is also a carrot. Rosie has had her since she was a toddler. She named her after the lady next door. Nobody has the foggiest idea why she chose a carrot as a comforter instead of a blanket or a stuffed toy. It goes without saying that there has been a long line of Denises. They are discreetly replaced when they become shriveled and gross. Rosie is no doubt aware of this parental subterfuge, but she chooses not to acknowledge it. We can only assume that in her mind, Denise's essence lives on no matter what body she inhabits — a bit like the Dalai Lama.

A few of Rosie's friends still have blankies. One even goes to bed sucking on a pacifier. But none of them cuddles up to a root vegetable. When Abby discussed Rosie's carrot fetish with a child therapist friend, she was told not to worry and that Rosie's need for Denise would eventually peter out. Meanwhile nobody should make a big deal of it. So we don't.

I find Denise on the floor next to the bed. She's long, but wrinkled and bendy and turning black at the tip. I make a mental note to replace her.

"Here you are, darling."

Like a church chorister with a candle, she wraps both hands around the carrot and holds it to her chest. "Night-night, Gran'ma."

I kiss Rosie's forehead and wish her sweet dreams. Then I go next door to check on Sam.

He is snoring softly in the single bed. I kiss him, too, and rearrange a leg, which has strayed from under the duvet.

The next morning I'm awake at five thirty. I have no idea why. It's not as if I have a great deal to do before taking the kids to school. They both had baths last night. Their school uniforms are arranged neatly on their beds. Reading folders are by the front door. I don't have to make them sandwiches, because the school provides a cooked lunch. All that's required of me is to make sure they have something inside them before they leave. Abby insists the kids have a decent breakfast — on the grounds that they can't hope to concentrate in school without something to nourish their brains. High-sugar breakfast cereals full of empty calories are off the menu. Instead they have eggs on whole-wheat toast, or organic porridge and berries.

I can't get back to sleep, so I take a shower and head downstairs to make coffee. While it's brewing I sit myself down at the kitchen table and check my e-mail. It's all spam. One invites me to "knock through walls with your cock."

I decide to take another look at the e-mail Abby sent me yesterday. The subject line is: Rosie and Sam — Operating Instructions. I reminded her before she wrote it that I have been taking care of my grandchildren since they were babies and I don't need instructions, but she said that she'd feel better knowing I had everything written down. By then she was so nervous about leaving the children that I didn't argue.

I skim-read the first page. It's mostly stuff

I know: bedtimes, school drop-off and pickup times, names of the kids' teachers. Some things I don't know, like phone numbers of mothers who will help out in an emergency.

The second page contains a timetable of Sam and Rosie's after-school activities:

Monday: Bogdan — Sam's new chess coach to house. He has your number and address. Rosie to drama. Tanya, Cybil's mum, will take both girls to drama. She'll also drop her home. Tanya and I usually rotate the pickup and drop-off, but she's happy to do it every week while I'm away. That way you'll always be there when Bogdan arrives.

Tuesday: Both to French Club. (Please take a snack — otherwise they tend to turn into hypoglycemic monsters.)

Wednesday: Rosie to science club. Sam to computer club. (Snack)

Thursday: Bogdan. Rosie to Zumba — again with Cybil. Tanya will take R and drop her home.

Friday: Reserved for playdates.

Saturday: Free. But they might get invited to friends' houses for sleepovers.

Sunday morning: Sam football practice. Rosie swimming.

Rosie never says much about her after-school activities — at least not to me. Sam only ever mentions chess. He has a real passion for the game. What's more, he's the best player in the lower school.

When it became clear that Sam had a talent for the game, the teacher who ran the school chess club took Abby and Tom to one side. He said that with some private coaching Sam would be good enough to compete in nationwide under-eleven tournaments.

Abby and Tom weren't sure about hiring a coach. They didn't want to put too much pressure on him and turn the game into a chore. In the end they left it to Sam to decide. He didn't think twice. If I remember rightly his reaction was something along the lines of "Awesome." The child was dazzled by the idea of becoming a chess champion — as was my mother. Now that Sam has won a couple of local tournaments, she refers to him as "my great-grandson, the chess master."

I often wonder if all these after-school activities are too much for the children. I worry that they wear them out — not to mention their mother, who, having put in her hours at the surgery, has to drive them from here to there in the school rush hour.

Then when she gets home she cooks and supervises homework and bath time. Depending on what shift he's on at the hospital, Tom may or may not be there to pitch in. For the moment I'm trying to forget that from next week — when activities start up again — I will be the one doing the ferrying. But at least I won't have been working all day, I've got Cybil's mother helping out and Mum will be doing most of the cooking.

I've always managed to bite my tongue over the school activities issue. It wasn't my place to offer Abby parenting advice. Rosie and Sam were her and Tom's kids, not mine. But during the weeks leading up to Christmas, they seemed to go down with one bug after another. It felt as if they were always off school. Abby must have roped me in to looking after them half a dozen times. Not that I minded. They were no trouble. I would make honey and lemon drinks and the three of us would snuggle on the sofa, covered in one of the kids' duvets, watching movies back-to-back. It was fun. Less so when I caught one of their diseases and ended up in bed for a week with a raging temperature, hacking cough and streaming nose. Abby dosed the kids up with Tylenol and was pretty gung ho about their various infections — the way doctors are. But I couldn't help thinking that they were getting sick because they were run down. In the end I decided to poke my nose in where I was pretty certain it wasn't wanted.

"Look, tell me to mind my own business," I said to Abby, "but do you think that maybe the kids are getting ill because they're exhausted?"

Abby was sorting clean laundry and barely looked up. "No, I think they're getting ill because it's winter. Kids and adults are dropping like flies. My surgery has been packed all week."

"I get that. But Sam and Rosie seem to be constantly on the go. I mean, they do so many after-school activities . . ."

"So do all the kids."

"But what about downtime? When do they get to sit and stare — to just be?"

"You're right," Abby said, folding a pair of Tom's socks into a bundle. "They probably don't get enough time to themselves. But nor do any of their friends."

"The thing is — I don't understand what it's all for. When you were young you had your piano lesson on a Saturday morning and that was it. During the week, you'd come home from school, I'd make you a sandwich and then you'd lie on the sofa and zone out in front of *Top Cat* or *Scooby-Doo*. It did you no harm. You always did well at school."

"That was thirty years ago. Things have moved on. These days it isn't enough for kids to do well at school. If they want to get into a good university, they must have other interests. They need a 'hinterland.' "

"But Sam and Rosie aren't much more than babies. How can you even be thinking about university?"

"It's the way it is. Round here five-year-olds have Mandarin lessons."

"Don't you worry about putting them under too much pressure?"

She put down the T-shirt she was folding. Finally I had her attention. "Of course I worry. How could you think I don't worry? You know how we dithered about getting Sam a chess coach. But these days all middle-class parents are caught up in this madness. People are too scared to take their foot off the gas. What would you do if you were me?"

I told her I didn't know. Then I reminded her how her dad used to take her out for ice cream and talk to her about history and the universe. "That was his idea of giving you a hinterland."

For a few moments, she looked wistful.

Then she turned to me. "I'll never forget him teaching me about infinity. I used to lie awake for hours trying to understand it. But I couldn't imagine something so vast — something that never ended. Then my brain would start to feel all weird. I'd get panicky and come running into your room. I'd tell you I was scared of infinity and you'd wake Dad up and tell him off."

I'm smiling as I remember.

Abby assured me that Sam and Rosie were fine — that all the kids did too much and got exhausted toward the end of term. She would make sure they had plenty of down-time during the school holidays. I let the subject drop.

There's yelling coming from upstairs.

"Gran'ma! Sam hit me."

"You're such a liar!"

I abandon my mother, who has just got up and is in her dressing gown poaching eggs. I get upstairs to find Sam is curled up on Rosie's double bed. Rosie is digging him in the back with Denise.

"Yuck . . . get that thing off me! It's disgusting."

"Rosie! Stop that."

"But he hit me."

"I did not."

"Yes, you did."

"OK — but only because you tried to steal my dinosaur book." Rosie gives her brother another poke with the carrot.

"Rosie — that's enough. If you carry on like that, your carrot will break. Then you'll have nothing to put under your pillow when you go to bed."

Rosie gives me a furious, squinty-eyed look. "She's not just a carrot. She's Denise."

Sam's cue to start taunting his sister. I catch my grandson's eye and hope that my expression is sufficiently steely to silence him. He mutters, "Baby," under his breath but takes it no further.

"I'm sorry," I say to Rosie. "I sometimes forget it's called Denise."

"She's not an it. She's a she. And she's my friend."

"Well, if she's your friend, then surely you don't want to break her."

Rosie hugs Denise to her chest and tells Sam that he smells.

"Your carrot smells. It stinks. You're a baby."

"I am not a *baby.* I'm *five.*"

"Baby."

Rosie drops Denise and lashes out with her fists. I grab her and pull her off the bed. She stands, looking daggers at her brother.

"OK," I say, "I think the only way to end this is for you both to say sorry."

"Sam needs to say it first," Rosie harrumphs, arms crossed in defiance. "He started it."

"No, Rosie. You started it. You tried to steal his book. Now you say sorry first."

"No."

"Come on. And when you've said sorry, I'm sure Sam will apologize for hitting you."

Rosie still looks furious and doesn't say anything. Then: "I'm sorry. There, I've said it."

"You don't mean it," Sam says. "Say it again and mean it."

"No."

I'm looking at the bedside clock. It's gone eight, both children are still in their pajamas and they haven't had breakfast. School starts at nine fifteen. That's not a problem, so long as there's no traffic. Nevertheless, I'm starting to panic. "Right, this stops now. I want you both dressed and downstairs in five minutes."

I send Sam to his room to find his school clothes. He heads off and then turns around.

"What day is it today?"

"Wednesday."

"That means I have to take something for show-and-tell."

"But why didn't you remind me last night? We could have sorted something out."

"I forgot."

I suggest he go downstairs and choose a photograph from one of the selections pinned to the corkboard in the kitchen. "What about one of Rosie as a baby? You could talk about how you felt when she was born."

"No way. I hated her." That's true. Sam's first words on meeting his baby sister were "Take her back to her own garden." To this day nobody — least of all Sam — understands the significance of the garden. But his feelings were clear. He didn't want a sister.

"Take one of your baby snaps, then."

"No. Everybody would laugh."

"Gran'ma," Rosie pipes up, "if it's Wednesday I need my sports kit. We do games on Wednesday."

"So where is it?"

"I don't know. It's in a red sports bag. I think Mummy remembered to bring it."

I tell her I'll go and have a hunt around downstairs.

"I know what I could take," Sam says. "You know when Granddad died and you had him cremated . . ."

"Yes."

81

"Did you get given one of those urn things full of his ashes?"

"I did."

"Cool. So why don't I take Granddad's ashes to show-and-tell?"

"Sam, you are not taking Granddad's ashes into school."

"Why not?"

"Because it's inappropriate."

Rosie wants to know what "in'ppropriate" means.

"It means that people would be a bit shocked and upset."

Sam isn't convinced. "But I could talk about how Granddad was this big strong man who used to play football with me and that I really loved him and now he's just a pile of dust."

"Sam, I know you loved Granddad, but . . ."

"I loved him, too," says Rosie. "I cried for days and days and days when he went to heaven and couldn't come back."

"OK . . . you both loved Granddad. And he loved you, too . . . very much. But, Sam, you are not taking his ashes into school. I keep them here because they are precious. Please take one of the baby pictures . . . Now, both of you — go and get dressed."

I leave them and go downstairs to look for

Rosie's games kit. I find it straightaway. Abby has left the sports bag under the coat hooks in the hall. I can't think how I missed it.

By now Mum is at the foot of the stairs calling up to the children to say their eggs are ready. They come charging down. Sam has made no effort to get dressed. Rosie is in her school sweatshirt, regulation tartan kilt and tights. "Gran'ma, I can't find my shoes."

"They're on the floor at the end of your bed."

"They're not. They've gone."

I trudge back upstairs and find them in the bathroom. Rosie must have put them there, but I can see no point in turning it into an issue. I'm just glad to have found them.

In the kitchen, the kids are moaning about their eggs. Abby makes them soft-boiled eggs. With Marmite soldiers.

"But Nana's done you poached eggs on Marmite toast. What's the difference?"

The difference is, you can't dip the toast.

"When I was growing up," Mum starts, "children ate what was put in front of them and they were grateful." She grimaces and starts rubbing her back. The children take pity on her — which is no doubt what she had in mind — and start eating.

I remind them that we have to be out of the house in ten minutes.

"Nana, do you think I should be allowed to take Granddad's ashes to school for show-and-tell?"

Mum looks at me. "He wants to take Brian's ashes to school? Why would he want to do that?"

"It's for show-and-tell," Sam says.

Mum tells him he should show his grandfather some respect.

"But he's ashes. You can't respect ashes."

"My grandson the smart-aleck."

"But I'm only saying."

Mum fetches her handbag and sits down at the kitchen table. "Here . . . I've got something interesting you can take."

She pulls out her large purse and opens the wallet section. "Here you are." She slides a faded, dog-eared black-and-white photograph across the table. "Who do you think the little girl is?"

I've seen the photograph dozens of times. The little girl in the cloche hat and brand-new coat with a velvet collar is my mother, age seven.

"She's pretty," Rosie says.

"Look how chubby I am." Mum smiles. "My mother fed my brother and me too much schnitzel and strudel."

"So, it's you," Sam says.

"It's me on my very first day in this country. I came here on my own — all the way from Germany."

I could see where this was going. "Mum, please. Not now."

"They should know about these things."

Rosie wants to know why Nana Frieda was on her own. "Where were your mummy and daddy?"

"What things should we know about?" says Sam.

I give my mother a hard stare. "They're too young."

"They're too young? What about me? I was seven."

Both children are demanding to be let into Nana's secret. But it's late (thank heavens). I tell them we have to leave it for another time.

"Aww."

"Right . . . Rosie, you get your shoes and coat on. Sam, you have precisely two minutes to get dressed." I pass the photograph back to Mum. She puts it away without looking at me. She's blaming me for wanting to protect the children.

"But what about show-and-tell?" Sam persists. "You won't let me take Granddad's ashes and now I can't take Nana's photo."

"Get dressed and I'll find you something."

"But it has to be something that belonged to Granddad."

I can't think. I'm not giving him Brian's watch to take to school, and Sam would hardly want a pair of his GoldToes from the clothes sack. Mum suggests giving him Brian's Death Valley snow globe.

"But what if he breaks it?" I say.

"Have you got a better idea?"

I haven't. I fetch the snow globe from the desk in Brian's study.

Sam reappears fully dressed and presents himself for inspection.

"Good boy. OK, you can take this." I hand him the snow globe.

His eyes are wide. "Wow. Thanks, Grandma." He's holding it in both hands, as if it's a bird's egg that might crack at any moment. "Granddad used to let me play with the snow globe all the time when I was little. It always reminds me of him."

"Promise me you'll look after it. I want it returned to me in one piece."

He promises. He'll give it to his teacher to keep in her desk drawer.

Rosie wants to know what's so special about a silly old snow globe.

"It's funny," Sam says.

"Why?"

"Because it's really hot in Death Valley. It never snows."

"I don't get it. . . . If it never snows somewhere, why would you put it in a snow globe? It's a stupid joke."

"You're stupid."

They bicker all the way to school.

CHAPTER FOUR

Thanks to roadwork and a broken-down truck, the ten-minute journey to school has taken half an hour. The kids are still arguing. Now it's about the color of air. Sam says it's invisible. Rosie insists it's blue. If I side with Sam, Rosie will get hysterical, so I opt to keep quiet. What with the traffic, the shenanigans before school, the constant quarreling and the fact that I didn't have time for breakfast, I'm not in the best of moods. And it's getting worse. We've done two laps of the school perimeter and I can't find anywhere to park. As I curse the SUVs for taking up too much room, Rosie breaks off from bickering with her brother to tell me that whenever her friend Flora's mum takes them to school, she chants for a space and it always works.

"Well, bully for Flora's mum."

"Sam, you smell like sick."

"Well, you smell like dog poo."

"You smell like dog poo and sick and farts."

So long as they're not hitting each other, I let the insults fly. As we approach the school gates for a third time, I have to slam on the brake so as not to mow down a mother and her children who have stepped into the road, oblivious of the traffic. I come to a halt no more than four feet from the group, but the mum — fur gilet vest, dinky ankle boots, newborn in a harness — doesn't look up from her phone. Carnage averted, I carry on cruising for a space. I can't help noticing that even the women in gym gear have freshly blow-dried hair. That means they shower before they exercise. Why would a sane person do that? More glossy, immaculate children and their mothers emerge from Range Rovers and Cayennes that are parked so tight they're practically sniffing one another's fenders. Women join other women and stroll toward the gates, ponytails and totes swinging.

There are some dads tagging along with the women. That was something you never saw in my day, busy dads making time to bond with their kids on the school run.

One of the dads is carrying a giant, superbly executed model of an erupting volcano — which I'm certain his child had little hand in making. He peers round the volcano and greets the woman in front of him with a double kiss — as if they're at a cocktail party. Private school.

According to Abby, most of the women at Faraday House Prep are stay-at-home mothers. Many — like Gilet Woman — have babies as well as older children. Not that you'd think it to look at them. When did the school run turn into the runway?

After Abby was born, I became a full-time mum. I slept when she slept. Since she was awake nearly all day — mostly with her gums clamped to my nipple — and woke to be fed every couple of hours during the night, neither of us got much sleep. With no time to myself I went days without washing my hair. I lived in my old maternity jeans and Dr. Scholl's. I only wore a bra if somebody was coming to visit — which didn't happen very often. Back then — long before mummy-and-baby groups and coffee shop meet-ups — mothers were far more isolated. I have a vivid memory of the time I invited a couple of Jehovah's Witnesses in, just for the company.

I swear that none of these Faraday House women has ever pooped with a toddler on her lap or sniffed her underwear and decided: "Yep, good for another day." That's because they all have au pairs and/or full-time nannies. Maybe I'm just old and bitter, but to me there's something sexless about these mannequin mummies. There's nothing earthy or, God forbid, slutty about them. I swear they all have pixilated vaginas.

When Abby went back to work, she put Sam and Rosie in day care. It was cheaper than hiring a nanny. Sam was four when he started — a few months off starting big school. Rosie wasn't even a year old.

Abby didn't want to go back to work so soon, but she had no choice. She and Tom (whose NHS salary was decent, but unremarkable) had a hefty mortgage and they needed the money. They still do. Even now they don't earn enough between them to pay two sets of school fees. So Tom's parents — who used to own a small chain of furniture shops — help out.

Abby was always against private education. She got it from her dad. He was adamant that a decent education was a right and not a privilege. Money had no place. Like her father, Abby believed that state school standards would never improve until voluble, demanding middle-class parents sent their kids to them.

Tom, on the other hand, wasn't keen on using their children as part of a social experiment. They argued the toss. I kept well out of it. Had I been asked for my opinion, I would — albeit reluctantly — have taken Tom's side. But in the end the argument was settled for them. Just as Sam was approaching school age, three of the local primaries failed government inspections and were put on special measures. One decent school remained, but Abby and Tom lived too far away to stand a hope of Sam being accepted. They enrolled him at Faraday House. To his credit, Brian never challenged their decision. Even he knew they were doing the right thing — not that he would ever admit it.

Eventually I find somewhere to park — right outside the school entrance. "Hoo-bloody-ray." I switch on my indicator and creep past the space, intending to reverse in. I've just begun the maneuver when one of those chichi baby Fiats nips in and claims the space. I look into my rearview mirror. I am expecting to see a blonde, with giant sunglasses on her head. Shades — albeit used as hair accessories — appear to be de rigueur even on a slate gray day like this. But the person I see in the mirror is a man. "Right. I'll sort him out. Bloody cheek." I yank on the hand brake.

"Gran'ma, don't say anything. It's Sarah's dad."

"I don't care whose dad it is."

I'm out of the car. The chap — in a beautifully cut suit — rolls down his window. He's far too big for the Fiat. His head is almost touching the ceiling. Probably borrowed the nanny's car. "Sorry . . . is there a problem?"

"Too right there is. You could see I was about to back into this space. You people think you're so damned entitled. . . ."

He is already apologizing, explaining that he's running late and got confused. He didn't see my reversing lights and thought I was double-parked up ahead. His remorse, which seems genuine, takes the wind out of my sails. But not as much as what happens next. As he starts to pull out of the space, I see that the girl sitting next to him has both legs in metal braces. My hand flies to my face. I'm a monster. I start running down the road after him, shouting apologies and waving my arms like a crazy woman. He either doesn't see me or pretends not to.

"You could have warned me," I say to the kids as I let them out of the car.

"We did."

"No, you didn't. You just told me he was Sarah's dad."

"But everybody knows that Sarah can't walk properly."

"I don't."

We fall in behind a couple of women in gym gear. They have perfect bottoms. One is pushing a heavy-duty cross-country stroller.

". . . and there she was, in the kitchen snorting her son's Ritalin."

"Nooo."

"I kid you not. . . ."

Faraday House is a magnificent Georgian manor, surrounded by tall hedges and bowling green lawns. There are tennis courts, rugby and cricket pitches, indoor and outdoor pools and a performing arts center. The original eighteenth-century building is dwarfed by the new glass-and-steel additions, which have been built to accommodate the ever-increasing population of the senior school.

Despite everything this place has to offer, I worry that it's too privileged, too white — that it doesn't reflect real life. Abby agrees and despite their emphasis on altruism she worries about the kids turning into brats who take advantage for granted. Once they start senior school she is going to insist that they donate a percentage of their allowance to charity.

Because it's the first day of term, Mrs. Spencer Jupp, the head, has stationed herself in the wood-paneled entrance hall to welcome back children and parents. An enormous glass chandelier glistens and glimmers above her. To her side is an antique velvet sofa and a walnut occasional table. Mrs. Spencer Jupp — known to everybody as Mrs. S.J. — is wearing a pale blue woolen shift dress and matching pashmina. She looks as if she is receiving dinner guests at her country estate. Instead she is ever so politely marshaling children, as well as issuing directives to the stragglers like Sam and Rosie. "Do giddyap, chaps. The bell went two minutes ago."

Much as they might want to giddy, they can't because so many of the children want to stop and chat with the head. "Hi, Mrs. S.J., did you have a good Christmas?"

"I did, Ben/Olivia/Arthur. How was yours?"

There are two hundred pupils in the lower school and I'm guessing that Mrs. S.J. knows each of them by name. This is what you pay for — the personal touch.

I wave good-bye to Sam and Rosie and watch them disappear into the thicket of children.

As I reach the bottom of the school steps,

I feel a tap on my shoulder.

Then comes the booming, almost regal voice. "Judy! Long time no see."

Ginny throws her arms around me as if we're old friends. "I just heard on the tom-toms about Abby and her husband going to Nicaragua. Good on them."

Abby sent a round-robin to her mummy friends at the school to let them know she was going. Now it appears to be on general release, which is good because it saves me having to explain. "What they're doing is amazing. Totally restores one's faith in human nature. You must be very proud."

"I am. But at the same time I worry about there being another quake, or that they might catch some terrible disease."

"Of course you do. It can't be easy, and naturally you daren't voice your worries in front of the children. Speaking of which, I think you're just as wonderful, stepping into the breach like this. Not many women our age would go back to full-time parenting. And you've already got your old mum at home."

I tell Ginny it's only for six weeks and fingers crossed, I'll manage.

"Well, if it all gets too much and you need somebody to take the kids off your hands for a few hours, you only have to shout."

I first met Ginny about a year ago. She was picking up her grandson Ivo from school — which she does every day. I was doing a one-off pickup because Abby had been held up at work. I remember her coming over to me, full of upper-class bonhomie: "Ah! Another grandma. At least I'm assuming you are. By the way, it's not your skin that gives you away. It's the Crocs. Aren't they amazing? So comfortable. I live in mine." She raised a large foot, encased in fuchsia rubber.

In fact, my Crocs belonged to my mother, who swore they eased her bunion pain. I'd borrowed them because I was running late and they'd been lying by the front door. Nevertheless I agreed that they were enormously comfortable and owned up to being a grandma. It was then that I noticed Ginny's T-shirt. Across her shelf of a bosom were the words *Being a grandma is God's reward for not killing your kids.* She was clearly a bit of a one-off — at least by Faraday House standards. She had a sense of humor. In my experience, the educated classes are often so in thrall to the high arts that levity scares them. God forbid they should laugh in case it makes them look lowbrow.

On top of that, Ginny's T-shirt and baggy

jeans — not to mention the Crocs — indicated that she had no interest in fitting into the school's elevated sartorial mold. I admired that. Indeed I, too, took a perverse delight in turning up at the school gates looking a bit slovenly. That day I was wearing faded black leggings and an ancient waterfall cardigan covered in bobbles. I think we both took one look at each other and recognized kindred spirits.

Once we'd finished discussing Crocs, we moved on to our grandchildren. Ginny's grandson Ivo was in the same year as Rosie. He belonged to her son and daughter-in law. She had two more grandchildren, by her daughter. For some reason, she seemed reluctant to say much about them and I was too polite to push it.

We learned so much about each other in that first, short encounter. I told her I'd recently been widowed. She revealed that her husband had run off years ago, leaving her with two small children. "Put me off men for good, I can tell you."

I can't remember the last time I saw Ginny. Abby hasn't asked me to do the school run in ages.

"Judy," she's saying now, "I want to apologize."

"What on earth for?"

"For not calling you. I see Abby most mornings, dropping off the kids. We always nod and I've kept meaning to stop her and ask for your phone number. I wanted to check how you were doing. The thing is, when people are grieving, one never knows if one's interfering. But I suppose you could always have told me to bugger off."

Another thing I like about Ginny is how she speaks like the Queen and curses like a trouper.

"I wouldn't have dreamed of telling you to bugger off," I say, touched that she's been thinking about me. "I'm always up for a bit of company that isn't my mother."

"Really? Now I feel even more guilty. Damn. Why didn't I pick up the phone?"

She insists we exchange phone numbers here and now. We've just finished texting them to each other when somebody calls out to Ginny:

"Don't forget, coffee at Claudia's this morning to discuss the spring fair."

Coming toward us is a woman with shoulder-length blond dreadlocks. These have been pulled into a giant, scruffy ponytail. I can't help thinking they must be a devil to keep clean. She has porcelain skin and a way with red lipstick.

"Hi, you must be Judy," she says. "I just

saw you with Sam and Rosie. I'm Tanya, Cybil's mum."

I've met Cybil several times at Abby's. She often comes over to play with Rosie. I've never met her mum. Abby doesn't know Tanya that well — work has prevented her from making many mummy friends at school, but she says Tanya's lovely.

"Tanya. Of course. You've offered to take the girls to drama and Zumba. Thank you so much. You're a lifesaver."

Tanya insists it's no problem because she has to take Cybil anyway.

"Well, I'm still grateful. . . . It's funny. I feel like I know you. Rosie's told me so much about you." But not about those dreadlocks. It's strange the things kids leave out — or just take for granted.

"Oh God. That sounds ominous."

"Not at all. She thinks you're great." Even with the dreads, Tanya is beautiful. I assume she's the token boho mum at Faraday House — another oddball like Ginny. I can see how the pair of them teamed up.

"Rosie likes me because I let her and Cyb eat crap all day long and stay up late when we were on holiday. . . . By the way, I got Abby's e-mail about Nicaragua. I think what she and Tom are doing is truly inspirational. There aren't enough people like them in this world."

She says if I need any more help with the kids, she's around.

"I'm allowed to work from home. It's a perk of sleeping with the boss." She explains that she and her husband run a small record company. "We specialize in rap artists mostly. Zane Needlzz is one of ours."

"Not sure I've come across him," I say — insinuating that there are other rap artists I have heard of. "I'm more Supertramp really."

"Oh, I love Supertramp," Ginny says. She starts singing: "Take a jumbo, cross the water. Like to see America . . ."

Tanya is laughing. "You old fogey, you. So, are you coming?"

"Where?"

"Claudia's coffee morning."

Ginny grimaces. "Really?" She tells me that parents in each year group take turns to organize the spring fair. "This year it's our turn. God help us."

"I'm sensing this isn't an event you're keen on."

"You sense correctly. . . . Don't get me wrong. I'm all for raising money for charity, but these things always descend into such a bitch-fight. Everybody competes to get the best stall and donate the best raffle or auction prize. Nobody really mucks in."

"Please, Ginny. You promised you'd come. Bloody Claudia has already roped me in and I'm not going on my own. You're my only ally."

"I'll go, but only if Judy comes, too."

"Me? But I'm not a parent."

"Nor am I," Ginny says, "but Rosie's in our year and right now you're her guardian. I promise you, nobody will mind. They're only interested in getting volunteers to run stalls."

"OK — I suppose I don't mind helping. . . . So tell me: what is it about this Claudia woman that you dislike so much?"

"You'll see," Tanya says.

Twenty or so mothers and a handful of dads are milling in Claudia's granite-and-steel basement kitchen-cum–living space. I can't help noticing how the women seem to hang on to the men's every word.

"To be honest," I hear one of the dads say to an eager-faced woman, "we've stopped the kids listening to pop music. The form is too simplistic."

"Oh, I couldn't agree more," says Eager-faced Woman with a coquettish flick of her hair. "We've just introduced Milo to Wagner. Of course his teacher had no idea it was spelled with a *W.*"

"Typical," another dad pipes up. "Actually Freddie's just started playing the French horn. He's loving it."

The man turns to another of his male companions and asks if his family had a good Christmas.

"Not bad. After the festivities, I gave my wife a break and took the kids on a French-language course in the Loire — just to give them a bit of an edge."

"Wow, you are amazing," simpers another woman. "I wish my husband would do stuff like that with our kids."

Tanya catches me eavesdropping. "Meet the stay-at-home tiger dads."

"Tiger dads are a thing?"

"You bet. Also known as DILFs."

"Sorry?"

"Dads I'd like to fuck. Well, not me personally. I don't get it. Most of them aren't even that good-looking."

"No, but they're around."

"Precisely. You wouldn't believe some of the shenanigans."

"Oh, I bet I would."

Tanya's eyes are scanning the room. "OK, that's Claudia, over there," she says with a jerk of her dreads, "holding court as usual."

Claudia is hard to miss. She towers above

the women she's speaking to. She has to be five-ten. Her body is slender and willowy. Auburn hair trails down her back. She's the type that looks good smoking a cigarette.

"I imagine she's very bendy," I remark.

"Funny you should say that," Ginny says, "because apparently she wanted to be a ballet dancer. She got into the Royal Ballet School, but then she shot up, so she was asked to leave."

"That's bad luck."

"Yes, but afterward," Tanya says, "she waltzed into Cambridge, came out with a PhD in child psychology, set herself up as a child care expert and now she's got her own radio advice slot . . . calls herself Dr. Claudia." She snarls as she says it. "Oh, and she also managed to bag a venture capitalist and produce two sickeningly gorgeous children." Hero is in Rosie's class. Sebastian is in the year above Sam.

"Are you sure you're not just a teensy bit jealous?" Ginny says.

"OK, I admit I wouldn't mind her money. But that's not it. I could forgive her the money and the fame if she weren't so bloody patronizing and superior."

"Well, I've never heard of her. And Abby's never mentioned her."

Tanya reckons that's because Abby prob-

104

ably has the sense to give her a wide berth.

"I think you're being a bit hard," Ginny says. "Claudia's all right. You just have to know how to handle her."

Meanwhile I'm finding it hard to get worked up about a person I haven't met. On top of that I'm starving. I've spied baskets of croissants and pastries on the long dining room table and suggest we dive in. Ginny pats her belly — which her sweatshirt is doing nothing to disguise — and says she's watching the old waistline. Tanya doesn't do wheat. I apologize for having to abandon them and make a beeline for an apricot Danish. I sink my teeth into the sticky pastry and thick, sweet custard. I appear to be the only person eating. All around me, huddled women are sticking to coffee and gossip. I eavesdrop as I chew.

"Of course there are far too many Japanese children at Faraday House. The way standards have risen is so unfair."

"What gets me is that their teacher has no idea how to give the class a sense of brand or uniqueness."

"Mimi is in the lowest group for maths, but I'm sure she's being used as an aspirational focus to inspire the less able children in the class."

I don't know how Abby puts up with these

women. On the other hand, she works, so she doesn't see much of them. And looking round the room, I can see a few more ordinary-looking folk: real women whose vaginas aren't pixilated and who have their roots and Gap labels on display.

Abby says that Faraday House is made up of two distinct halves. There are the well-off parents: one or both will be the corporate lawyers, bankers and hedge fund managers. Then there are lower-earning professionals: teachers, journalists and civil servants, who, like Abby and Tom, often need help to pay the fees. Either that or they live in small apartments and go without decent cars and holidays.

I've finished the Danish, but so far it's done nothing to raise my blood sugar level, so I help myself to a mini *pain au chocolat*. I'm in midchew when a couple of women approach me and tell me that I must be Abby's mum.

"She's so brave, flying off to minister to the afflicted. I take my hat off to her."

"Me, too," the second woman says. "On the other hand, I can't help thinking it would have been easier to send the afflicted a check."

I look around, or should I say up, to see that Claudia has joined our little group.

"Claudia," gushes Check Woman, "you must meet Judy. She's Abby Schofield's mother."

"Of course!" Claudia says. "I saw you at school with Sam and Rosie. Thank you so much for coming, particularly at such a busy time. Taking on two children can't be easy. You have my sympathies." She dispenses largesse as if she was born to it.

"I'm sure I'll get used to it."

"By the way," the friend of Check Woman says to Claudia, "now that I've got you, I wonder if we can have a word. Charles and I are convinced that Ollie has attention deficit disorder. Meanwhile his teacher insists he's just naughty and we need to come down on him more firmly. I've tried confiscating the iPad, but he just finds one of the spares."

Claudia manages to let drop that she wrote her doctorate on ADHD. "Why don't we have a chat about it later — after everybody's gone?"

"I don't want him taking Ritalin," the woman continues. "I've seen what that does to kids. It turns them into zombies."

Claudia rests a willowy hand on Check Woman's arm. "Listen to me. Nobody's going to prescribe Ollie Ritalin, just like that. First I'd need to see him in action and assess him. After that we can look at practical ways to modify his behavior. I've got plenty up my sleeve."

"Really? I can't tell you what a relief that is."

"See?" her friend says. "I told you Claudia would be able to help. Now stop getting yourself so worked up."

Claudia has turned away from Check Woman and is looking at me. Her head is tilted, her brow furrowed with concern. "So, how are Sam and Rosie coping with their parents being away?"

"They only went yesterday. But so far they seem to be fine."

"That's good to hear — because you never know how children are going to react when parents leave them for weeks on end. Some get very angry because they feel abandoned. Suddenly you're faced with a whole load of behavioral problems."

I don't get a chance to reply because Tanya has come out of nowhere and is already setting Claudia straight. "No chance of that. Ginny's just been telling me how much Judy's grandchildren adore her. She's like a second mother to them."

"Oh, I'm sure you are," Claudia gushes, touching my arm in the same proprietorial way that she touched Check Woman's. "But

I'm always here if you're worried about anything and feel like a chat."

"That won't be necessary," Tanya retorts. "Judy will be fine."

"I'll be fine," I repeat, starting to feel invisible because Tanya is speaking for me.

"Of course you will," Claudia simpers. "But it can't be easy being landed with two children, particularly when you're still coming to terms with widowhood."

My widowhood and how I'm dealing with it are nothing to do with her, but for the sake of politeness I decide to let it go . . . unlike Tanya.

"I think that's Judy's business. Don't you?"

Claudia looks at Tanya and narrows her eyes. For a moment I think the pair of them are about to lock horns. But instead she turns back to me. "Goodness . . . yes, of course. I'm so sorry if I overstepped a boundary. I was only trying to be of help."

As I smile at Claudia and tell her not to worry, I'm aware that she's looking over my shoulder, most likely searching for another group of women among whom she might distribute her largesse. She informs us that she really ought to mingle and goes on her way.

Check Woman and her friend are eager to

tell me how amazing Claudia is. They simply don't know how she does it. She writes books and articles, has her own private practice counseling parents and children and manages to run a home.

"I think you'll find that staff might be the answer," Tanya sniffs. She makes our excuses and steers me away from the table.

"That was a bit rude," I say, midsteer. "They seem pretty harmless."

"I know, but I couldn't help myself. Claudia gets on my top tits, but not half as much as her bloody acolytes."

"Tanya, please don't take this the wrong way. I know you were only trying to help back there, but I am capable of speaking up for myself. I don't need you to do it for me."

"Sorry. It's just that she and I had a run-in a while back and I didn't stand up to her. It felt easier somehow, doing it on your be-half."

I ask her what happened and she explains that she and her husband, Rick, got a bit merry at the school quiz night. "We weren't drunk — just a bit loud. We were having fun — as were loads of other people. Any-way, afterward Claudia took me to one side and asked if we were high. Said that work-ing in the music business as we do, it must be hard not to succumb to drugs and that if we needed help getting clean, she knew somebody."

"Getting clean?"

"Yes. God knows what she thought we were on. It's so ironic because Rick and I never take anything stronger than Tylenol."

"So, what did you say?"

"Nothing. I didn't owe her an explanation. I walked away. If I'd stayed I would have punched her."

"I'm guessing she took your silence as an admission of guilt."

"Too bloody right she did. You can imagine the gossip. It's died down now, but it was horrible at the time. I thought about having it out with her, but Rick said I might end up digging myself in deeper. So I kept quiet and tried to rise above it."

"She really is a piece of work. I think I shall do my best to keep out of her way."

"Good luck with that."

Ginny sees us and breaks away from a group of women she's been chatting to. Her dietary resolve appears to have fizzled out, because she is chewing on a croissant. "So, what were you and Claudia talking about?"

"She was offering me the benefit of her vast experience and wisdom, said if I was having trouble with my abandoned grandchildren I could always call her for a chat."

"That sounds about par for the course."

"Don't worry," Tanya says. "I told her to get stuffed."

We carry on chatting, Tanya and Ginny pointing out mothers and giving me the lowdown on each of them. "That one there — with the hippie skirt — her name is Hester. She gives her kids breast milk eardrops when they have an infection. And she gives her husband, Reiki, blow jobs."

"What, when he has an ear infection?" Ginny says.

The three of us are falling about. At the same time, Claudia is tapping a glass with a teaspoon, trying to get everybody's attention. We hear, but we can't stop laughing.

By now everybody else is standing in silence, staring down their noses at us. We finally pull ourselves together, but not before Tanya has let out one final snort of laughter. As Claudia waits for quiet, she is smiling and serene — as if she has risen above the smut.

"OK . . . if everybody is finally ready . . . I just wanted to say happy spring term to one and all — and to remind you that the school fair is only a few months away and that we really do need to get cracking."

The first item on the agenda is to elect a committee chairman. Claudia regrets that she won't be standing because she has too many work commitments.

Straightaway a woman announces that last year she organized the fair at her older daughter's school and would be more than willing to head up the committee. "I'll be in New York for the next eight or nine weeks, but I'm sure you can all work with me in my time zone. It's only a five-hour difference."

"No problem," Tanya says, her voice loud and heavy with sarcasm.

Claudia makes a point of ignoring Tanya and thanks the woman for offering her services. She does, however, suggest that maybe the five-hour time gap isn't ideal. Seconds tick by. There are no more volunteers. Nobody wants to take ultimate responsibility. Then:

"I know," Claudia says, "what about Tanya?"

"Me?" Tanya looks as if somebody has walloped her.

Ginny tells her that this is her come-uppance for telling Claudia to get stuffed just now.

"You think I don't know that? . . . Bitch. . . ." Tanya's face is pink.

"Please don't make a scene," Ginny says.

"Why the hell not? She's not going to tell

me what to do."

Claudia is smiling, head tilted, waiting for Tanya's reply. "So, what do you say?"

"I'll do it," Ginny pipes up. "Tanya has a job. She hasn't got time."

Claudia's smile vanishes. Her mouth becomes a thin line. She's angry and, for the time being at least, defeated. "Excellent. I'm sure we all appreciate you putting yourself forward."

Claudia goes on to say that she's sure Ginny will have no trouble recruiting fellow committee members and wishes her good luck. "Right, if there's no other business I'll organize some more coffee."

"Thank you," Tanya says to Ginny. "That's one I owe you. But you didn't have to volunteer. Organizing the fair is your worst nightmare."

"I know. But you were about to start yelling."

"I wasn't. Not really. Not in public. I was just going to say no and refuse to let her badger me."

"You mean I volunteered for nothing?"

"Kind of."

"Right. You really do owe me. I will expect your full and undivided support organizing this wretched event." I can't help feeling that Ginny's tone is similar to one Lady

114

Bracknell might have used to a minion.

"You got it."

Ginny grunts.

I tell her that I will help, too.

"That's very kind of you, Judy," she says with a smile. "I appreciate that."

Tanya says her good-byes because she needs to get home and start her day's work. Ginny and I stroll back to our cars, which are parked at the end of the street.

We get chatting and I find myself asking Ginny how she got to be so posh. She looks affronted, but amused and says she isn't remotely posh. I tell her that posh people always say that.

"Of course you are. You remind me of one of those formidable women who swanned around Bombay during the Raj."

She laughs. "Actually I was born in New Delhi."

"Aha — I rest my case."

"My father was an engineer. He went out there to build bridges and aqueducts. We moved back when I was ten. I don't remember much about it — apart from the heat. My mother used to lie in bed all day and get up at night to go to parties."

"I bet you had servants."

"Dozens. But life changes. I'm not who I once was. Haven't been for decades."

"What do you mean?"

"Let's just say that I fell from grace."

"In what way?"

She looks at the ground and back up at me. "Do you mind if we don't talk about it?"

"Of course not. I'm sorry. I didn't mean to pry."

"You weren't."

She says she has to run. She needs to pick up a prescription before the doctor's surgery closes for lunch.

CHAPTER FIVE

"Judy, can you come here? I'm a bit confused."

Mum is sitting at the kitchen table e-mailing on the laptop that Estelle Silverfish gave her. I'm surprised at how quickly she's getting the hang of the Internet. Tom was as good as his word. Before he and Abby left for Nicaragua, he spent an entire morning setting up the computer and getting her going. Despite her age, she's a fast learner. I can't help feeling rather proud.

She's been on the phone to all her friends telling them that she's now a Googler. "I never knew you could get so much off the computer." She's even set herself up as an unofficial health help line. "Let me know your symptoms and I'll Google them and tell you what you've got."

I gave her a long lecture on the dangers of consulting Dr. Google, but she's not having it. She's already successfully diagnosed her friend Lillian with bursitis and she's over-the-moon. Lillian less so.

"OK, what is it?" I say, regarding her request for help. Before she can explain, her cell phone starts playing "Amoré." She changes her ringtone all the time. Last week it was "Delilah." She picks up the phone and peers through her specs, fingers dithering. Finally she hits "connect."

"Hello. Frieda speaking . . . Hello? . . . Hello? . . . Is there anybody there?" Mum looks at me with a shrug. "Nobody there." She shakes the phone and puts it back to her ear. Still nothing. She shakes it again, harder. This time she also bashes it against the table.

"For crying out loud, Mum. What are you doing? You'll break it."

She carries on shaking the phone. She's like a child with a snow globe. "Damn stupid thing never works."

She hands it to me. No battery. "Mum, how many times do I have to remind you to charge your phone?"

She looks sheepish. "Is that what it is? I'm sorry. I keep forgetting."

I take the phone and put it on charge next to mine on the countertop. By now she's staring into the laptop again. "OK, so here's my problem. . . ."

She explains that over the last few days she's sent three e-mails to her cousin Miriam in Montreal and Miriam hasn't replied.

"Give her a chance. Maybe she doesn't check her e-mail that often."

"OK — but meanwhile I keep getting e-mails from somebody called Mailer-Daemon. I've got no idea who he is — or what his first name is. And I don't understand what he's trying to tell me, but I've replied to his e-mails. I thought it was rude not to."

"Hang on. . . . You're in correspondence with Mailer-Daemon?" Was that a thing? Could you even do that?

"So you know who he is?"

"Not as such. He doesn't exist. By that I mean Mailer-Daemon isn't a person."

"What do you mean, he doesn't exist? He's been e-mailing me."

I lean over her shoulder and stare at the computer screen. As I try to explain what Mailer-Daemon is and at the same time work out how she could possibly have replied to it, Rosie appears. She's carrying my laptop, which I've let her borrow. She puts it down next to Mum's.

"Nana, Nana — you have to watch this. It's my favoritest thing on YouTube."

"On what Tube?"

"Just watch."

On the screen a woman's fingers, nails covered in Mickey Mouse transfers, are removing the foil from a Kinder-style egg, but bigger. "Ooh, what do we have here?" purrs the disembodied voice. "Yum . . . lovely, creamy milk chocolate."

"Rosie, darlink — why are we watching a person unwrap a chocolate egg?"

"Shush. It's awesome. Keep watching."

The fingers crack open the egg. Shards of chocolate fall to an unseen surface. Inside one of the halves is a small plastic container. The fingers remove the lid and rummage inside. They produce a tiny plastic figure. "Who do we have here? Wow, it's Queen Elsa."

Rosie claps her hands. "It's Elsa! Yay! Maybe the next one will be Kristoff or Anna."

My mother looks at me. "What is this? Do you understand it?"

Meanwhile another egg appears and the process is repeated. This time Olaf emerges from the plastic box. Next up is the Duke of Weselton.

"Oh no! We hate the Duke of Weselton. Boo!"

"It's called unboxing," I tell my mother.

She frowns as she repeats the word. "But

what is it for?"

"It's not for anything. It just is."

I explain that, left alone, kids Rosie's age will spend hours watching chocolate eggs or even toys being unwrapped.

"And this is a good thing? This is healthy? Doesn't it mean they just nag their parents to go out and buy the toys?"

"Abby says not. It's the actual unwrapping they seem to love."

"I don't get it. What a world."

Mum has no trouble understanding Polly Pockets, Moshi Monsters, Furbies. As a kid, I had trolls, so these new creatures make sense to her. She gets them. She gets loom bands because I used to spend hours braiding odds and ends of knitting wool and turning them into bracelets. She gets Pokémon trading cards. My generation traded sweet cigarette cards. But unboxing is bizarre and beyond her ken. If I'm honest, it's beyond mine, too. I don't understand the satisfaction that Rosie and her friends get from such a mindless activity. But since I have no intention of relinquishing my Cool Grandma status, I will not be letting on.

When I tell Rosie that she's spent enough time watching her unboxing video and maybe she should find something to do that doesn't involve a computer screen, there are no cries of protest. For the time being at least, she and Sam are pretty much doing as they're told. But I'm guessing this honeymoon period won't last long.

Rosie disappears to her room. I go back to explaining Mailer-Daemon to my mother. "So what you need to do is phone Miriam and check that you've got the right e-mail address."

I hand Mum the landline and go upstairs to take a shower. It's Saturday lunchtime and I'm still in my dressing gown. All morning, I've been waylaid by kids' squabbles and demands that I play games or sit and watch TV with them. I haven't had the heart to refuse them. As I cross the landing, I can see into Rosie's room. My granddaughter is sitting on the bed unwrapping Polly Pocket figures, which she's wrapped in toilet paper. At the same time she's delivering a singsong commentary: "And who do we have here? It's Shani. Isn't she beautiful? I adore her hair. She loves fashion and music — especially the drums . . . OK . . . and this is Lila. She is such a drama queen like you wouldn't believe. . . ."

Abby says that these days she's too scared to ask her daughter what she wants to do when she grows up because she's pretty sure she knows the answer.

Next door, Sam is playing chess against himself. I watch him chewing his bottom lip as he considers his next move. He's wearing a red bucket hat. Once he's repositioned the chess piece, he turns the board around and swaps the hat for a baseball cap.

I decide that a bath will be more relaxing than a shower. I turn on the tap and pour in posh jasmine bubbles. As I lie in the tub, I realize how much I'm enjoying a few minutes' peace. Both children are playing quietly in their rooms. There is no fighting. Nobody is demanding bits of me. Downstairs, Mum seems to have come off the phone, because I can smell bacon frying. Bacon bagels for lunch. For as long as I've known her, Mum has refused to keep kosher. She has no interest in religion. The only time she'll set foot in a synagogue is for a wedding or bar mitzvah.

It's not long before I find myself thinking about Brian. Since the night Abby and Tom left, I've hardly given him a thought. Usually even when I'm busy I make sure that after I've gone to bed we have one of our one-sided chats. "Hey, Bri . . . it's me. I'm doing a bit better. But I still can't bring myself to throw away your clothes. Oh, and by the way, where did you hide the Allen key . . . you know, the one you always used to bleed the radiators? Can't find it any-where. Try to give me a sign to indicate its whereabouts. Miss you. Love you. . . . Bri . . . are you OK?"

I'm always asking him to give me signs. Not that he ever does and not that I really expect them. I know that stuff only happens on *Ghost Hunters.*

These last few days, the gap between climbing into bed and falling asleep has been reduced to moments. I've been too tired to make conversation with my late husband. I'm starting to remember what it is about children that's so exhausting: They run everywhere, usually yelling as they go. They're self-obsessed. They have egos that require constant boosting and massaging. They couldn't care less about anybody else. In a nutshell, they are loud, pint-size narcis-sists with the energy of puppies.

As I scrub myself with the loofah, I say sorry to Brian for being absent these last few days. I imagine his reply. "Will you stop apologizing? You're getting on with your life, and about bloody time."

Eventually I realize that I'm lying in lukewarm water. I could top it up with hot, but lunch will be ready in a minute. I haul myself up. My knees ache. I find myself wondering, as I often do, when my body started to feel so heavy. I step out, dripping onto the mat.

"Grandma — I want to do some painting. Where are my paints? And I can't find any paper either."

I have forgotten to lock the bathroom door. Rosie is standing in front of me. She carries on yammering about her paints and paper and where she had them last. Finally she tilts her head to one side. "Grandma, why are your boobies so long? Mummy doesn't have long ones. Hers are more round and doughnutty. Yours are like sausages."

"It's all about gravity, my darling."

I manage not to make a sudden grab for a towel. I don't want to give Rosie the impression that I'm embarrassed about her seeing me starkers — particularly as Abby and Tom waltz around the house naked in front of the children. They're determined that the kids should grow up at ease with nudity and not see it as something smutty. So I reach out, casually remove a towel from the rail and wrap it around me.

"We did gravity in school. So, will I get long boobies? Do they sway from side to side as you walk?"

"Only if I'm not wearing a bra."

Any second now, she's going to ask me to

swing them over my shoulder like a continental soldier. Then I remember that according to the wartime song, it was balls, not boobs.

I am saved from further humiliation by my mother calling upstairs to say lunch is ready. I tell Rosie I'll be down in a sec and I'll help her find her paints.

"Miriam had given me her old e-mail address," Mum says.

"That figures."

She hands me a bacon bagel and tells me it's my fault the bacon's gone cold. "How long does it take to get dressed?"

"Sorry."

I don't tell her that I was standing in front of the mirror scrutinizing my breasts and wondering if at my age it was worth getting them lifted. I decided it wasn't. Not because I'm too old, but because of the barbarism factor. Nobody is going to hack into my breasts, slice off my nipples and stitch them back on.

I turn to Sam and ask him how his chess game is going.

"Great. I opened with the queen's gambit. The clever thing about the queen's gambit is that white sacrifices a pawn for rapid

126

development and usually gets its pawn back."

I have no idea what he is talking about. "Wow. Sounds complicated."

"Not really. I've been studying it with Bogdan. He's my chess coach. Bogdan's Russian, but he knows a lot about English history. He says the queen's gambit goes back hundreds of years — to before Henry the Eighth."

"Huh, nearly as old as me," Mum says. "So, what's he like — this Bogdan?" My mother doesn't care for Russians because of the pogroms and because at the start of the war they sided with Hitler. Then decades later they wouldn't let Jews emigrate.

"A bit scary," Sam says.

Mum rolls her eyes. "They all think they're bloody Cossacks."

"You know what, Nana, I could teach you to play chess."

"Nah — I'm too old."

"You've managed the Internet."

"No, I haven't. I can do a few basics, that's all. I couldn't get my brain around chess. Chess is for clever people."

"Sam isn't clever," Rosie pipes up. "He's stupid. When he was little he thought fish sticks could swim."

"Yes . . . when I was little. . . . At least I

didn't think teachers lived at school."

Rosie looks like she might burst into tears. Her hand is making a fist.

"OK, that's enough. Who'd like some pineapple?"

They both would. Mum declines. Pineapple gives her heartburn, which means she has to take an extra proton pump inhibitor.

I ask Sam if he's looking forward to the county chess tournament he's got coming up in April.

"I'm a bit nervous. Bogdan says that if I'm going to do well, I need to up my game and start focusing. He says I'm only fair to middling and that there are loads of kids who could wipe the board with me. So I've got a lot of work to do."

"You have to work for what you want in this world," Mum says. "You get out what you put in."

Sam shrugs. "I guess." He seems subdued all of a sudden. I'm not sure I like the sound of this Bogdan.

I'm gathering up plates when my phone rings. Mum tells me to go ahead and take it — she'll load the dishwasher.

It's Ginny. She's at a loose end and wants to know if I feel like popping over to hers for a cuppa and to brainstorm creative ideas for the spring fair. "I'd say let's meet somewhere halfway, but my daughter has borrowed my car."

"I'd love to come over. But I've got the kids. I'm not sure if Mum can cope on her own."

"Go," Mum says with a wave of her hand. "Rosie has found her paints, so she's going to busy herself with them while I wash up, and after that she's going to teach me how to make loom bands."

Mum is making a real effort to play with Sam and Rosie. When I was a kid she almost never played with me. She was always cooking, cleaning and resting. My dad was the one who read to me and got down on the floor to build bricks and play Snakes and Ladders.

I'm more convinced than ever that my mother is experiencing some kind of renaissance. But last night, when I suggested that the children being here was doing her a power of good, she wouldn't have it. She got huffy, as if I'd insulted her, and insisted that she was simply "keeping my chin up because I don't want them to see me miserable."

I tell Ginny that Mum is happy to look after Sam and Rosie. She gives me her address — a street on the Butcher's Row Estate.

I'm confused. How does somebody as well bred as Ginny end up in public housing? Presumably it has something to do with her "fall from grace."

"I hope you don't mind coming over to the dark side," she says, sounding as gung ho as ever. "There are those that do." Then I hear it, the faint hint of anxiety in her voice that says "Now that you know I don't have much money, will you still want to be my friend?"

The unpalatable truth is that there are those who wouldn't. Around here, in the privileged organic-squid-ink-and-tapenade ghetto that is Eden Hill, people rate people by how close they live to Butcher's Row. I am overcome with the need to let Ginny know that I'm not one of them. I want to tell her that Brian and I bought in to the neighborhood years ago, before it became gentrified; that I almost never shop at Whole Foods because I agree with my mother that their prices are a chutzpah. I want to enlighten her about my house, which by Eden Hill standards is an eyesore. There are no plantation shutters. The porch isn't guarded by twin bay trees in zinc pots. My front door is not painted a matte gray. Instead it is covered in cheap and chipped red gloss. There is no brushed chrome house number, letter box or doorknob. My door furniture, such as it is, came from Home Depot circa 1981. But I'm worried that if I blurt all this out, Ginny will think I'm protesting too much. So I say nothing about Whole Foods or the house.

Instead I tell her not to be so daft. Why on earth would I mind where she lives?

The estate is a ten-minute drive away. I know the streets well. For twenty years they were my shortcut to work. The place has its share of dog shit, discarded needles and rusting jalopies minus their wheels, propped up on bricks. It's pockmarked with satellite dishes. There are problem families. The teenage arsonists and drug-dependent burglars make headlines in the local paper, which in turn stir up fear among the residents of Eden Hill. Then again, the appearance of a car more than five years old stirs up fear in Eden Hill.

Despite all this, Butcher's Row is less crime-ridden and easier on the eye than a lot of public housing estates. The prewar semis are pebbledashed and cottagey and have decent-size gardens front and back. The pavements are lined with trees and there's a brand-new kids' playground. Thanks to Margaret Thatcher, many of the residents have been able to buy their homes.

Some people — me included — think that reducing the public housing stock was one of Thatcher's worst crimes, but there is no doubt that over the years, private ownership has improved the look of the place. There is more than a handful of tidy, freshly painted houses with neat gardens and nice cars outside and solid aspirational families inside.

Ginny's front garden with its trimmed, wraparound privet hedge is particularly well tended. Pruned rosebushes line the crazy paving path to the front door. Between them, snowbells are starting to appear. On the porch, a garden gnome is smoking a pipe as he reclines in a deck chair.

Ginny must have seen me pull up, because she opens the door while I'm still admiring the gnome. "His name's Gilbert," she says. "I named him after a favorite uncle."

She ushers me into a small living room. I'm struck by the original thirties fireplace with its reddish brown tiles. To one side, arranged at an angle, is an art deco armchair. The bentwood arms are scratched and bashed about. Horsehair is escaping from a split in the beige leather seat. A few hundred quid would see it right. Ditto the sagging bergère sofa, its wickerwork in holes. Ginny has covered it in a purple mohair throw and added velvet cushions.

"Sit your body down," she says, picking up a copy of the *Guardian* lying on the sofa. I accept her offer of tea and she disappears into the kitchen to put the kettle on.

"I love this sofa," I call out to her. "And the chair. You've got a great eye."

"Thank you. I just wish I had the money to do the restoration. I picked them up at a flea market years ago and they've been in this state ever since."

She returns with a plate of chocolate digestives, which she places on the coffee table. A Clarice Cliff jug stands toward one end, filled with dried flowers.

"So, come on, be honest," she says, heading back to the kitchen, where the kettle is gurgling loudly as it comes to the boil. "Were you shocked when I told you I lived here?"

"Ginny, it's none of my business where you live. And anyway — why does it matter?"

She doesn't answer. I can hear the tinkling of teaspoon on china. In a moment she's back carrying mugs of tea. They both say Tamiflu. I'm guessing another flea market find.

"It doesn't matter," she says, lowering herself into the deco armchair. "Not in the grand scheme of things. But some of the mothers at Faraday House won't let their children come on playdates with Ivo if I'm looking after him here. They make absurd excuses about it being too far. I don't know what they think is going to happen. I keep telling them the neighbors only bugger the children when there's a full moon."

I burst out laughing. "Please tell me you didn't actually say that."

"No, but I wish I had. These people are such idiots."

We both help ourselves to chocolate biscuits. Ginny dips hers in her tea and takes a bite. She looks thoughtful, as if she's gearing up to tell me something.

"I owe you an apology," she says.

"Really? What for?"

"For the other day. I mentioned my fall from grace and then I cut you off without an explanation. It was rude of me."

"No, it wasn't. Your life is your business. You owe me nothing."

"Maybe not, but I'd like the two of us to be friends and I'm not sure it can happen if there's a dirty great elephant in the room. So, if you're happy to listen, I'd like to explain."

It's not a long story. Ginny's parents were both independently wealthy. Her father

134

became an engineer because he wanted a career, not because he needed one. They owned two houses — a villa on Hampstead Heath and a manor house on the Devon coast. "They sold the Devon place decades ago, but when I was a child my mother and I spent long, glorious summers there. My father came when he could get away from work. There were horses, tennis courts, a private beach with rock pools where I used to hunt for crabs with my cousins. There were picnic lunches, croquet and cream teas. It was pretty idyllic."

Ginny went to boarding school and on to university. To her parents' horror, instead of choosing a suitably ladylike subject such as English literature, French or art history, she chose politics and sociology. "I'd been sheltered from politics all my life. Then when I was still at school, a teacher gave me a book on the Russian Revolution. After that I started reading about British socialism and the history of the Labour Party. I became somewhat smitten with left-wing politics. You could say 'fuck' in my family, but not 'socialism.' My parents were appalled. Of course that was like a red rag to a bull. I would quote Marx at them over breakfast — inform them that the history of all hitherto-existing society is the history of class struggle. At first, they patronized me, informed me that I was going through a phase and that I'd grow out of it. It took months of nagging to persuade them to let me take politics at university. In the end I simply wore them down. Toward the end of the first term, I fell in with a bunch of Maoists who lived in a squat in Brixton. I dropped out in my second year. By then I'd hooked up with a layabout car mechanic named Kev. Of course the inevitable happened and I got pregnant. At the time, my father was abroad working, but my mother was scandalized and in complete and utter despair. In an ideal world she would have banished me to a nunnery. Instead she insisted I have an abortion and go back to university. I refused. I was determined to keep the baby. We had a huge fight, which ended with her throwing me out and telling me never to darken her door. I eloped with Kev. We moved into a single room with a shared bathroom over a pub. Emma was born a few months later."

"But what about your father? Did you contact him?"

"He went along with my mother. Said I'd let down the family name. I was sure that once they met their granddaughter, their hearts would melt and we would be reconciled. But it wasn't to be. Six weeks after Emma was born, my father had a heart attack and died. My mother wrote to me, blaming me for his death. She banned me from the funeral and told me again that she never wanted to see me or 'the child.' So there we were, living with a baby on Kev's wage, which barely covered the rent."

"How on earth did you manage?"

"You just get on with it. I had no choice. My darling uncle Gilbert took pity on us and sent checks several times a year. His money kept the wolf from the door. We didn't starve. But when I got pregnant a second time, Kev couldn't handle it. He started drinking, seeing other women. Then one night he didn't come home. A day or so later he called from a phone box to say the marriage was over and I shouldn't try to find him. When Uncle Gilbert died a few years back, he left me a few thousand, so I hired a private investigator to try and find Kev. I'm not sure what I was hoping to achieve. I didn't want money. In fact, I assumed he wouldn't have any. I think it was curiosity more than anything. The investigator located him almost immediately: in the cemetery. He'd died years before in a car crash. The report in the local paper said he'd been seven times over the alcohol limit."

Ginny said that after Kev walked out, it was three years before she and the children were rehoused by the council. The single room over the pub was replaced by a two-bedroom apartment in a new social housing development nearby. Later on they moved to the house they live in now. Friends babysat while she cleaned offices and waited tables. After her children started school she did an Open University degree and qualified as a social worker. "On my salary buying even a small flat somewhere like Eden Hill was out of the question. So the kids and I were forced to stay here. Then two years ago Social Services made me redundant. By then I was sixty, so I have my pension. I get by."

"OK, tell me to mind my own business, but surely your son could help you out financially?"

"He could and he's offered a hundred times. As has my brother, William, who's also loaded. They've both offered to buy me a flat. But I don't want their money. It would make me feel dependent, constantly indebted. I can't think of anything worse. Plus I need to be here."

"Why?"

Ginny stares into her mug of tea. Seconds pass before she looks up.

"My daughter lives two doors away." She lets out a soft, bitter laugh. "Talk about history repeating itself. Emma also fell for a layabout — although she had the sense not to marry him. She got pregnant by him at sixteen and again at eighteen. Then he left her. The difference between her situation and mine was that she knew where to find him. She hauled the blighter in front of a judge and managed to get a few quid a month off him in child support. But he has no interest in the boys."

"Poor girl. Poor kids."

"I blame myself. I'm afraid I wasn't a very good role model. . . ."

"Of course you were. Look at you. You pulled yourself up. You got a degree. And Ben has done really well for himself."

She shrugs. "He has and I'm proud of him. But Emma worries me. She's bright. She's got a great eye for fashion. She buys and sells vintage clothes online. What she'd like to do is open her own shop and maybe even start a chain, but she can't do that without capital."

"And her rich brother and uncle?"

"They think that because she dropped out of high school, she's lazy. They're happy to give her the money to study fashion, to get some qualifications, but not to build up the business. They think that even though she's in her thirties, she needs to get a degree, work in fashion for a few years, see how the business works and then go out on her own."

"They could be right."

"They're not. My daughter is many things, but lazy isn't one of them. That girl works day and night trying to make ends meet. All she does is sit in front of her laptop. She runs herself ragged hunting all over the world for bargains. And she's good at it. She makes a decent profit, just not enough to live on."

"Can't be easy."

"It isn't. And the other problem is that because she's always working, she tends to ignore the boys and let them run wild. They're only ten and twelve, but they're starting to get into mischief. I help out a lot of the time, but when they're on their own they're always getting into fights with kids in the neighborhood. They've been caught letting down car tires. The other day, a neighbor found them playing chicken on the main road. They're also getting a reputation at school. On top of all this they never get to see Ivo because Madeline, my daughter-in-law, doesn't like him mixing with them. It's so sad. I hate the idea of these cousins growing up not knowing each other."

"Ginny, I am so sorry. I had no idea you were going through all this."

While she's been telling me her story, her eyes have become glassy. She wipes them with the heel of her hand. Then, in a few seconds, she's back to herself. "Right, that's enough self-pity for one day. How about another cup of tea?" She picks up both our mugs. Mine is still half-full, but she doesn't notice.

"What's wrong with a bit of self-pity?"

"Everything. Moaners are so tedious. Chin up, chest out . . . that's what I was taught. If life throws you a curveball or two, you get on with it."

"And what if you can't get on with it?"

"You have to."

With that she disappears into the kitchen again. She returns with fresh tea and a note-pad under her arm. "Right . . . the school fair. I've jotted down a few ideas."

When I get home, Mum is sitting on the sofa with the kids. Rosie is gabbling into the phone. "We had fun today. Me and Nana made loom bands — mine's pink, and

Nana's is green. At first hers went a bit wrong, but I helped her sort it out. Then we made one for Sam — his is blue."

"Let me talk. It's my turn." Sam tries and fails to wrestle the phone from his sister.

"Go away." She pushes him in the chest and puts the phone back to her other ear.

"But you've been talking for ages."

"I made you a loom band."

"So what? That doesn't mean you get longer on the phone."

Rosie takes Denise out of her jeans pocket. She screws up her face and holds the carrot aloft — a crucifix against the vampire. I do wish she'd keep Denise in her bedroom. But since I swapped her for a fresh carrot, at least she isn't oozing anymore.

"They're talking to Abby and Tom," Mum whispers.

Since they arrived in Nicaragua, the Internet has been down. So instead of Skyping, Abby and Tom have been calling us from the MediGlobal satellite phone. The problem is that all the medical staff wants to call their families, so the pressure on it is huge and we only get a couple of minutes at a time.

I tell Rosie to let her brother have a turn.

"In a minute."

"No. Now."

"But —"

"Rosie . . . I said now."

Another grimace. Then: "Bye, Mummy. Bye, Daddy. Miss you. Love you." She's still making kissing noises down the phone when her brother grabs it off her.

While Sam chats away, I ask my mother what sort of an afternoon she's had with the kids.

"Lovely. We made loom bands. We chatted."

"What about?" My question isn't innocuous. It's loaded. I'm worried she's been talking to the kids about the war.

"Oh, you know. This and that."

"What sort of this and that?"

She doesn't get a chance to reply because Sam breaks in to tell me that Abby wants a word. He hands me the phone.

"Hi, darling. How's it all going?"

"We're fine."

She sounds exhausted.

"Are they managing to get food supplies in? Are you getting enough to eat?"

"Yep. It's all good."

I bet they're living on rice and beans.

"I hope you're managing to get some rest."

"It's still pretty full-on. Tom operated on more than a dozen people yesterday. Broken bones mainly. I had a couple of kids with

143

internal injuries die on me in the night."

"Oh, sweetheart, that's awful. It must have been gut-wrenching. But what about you? When did you last sleep?"

"I'll grab a few hours later."

I'm imagining her heavy-eyed, the weight falling off her.

"Please take care. Both of you."

"We are. How are the kids? They sound great. But I worry and I still feeling guilty about leaving them."

"Abby, listen to me. You have to stop this. Each time you call I tell you the kids are fine. They tell you they're fine. You have to start believing it. If you carry on fretting like this you're going to make yourself ill. Then you'll be no use to anybody."

"OK. I'm sorry." She's sounding sheepish now. "And you're OK? You're coping?"

"It's all good. I promise."

She says she has to go. There's a queue of people wanting to use the phone.

"Go. Take care. Love you. Love to Tom. And get some rest. . . ."

The kids are a bit upset they don't get a chance to say good-bye, so we have hugs on the sofa instead. Pretty soon they've cheered up and they're showing off their loom bands. Meanwhile Mum is checking on the chicken she's got in the oven.

After we've eaten I start running baths. Once they're in their pj's we have half an hour of *Shrek* and then I announce it's bedtime. They protest and beg to finish the film. I offer them another fifteen minutes. We finally agree on thirty.

Sam has grown out of bedtime stories and prefers to read to himself from what Rosie calls "chapter books." He disappears to his room. I tell him I'll be in to say good night after I've read to Rosie.

After a few more pages of *Aliens in Underpants Save the World,* I pull the comforter up under Rosie's chin and kiss her night-night. Then she can't find Denise. I finally locate her in the bathroom, under a pile of damp towels.

Rosie rolls onto her side, clutching Denise in both hands. I go to turn off the lamp.

"No, leave it on. I'm scared. And before you go, can you check under my bed?"

"Darling, there are no burglars. A burglar couldn't even fit under this bed. It's too low."

"I don't want you to check for burglars. I want you to check for Hitlers."

Downstairs Mum is watching one of her programs — some hospital drama.

"This chap's dying of lung cancer. Did

145

you know that when you get lung cancer, the secondary growth often appears first? With him it was a brain tumor. They managed to get rid of the brain tumor, but —"

I've switched off the TV.

"Hey — why did you do that?"

"We need to talk. What have you been telling the children?"

"Nothing. Switch the TV back on."

"No." To make my point, I position myself in front of the screen. "And if you didn't say anything, then why did Rosie just ask me to check under the bed for Hitlers?"

"They asked me about what it was like growing up in Germany."

"And you told them."

"They should know the truth — what human beings are capable of."

"Mum — they're children. Rosie's not much more than a baby. They need to be protected."

"I was a child. Who protected me?"

"Nobody. And that was a tragedy — a catastrophe. But what were you hoping to achieve by telling the kids your story?" I take a breath. "Please tell me you didn't tell them about the camps."

"Of course I didn't. You think I'm mad?"

"You told me. I was six when I found out what Belsen was. Just because you had your innocence snatched from you, it doesn't give you the right to do the same to other children. You did it to me. That was bad enough."

It's a low blow. I regret it at once. "I'm sorry. I shouldn't have said that. You didn't tell me about it to hurt me. But at the same time, I feel that I should have been shielded from it until I was older."

Mum's face crumples. Sitting in the armchair, she looks even smaller and more vulnerable than usual. "I don't know what to say. I'd experienced such terrible things. I wanted you to know. I thought I was educating you." She looks as if she might break down, but she doesn't. "Maybe I was wrong to tell you when you were so young. But you coped."

"Only because I had Dad to talk to. And now you've scared Rosie. The poor kid's petrified. It's taken me ages to calm her down. If she has nightmares it'll be your fault and you'll have to explain to Abby."

Suddenly my mother is back on the defensive. "You're overreacting. She'll get over it."

The day I heard my mother's story for the first time, she and I were in the kitchen. She was standing next to the cooker, stuffing a chicken neck. I was crayoning at the blue Formica table. She'd been telling me about the terrible food at Dad's cousin's wedding. "And such small portions." I was almost certainly bored and probably wondering how to change the subject. Mum didn't talk about her childhood in Germany very much. All I knew was that she'd been born in a place called Berlin and that her parents had died a long time ago. I was curious to find out more.

Mum carried on shoving thick yellowish gloop into chicken skin. She seemed thoughtful and happy to talk.

"Berlin was a beautiful city. And we had such a lovely house. It was nothing like this one. Much bigger. My bedroom had frilly curtains and rosebud wallpaper. There were two cherry trees in the garden — and a swing and a hutch for my pet rabbit. She was called Adelheid."

"That's a funny name."

"That's because it's German."

"Say something in German."

"OK . . . *Ich heisse Frieda und ich habe eine tochter. Sie heisst Judy. Sie ist sehr schön.*"

"It sounds funny."

Mum laughed and translated. I discovered that *tochter* meant daughter and *schön* meant pretty.

"Am I really pretty?"

Mum came to the table, holding out her matzo-meal and chicken-fat hands. I remember thinking she was going to cup my face in them. But she didn't. Instead she kissed my forehead and both cheeks. "You are more than pretty — you are beautiful. You are a *shaineh maidel* . . . a beautiful young girl."

She went back to her story. It wasn't long before she got to the scary bit. There were bad people called Nazis who hated Jews. One night, they smashed the windows of Jewish shops and started taking Jews to "the camps." I imagined fields of brightly colored tents. Then she explained. She spared me nothing. It was odd, but I wasn't frightened. I'd been learning about Henry VIII in school. I knew all about him chopping off people's heads and people getting burned at the stake. It felt a bit like that. Just history.

"So, what happened to you and your mummy and daddy?"

"By 1939 it was almost impossible for Jews to leave Germany. But Jewish charities in England offered the Nazis money to let the children go and they agreed. That's how the Kindertransport got started."

I repeated the word. I liked the way it sounded. My mother explained that thousands of children left Europe on Kindertransport trains.

"You mean they had to leave their parents?"

"Yes."

That's when I got upset. These were children just like me. How was it possible to hate them for no reason and then drag them away from the people they loved most in the world?

"So, did you have to leave your mum and dad?"

"I did. I left Berlin in May. It was such a beautiful day. 'Führer weather,' they called it. I remember saying good-bye to my brother, Joseph. He was eighteen and too old for the Kindertransport. 'Bye, sis,' he said. 'See you in a few months.' Then he handed me a bar of Ritter chocolate for the journey. My mother begged me to hug Joseph good-bye, but I refused." My mother was managing to weep and chuckle at the same time. "I was going through a phase of not liking boys. So . . . after I'd waved my brother good-bye, we took the tram to Friedrichstrasse Station."

I asked her why the Germans had such long words for everything. She said she didn't know and promised to teach me how to say her favorite German word: Bezirksschornsteinfegermeister. It meant head district chimney sweep.

"Anyway, we reached the station. There was a woman struggling to get her baby carriage up the stairs. She yelled at my father, who with his dark complexion and black beard couldn't have looked less Aryan, 'You . . . Jew scum . . . I have given the Führer a child. Help me up the stairs.' And he did. He was so polite. He never said a word."

"And the woman never said 'Thank you' . . . right?"

"Right. That morning, fifty of us children got on that train. Some were young like me. Others were teenagers. The older kids understood what was happening. We little ones didn't. Our parents told us we were going on an exciting adventure and that we had to be brave and grown-up. But most of us were crying. A few of the boys were trying to make light of it. They were laughing and sharing sweets, trying to be big, fearless men."

"So, where did the train take you?"

"To the Dutch coast. At that stage the Germans hadn't invaded Holland. From there we took a boat to England."

151

"And did you have friends on the train?"

"No. My friends left before me. So I was all by myself. I remember sitting on the wooden seat, cuddling Lotte, my doll. I had a manila luggage tag round my neck. It had my number on the front and my name on the back. We were allowed one small suitcase. Mine was full of brand-new clothes. My mother didn't want the people who took me in to think she didn't have standards."

Mum was choking back tears.

"Mutti held my hand through the window. 'Write to us,' she said. 'And be good. Your father and I don't want to hear bad reports. You mustn't worry. Soon we'll all be together again.'

"As the train pulled out of the station, she ran alongside. Vati didn't move. He stood there in his gray overcoat with the yellow star, barely waving. As the train gathered speed Mutti couldn't keep up and she was forced to let go. I can still hear her howling from the pain while my father tried to comfort her. She wasn't the only one weeping. As I looked out of the window, all I could see was pitiful mothers waving handkerchiefs. There was one father who refused to let go of his son. While the train was moving, he pulled him by his arms back through the window. He must have used so much force because the child fell onto the platform, crying out and bleeding."

"So he got to stay with his parents."

"Yes . . . for all the good it did him."

I didn't ask what she meant by that. Young as I was, I could work it out.

"When we reached England, we were put on another train to London. I hadn't slept for two days and two nights. By the time the train pulled in, I could barely keep my eyes open. We were ushered onto the cold platform where we waited for people to come and claim us. I had never felt so frightened and alone. The only words of English I knew were the ones my mother had taught me: please and thank you."

Frieda was seven. She never saw her parents or brother again.

She was taken in by an orthodox Jewish couple who lived in North London. The Lewins loved her and raised her as one of their own. "Some children weren't so lucky. People treated them like unpaid domestics." To this day my mother refers to the Lewins' three natural children — all of them now dead — as "my brother and sisters."

By the time she reached her teenage years, my mother was done with God and religion — much to the despair of the Lewins. They took the view that everything — even the worst catastrophes — happened for a reason. God had a grand plan that we on earth weren't privy to or meant to understand.

The Lewins began to fear that Frieda would marry out of the religion — and she did. They were heartbroken. They felt they had failed Frieda's parents. Frieda fell out with them when they refused to come to her registry office wedding — to see her marry Jack Harris, to whom she would remain devoted until the day he died. Affectionate relations with the Lewins only resumed after I came along.

During the war, Jack, his mother and his siblings had been evacuated to a farm in Devon. He chased sheep, collected eggs and fed baby lambs. He always felt guilty that my mother had suffered so much while he had this idyllic life in the country.

But my mother had her own guilt. Survivor's guilt, they call it. Time and again she would break down and ask the same question: "Why was I saved when so many perished? I had no right to live. It should have been me that died."

Growing up, I had no problem understanding why my mother felt guilty. What baffled me was her need to be ill all the time. It wasn't until I started reading books about the lives of Holocaust survivors that I understood. My mother believed that because she had survived she didn't deserve to be loved — at least not for herself. A sick person, on the other hand, always deserved love and compassion. I'm also guessing that she saw physical pain as her penance, the price she had to pay for being spared.

I couldn't keep up with her ailments. If it wasn't her head or her back, it was her heart or her stomach. It felt like every week she was finding "blood in my business." She had a specialist for every condition. And they didn't come cheap. At the same time, Mum longed to move into a bigger house.

"Fine," my father would say. "Give up your specialists — or at least start seeing doctors for free on the NHS — and you can have a bigger house tomorrow." But she was hooked on being ill. It was strange how the woman who thought she didn't deserve to be loved insisted on consulting the best doctors in the land.

"Take my advice," she would say to her friends, "and only make appointments with doctors who have long waiting lists. If he says he can fit you in immediately, he's a lousy doctor." Years later when I relayed my mother's theory to Abby, she laughed and admitted there was more than a grain of truth in it.

Whenever I got ill as a child, Mum fussed around me, fed me junior aspirin, bought me comics and lemonade. But even if I'd wanted to, I could never have competed with her on the sickness front. I was off-color. She was always at death's door.

Brian despaired of the way Dad and I — not to mention everybody who knew my mother's story — walked on eggshells around her. "You're letting Hitler win all over again. A kick up the backside, that's what she needs to bring her to her senses." He was speaking figuratively, of course. Even so, nobody — least of all he — was prepared to administer it.

But once my father died and there was nobody looking over my shoulder telling me how emotionally frail my mother was, I found the courage to confront her. One day, we were sitting in her kitchen having coffee and cake when I dared to suggest in the most tentative, round-about way that maybe she wasn't quite as ill as she thought she was.

"You're calling me a liar?"

"No, of course not."

"You think I enjoy being ill and in pain all the time?"

"No — not exactly."

"Not exactly? Then what?"

"All I'm saying is that the mind is complicated. Sometimes feelings and emotions are hard to unravel."

"So now I'm insane?"

"Of course you're not. All I'm saying is that what happened to you during the war has taken its toll."

"You're not wrong there."

"So maybe you need to find some way of dealing with those feelings."

"You mean see a trick cyclist?"

"Maybe."

"What are you trying to do? Get me put away?"

"Oh, for God's sake. Of course I'm not."

"Let's get one thing straight. I am not crazy. I will never see a head doctor. I don't know how you can even suggest such a thing."

Then she said I was giving her palpitations, so I shut up.

Over the years, I'd raised the subject a few more times, but the response was always the same.

Back in the living room, Mum is telling me that my outburst has made her acid reflux worse. She's going to pop an extra PPI and have an early night.

She heaves herself out of the armchair.

157

"I'm sorry if I said the wrong thing. I suppose times have changed. These days children are shielded from all the terrible things that go on in the world. I suppose that's a good thing. . . . But Sam couldn't get enough of my story. He thought it was really exciting. He told me I was really brave."

"Of course he did. Sam is older and more robust than Rosie. She still believes in witches and monsters. She thinks you can fit a burglar under her bed. She's petrified that Hitler is about to make a comeback."

"I'll speak to her, tell her I didn't mean to upset her."

"That might be a good idea."

"Right, I'm off to bed."

"Mum — before you go . . . I'm sorry, too. I didn't mean to upset you. You did your best when I was growing up. You'd been through hell. You thought you were doing the right thing."

I hug her and kiss her on the cheek. Finally she pulls away. I wipe the tears from her face. "I'm a stupid old woman."

"You are, but I still love you. Come on, let's forget it."

"So, are we OK?" she asks.

"Of course we are. Now go to bed."

I offer to bring her a mug of cocoa and she says that would be lovely.

She trudges upstairs, her hand pressed into the small of her back.

"I thought you had heartburn."

"I do. Now my back's playing up."

After I've taken the cocoa up to her, I lie on the sofa and wonder how you get rid of Hitlers under the bed. It takes a while, but finally I have it. Führer spray.

CHAPTER SIX

I am standing at the kitchen sink, screwing the top off an almost empty bottle of Windex. Mum is in the shower. The kids are playing in their rooms, having demolished their nana's special Sunday breakfast of crêpes with chocolate sauce.

I pour what's left of the Windex down the sink and rinse the bottle in hot water. Finally I pour in a few drops of red food coloring, dilute it with water and screw the top back on. Ta-da. Führer spray. When Abby was small — and depending on what fiends she was terrified of at the time — it was known as monster spray, Dalek spray or ghost spray. We got through gallons of the stuff.

I head upstairs armed with my secret weapon. Rosie is sitting cross-legged on her bed, commentating as she unwraps I know not what.

"Sweetheart — sorry to interrupt, but I've

got something that might help with the Hitlers." I perch on the edge of the bed and show her the magic spray. "It's amazing. Never fails. I'll spray the room and the Hitlers will be gone in an instant."

"That's stupid," she says.

"Why?"

"It's for babies. When I was little and I was scared of monsters — that's before I got scared of burglars and Hitlers — Mum used to make monster spray to get rid of them. But it wasn't real. It was just red stuff and water. Sam told me."

Of course he did.

"So I'm guessing it never worked."

"Nope."

Fabulous.

There's a tap on the open door. "Mind if I come in?" Mum says. But she's already in and asking me to budge up so that she can sit on the bed. I explain — perhaps too pointedly, seeing as I'm supposed to have forgiven my mother for telling Rosie about the Nazis — that we are looking for something to get rid of the Hitlers.

"Well, I think I might have just the thing." She reaches into her apron pocket and pulls out a faded blue velvet box. I recognize it at once. She hands it to Rosie and tells her to open it. "This was mine and now I want you to have it."

"Mum, are you sure?" Along with a handful of family photographs, the piece of jewelry inside the box is my mother's most precious and treasured possession.

"Shh."

Rosie lifts the lid and unfurls a long gold chain. Hanging from it is a tiny Star of David. It was a present from my grandparents to my mother. They gave it to her the day she left Berlin. I can't believe she is parting with it.

"It's very pretty," Rosie says. "And it's really for me?"

"It is."

"Wow. Can I put it on?"

Mum secures the chain around Rosie's neck and lines up the star. "Perfect."

She explains how the necklace came to her and that the star is an important Jewish symbol.

"I'm Jewish. Mummy told me."

Mum tells her that's correct and explains how Jewishness is inherited entirely through the female line.

"And the star will look after you," my mother says. "Just like it looked after me."

"When you were escaping from the Nazis?"

"Yes. I promise — nothing will ever hurt you."

"Including Hitlers?"

"Especially Hitlers."

In my head I'm questioning the wisdom of telling Rosie that nothing will ever hurt her, but bearing in mind how frightened she was last night, it's probably not such a bad idea.

"And I'm sorry I frightened you. The things I told you happened a very long time ago. We live in a different world now." She kisses Rosie's forehead.

"Apart from ISIS."

What? The child knows about Muslim fundamentalists? "Good God, Rosie, who told you about ISIS?"

"Mum and Dad. It was when kids in the playground were calling Abad in year four a terror-something."

"Terrorist," I oblige.

"That's it. I didn't understand, so Mum and Dad explained to me and Sam. But I'm not scared of terrorists, because they're a long way away."

"Of course they are," Mum and I say, practically in unison.

"So, can I take the necklace to school?"

Mum says she'd rather Rosie didn't because it might get lost.

"Is it worth lots of money?"

"No, darlink. But it's still very precious." She says that Rosie should only wear it on special occasions. "When you go home, I think you should let Mummy look after it."

"OK." But she insists on wearing it for the rest of the day. "And, Nana . . . thank you." With that she throws her arms around her great-grandmother.

"My pleasure, darlink. May you have the health to wear it and the strength to tear it."

Rosie looks confused but doesn't say anything. She's used to her nana's strange sayings from the olden days.

We leave Rosie to get back to her unboxing and head downstairs.

"You just did a wonderful thing," I say, tipping Führer spray down the kitchen sink.

"I always meant for you to have it after I died. Are you angry with me?"

"What? Of course not. It's a child's necklace. Rosie should have it."

"Just make sure she looks after it, that's all."

"I will. I promise. I'll speak to Abby when she gets back."

When Sam finds out that Rosie's been given a special present, he's not best pleased. "It's not fair. Why should she get something precious and not me?"

I explain about Rosie being scared of Hitler and how Nana thinks the Jewish star will protect her.

"You mean like a lucky rabbit's foot?"

"Kind of."

"Well, Dad says only stupid people believe in rabbits' feet. He says it's just superstition. I agree."

"And you're probably right. But will you please do me a favor and not share your opinion with Rosie?"

" 'K. . . ."

"No, that's not good enough. You absolutely have to promise."

"Fine. I promise."

Even though he's only just finished his breakfast, I shove a packet of prawn-cocktail-flavor Monster Munch into my grandson's hands to say thank you.

It's been sheeting with rain all night and it still hasn't stopped. At eight o'clock I got a call to say that Sam's football practice had been canceled. Rosie said that as Sam wasn't going to football, she wanted to skip her swimming lesson and stay home, too.

"But your mum and dad have already paid

for your swimming lessons. You really ought to go."

"But it's just this once. I'd rather stay here and do stuff with you and Sam. We could play Jenga."

I didn't take a lot of persuading. Jenga was fun, whereas drinking stewed coffee in the municipal poolside café while my hair and clothes soaked up burger and fries smell was not.

While Sam went to find the Jenga box, Mum made a start on a cheesecake. Estelle Silverfish was dropping by later.

We've been playing Jenga for over an hour. Rosie's cross because Sam is more dexterous than she is, and she's getting more and more frustrated that she can't move the bricks without the tower collapsing. She tells me to go away when I offer to help. She wants to beat Sam on her own. I admire her grit, but I know it's going to end in tears. When her clumsiness destroys the tower yet again, she starts throwing Jenga bricks around and kicking Sam.

"Hey — what was that for?"

"I hate you."

"Why? Just because I'm better at Jenga than you and you're a stupid mal-co."

Mal-co. Bully-speak. Short for mal-coordinated. Despite being banned, it's commonly used at the kids' school, typically during a football match when the goalie misses an easy save.

"I am not a mal-co," Rosie yells. She leans across to hit her brother, but I manage to grab her arm.

"OK — Rosie, that's enough. You need to calm down. It isn't Sam's fault that he's older than you and he's got a steadier hand. . . . Sam, that word is nasty and unkind. You are never to use it again. Do you understand?"

"But she said she hated me."

"I know. That doesn't give you an excuse to call her names."

"Yes, it does."

"You're a mal-co, too!" Rosie said.

"Rosie, did you hear what I just said to your brother?"

"Don't care. He is."

At this point Mum appears, wiping her hands on her apron. "Vot on earth is all this noise? What would your parents say, hearing you shouting like this? You both deserve a smack tush. Now both of you — go to your rooms. And don't expect any lunch."

In all the time my mother has known her great-grandchildren, she has never raised her voice to them. So taken aback are they

by her scolding that they make no attempt
to argue. Glaring at each other, they leave
the room.

"Mum, you were brilliant."

"What can I tell you? I'm a natural disci-
plinarian."

"No, you're not. When I was growing up
you left all that to Dad."

"That's all you know. I used to send you
to bed without supper."

"Once maybe."

"More than once."

"But we can't let them miss lunch."

"Why not?" Mum says. "It will be good
for them. Bad behavior deserves consequences."

"I know. But you can't starve them."

"Don't be ridiculous. They're not going to
starve. OK, I tell you what . . . They can
have bagels for lunch, but no smoked
salmon. Just cream cheese. How's that?"

My mother remembers when the average
weekly wage was twenty pounds and
smoked salmon cost a pound a pound. To
her it will always be a luxury.

"Fine." The kids prefer cream cheese anyway.

But in the end no further punishment is
required. Sam and Rosie manage twenty
minutes in their rooms. They come down

looking sheepish and full of apologies. "We've made up, so please don't send us back to our rooms."

Mum pretends to be weighing up their request. "I'm not sure."

"Please?"

She shrugs. "Fine. But no more fighting."

" 'K."

"Now come here for a kiss. Then you give your grandma a kiss. She's doing her best to look after you. I won't have you upsetting her."

Without the kids seeing, I mouth a thank-you to my mother.

Kisses and hugs done, I suggest the kids do their homework before lunch. My motive is purely selfish. I have my sights set on sitting down with a cup of coffee and the Sunday papers. The children have other ideas. While they were upstairs they hatched a plan. They want to teach Mum and me how to play *Minecraft*. I'm instantly looking for an escape route. To me, computer games — even highly sophisticated ones — seem arid and monotonous. I would much rather escape into real-life drama — albeit fictionalized. I need characters to care about, to root for — even ones in some crappy soap or a made-for-TV movie. I see nothing mind-enhancing about pitting my wits against brutes and beasts in some cartoon-ish virtual world.

Mum seems to be intrigued and raises no objections. Meanwhile I make my excuses. I really need to put in a supermarket order. The carpets need a good Hoover. But they're not taking any notice. Sam's Play-Station is all set up and ready to go. Sam and Rosie climb onto the sofa and squeeze in between Mum and me. "OK, watch this."

A strange terrain appears on the screen. We have entered some kind of barren robot world where the trees, hills and even the sun are made up of cubes.

"Couldn't they have made it a bit more realistic?" Mum says. "I thought these computer people were meant to be clever."

"They are clever," Sam says. "Just keep watching. OK . . . so during the day we collect resources. At night we fight baddies."

Mum is leaning in. To show willingness, so am I. "What sort of baddies?" Mum says.

Rosie explains that there are exploding zombielike creatures called Creepers who attack at night. "So we need to build a house quickly, before dark." Soon they have my mother left-clicking the mouse on a tree trunk to make wood.

"Ha! Well, will you look at that? It's all very clever, Judy, don't you think? Can I do it again?"

Once Mum has gathered enough wood, the kids have her building something called a crafting table. Soon she's making spades and pick-axes and burning wood to make charcoal. She's *ooh*ing and *aah*ing. The children are laughing — tickled that she's enjoying it. I'm trying really hard to work up any enthusiasm. The kids pick up my antipathy.

"Gran'ma thinks it sucks," Sam says to his sister.

"I don't think it sucks exactly. . . ."

"But it's so exciting," Rosie says. "Why don't you like it?"

"I guess I just don't see the point. Are you disappointed that I don't like it much?"

"Uh-uh. Mum doesn't get it, either."

My mother, on the other hand, appears to be hooked. "Right, so how much time do we have left to finish the house? I don't want the baddies getting us."

I'm baffled. I can't begin to explain why my mother has taken to *Minecraft*. Maybe it's more about her enjoying connecting with the kids. Meanwhile I am desperate for the phone to ring, for somebody to knock at the door — anything to take me away from this. So when Mum says the cheese-cake should be done by now, I'm on my feet before you can say sour cream topping.

"Stay where you are, Mum. I'll go and check on the cake."

I leave the cheesecake to cool. The bundle of Sunday papers is still lying on the door-mat. I shove i t under my arm, head upstairs to the bedroom and close the door.

Estelle Silverfish arrives just after three. "Look at me. I'm drenched. I only walked from the cab to here and I had an umbrella." Estelle Silverfish shares my mother's fondness for exaggeration. Brian used to call it tabloiding. She has a few spots of rain on her leather coat. Mum takes the umbrella while I help Estelle Silverfish off with her coat. I hang it on the coat stand in the hall. Meanwhile I can hear her asking Mum if she thinks the water will stain.

"You didn't Scotchgard it?"

"I forgot."

"How could you forget? The first thing you do when you buy leather is Scotch-gard."

Unlike my mother, who values comfort and practicality over style, Estelle Silverfish is all about style. Over the years, if she'd had the inclination, Mum could have looked as elegant as Estelle Silverfish. She had everything going for her. She was just as slim and attractive. Dad used to say she was way more attractive, that she had prettier eyes and higher cheekbones. But fashion never interested my mother. If she's neat and tidy, she's satisfied. Dad adored Mum as she was and always encouraged her indifference to things sartorial — on the grounds that it saved him a fortune.

Today Estelle Silverfish is wearing knee-high suede boots with a kitten heel and a rust-colored tunic over skinny charcoal trousers. She's pulled the outfit together with a double string of rust-colored beads and matching earrings. Unlike Mum, she isn't naturally thin. When you ask her how she keeps her figure, she laughs and tells you she hasn't eaten since 1979. Phil Silverfish, on the other hand, weighed nearly two hundred and eighty pounds when he died. The three junior Silverfish — two boys and a girl — are also overweight. "Estelle's a feeder. What can I tell you?" Mum said when Naomi Silverfish got a gastric band. "She can't enjoy eating, so instead she force-feeds her family."

Mum disappears to fetch the new spring coat she finally bought. I've seen it, but she's been desperate to show it off to Estelle Silverfish. She comes back wearing the three-quarter-length camel coat, which is slightly too wide on the shoulders and too long in the sleeve. I'm less than keen, but I wouldn't say anything for the world. Estelle Silverfish is looking as if she's struggling to find something polite to say. But Mum doesn't notice because she's too busy giving us a twirl.

"So go on. You have to guess. How much do you think I paid for it?"

"I don't know," Estelle Silverfish says. "A hundred."

"Ten."

Estelle Silverfish's eyes widen. Even she can see it's worth more than ten quid.

"It's secondhand, but it's hardly been worn. I got it on eBay. You won't have heard of it because you're not online, but you can buy and sell anything. I was surfing and I just stumbled across it. I even opened a Pay-Pal account."

"A what?"

"It's for people who do a lot of Internet shopping. You wouldn't understand. So, what do you think?" Mum turns back the sleeves and gives another twirl.

"It's very practical."

She hates it.

Just as we're sitting down to tea and cake, the kids burst into the kitchen demanding snacks. While I go in search of nuts and raisins, Estelle clucks over the children: how they've grown, how Rosie looks just like one of the daughters in *Fiddler on the Roof,* how with those big brown eyes Sam's going to break a few hearts when he gets older.

Once the kids have disappeared back to their rooms, I congratulate her on her granddaughter's upcoming nuptials.

"What can I tell you? Both girls are wearing trouser suits. How's that going to look in the photographs? I've offered to buy them wedding dresses. They don't want to know."

"You need to pull back," Mum says. "It's their day, not yours."

"I know, I know. But they're both such beautiful girls. Would it hurt them to wear dresses?" Estelle Silverfish places her hand on my mother's. "Frieda, please change your mind and say you'll come to the wedding. I really want you to be there . . . for moral support."

"You need my support because the two brides refuse to wear dresses?"

"It upsets me what people will think."

"People will think they're lesbians."

"Fine. But I'd like you to come anyway. You're my best friend."

Mum makes her misery face. "I don't know. I don't have the energy I used to have."

I remind my mother that for over a week she's been preparing three meals a day for four people. "You have plenty of energy."

"That's what you think."

"It's what I know."

"You don't know how I feel." She turns to Estelle Silverfish. "I'll think about it."

"Good. And I'll keep on nagging."

I leave them to gossip, but not before I've helped myself to a second slice of my mother's sour-cream-and-vanilla-infused cheesecake. Back in the living room, I'm chowing it down and eavesdropping.

The pair of them is cackling. That's twice I've caught my mother laughing today. "He looks nice," Estelle Silverfish is saying. "I like a man with a strong chin. Nice eyes. I'd say he's a kind, reliable sort. . . . Calls himself Big Max." The cackling gets louder. "Omigod, this one's wearing a gold chain . . . No, I don't like the look of him . . . too flash. And look at his nose hair."

"That's not nose hair. It's a bit of schmutz on the screen."

"I think I like Big Max best. I wouldn't mind giving him a try. So what do I do now? I read somewhere about how you need to poke people?"

"No, you message him on the Web site. . . . Here, I'll show you. 'Hello. . . . My . . .

name . . . is . . . Estelle. I . . . am . . . seventy-five years young. . . .' "

"Good idea to lie about my age. We don't want him to think I could keel over any minute. OK . . . you need to tell him I am a widow, well preserved, a size ten . . . that I'm in good shape . . . have all my own teeth . . . that I'm not on too many pills . . . just a blood pressure tablet and the occasional Tums."

"Very sexy."

"You're right. So maybe I won't mention my hip operation?"

"Best not."

I must have dozed off, because the next thing I know, Mum and Estelle Silverfish are waking me up with another cup of tea. Estelle perches on the sofa, practically next to my head, the laptop on her knees.

"So, Judy . . . your mother and I . . . we've been on the computer and we've found a couple of chaps you might like."

"No. Not this again."

"Just listen," Mum says.

I sip my tea and decide the easiest thing to do is to give Estelle Silverfish the floor and let her words wash over me.

"One's bald, but he's got a nice face and at your age you can't be too fussy."

"I'm sorry — bald or not — I'm really

177

not interested." So much for letting her words wash over me.

"Maybe not, but why don't you just take a look at their profiles?"

"Honestly I'd rather not."

"What did I tell you?" Mum says.

I try to stay calm. "Look, I know you both mean well, but I'm not ready to start dating."

Estelle Silverfish looks at Mum. "What do you do with her? She's such a good catch. Nice figure. Trendy haircut. Her face is holding up."

"I've told her. She won't listen to me."

Estelle shrugs, looks at her watch and says she has to run. Her son and his wife are taking her out for Chinese. "The rain has stopped, so I'll take the bus."

She fusses over her leather coat, which appears to have a couple of watermarks. She'll show it to her dry cleaner, who apparently worked miracles on her silk blouse.

"So," Estelle Silverfish says to Mum, lowering her voice. "You'll let me know if I get a message from . . ." She mouths the words "Big" and "Max." She has no idea I overheard her and Mum while they were on the dating Web site.

"Will do."

After Mum has seen Estelle Silverfish out,

178

she starts on me again: "What's wrong with you? Why are you so against entering the world of the living?"

"I've told you, I will think about dating when I'm ready. And anyway — what about you?"

"What about me?"

"You're happy enough to sort Estelle out with Mr. Whopper or whatever his name is, but since Dad died you've never even looked at another man."

"Don't you know it's rude to eavesdrop?"

"I couldn't help it. The two of you were cackling like Macbeth's witches."

"Well, maybe if I'd had a mother giddying me up and nagging me, I would have started dating again."

For the very first time, it's dawning on me that Mum might regret spending the past three decades alone.

"You need to live your life. That's all I'm saying."

"Mum, please give me a break. Having the kids to stay is a big step for me. I'm trying to get back into the world. I really am."

"You must. Don't let life pass you by. Time goes so fast. I don't want you to reach my age and have regrets."

So I'm right. My mother isn't happy be-

ing alone. She disappears into the kitchen
to start dinner.

CHAPTER SEVEN

Bogdan, Sam's chess coach, is prone to rants. They go something like this: "Eed-y-ot! What have you done? You just moved your knight in front of your bishop and got nothing for it. You need to think, Sam! Think and plan!"

Sam is pretty robust, but in the last week or so — ever since Bogdan started coming to the house to wave his arms, bash the table and shoot spittle — my grandson has become anxious and fretful. Compared to his previous coach — a limp, geeky type called Tim — Bogdan is a pit bull.

Minor problems are tipping Sam over the edge. Last night he had a meltdown just because he lost one of his Dude Dice. On top of that, the child is spending every spare minute shut in his room, trying to improve his game. Sometimes he plays solo chess with the hats. Sometimes he plays against the computer. If he's not playing chess, he's reading about it. Now when he messes up a game, he even calls himself an idiot. Or worse: a retard. This is all down to Bogdan. The man is a bully and I want him gone.

Rosie is no fan either. "Bogdan has coffee breath and his trouser legs end before they get to his ankles. He's weird."

The first time Bogdan yelled at Sam, it was as much as I could do to stop myself from barging in on their session and telling the man his fortune. Mum stopped me. She said that making a scene would embarrass Sam and make him feel worse. So against my better judgment I didn't. Instead — making sure I stayed out of sight — I kept an ear on things from the doorway. After Bogdan had gone, I sat Sam down and asked him if he was OK.

"Sure."

He didn't sound — or look — as if he meant it. "Nobody has the right to shout at you like that. I'm going to tell him not to come again. It beats me why your mother hasn't got rid of him."

"But Bogdan is meant to be the best there is."

"Well, I'd hate to see the worst."

"Mum says he sets really high standards and he's strict because that's how you make people stay focused and get the best out of them."

"Your mum said that? OK, leave it with me. I'm going to speak to her."

If this isn't enough, I'm worried about Rosie, too. She's having trouble sleeping. I've asked her if she's still afraid of the Hitlers. She says not.

"They don't scare me anymore because I've got my star necklace to protect me. I don't know why I can't sleep."

"Do you think it's because you're missing Mum and Dad?"

"I am missing them, but we talk on Skype. I don't think it's that."

I've asked if there's something bothering her at school. Is she struggling with her lessons? Has she fallen out with her friends? She says school is fine.

Each night I make her a cup of warm milk and she drinks it in bed while I read to her. After twenty minutes, I'll close the book and tell her it's time to go to sleep. But she begs me to stay and read some more. I don't want her to get upset, so I carry on. Sometimes I end up reading for an hour or more. Eventually she'll let me kiss her good night and allow me to go. Ten minutes later she'll come trotting downstairs with Denise, asking for a cuddle. The last couple of nights

I've taken the pair of them into my bed. Sometimes it's gone eleven before she drops off. Of course she's finding it almost impossible to get up in the morning. I've already let her have a couple of days off school to catch up with her sleep. I can't keep on doing it.

An exhausted Rosie plus an anxious Sam equals conflict. They seem to be fighting all the time. I'm coping, but the noise and rows are getting too much for Mum.

"All I did was ask one of them to hand me the TV remote," she told me the other day, "and as Rosie went to get it, Sam snatched it from her and made her cry."

They're squabbling about nothing and anything: who gets in or out of the car first, who has the most bubbles in their milk, who has the biggest plate of food, who has the biggest brain. Last night Rosie was having an imaginary tea party with some soft toys and Sam ate all her imaginary biscuits. She chased him round the living room, trying to wrestle the imaginary plate from his hand, but he locked himself in the loo and made loud munching noises. Rosie was beside herself.

The following day I got a call from Sam's teacher, Mrs. Gilbert. She announced that Sam had produced a plastic assault rifle during show-and-tell and started firing indiscriminately. She reminded me that the school has a strict anti-toy-weapons policy and that bringing a gun to school was highly inappropriate.

"But Sam doesn't own a rifle."

"He most certainly does. It's called the Sniper. I have it locked in the cupboard under my desk."

Then I remember. Tom's parents sent it for his last birthday. It's an exact replica of an army assault rifle — albeit scaled down — and makes a terrifying noise — a bit like a busted popcorn machine — when you fire it. Sam adores it. I remember watching him unwrapping it. Abby and Tom were furious when they saw the thing. They are emphatically against children bearing plastic imitation firearms, but since they didn't want to offend Tom's parents they had to let him keep it. He's allowed to play with the gun in the garden, but only on his own. If his friends saw it they would report back to their parents. I had no idea that Sam had brought his assault rifle with him when he came to stay, let alone taken it to school — I assume hidden in his sports bag. Meet my grandson, the gun smuggler.

"I don't want you to worry unduly," Mrs. Gilbert went on. "The children thought it was great fun. Nobody was traumatized."

"Thank the Lord for that. I had no idea he had taken it to school. I can only apologize and assure you that he will be punished and it won't happen again."

"Good. I do have one slight concern, though."

"What's that?"

"All the children know that guns aren't allowed in school. Sam purposely disobeyed the rule. He's usually such a good, well-behaved boy. This is so out of character. I'm wondering if he's slightly troubled at the moment. After all, both his parents are away. I'm wondering how he's coping with that."

Was Mrs. Gilbert suggesting that because Abby and Tom had gone to Nicaragua, my nine-year-old grandson was a school rampage killer waiting to happen? Did we need to "talk about Sam"? "Mrs. Gilbert, are you telling me that you think Sam has psychological problems?"

"What? Good heavens, no. Sam said he brought the gun in as a joke and I believe him. But at the same time I can't help thinking he might be attention seeking."

"I don't think it's that."

I explained about Bogdan and the chess tournament. "Poor mite's really stressed.

He's also taking it out on his sister."

"That's not good. But it does make sense. OK, leave it with me. I'll talk to him again and see if I can't calm him down."

"Would you? I'd really appreciate it. And my apologies again. Send him home with the gun and I'll hide the damn thing."

When I sat Sam down to discuss the assault rifle episode, he said he'd only taken it to show-and-tell because he couldn't think of anything else to take. What's more, because Mrs. Gilbert had laughed really hard at the Death Valley snow globe, he felt he had a standard to maintain. He thought the gun would be fun. I told him I understood, but I was confiscating it until his parents got back. He protested, but I took it anyway.

Mum says that all the noise and fighting between the children is giving her tension headaches and that I need to get to the root of the problem. The one thing that doesn't bother her is Sam taking a gun into school. "So what? It's only make-believe. It doesn't mean anything. You played with guns — all the kids did. I used to buy you caps for it."

I'm not going to argue the toss about toy guns with my elderly mother. I'm more concerned about Bogdan. I am in no doubt that he is the root of Sam's problem. His bullying is making Sam anxious and bad-tempered. Rosie's irritability, on the other hand, is due to sleep deprivation. I would put money on this being caused by all her after-school activities. She gets overstimulated, not to mention overtired, and can't sleep.

The truth is that neither of my grandchildren is getting enough downtime. On top of his chess, Sam is doing other after-school activities. These have to be adding to his stress. Then there's all the homework: spellings to be learned, tables to be recited, the difference between igneous and sedimentary rock to be Googled. By then it's eight o'clock and time for a bath and bed.

Despite the memories Abby has of coming home from school and unwinding in front of kids' TV for an hour or so, she doesn't let Sam and Rosie do the same. Along with all the other Faraday House mothers, she makes sure her children are still learning and supposedly expanding their brains way after school has ended. Not for the first time, I wonder what happened to daydreaming, doing nothing. But like Abby says, times have changed. Kids are competing from the time they start pre-school. Daydreaming is a luxury.

■ ■ ■ ■

After Bogdan's first outburst I told Abby how I felt about him. "You don't get the best out of people — especially kids — by terrorizing them. He's a horrible man."

Abby insisted that he wasn't horrible, just Russian. "You need to understand the Soviet temperament," she said. "It goes back to communist times. These people mentor with fierce, almost military discipline. And they give off all this fiery emotion. Do you have any idea what Russian athletes go through when they're training for the Olympics? Their coaches have no time for carrot. With them it's all stick. That's why they produce so many champions."

Then it hit me. Despite everything Abby had said about not putting pressure on Sam, she wanted him to be a champion.

I told her there was a difference between discipline and striking fear into a person and that I intended to tell Bogdan he could stick his fiery emotions where the sun don't shine.

"Mum, please don't. Bogdan isn't just a coach — he's a guru, and he's costing us a fortune. Get rid of him and Sam's chances of doing well in the tournament go up in smoke."

So I did nothing. Then Sam started getting anxious and I had another conversation with my daughter.

"But he's worrying me," I told her. "He starts fights with Rosie and he shuts himself away playing chess as if his life depended on it. I don't like it."

"He's tense because this is a regional tournament. It's his first really big competition. He'll calm down when it's over. You have to stop worrying. Tom and I will give him another pep talk."

And they did. Rosie went upstairs and left them to it. She has no interest in "Sam's boring chess." I hovered in the doorway.

"So, Sam," Tom said. "Grandma is worried that Bogdan yells and you're getting upset. Do you want me to speak to him?"

"No. It's fine. Bogdan yells a bit. But it's only because he thinks I'm capable of doing better. If he thought I was useless he wouldn't bother."

"Good for you, darling," Abby said. "That's the spirit. Bogdan doesn't mean to be unkind. It's just his way. Everybody we've spoken to about him says his bark is far worse than his bite. But you mustn't work too hard. You need to take time out to relax."

"I know. But I have to keep working on my game. It's the only way I'm going to win."

"OK," Abby said, "so long as you're not wearing yourself out. Sweetheart, I want you to know that Dad and I are really proud of you. It's not easy preparing for a big tournament when we're so far away. But we've got tremendous faith in you. You have such talent."

"Your mum's right," Tom said. "You just need to go out there and show the other kids what you're made of. Who's the best?"

"I am."

"I didn't hear you. Who's the best?"

"I am!"

Abby and Tom are thousands of miles away healing the sick and injured. Their only reward is gratitude and the satisfaction that they've eased some of the suffering in the world. Every time I speak to Abby she tells me there's still a constant stream of casualties being stretchered into the field hospital — many with crush injuries that have caused internal damage. "We don't have the facilities to treat those patients. So they have to be airlifted out. It takes time. There are rows and rows of them on mattresses waiting their turn. All we can do is give them

191

morphine for the pain. Many die before they make it out. Then there are all these distraught people wandering around, looking for lost relatives. The place is chaotic." She's lucky if she and Tom get four hours of sleep a night.

My daughter and her husband are good people. They are exceptional people. But there's no getting away from it — they've changed. Abby has changed most. Back in the day, when she still walked in her father's footsteps, she didn't want the children to go to private school. Tom did. He'd been educated privately and wanted his children to benefit the way he had. At the time the local state school was underperforming and Abby took a leap of faith. They convinced themselves that it was possible to have kids at private school and still be cool, relaxed parents. Then the after-school activities started. Now that they could have a chess prodigy on their hands, they want him to win. Even the likes of Abby and Tom haven't been able to resist being sucked into the Faraday House vortex of competition and ambition. They've become what they said they would never become — pushy parents. But I wouldn't dream of adding to their stress by telling them.

Instead, a day or so later, I confide in

Ginny and Tanya. We've just dropped the kids off at school and, along with other groups of mums, we're hanging around chatting outside the main building. When I tell Ginny and Tanya that I think Abby and Tom might be turning into tiger parents, Ginny laughs.

"Well, they're hardly the worst offenders. Don't get me wrong. I can't say that I approve of all this hothousing, but right now I could point out half a dozen mothers who've had their kids up since six practicing piano or violin."

"Well, I think Sam and Rosie are being pushed too hard — especially Sam."

"You're probably right," Tanya says. "Abby and Tom have been turned. But you can't blame them. Being a parent at this school is a bit like being in a cult. If you're not part of it, you have no place. And God knows I've tried to be out of it. I was dead against Cybil doing too many after-school activities, but in the end she made such a fuss about wanting to keep up with her friends that I gave in."

Ginny says that by coincidence she was reading an article on tiger mothers in yesterday's *Guardian.* "Apparently what these women don't realize is that quiet time gives children the chance to consolidate

193

what they've learned. It also breeds creativity."

This jogs a distant memory — of the poems Abby would write when she was nine or ten, usually when she was alone, messing about in her room. They were mostly tragic odes to childhood suffering. Even then Abby was big on suffering. They had odd, melodramatic titles. "He Vows to Die with Sacrifice" sticks in my mind. I remember Brian joking that she was going to be Homer when she grew up and me saying she couldn't be Homer and Mother Teresa.

"The thing is," Tanya says, "when you ask parents what they want for their kids, they always say they want them to be happy. But in the upper school, loads of kids are self-harming or have anorexia — boys as well as girls — because they can't take the pressure. Where's the happiness in that?"

Tanya is in the middle of telling me about this amazing woman she knows who teaches kids mindfulness techniques when we hear yelling. Claudia is coming toward us. Hero is a few paces behind her mother, bawling her head off. There are tears and snot running down the child's puffy red face.

"Will you look at that?" Tanya says. "Oh, this is pure joy. . . . St. Claudia's kid is having a tantrum."

But Tanya's elation is short-lived. Claudia has seen us and as she crouches in front of her daughter, I get the feeling we're about to be treated to a master class in dealing with a temper tantrum.

"OK. That's enough." Claudia's tone is calm but firm. "Hero — listen to me. We're late. I need to get you into school. This has to stop."

Hero ratchets up the decibels. Tanya is practically punching the air.

"Hero . . . I need you to focus. Come on . . . focus on Mummy. Look at me."

Hero isn't having it.

"I have to video this," Tanya says, rooting around in her bag for her phone.

"Don't you dare," Ginny barks. "It's not fair on Hero."

"Hero wouldn't see it."

"Even so."

Tanya pulls the zip back across her bag, grumbling that she can't see what harm it would do.

"Hero, that's enough. . . . Tell you what. . . . Let's practice our breathing exercises. Take a deep breath. . . . Come on, you can do it. . . . That's it. . . . Take a breath and let it out slowly. Let go of all that nasty anger and frustration. . . . That's it. . . . Breathe in and out . . . and slowly feel the tension float away."

Hero takes a series of short gasps.

"Good girl. Excellent. And again."

This time she manages a proper deep breath. The child is calming down.

"That's it! Well-done!"

"Crap," Tanya says. "How did she do that?"

"Now, tell me again why you're so upset," Claudia says, "but slowly this time so that I can understand."

"I've forgotten" — gasp — "Josie's" — gasp — "reading folder that she left at our house."

"And how does that make you feel?"

"Scared."

"Why would you be scared?"

"Miss Carter will get cross with Josie for not bringing it to school and it will be all my fault."

"No, she won't. Miss Carter is lovely and kind. She never gets cross — you know that."

"But I'm frightened she might this time and then Josie will cry."

"And how do you feel about Josie crying?"

"Guilty."

"Goodness. That's a very grown-up feeling. And it's not a very nice one, is it?"

Hero shakes her head.

"OK, so would it help if I came in and had a word with Miss Carter?"

Hero gives a nod of her blond curls, some of which are damp with sweat and plastered to her forehead.

"Fine — let's go."

Claudia gets up and takes Hero's hand. "What a morning," she gushes in our direction. "I've got Sebastian at home with some bug that's doing the rounds. Now this. I'm exhausted before the day has even started. But I can't blame Hero. She's such a people pleaser. Upsetting others is one of her greatest fears, and irritating as it is, she's showing an emotional intelligence way beyond her years."

Claudia bids us cheerio and she and Hero disappear into school.

"Oh, fuck off," Tanya mutters.

"That's a bit strong," Ginny says.

"Well, it's how I feel. Why does her kid get the cute, socially acceptable neuroses?" Ginny and Tanya want me to come to the coffee shop with them, but I can't. I'm taking Mum for her annual physical. The NHS offers one, but Mum insists it's not thorough enough. There's no MRI scan or colonoscopy. So she pays. The investigations are so extensive that they take nearly all day. She loves it more than Christmas. It's her

197

one treat to herself. I usually drop her off at the clinic. When it's all over, she gets a cab home. Today I'm particularly grateful that she's making her own way home because I have been called in for an after-school meeting with Rosie's teacher.

Claudia is right about Miss Carter never getting cross. She is sunny and kind and American. She calls her pupils honey pie and sweet pea. Miss Carter is the kind of person who hugs herself while declaring: "I'm so glad I live in a world where there are Octobers." The kids adore her.

I collect Sam from his class and suggest he and his sister wait for me on the playground.

"But why does Miss Carter want to see you?" Rosie says. "Have I been bad?"

"Of course not. I suspect she's noticed that you've been looking a bit tired lately and that you've been taking time off."

"Promise you won't tell her about Denise. She'll laugh. Or the Hitlers."

"It's OK, darling. I promise."

I send the kids on their way, but they don't move.

"I reckon you did do something bad," Sam says.

"Shuddup. I did not."

"I bet you farted and everybody smelled it and felt sick."

"No, I didn't!" Rosie kicks her brother's leg.

I tell Rosie to stop kicking and warn Sam that I will take away his chess set if he doesn't stop taunting his sister. "Now say sorry. Both of you."

Grumpy apologies are exchanged and I shoo them off. Sam charges ahead of Rosie toward the playground.

I'm a few paces from Miss Carter's classroom when I see Claudia coming out. At her side is a smiley, much-cheered-up Hero. "I just wanted to check with Miss C that Hero had a good day. Apparently she did."

"I played in the Wendy House," Hero says with a nod of her curls.

"Good for you," I say.

Hero asks if she can go to the playground for a few minutes. "Yes, but literally for a few minutes. We mustn't be late for ballet."

Claudia turns back to me. "So, how is everything going? Hero let it drop that Rosie's been having a few issues. But it won't go any further. You have my absolute word. These things happen."

"Oh, I wouldn't worry. It's hardly a secret."

"Really? You surprise me."

"Rosie's a bit tired, that's all. She's finding it hard to sleep."

Claudia looks confused but doesn't say anything, so I carry on. "If you ask me, she does too many after-school activities and her brain gets overstimulated."

"Don't they all?" Claudia says with an I-feel-your-pain eye roll. "In fact, I've just submitted a paper to one of the psychology journals on the dangers of hothousing children. These kids are going to burn out if their parents aren't careful. And to my shame, I'm just as guilty as the next mother. But I have to say that Hero handles the pressure better than most. I've taught her lots of coping strategies."

Of course she has. I've finally decided I don't much care for Claudia. I tell her it's been nice chatting, but I should get going because Miss Carter is waiting for me.

"Absolutely. . . . Oh, before you go, I forgot to ask — how's Sam doing?"

"Oh, you know . . . getting himself a bit wound up about this big chess tournament."

I must stop giving this woman so much information. She's only going to use it against me.

"He's such a talented boy. His parents must be so proud of him."

"We all are."

200

"But you must wonder if Sam and Rosie would be doing better if their parents hadn't chosen to leave them."

I'm considering boxing Claudia's ears with my handbag when Miss Carter — ponytail, ballet pumps — appears at the classroom door. "If you'd like to come in, Mrs. Devlin, I can see you now."

I mutter, "Bye," to Claudia and follow Miss Carter inside. We squat opposite each other on tiny plastic chairs. Miss Carter thanks me for coming. I'm aware that she isn't quite her gladsome Anne of Green Gables self.

"OK, I'll get straight to the point," she says. "I don't want to worry you, but I'm concerned about Rosie."

"I know what you're going to tell me. The child's exhausted. She does too much after school. Her brain is always on the go and she's not sleeping. I'll discuss it with her mother and see if we can't take some of the pressure off her."

"Sounds like a good idea. I have noticed Rosie looking a bit out of sorts lately and she has been absent a few times. But that isn't why I asked to see you. I'm pretty sure that the issue I'm concerned about isn't related to her lack of sleep."

Miss Carter explains that a few days ago

when the children came in from morning play, she asked them to sit down on the floor mat. "I clapped my hands and said 'crisscross applesauce,' which is what we say to the kids back home when we want the class to sit down quickly and cross their legs. One boy didn't hear me. Rosie, who was already sitting down, looked up at him and told him: 'Miss Carter said crisscross applesauce . . . motherfucker.' "

It's so shocking and yet so cute that it's hard not to laugh. "Excuse me?"

"I'm sorry, but that's what she said."

"Good Lord. Are you sure?"

"I'm afraid so."

Then it hits me. This is what Claudia was driving at just now. Hero didn't tell her mother that Rosie was coming to school tired. She told her that Rosie had said motherfucker. If she heard, then all the kids must have heard — which means all the parents must know. Although it was odd that Ginny and Tanya hadn't said anything this morning.

I'm nonplussed. "But where on earth did she get it from?"

"I was hoping you might be able to tell me." The lovely Miss Carter's perfectly tweezered eyebrows are knitted in concern. I can tell she feels sorry for me.

"I have absolutely no idea." That's not quite true. I know Rosie is familiar with the F word because that day over lunch, before Abby and Tom went to Nicaragua, she was demanding to know when she would be allowed to say it.

"Could it have come from the TV?" Miss Carter says.

"No. She doesn't watch adult shows. Maybe she picked it up from one of the other kids?"

"I admit that I didn't ask her, but I sincerely doubt it. I have never heard that word used in the lower school."

"I take it that all the children heard her say it."

"A few did, but they don't know what it means and I didn't make a big deal of it. None of the parents has complained, so I'm pretty sure it was forgotten by home time."

But it wasn't. Hero remembered and told her mother.

I apologize profusely to Miss Carter, tell her I'll investigate and get back to her.

As I'm leaving she hands me a small pile of Rosie's paintings. "I've just taken down a whole bunch of the kids' artwork to clear some wall space. I thought Rosie might like hers."

"I'm sure she would." I've barely got the

sentence out when the painting on top of the pile catches my eye. It's a picture of a lone naked woman with long tubular-shaped breasts. I know it's me because she's written *Granmar* at the bottom in fat black letters.

"Good Lord. I don't know what to say. What must you think of our family? You see, I was getting out of the bath the other day and Rosie came barging in and . . ."

Miss Carter is laughing. "Please don't worry. The children often paint pictures of their parents naked. Alarm bells only start going off if we see an erect penis."

Anne of Green Gables just said penis.

"Well, thank the Lord for that." I stutter my thanks, apologize again and can't get out of the door fast enough.

By now we're too late for French class, so I tell the kids we're going straight home.

"Yay!"

I decide that their delight speaks volumes about their after-school activities.

"So, what did Miss Carter want?" Sam says. "Has Rosie done something bad?"

"Sam, I've already told you. Miss Carter called me in to talk about why Rosie isn't sleeping. Now will you please mind your own business?"

When we get home, Sam takes his cheese

and Marmite sandwich to his room. He wants to play chess. Rosie decides to eat hers at the kitchen table. I make myself a cup of tea and join her.

"Sweetie, I need to ask you something. Miss Carter didn't just want to talk about you being tired. She mentioned something else, too. She said you used a bad word in class the other day."

"You mean motherfucker?"

Again I'm fighting the urge to laugh. This innocent, cute little girl who sleeps with a carrot seems so at home with the word.

"I do," I say with what I hope is appropriate gravitas.

"Miss Carter didn't tell me off. She just said it wasn't very nice and I shouldn't say it anymore. So I haven't. Except for now. But that's only because I'm explaining."

"That's fine. But what I'd like to know is where you got it from."

"Some big boys were saying it."

"Big boys? You mean in the senior school?"

"Yes, they were really big. Nearly as big as Daddy."

"And where did you hear them say it?"

"At lunchtime. We had to eat lunch in their dining hall because ours was cold. Miss Carter said the heating broke down."

"OK . . . and you're certain you're telling

me the truth?"

"Yes. It was definitely the big boys."

"Fine. We won't say any more about it. But please — don't ever say it again."

"I won't. I already promised." She pauses. "Grandma, please don't tell Sam I said a bad word 'cos he'll tease me."

"OK. It can be our secret."

"Good. But you can tell Mum and Dad."

"I can?"

"Yes, 'cos they're too far away to punish me."

"But I might punish you."

"No, you won't."

"What makes you say that?"

"Because you're my grandma. You have extra-special love for me and Sam, and that's why you spoil us. It's the same with all grandmas."

There are no flies on this child. "You think?"

"Yes." She starts grinning. "I'm right, aren't I?"

"Maybe . . . but woe betide you if I catch you saying it again."

"What does woe betide mean?"

I'm in the middle of explaining when Mum appears. "You won't believe the day I've had. They put needles in my arm, electrodes on my chest. I was pushed and poked and prodded. They shoved cameras up my behind. . . ."

Instead of giggling, Rosie looks thoughtful. "They must be very small cameras to fit up your bottom."

"They're not that small — believe you me."

"So, could you see all your insides?"

"The doctors could. I couldn't bear to look."

"Of course you looked," I say, laughing. "Don't fib. You loved every minute of it."

"I did not. I hate it. I simply accept that it has to be done. Anyway, you'll be pleased to know that for a woman my age, I'm in pretty good shape."

"That's great news."

"Ach . . . what do doctors know? I'm telling you, people have all these tests, the doctors tell them they're fine and a week later they drop down dead."

"So why do you put yourself through it all? It costs a fortune."

"I do it for you — because it gives you peace of mind."

CHAPTER EIGHT

"So it's all Zane Needlzz's fault," Ginny says. "Well, I hope you're going to read Mr. Needlzz the riot act."

Ginny thinks the whole thing is a hoot and can't stop laughing. Tanya, on the other hand, is beside herself and can't stop apologizing.

The three of us are sitting at the long teachers' table in the school dining hall. The first meeting of the spring fair committee is due to start in ten minutes. We are the first to arrive and I have been telling Ginny and Tanya about motherfucker-gate. I've barely begun when Tanya stops me. "Oh God. Crap. This is my fault."

"What do you mean? How can it be your fault?"

It turns out that a couple of Sundays ago, Tanya and her husband, Rick, invited Zane Needlzz and a bunch of other hip-hop artists on their record label to their place for lunch. "With these guys, every other word is fuck or motherfucker. But in our business you barely notice. And there was Cybil, being as good as gold, watching kids' shows on her iPad. I had no idea she was taking it all in. I'm so, so sorry. She must have told Rosie. Christ, I'm such a shitty mother."

"OK, first of all, you're not a shitty mother and second of all, you can't be certain that Cybil told her. Other kids in the class could easily have picked up the word."

"It was Cybil. I know because she's been going round the house calling Rick and me motherfuckers. When we asked her where she got the word from, she said it was from Zane and his friends. This is totally down to me. I'm really sorry. I feel so guilty."

I tell her she has no need to feel guilty and that these things happen. But she says she wants to confess to Miss Carter. Ginny and I can't see the point.

"Let sleeping dogs lie," Ginny says.

Ginny is shaking her head and smiling. "You know what's sweet? That Rosie concocted that story — about older boys using the word — in order to protect her best friend."

"She's a good kid," Tanya says.

Ginny says she'll second that. "That is a very sophisticated lie. It would seem that it isn't just Hero who has emotional intelligence beyond her years."

I can't help agreeing with them that Rosie's loyalty is commendable. But I will not let her get away with lying. They both insist I don't come down too hard on her.

"I won't." Like Rosie says, I'm her grandma. I have special love. Plus she was lying for the best of motives. "The more important problem is that since Claudia has hinted heavily that she knows Rosie swore in class, should I be worried about her gossiping?"

"Of course she'll gossip," Tanya says. "It will be round the school in no time."

"Great. But at least she doesn't know it was Cybil who told Rosie, so you're in the clear."

"Maybe. But Cybil's six. There's nothing to say she won't start boasting to the other kids that she was the one who told Rosie. At some level she still thinks it's cool." She pauses. "I suppose you two know Claudia's giving a talk this afternoon in the school hall."

We tell her that we did not know that.

"Haven't you seen the notices? They're all round the school. The woman's got a new parenting book out. She's off on a lecture tour to publicize it and she's starting it here."

"How very thoughtful of her," I hear myself say.

Tanya says she would rather wipe her arse with sandpaper than go. Ginny and I are inclined to agree.

We have to break off because mothers are starting to file in for the spring fair meeting. Ginny gets up. "Over here, ladies. Pull up some extra chairs if you need to."

Here they come — fifteen or so stay-at-home mums, bright-eyed and ponytailed. I suggested to Ginny that we have the meeting in the evening to give the working mothers a chance to play a part in organizing the fair, but she and Tanya were adamant that none of them would come. They took the view that most of them were in high-powered jobs, which meant they worked late. Or they thought getting involved with school fund-raisers was beneath them. They preferred to donate fancy raffle prizes. "Which is absolutely fine by me," Ginny said.

"Not exactly a huge turnout," I say to Ginny.

"It'll do. I don't want too many cooks spoiling the broth. A small group of volunteers is easier to manage."

Several women are pushing those big three-wheeled industrial-strength strollers, which cost a fortune. I remember the stroller I had for Abby. It weighed ounces and folded up in seconds. How on earth do they get these things on the bus? I'm laughing to myself. What am I thinking? This lot doesn't take the bus. What's more, I am reliably informed by Abby that most of them have two strollers — one for strolling and a lighter one for traveling that is stored in the Range Rover. Abby says I wouldn't believe the extent to which stroller competition is a thing. I don't think it was when she was small. In my day everybody went for cheap and lightweight. But Mum said that back in the forties and fifties, all new mothers aspired to a grand, coach-built pram like the one the Queen had for Prince Charles.

All except one of the babies is napping. A chubby chap named Freddie is sitting on his mother's lap, chewing on his Celeste the Penguin teething toy. I seem to remember Abby making do with a plastic teething ring. Now babies — the middle-class ones at least — have Celeste, who comes impregnated with vanilla and is made from the sap of the hevea tree.

Freddie's mother is a ruddy-cheeked woman with a head of prematurely gray hair. I recognize her at once. Tanya pointed her out to me at that first meeting at Claudia's house to discuss the school fair. Her name is Hester. She's the one who gives her children breast milk ear drops and her husband, Reiki, hand jobs.

Pinned to Hester's fleece is a Friends of the Earth badge. She's clearly a member of Faraday House's "other half." I wonder how at home she feels among the Marc Jacobs totes and expensive highlights.

Freddie has a moon face and eyes the color of bitter chocolate. He's gorgeous — what my mother would call "a nosh." Pretty soon I'm out of my seat, blowing raspberries on the back of his hand. Each time I make the noise, he laughs. "You're more than welcome to hold him," Hester says. "He's very good with strangers."

"Really? I'd love to." I lift him from his mother's lap. "Come on, little man. Oh, aren't you a cutie?" Freddie is all smiles and gurgles. "Who's a booful boy, then? Who is? You is. Yes, you is."

It takes a moment before I become aware of a distinct lack of padding between Freddie's bottom and me. She can't have. Surely not. "Goodness," I say to Hester, "I think you've forgotten to put a diaper on him."

"I didn't forget," she says, looking rather pleased with herself. "He only wears one at night. During the day, he's dry. He's completely potty-trained. You won't believe the amount we save on diapers. And of course it's environmentally sound because we're doing our bit to reduce all the methane produced by landfill sites."

"But he's six months old."

"Five actually."

"And he's potty-trained at five months? That's a thing?"

Out of the corner of my eye I can see looks being exchanged among the other mothers. Ginny mutters: "What balderdash. Now I've heard everything."

"It's not remotely balderdash," Hester says. "Several books have been written on early potty-training. You learn to look for that screwed-up, urgent expression on their face and then you know it's time to produce the potty." She takes a travel potty with a disposable — no doubt biodegradable — liner from her burlap bag.

"I had no idea," I say.

"He'll be fine. I promise."

I'm not sure what to do. The woolen skirt I'm wearing is almost new and dry-clean only. "I'm sure he will. And it's not that I don't trust him. But just for now, I think I'd rather give him back. Maybe another time." I can't get rid of Freddie fast enough.

"Suit yourself," Hester says, going all snarky on me. I ignore her and return to my seat.

The meeting lasts less than half an hour — partly because most people want to get to Claudia's talk — but mainly because Ginny, ever the Girl Guide, is so organized. She has made a list of all the usual stalls — face painting, ring toss, guess the weight of the cake and so on — as well as the jobs that need to be done. People are quick to volunteer and suggest ideas for new attractions, such as throwing wet sponges at teachers and a stick-on-tattoo parlor. Somebody says she can get a deal on a merry-go-round. We vote on each of these. Everything is carried unanimously. "Text me if you have any problems," Ginny says. "I will send out e-mails and leaflets nearer the time reminding people to get baking for the cake stall. Oh, and we'll need some volunteers to man the barbecue. Mrs. S.J. has given me a float from school funds, so I'll order the burgers and buns. Right, I think that just about wraps it up. . . ."

Talk of the devil. In swans Mrs. S.J.: flawless blow-dry, lipstick freshly applied. "Sorry to interrupt, ladies. I know you're doing terribly important work, but I just want to remind you that Dr. Connell's talk is about to start in the hall."

Chairs are scraped back. I find myself watching Hester as she stands up, Freddie still cradled in her arms. What she can't see and I can is the wet patch on his dungarees, which is growing by the second. Since fresh pee is warm, it takes her a while to react. Then the woman who has been sitting next to her notices.

"I think you'll find that Freddie has just wet himself and you," she says, barely able to suppress her joy. Freddie's mother removes her hand from underneath her son and looks at her wet sleeve. Then she sniffs Freddie's bum, as if there is a possibility her son is excreting organic elderflower cordial instead of pee. Her shock turns to indignation. "Well, it's never happened before," she says. "I think he must be coming down with something."

I'm about to dash into the school kitchen to grab some paper towels when a second woman, whose baby daughter is wearing a necklace made of amber beads, steps in with a wad of baby wipes.

I nudge Tanya. "Doesn't that child's mother realize she could chew on those beads and choke?"

"You'd think. But the babies all wear them. The amber is supposed to contain properties that relieve teething pain."

The nurse bit of me kicks in. "And presumably they've checked the scientific evidence — the peer-reviewed studies."

"What? You have to be joking. They don't care about science. It's word of mouth that matters. I'm telling you, some of these women are crackers."

By now Ginny is staring at the little girl as well. "But eventually a child is going to die."

"Not possible," Tanya says. "The beads possess magic powers that send out a force field to stop babies chewing them."

"God, life can be depressing," Ginny mutters, putting her legal pad in her bag. "Come on, let's get out of here and adjourn to the coffee shop. I could murder a doughnut."

With so many people heading toward the school hall, traffic is moving slowly in the corridor. I suggest that to save time we leave through the emergency exit next to us. I'm lifting the bar when Mrs. S.J. appears.

"Goodness, ladies, surely you're not leaving?"

"We don't want to," Ginny says, "but there's still so much to discuss for the school fair. It will be upon us before you know it."

"Oh, but surely you can take an hour or so off? Dr. Connell is such an excellent speaker. What's more, there's tea and cake in the hall. Do come. I promise I won't tell on you to the other volunteers." Mrs. S.J. offers us a conspiratorial wink.

We've been railroaded.

Just inside the door, a table is piled high with Claudia's book. The cover is full of smiley, bouncing and skipping ethnically diverse children. It's called *How to Parent.*

"A suitably modest title," Ginny remarks.

There is a notice saying that Dr. Connell is charging a pound above the cover price and donating it to the school fund. None of us — Tanya in particular — feels inclined to put our hand in our pocket. Instead we help ourselves to cups of tea. Ginny takes a slice of sponge in lieu of a doughnut and I find the last three seats next to one another. They're in the second row, which is good, but they're also in the middle, which means we can't slip out after five minutes.

Mrs. S.J. and Claudia are already seated on the stage. Claudia is wearing a navy pencil skirt and a matching tailored jacket. Her hair has been gathered into a French pleat. Her long legs are tucked neatly to one side, the way the Queen does it.

Once everybody is seated, Mrs. S.J. stands to make her introduction. "Ladies . . . and I think I spy one or two gentlemen . . ." Cue polite laughter. "As some of you will know, Dr. Connell has written six hugely successful books on child care. *How to Parent* is her seventh and I have no doubt that it is racing up the bestseller charts as I speak. I think you will agree that we are extremely fortunate to have such a distinguished expert in our midst. So without further ado I would like to hand you over to Dr. Connell."

As the audience applauds, Claudia gets up from her seat. Once she's arranged her iPad, she grips the sides of the lectern with both hands. As she waits for silence, her eyes scan the room. Her nude lips are fixed in a smile. There are no nerves — at least none that I can detect. She has the poise of a seasoned public speaker. After turning to Mrs. S.J. and thanking her for her kind words, she takes a moment before she begins: "I have five golden rules of parenting. They are as follows: Shape, don't control. Listen, don't preach. Celebrate the positive. Don't be frightened to say no. And finally remember to look after yourself. Wine o'clock is a lifesaver and should never to be underestimated."

This sets off a ripple of applause and a few hear, hears. At the same time, Tanya is stabbing the keyboard on her phone composing an Amazon review of Claudia's book. I'm assuming it's going to be less than complimentary.

"But you haven't even read it," I hiss.

"And your point is?" She carries on typing.

Meanwhile Claudia is talking about the best way to punish naughty children. "Try not to overreact," she soothes. "Make sure the punishment fits the crime. If you always resort to heavy punishments, you will end up with nothing left in your armory. If you take your children's iPads away just because they have talked back to you, what are you going to do when they punch their siblings? Also . . . whichever punishment you choose, the most important thing is to carry it through. Constant threats don't work. Children end up laughing at you and thinking they can get away with murder."

"It pains me to say it," Ginny says to me, "but the woman is talking sense."

"I know. It's infuriating."

Tanya isn't listening to us or to Claudia. Her Amazon review posted, she's checking her Facebook page.

Claudia spends the next forty-five minutes

giving advice about dealing with everything from bed-wetting to picky eaters to bullying. She has a great deal to say about the latter: "Even when schools have excellent antibullying initiatives in place" — she offers Mrs. S.J. a nod of recognition — "it's hard to banish bullying completely. That's where parents come in. Children who are being bullied must never be left to suffer in silence. They must feel able to confide in their parents. The key word here is 'intimacy.' Loving children isn't enough to protect them. Your relationship with your kids needs to be intimate as well as affectionate. They must be encouraged to share their deepest thoughts and fears with you. That way, if your children are being bullied, they are more likely to confide in you and trust you to deal with the situation appropriately."

When she's done, the applause is enthusiastic and lengthy. Ginny and I even find ourselves joining in. Tanya glares at us, arms folded.

Mrs. S.J. announces that Dr. Connell will now be taking questions. One of the dads kicks off. He's worried that as a single parent he's overprotective and interferes too much in his children's lives.

"That's Jim Ferguson," Tanya whispers.

"He's known as Tragic Jim. Terrible thing. Wife died in a car crash a couple of years back. Left him to raise twin girls."

Tragic Jim says that on the one hand he wants his daughters to bring their problems to him. On the other he's worried that he's denying them space.

"It's about finding the right balance," Claudia says. "It isn't easy. As parents, we must respect our children's privacy, but at the same time, we need to be on their case. It's also vital that they know we're emotionally available and that it's safe to bring problems to us. On the whole my two do discuss problems with me."

"Course they do," Tanya snorts, eyes rolling.

A second woman wonders how she can best deal with her children whose behavior has deteriorated since their father took a four-month engineering contract in Brazil. "He'll be back in three months, but things are so bad, it might as well be three years."

"You have my sympathy," Claudia says with a tender smile. "This is separation anxiety, pure and simple."

She emphasizes the importance of phone and Skype contact along with messages of love from Dad in the form of old-fashioned letters and cards. "It's important that he keeps telling the kids he misses them and loves them and can't wait to come home. I also suggest you start planning a family vacation for when Dad gets back. This will give the children something to focus on and look forward to."

"That's a great idea. I hadn't thought of that."

For the next fifteen minutes, hands keep going up. It seems like half the audience has questions. Claudia manages to answer four or five before Mrs. S.J. gently interrupts to say that the bell is about to go for end of school. She thanks Claudia for her insight and inspiration, wishes her well with the new book and asks everybody to give her a big hand — which they are more than delighted to do.

Mrs. S.J. makes a quick exit. I'm guessing she has no desire to stick around to be accosted by mothers demanding to know why Milo or India hasn't been put in a higher maths set.

Some people head outside to wait for their children to come out of class. Others make their way to the book table. Meanwhile a large crowd has gathered around Claudia — presumably to pay homage to ask for her advice.

"You're staring at her," Ginny says to me.

"I know. I'm just wondering what it must feel like to have adoring fans."

"Wonderful for the old ego, I guess. But I would never want to be a fan — at least not one who chases after luminaries to touch the hem of their garment. It's so demeaning. Turns you into just another member of the public."

"But isn't that what we are — members of the public?"

"You might be. I'm not."

Tanya is listening and smiling. "You know, Ginny, in your own way you're such a snob."

"Me? A snob? Get out. You're talking to somebody who lives in public housing. All I'm saying is that people shouldn't assume that there is a natural order of things — that they are destined to spend their lives in awe of the great and the good rather than nurturing their own talents. Too many lives are wasted that way." She pauses. "I'm always trying to drum this into my daughter's children."

Just then I notice Claudia waving at me and beckoning me over. "I wonder what she wants," Tanya says. "Whatever it is, watch your step."

Claudia is chatting to the woman whose husband is in Brazil. As I approach they break off. "Judy, I want you to meet Alice. I thought that since Sam and Rosie have been having separation anxiety problems, it might help if you two got together."

I am aware that there is a gaggle of women around us, taking this in.

"Actually Sam and Rosie are fine. So far, they're doing really well." I turn to Alice. "I'm sorry you're having such a rough time with your kids and of course I'd be more than happy to have a chat over a cup of coffee, but for some reason — probably nothing more than luck — my two are OK."

"Oh, come on, Judy," Claudia says, "that's rather disingenuous of you."

"I don't think it is."

"But surely Sam and Rosie's problems are public knowledge? Kids have problems. It's nothing to be ashamed of."

"I agree, but my grandchildren are not having problems."

"But everybody knows Sam brought a gun to school. And not just any old gun. I think I'm right in saying it was an army assault rifle."

"Oh, for goodness' sake. It was a toy. He did it for a joke."

"And what about Rosie? Is it a joke when she calls one of her classmates a motherfucker?"

I carry on looking at Claudia. That way I

can't see the collective eyebrow-raising that I assume is going on.

"And what about her painting inappropriate sexual images?" There are several gasps.

"Excuse me? What the hell are you talking about?"

"Hero told me she paints pictures of naked people."

"Oh my God. You really are scraping the barrel now. Rosie saw me getting out of the bath the other day. The painting is completely innocent. Even Miss Carter said so."

"With all due respect to Miss Carter, she doesn't have my expertise in child psychology."

I can feel my hand making a fist. "This would be funny if it weren't so malicious. What are you suggesting? That I am behaving inappropriately around my grandchildren?"

She doesn't say anything.

"Come on. Answer me. Are you or are you not accusing me of inappropriate behavior? It's a simple question. I'm sure everybody is gagging to know."

"I'm not."

"Good."

"I do think they have some issues, though."

"What issues? There are no issues. You've

blown everything out of proportion. What's more, you've done it in public, for the benefit of the entire school — in order to hurt and humiliate me."

"Don't be ridiculous. Why would I want to humiliate you?"

"You tell me."

"Look . . . the point I'm trying to make is that Sam and Rosie are acting out because they feel abandoned and bereft — bereaved even."

"Just like mine," Alice pipes up, looking at me. "I do think Claudia's right. You're being too hard on her."

I am anxious not to take out my fury on Alice, who seems like a decent soul, if a bit meek and ineffectual. I say again that I'm sorry she's having a bad time. "But I really don't think I'm the best person to help you."

Fighting to stay calm, I turn back to Claudia. "Since you have so generously diagnosed my problem, let me return the favor. You are an addict. You have an obsessive need to rescue people you consider to be lame ducks so that you can build them up again, restore them to health. Then you sit back and bask in the glory."

Claudia frowns. Her head and neck jerk back. For a second she looks like a chicken dodging a bullet. "That's nonsense. I have no idea what you're talking about."

"Your ego. That's what I'm talking about. Now, for the last time, my grandchildren are not suffering from separation anxiety and I would thank you to keep your nose out of my affairs."

"Judy, please don't be like this. I'm sorry if I've upset you. I honestly didn't mean to. But I do think it's best and fairer on the children if things are out in the open. I can hear that you're angry —"

"Angry? Angry doesn't begin to describe what I'm feeling right now."

Nobody knows where to look. People are staring at their feet. But not a soul has moved away. This is gossip gold and nobody wants to miss a second.

"But my intentions were and have always been completely honorable," Claudia says.

"The hell they were. Do you think I was born yesterday?"

"Judy — you need to calm down and take a breath."

"Don't you dare patronize me. Your caring, compassionate persona may fool this lot, but it doesn't fool me."

"Actually . . . I'd like to say something if I may." It's Tanya. She's edging through the crowd toward Claudia and me. "Just to set the record straight, it was Cybil who taught

Rosie to say motherfucker. So if anybody's to blame, it's me. She picked it up from a friend of mine. I don't want anybody blaming Judy and certainly not Rosie. It's entirely my fault."

Claudia has the decency to turn red. She stammers an apology. "I'm sorry if I got that part wrong. But I don't think it changes the overall picture of what's going on with Sam and Rosie."

"How dare you . . . you —" I'm about to call her a bitch, but Ginny interrupts.

"Come on," her voice booms over the melee. "Time to go."

She's right. I'm done. A slanging match would achieve nothing. The crowd parts like the Red Sea. Twenty pairs of eyes are on me as I head to the door, followed by Ginny and Tanya.

"You didn't need to own up," I say to Tanya.

"Of course I did. I wasn't about to let you take the blame for my mistake."

"Well, I'm very grateful. Thank you."

Ginny puts her arm across my back. "Well-done, you, for taking Claudia on. You were bloody brilliant."

When we get outside, Cybil and Ivo are already there. Rosie and Sam have yet to appear. They both had PE last lesson and are probably still getting dressed.

"Hi, Rosie's gran," Cybil says, all freckles and long eyelashes.

"Hi, darling."

Ginny nudges Ivo. "Come on, you know Judy. Say hello."

"Hi." Ivo's voice is a whisper. He doesn't look at me. He rarely does. He's painfully shy. Ginny blames his mother. She says she's too strict and controlling and that once Ivo's testosterone kicks in, she won't know what's hit her.

"Rosie's gran," Cybil says, "you look cross."

Tanya tells her not to be rude.

"But I'm only saying." Cybil turns back to me. "So, are you cross? Sometimes when I get cross it's because my blood sugar's low. Would you like some of my egg mayo sandwich from lunch? It's a bit squished, but it's very nice. Much better than the school lunches you get here. They had stinky fish today. Yuck."

"Cybil, please. Judy is fine."

Cybil is pretty and engaging, just like her mother. But she's in a pickle. One sock is up, the other is down. Her school cardigan is inside out. The backs of her hands are covered in Biro doodles and sparkly stickers.

I assure Cybil that I'm fine. But I'm not. My heart's still pounding and pumping adrenaline. I'm thinking that I could do with a very large Scotch. I want to get home.

"Kids — tell you what. If Ginny and Tanya don't mind, could you pop back into school and see what's happened to Rosie and Sam?"

"Sure."

The children charge off, only too eager to oblige. Meanwhile I'm holding my hand out in front of me.

"Look. That bloody woman has made me so angry I'm actually shaking."

Ginny says I need to take a breath and calm down.

"I can't calm down. She's a manipulative, in-your-business, ego-maniacal, self-aggrandizing bitch. I loathe her. I absolutely loathe her."

"Wow — she sounds like a piece of work. So, is this a private conversation or can anyone join?" The three of us turn toward a man's voice. Standing in front of us is a chap about my age: close-cropped silver hair, trendy horn-rimmed specs and a jokey grin. I've never seen him before and I can tell from Tanya's blank expression that she doesn't know him either.

"Mike, hi," Ginny says. "How are you?"

"Oh, you know — getting older."

"Ha. Aren't we all? But look at you with your trendy specs and posh jacket. You've got nothing to worry about. You don't look a day over fifty."

"That's a nice thing to say to a man of forty-five."

"Idiot!" Ginny gives Mike a friendly slap on the shoulder. They're clearly old friends. "So, are you here to pick up the kids?"

"I am."

Ginny is moving herself into position to introduce Mike to Tanya and me, but he doesn't give her a chance. "So come on, which one of the teachers has got you lot so worked up? Or is it Mrs. S.J.'s new secretary? I've heard she yells at the kids and everybody hates her."

I watch Ginny hesitate, so I jump in: "Actually it's not a member of staff. It's one of the mothers."

Ginny shoots me a strange look. It manages to be both fearful and beseeching. I have no idea what she's trying to say. Tanya looks just as confused.

"Well, whoever she is," Mike says, "she sounds horrible."

I tell him she is. "Her name's Claudia Connell. If you have any connection to this school, you're bound to have heard of her."

"Oh God," Ginny mutters. She's looking at the ground. She clearly wants it to swallow her up. But because I'm still so caught up in adrenaline-fueled emotion, I'm confused and can't work out why.

Mike is frowning. "Really? What's she done?"

"She's told the entire school that my grandchildren are having behavioral problems when they don't. Granted Sam brought an assault rifle into school and Rosie said motherfucker and painted a nude picture of me, but Claudia took it entirely out of context. All she's interested in is spreading dirt. She's a vile, hateful woman and I want to throttle her."

"Oh, I'm sure you don't," Ginny simpers. Ginny isn't prone to simpering, so it sounds almost comical.

"I bloody do."

"Well, I can quite understand why you would," Mike says. "That's a terrible thing to have done." He glances at his watch and starts to move away. He looks embarrassed and agitated — as if he's desperate to make his escape. "Sorry. I should go and look for my daughter and her children. She's got a train to catch and I need to get her to the station. Do excuse me."

Mike disappears into the school.

"Strange man," I say to Ginny. "Who is he?"

"Claudia's dad."

CHAPTER NINE

"And in other news this Sunday lunchtime: Thousands of homeless survivors of the recent earthquake in Nicaragua are facing what a UN spokesman has described as a serious and concerning outbreak of typhoid and cholera. In a press conference to be held later today, the Nicaraguan president Daniel Ortega will appeal for more doctors and international aid. . . ."

"I hate cholera and typhoid," Sam says, chewing on a cheese and Marmite bagel.

"I don't think anybody's keen." I break off from unloading the dishwasher and hit the off button on the radio. He's heard enough. I should have turned it off the moment the item came on.

"But I hate it because it means that now Mum and Dad will be staying longer in Nicaragua."

"I know, darling. It's rotten for everybody. But maybe the doctors will cure all the people quickly and stop others from getting sick. If that happens Mum and Dad will be home sooner than you think."

The outbreak of typhoid and cholera has been a game changer. Abby and Tom Skyped last night and broke it to the children that they might be away for more than six weeks. "The thing is," Abby said, "people are getting very sick and there just aren't enough doctors."

"Are children getting sick?" Rosie said.

"I'm afraid they are."

"So, if you came home instead of helping them, would they die?"

"They might."

"Then you have to stay and make them better. Sam and I are fine with Grandma and Nana. And I've got my star necklace to look after me."

"That's good. But remember that the star necklace is very precious. I hope you're looking after it."

"I am. I promise."

Sam agreed with Rosie. Their mum and dad had to stay.

"But if I get worried or sad," Rosie said, "I can still tell you, can't I? You won't be too tired and busy to listen?"

Despite all the pixels on the screen, I could see that this had both of her parents close to tears. "Oh, sweetie, of course we won't," Abby said. "No matter what we're doing, Dad and I will always make time for you."

"And if anything serious happened," Tom said, "like you were really unhappy or you weren't well, we'd be home in a flash."

" 'K."

"Where did we get such wonderful, mature kids?" Abby said a few minutes later, after Sam and Rosie had disappeared and we were able to Skype alone. I decided this probably wasn't the time to tell her about the assault rifle incident or Rosie saying motherfucker and lying about where she heard it. Ditto my spat with Claudia. I also chose not to mention that I'd taken Bogdan to task. No matter what Abby says, I won't have him bullying Sam.

It was during his Thursday evening lesson. Bogdan was laying into Sam as usual. "Nyet. Eed-y-ot! What are you thinking? Stupid boy. What have I told you about developing your knights before your bishops and not bringing your queen out too early? And look at you — weakening your pawns in front of a castled king."

I was eavesdropping from the doorway as usual. All I could hear was Bogdan shouting and bashing the table: "No! No! No! Remember, look at the whole board! . . . Nyet! I geev up . . . What have I told you? Castle early and often."

By the time the session was over, Sam was white and exhausted. I went into the room, handed him a bar of chocolate and told him he could go and watch TV. Bogdan was standing with his battered briefcase under his arm. For my benefit he was all smiles. "Sam is coming along very well. He needs to concentrate more. But he is excellent pupil. My best."

"Then for goodness' sake, why don't you tell him that?"

"I don't understand."

"I've heard you. You're always so hard on him. You're always calling him an idiot."

"This is good. He shouldn't get beeg head."

"But he needs encouragement. You're undermining him. He's losing his confidence."

"No. I make him tough."

"That's ridiculous. What you're doing is turning him into a nervous wreck. Please — you need to ease up on him and stop calling him an idiot."

By now Mum has joined us. "What my daughter is trying to say is this . . ." She moves in on Bogdan, so that she is inches from his face. Then she speaks to him very quietly, in fluent Russian. Since when did my mother speak Russian?

Whatever she has said, it seems to have worked, because Bogdan is red in the face and can't get out fast enough.

"Bloody hell, Mum, what did you say to him? He looked like a scared rabbit. And where did you learn to speak Russian?"

"I once dated a Russian Jewish refugee. So I told Bogdan that if he carries on bullying Sam, you would cut off his balls."

"What? You didn't."

"I most certainly did."

"Marvelous. You do realize he'll never come back. Have you any idea the trouble you've got me into?"

"Don't worry. He'll be back."

"How do you know?"

"He wants another champion to add to his list. Why wouldn't he come back?"

Back on Skype, I was reminding Abby that contrary to her belief, she was doing a fantastic job of raising her kids.

She wasn't so sure. Here they were, on the other side of the globe, putting other people — albeit injured and sick ones — before their own children. "It's bound to have an effect. I don't want them growing up with abandonment issues."

I wanted to say something along the lines of "Oh God, you're as bad as bloody Claudia." But I didn't. Instead I told her the kids were fine and that she and Tom needed to focus on their work and stop fretting.

I've just put away the last of the clean dishes when Rosie appears, all dressed up. She's going to Lilly's birthday party this afternoon. Lilly isn't one of her special friends, but — as per school etiquette — her mother has invited the whole class to the party. I left it to Rosie to choose her outfit. She's teamed a bright pink layered net skirt with stripy tights, a Save the Tundra T-shirt and a sparkly headband that has a fluorescent yellow rose at the side.

"Wow, look at you, pretty girl."

She does a twirl. "Do you like it?"

"I love it." My granddaughter is only five and already she's pulling off boho chic.

"Well, I think you look stupid," Sam says.

"I don't look stupid! I look pretty. Grandma said."

"Sam, that's a horrible thing to say. Why are you being so mean?"

"And that's my tundra T-shirt," he says.

"It's not! It's mine!"

"Liar. And anyway, you're a baby. You don't even know what tundra is."

"I do. It's lots of snow." Rosie is pink with

fury. She's fighting back tears. Any second now she'll lash out at Sam.

"Sam, what on earth has gotten into you?"

"She stole my T-shirt."

Rosie bursts into tears. "I didn't. I didn't. It was in my stuff."

"No, it wasn't — you stole it. And you know it."

Rosie lunges at her brother and starts punching him. "I didn't steal it. I hate you. I hate you." Sam is bent over the table, his arms protecting his head.

I pull Rosie away, but she's struggling and yelling at me to get off. "Rosie. That's enough. Calm down."

"I won't calm down. He called me a liar. I'm not a liar."

"I know you're not."

"Well, tell him."

"I will, but only if you stand still and stop punching."

I point out to Sam that the tundra T-shirt is far too small for him and that I'm guessing his mother realized that and passed it on to Rosie.

Sam doesn't say anything. Instead he pokes his tongue out at his sister and stomps off, taking what remains of his bagel with him. I give chase and catch him at the bottom of the stairs. "Sam, what on earth's the matter with you? Why are you being so horrible lately?" Stupid question. I know why.

"I'm going to play chess in my room," he says by way of reply, and carries on upstairs. I let him go. There's no point trying to talk to him while he's like this.

Meanwhile Rosie is fretting about something else. She can't find her sparkly shoes. I tell her to check under her bed.

Once Rosie has her shoes on and I've wrapped Lilly's present — a decorate-your-own twinkly tiara and necklace set — I head into the living room to say good-bye to Mum. She's minding Sam while I'm out. They were planning to play *Minecraft,* but I'm not sure that Sam is going to feel like it. I'm not sure my mother is either. She's been a bit odd, a bit remote ever since she found out that Estelle Silverfish is dating Big Max. Right now she's sitting with a book on her lap and staring into the middle distance. It's the reason I haven't said anything to her about my confrontation with Claudia. She's far too wrapped up in herself.

"Mum, you all right?"

"Goodness, you made me jump," she says, slapping her hand to her chest. "I'm fine. Why shouldn't I be?"

"I dunno. Lately you seem a bit out of it, that's all. I was wondering if it had anything to do with Estelle."

"Estelle? Why should it have anything to do with Estelle? I've got a bit of a backache, that's all. I'm not sleeping. It's that mattress."

The mattress is new. That's not what's upsetting her. My elderly mother is jealous that Estelle Silverfish is seeing somebody.

Lilly's mother, Felicity, is greeting parents in her grand oak-paneled hallway and insisting they stay for a glass of "fizz." Most seem more than delighted to accept. As I join the queue to say hello and deposit Rosie, a couple of mothers behind me are trying to arrange a playdate for their daughters. They're both checking the calendars on their phones. "OK . . . Tamsin can do next Saturday — Oh no. Oops, it's Mabel's party."

"Really? That's odd. Livvy hasn't had an invitation. I wonder if her mum made a mistake. I should speak to her. . . . OK . . . Livvy can do the twenty-fifth. She's just had a cancellation. How would that work?"

"Sorry, no. Tamsin's got ballet."

"What about the twenty-ninth?"

"Fully booked, I'm afraid."

"Thirtieth?"

"Mandarin. Ooh . . . she's got a slot on Saturday the first, though."

"Yes, that's good. But it would have to be after her trombone lesson and she's got a bowling party late afternoon."

"Perfect."

When did kids get to be so busy? And when did mums turn into their diary keepers? When Abby was growing up, weekends were pretty much commitment free. If there was a birthday party, it was attended by a handful of the birthday girl's or boy's closest friends. Playdates weren't called playdates. They weren't called anything. Mums would approach other mums in the playground and ask if so-and-so would like to come for tea. Kids were never "fully booked." I never had to check my diary.

I get exhausted just thinking about this hectic new world, where kids and mothers are always on the go. Lilly's mum gushes a greeting, says how lovely it is to meet me and tells me how proud I must be of Abby. "You absolutely must stay for a drink."

I explain that I can't stop because I need to get to the supermarket. Mum has given me one of her lists. Not only is it very long, but it involves going to the regular supermarket for basics, then on to the kosher butcher — where there's never anywhere to park — for meat and chicken fat. After that it's another ten-minute drive to the only Jewish bakery that sells wholemeal matzos. "Oh, and get some bagels for the freezer," she said as I left. Since Mum moved in, the freezer has become another mouth to feed.

Felicity says it's a shame I can't stay. "Maybe we could just have a quick natter." She ushers me toward the staircase. "I just wanted to let you know," she says, lowering her voice, "that I heard about what happened between you and Claudia and that I'm totally on your side. That woman needed taking down a peg or two, and by all accounts you did a great job. I just wish I'd been there."

"I didn't set out to put her in her place. She upset me, that's all."

"And you stood up to her. Good for you. Claudia will always have her fans and hangers-on, but you should know that there's a significant minority that see through her."

"Well, it's good to know I'm not alone."

"Of course Claudia isn't the only problem. There's been a lot of gossip about Tanya. I know she's a friend of yours, but I thought you should know. The thing is, it's not just the swearing. . . . It's the drugs."

"What drugs?"

"Tanya and Rick are known for it."

"And you have proof of this?"

"You don't need proof. They're in the music business. They hang out with all these rappers. Come on . . . don't be naive. Of course it's Cybil I feel sorry for."

We're joined by another woman who has clearly been eavesdropping. "Me, too. It's always the children who suffer. So sad."

"And it's not just weed," Felicity says. "I heard they do a lot of coke, too."

I'm about to express my views on malicious, unsubstantiated gossip, which I know for a fact was started by Claudia, when Tanya appears with Cybil. Felicity and her friend fall silent and exchange embarrassed glances.

"Please don't stop on my account," Tanya says as she directs Cybil toward Lilly and the untidy queue of children trying to hand over gifts. She offers me a thin smile. Crap. Does she think I'm part of this witch hunt?

"Sorry, ladies. Must dash. I'm meeting my supplier."

She kisses Cybil good-bye and she's out of the door. I chase her down the path. "Tanya, wait. . . . Please . . . I had absolutely no part in that."

She stops and turns around. She looks

246

shamefaced but at the same time close to tears. "It's OK. I know you didn't."

"Thank heaven for that."

"I thought the gossip had died down. But since this swearing thing, it's all kicked off again."

"I'm so sorry. I don't know what to say."

"Just because we're in the music business, they think we sit around all day cutting coke or with needles in our arms."

"Listen . . . would it help if I picked Cybil up from the party later and dropped her home?"

"Would you mind? That would be great. I'm not sure I can face those women again today."

"Of course I don't mind."

I walk Tanya back to her car. "You going to be OK? I'd offer to come home with you, but I need to do a food shop."

"Thanks, but Rick's there. I think we might sit and watch a movie." She pauses. "I hate these women. I hate the gossip. It's like being in a Jane Austen novel. I've got this sudden urge to become an invalid and retire to my bed for a year or two."

I tell her that I feel like doing the same — anything to avoid bumping into Claudia's father again.

Tanya's face brightens. "You were hysterical. I sensed there was something in the air. I was trying to tell you to shut up, but you weren't getting it."

"I know. I made an utter fool of myself and I could see I'd upset the poor man. It's not his fault his daughter is so horrible."

"On the other hand, you probably didn't say anything he doesn't already know."

Then it occurs to me that since Claudia is away on her book tour, he might well be dropping Hero off at the party.

"I'm sure her dad will bring her," Tanya says.

"Maybe, but I should scoot. . . . God, what if I bump into him later when I'm picking the girls up?"

"So what? Just go up to him and apologize."

"But what if he starts yelling at me? I've caused enough drama lately. I don't want to start any more."

I decide to get a cup of coffee before hitting the supermarket. I head for the new café-boulangerie in the high street. For once there's a parking spot right outside. I order a large cappuccino and — as a treat — a slice of coffee and walnut cake. There's an empty table for two in the window. I sit facing the street, gazing at the chichi flower shop over the road. Oversize containers full of spring flowers are arranged on the pavement. Some tulips the color of cantaloupe catch my eye. When I've finished my coffee I will award myself another treat and buy a bunch.

After a while I turn away and start stirring the cocoa into the cappuccino foam. In my head I tell Brian that I'm feeling a bit blue and could do with cheering up. I'm worried about Sam. I'm worried that Rosie still isn't sleeping. I hate the way they're fighting. I still haven't come down from my contretemps with Claudia or the fact that I upset her father. And now I'm worried about Mum being jealous of Estelle Silverfish. I use my coffee spoon to skim some thick coffee butter icing off the slab of cake. As it dissolves in my mouth, I imagine Brian telling me that everything will sort itself out and there's nothing to be gained by worrying.

"You always say that," I inform him aloud. "But what if it doesn't sort itself out?"

That's when I hear the voice. Only it isn't Brian's. He never speaks, other than in my imagination. "Did you know," says the voice, "that talking to yourself is the first sign of insanity?"

I give a start and look up. It's Claudia's

dad. Of all the café-boulangeries in all the neighborhood, he has to walk into mine. What do I say? I settle for "Mike, hello. Well — this is rather embarrassing."

"Why? Because I've discovered that you are sliding into insanity?" He has a nice smile.

"Partly that. I was talking to my late husband. I do it a lot — mainly in my head, I might add. And for the record I make up his replies, which are based on my having known him for over thirty years." I pause. "I'm Judy, by the way."

"I know. Ginny told me."

"Ah."

"Don't worry. We weren't gossiping. I was curious to find out what happened between you and Claudia, that's all. I am aware that she rubs some people the wrong way."

I decide not to rub salt in the parental wound by expounding any more of my opinions on Claudia. Instead I insist that I behaved badly, too. "After Ginny told me who you were, I should have come after you and apologized. Claudia's your daughter and whatever my feelings are toward her, you don't deserve to be privy to them. My only excuse is that I was terribly cross."

"I understand. You really don't have to apologize. I know what Claudia's like. It's not news to me. I'm sure she should be the one saying sorry."

At that moment two boys come ambling over from the direction of the loo. "Granddad. Please can Josh and me get milk shakes and cake now?"

I don't recognize either of them, but I assume the one campaigning for shakes and cakes is Mike's grandson, Sebastian.

"Seb, I'm in the middle of a conversation. Don't they teach you anything at that posh school of yours? Don't you know it's bad manners to interrupt?" His tone is jolly. Nevertheless he makes his point. Sebastian apologizes.

"But the thing is, Josh and me are hungry and you're busy talking. So if you give us the money we can buy what we want on our own." Sebastian is tall like his mother and he has her green eyes, but that's where the resemblance ends. I'm assuming that with his brush of red hair and a face full of freckles he takes after his dad. He reminds me of that kid in *Happy Days*. What was his name? Went on to be a film director. It'll come to me. Ever since menopause I've had a problem remembering names — nothing else, just names. I often wonder if there's a link between lack of estrogen and identity recognition. I should get Mum to Google it.

"All right," Mike is saying to Seb, "you can buy your own drinks and cake. But be careful. Make sure you get a tray. Oh, and if you can manage, would you be kind enough to get me a latte?" Mike reaches inside his jacket, takes out his wallet and hands Sebastian a twenty-pound bill.

"Thanks, Granddad."

"Yeah, thanks, Seb's granddad."

The two friends head to the counter. "So, are you helping with the children while Claudia's away?"

"I am. Laurence — he's my son-in-law — isn't great at coping on his own, so he tends to rope me in. Not that I mind. I love spending time with them."

I notice that Josh is holding a strange multipropellered flying machine with a small camera attached.

Mike catches me staring. "It's a drone. We've been flying it on Hampstead Heath."

I tell him I've never seen one before. "So, what were you doing? Spying on the likes of Harry Styles and Boy George?"

This makes him laugh. "No, just filming the landscape. Seb and his friend took it to two thousand feet — quite illegal, I might add — and got some astonishing footage." He hesitates. "Would you mind if I joined you?"

"Not at all, please do."

As he pulls out a chair, he offers to get me another coffee. I thank him and tell him maybe later, as I've hardly started the one I've got.

"You know," I say, "you really don't have to apologize for Claudia. She may be your daughter, but she's an adult. She isn't your responsibility."

"You're right. But I can't help it. Parental responsibility tends not to wear off. It lasts until you die."

"You may have a point there."

Sebastian appears with a latte in a tall glass cup. His hands are shaking. A good deal of coffee has spilled into the saucer. He places it carefully on the table and presents his grandfather with his change. Mike thanks him, tells him well-done and doesn't mention the spilled coffee. I can't help wondering how Bogdan would react in such circumstances.

"Is it OK if we go and sit over there?" Sebastian says, pointing to a table by the door. Josh is already there tucking in to chocolate fudge cake. "Then we won't be in your way."

I tell him that he and Josh are more than welcome to pull up another table and sit with us. "I'm Judy, by the way. My grandson, Sam, is in the year below you."

"Hi, Judy. Pleased to meet you. I'm Seb."
He turns back to his grandfather. "The
thing is that Josh is already there now."

Mike says it's fine for him to sit with Josh
and shoos him away.

"What a self-possessed, well-mannered
lad," I say when he's out of earshot.

"Isn't he? Claudia does manage to get
some things right."

"Well, I guess his father must have some
input, too."

"True."

Mike sips his coffee. He looks thoughtful.
"Claudia doesn't mean to upset people, you
know."

"I'm sure nobody sets out to offend."

"She had a rotten childhood."

Oh, please. I can't believe he's playing the
crap childhood card. "Maybe she did, but
so have millions of people and they turn
out OK. And anyway, you really don't owe
me an explanation. We barely know each
other."

"I know. But I'd like to explain — give
you a bit of background . . . if you're happy
to listen."

Frankly I'd rather not. I don't give a damn
about Claudia's childhood. But Mike is a
nice man and I don't want to appear rude.
"Sure."

"OK . . . So, when Claudia was five, her mother left me for another man. He was a bully and he insisted she leave Claudia with me. Eventually they went to live in Paris. After a few months he made her cut off all ties with Claudia. My ex did as she was told and didn't see Claudia for twenty years. She abandoned her only child." He pauses. "Actually that's not quite true. She made contact when Claudia was accepted at the Royal Ballet School. It was something to brag about. But when Claudia grew too tall and lost her place, she disappeared again."

"Good God. That's appalling. I'm so sorry." Now I don't know what to think. Have I been too hard on her?

"These days, she has a tentative relationship with her mother, but it's still not great. She still has a lot of issues."

"That's pretty obvious."

"So it's not hard to understand why she threw herself into becoming a parenting expert and why she has the overwhelming need to rescue people."

"I get all that. But what I don't understand is why at the same time as wanting to look after people, she manages to be so unkind and manipulative. She's been spreading rumors about people taking drugs when they're not. She also seems hell-bent on

255

making it appear that my grandchildren are suffering separation anxiety while their parents are away — the insinuation being that I'm not coping." I realize I'm getting worked up again. I've still barely touched my coffee and cake and walnut is my favorite.

Mike puts down his coffee cup. "She would never admit it, but she's unhappy. Unhappy people behave badly. It's the only explanation I can offer."

"But what she's done to this other couple — accusing them of taking drugs — is far worse than what she's done to me. It's hateful. And I know it's not true."

"I think Claudia spends her life petrified that her friends are going to abandon her. She creates juicy gossip to keep them close."

"But she has a doctorate in psychology. It seems crazy that she can't see what she's doing."

"It is crazy. I've told her. Laurence keeps telling her. Funnily enough, he and I are the only people she doesn't try to manipulate. She knows we wouldn't put up with it. No matter how often we try to make her understand, she refuses to admit she has a problem. It doesn't help that she's surrounded by all these groupies who think she's some kind of guru and hang on her every word."

There's a commotion coming from the boys' table. Sebastian is holding a piece of drone and Josh is bent over him, trying to offer comfort. "Oh God. I didn't mean it. I didn't mean it." Sebastian gets up and comes tearing over to Mike. Josh hangs back — possibly because he wants to avoid any flack.

Sebastian is almost in tears as he hands the broken part to his grandfather. "I didn't mean to break it. It was an accident. I'm so sorry. I'll pay you back out of my pocket money. . . ."

"What, all two thousand pounds?"

"Excuse me — you're letting nine-year-olds play with something that cost two grand?" It's none of my business what Mike does with his drone, but I'm so shocked that the words fly out of my mouth before I have time to think.

"It didn't cost me anything," Mike says to me. "I've got it on loan from the manufacturer."

"Granddad's a tech journalist," Sebastian says, brightening between sniffs. "He gets to try out all this really cool stuff and then he writes about it in the newspapers."

"So I'm guessing," I say, "that so long as the drone people get a good write-up, they

257

won't mind too much if it's damaged."

"That's right. They might even send me a spare part if I ask nicely."

"Really?" Sebastian says with wide eyes. "You mean they won't be cross? But if they are, you will tell them it was an accident, won't you? I really didn't mean it."

"It's OK, Seb. It'll be fine. I promise." Mike turns to me. "Seb's a bit of a worrier. Aren't you, son?" He smiles and pulls the lad in for a hug.

"Granddad, stop it. Not when there are people."

Mike rolls his eyes and lets him go.

"You know," I say, feeling I should step in and ease the familial tension, "I'm not sure I'd spend two grand to spy on Boy George."

"There are fans that might," Mike says, smiling. "Right, I think I'd better get these boys home. I told Seb's dad we'd be back by four." He gets up and asks Sebastian to fetch Josh. "It was great to chat, Judy. Thanks for letting me explain everything. I know it doesn't help, but I like to think of Claudia as a work in progress. One day she'll fathom it all out."

"I hope so. And my apologies again for being so rude the other day."

"No problem."

I wave him and the boys off.

"Granddad," Sebastian says. "Who's Boy George?"

By now I've calmed down. I start tucking into my cake. Then it comes to me: Ron Howard.

CHAPTER TEN

"Grandma, if I'm still living at your house
when it's my birthday, can I have a Cinderella party?" Ever since she got home from
Lilly's party, Rosie's been busy planning
her own — which isn't for six months. Last
night she wanted a *Frozen*-themed bash,
but by bedtime she decided against it
because lots of girls were doing *Frozen*.

"Of course you can have a Cinderella
party. That's a great idea. You can invite all
your friends over to clean my house."

"Hang on . . . what about mine?" Ginny
says. "I'm guessing your house is spotless.
It's my place that could do with a once-
over."

I'm laughing, but Rosie doesn't get the
joke. She wants to know why having a
Cinderella party would mean her friends
having to clean Ginny's house.

It's school pickup time and Ginny and I
are hanging around outside, shooting the

breeze. Ivo and Rosie have emerged, but it seems like Sam's class hasn't been let out yet. Rosie says they're probably still tidying up after art class.

"Fancy coming to mine for a cuppa?" Ginny says. "I have to drop Ivo off. He's got a playdate with a boy from another school. Then Emma's coming round and leaving her boys with me for a few hours — so your kids will have company."

I tell her I'd love to come, but it's Tuesday. The kids have French Club.

"I hate French Club," Rosie harrumphs. "Everybody can talk it 'cept me. Delphine gave us volcablry to learn last week, and I lost the bit of paper. I know she'll be cross with me."

"I'm glad I don't do French Club," Ivo says. "It sounds strict and horrible."

As if on cue, Sam appears. "It is. All we do is sing silly babyish songs or get tested on words. I don't see why we have to learn French when practically the whole world speaks English — apart from the Chinese. I learned that from my book of facts."

"And French people eat frogs' legs," Rosie says. "Why would you want to eat poor little frogs?"

"Actually frogs' legs are rather nice," Ginny says. "Can't say I have much time for the Frenchies. What bothers me is that in 1558 we handed them Calais and all they gave us in return was the bloody bidet."

Both children are clamoring to be let off French Club. "Please, please . . . just this once. We won't ask again. Promise."

I give in for selfish reasons more than anything. Having spent the day changing beds, doing laundry and spring-cleaning kitchen cupboards, I'm bushed. I'd much rather have a cup of tea and a gossip at Ginny's than drive two miles to French Club in traffic and then sit in the car for an hour and a half while the kids learn to conjugate *avoir* and *être*.

Soon after we arrive at Ginny's, her daughter, Emma, appears with her two boys, Mason and Tyler. It's hard to believe that Ginny and Emma are mother and daughter. Ginny is stocky and lives in sweatshirts and jeans, whereas Emma is tiny and looks like she's heading to a rockabilly convention. Her Rosie the Riveter head scarf has been accessorized with a tight red-check shirt, pedal pushers and clumpy fifties slingbacks. Like Tanya, she's a whiz with scarlet lippie.

She's full of warmth and smiles when she greets us and she makes a particular fuss over Sam and Rosie. But I can't help thinking that her cheerfulness is affected. There's something about her manner, the occasionally taut facial expression, the way she picks at her nails, that suggests all is not well.

"So, did you sell much today?" Ginny says, coming into the living room with a tray. There's tea for us — sandwiches, potato chips and juice for the kids. She sets it down on the dining room table.

"A bit."

"What does that mean?" Ginny says, swatting the back of Emma's hand to stop her picking at her nails.

Emma pulls away. "It means you have to stop nagging."

"Fine. I apologize." She hands out mugs of tea.

"Sorry," Emma says. "I didn't mean to snap. The boys are getting me down, that's all. They won't stop fighting. I don't know what's got into them lately. They used to play really well together."

"Join the club," I say.

"Your two fight? Seriously? They look like butter wouldn't melt."

I can't help noticing the way Emma speaks — only because her accent is something else that separates mother and daughter. Whereas Ginny sounds like somebody who regularly revisits Brideshead, Emma's accent is pure London street.

For the last half hour, the children have been upstairs in Ginny's spare bedroom playing Scalextric. So far there have been no skirmishes. The only sounds have been good-natured cries of victory or defeat.

Ginny calls them downstairs for snacks and insists that they eat at the table. Mason and his younger brother, who are both wearing Manchester United shirts, want to take their sandwiches into the garden, where there's a trampoline. But Ginny's not having it. "You eat at the table like proper people. Then you can go into the garden." Sam and Rosie get up to the table. Mason and Tyler don't move.

"That's crap," Mason says.

Emma is on her feet and in Mason's face. "Don't you dare talk to Granny like that. Now apologize. I don't know what Rosie and Sam must think."

With the sullenness of a sixteen-year-old, Mason mutters an apology. Both boys get up to the table.

"It's OK, Mason," Sam says. "Everybody at my school says 'crap,' even though you're not meant to."

I tell Sam that's enough and that we've had enough swearing for one day.

"Well, I bet they don't say 'shit' or 'fuck,' " Mason says.

"Mason!" Emma turns to her mother and shoots her a plaintive look. "What do I do with him?"

"OK, folks," Ginny says, "do you think we could possibly change the subject?"

Sam chooses not to hear. "They do say the *F* word," he whispers. "But it's really naughty."

"Well, at our school we say it all the time. The teachers don't care."

"Yeah, they do," his brother says. "You got sent to the head for saying it."

"I did not."

"You did."

"You're such a liar."

"I am not."

With that Mason thumps his brother's shoulder. Tyler returns fire with an identical blow. Before anybody has time to react, they are on the floor punching, biting and pulling hair. This isn't the usual sibling set-to. The boys' faces are red and contorted with rage. They really want to hurt each other. Emma makes a halfhearted attempt to separate them. "Stop it, you two. I said, stop it."

Rosie is wide-eyed and clearly a bit scared, but Sam is kneeling on his chair to get a better view. He's enjoying this.

Emma looks on, close to tears. "I give up. I dunno what to do with them."

Ginny puts down her mug of tea and wades in. "Right. This stops now," she bellows. She grabs Tyler by the arm and heaves him, protesting, off his brother. "How many times have I told you I will not have fighting in my house? Now both of you sit down and eat your sandwiches — or you will go straight home. This is appalling behavior. I cannot tell you how disappointed I am."

Tyler looks at her, sweaty and defiant, as he rearranges his football shirt. "But Mason started it."

"I did not. You called me a liar."

"I don't care who started it. How dare you misbehave — particularly in front of visitors? Now, I won't tell you again — sit down." Ginny's arm is outstretched, her finger pointing at the table.

The boys do as they're told and the four children eat in silence.

Ginny is still trying to get her breath back as she sits down. "For God's sake, Emma," she says, lowering her voice, "you have to start showing those boys who's boss. If you don't, they will be out of control before you know it. Heaven help you when their hormones kick in."

Emma is holding her mug of tea in one hand and wiping her eyes with the other. "I do my best. You know I do. But I'm trying to run my business and look after them on my own. It's not easy raising kids in this neighborhood — particularly boys. You've no idea what it's like."

"Of course I know what it's like," Ginny barks. "I raised you here, didn't I?"

"It wasn't as rough back then. Kids weren't roaming the streets with knives."

I find myself thinking — not for the first time — that the parents at Faraday House have no idea how lucky they are.

After they've finished their snacks, Ginny says the children can play on the trampoline. They put on their coats — with no arguments — and charge outside. Standing by the sliding glass door, I can see that Ginny's secondhand trampoline doesn't have a safety net around it. It's also getting dark. I'm imagining broken heads, but I don't have the heart to stop the fun. Emma follows the children outside. "Mason, you're the oldest. You make sure that everybody gets a turn. And no fighting . . . and don't say fuck."

"I worry about the boys so much," Ginny says to me, closing the door against the icy blast. "They're not bad kids, but they're always fighting — either with each other or with kids at school. And then there's all this other mischief — like playing chicken on the main road."

"If you ask me, that's not mischief. They could get killed."

"Don't I know? The thing is that round here all the kids play in the street. The only alternative is to keep them inside. But they don't have Xboxes and iPads like other kids . . . They'd go stir-crazy."

Emma comes back into the living room and says she'd better get going. Her class starts in half an hour. As she picks up her bag and fake leopard-skin coat, she thanks her mum for agreeing to look after the boys.

"No problem. Just go."

"Great to meet you, Judy. I'm really sorry about my kids playing up. I don't know what you must think."

What do I say? I'm not about to tell her that Ginny's probably right and that she could have serious trouble brewing. Instead I tell her not to worry and that all kids have their off days.

"With my two, every day's a bloody off day." She gives a quick glance into the garden and is gone.

Ginny explains that Emma is doing a business start-up course. "It's the first step to opening her own shop. But without the cash I can't see that happening anytime soon."

"Still no joy from her brother and uncle?"

"Uh-uh. They take after each other, those two. Bloody hard, the pair of them."

I can't think of anything that might console her. For a few moments we drink our tea in silence. Finally I mention that I haven't seen Tanya yesterday or today.

"Didn't she tell you?"

"Tell me what?"

"She's decided to stop working from home. She's back at the record company's office in Soho."

"Why?"

"All this drugs gossip is getting her down. She can't face people. So she's decided to stay away for a while."

"Bloody Claudia."

I tell Ginny that I'm not sure she's doing the right thing. I tend to think it's better to stay and fight. But Ginny says her mind was made up.

"I'll give her a call. . . . Oh, by the way, guess what — I bumped into Mike."

"No! What did you say?"

"I apologized for not coming after him to say sorry for my outburst. He apologized for Claudia. Believe it or not, it was all very easy."

269

"He's a lovely man. But he must be so torn. He knows Claudia's a head case. On the other hand, she's his daughter. He has to remain loyal."

"I agree. He's in a rotten bind. . . . So, are you and Mike friends? You seem to know him quite well."

"Not really. I met him the same way I met you. He picks up his grandkids from time to time and we got chatting. I've known him for ages. Actually it's strange your paths haven't crossed before." She pauses and goes all quiet and conspiratorial. "He's rather good-looking, don't you think? Slim, trendy clothes . . . single."

I can feel a grin forming on my face. "My God, you've got the hots for him."

"Me? Don't be daft. First of all, I have no interest in dating and second, even if I did, Mike's not my type. He's far too nice. I'd eat him for breakfast."

I'm laughing. "You sure?"

"Positive. I need a man who would stand up to me. Give as good as he gets."

"A sturdy cattle farmer — that's what you need."

She laughs and tells me I could be right.

"So, has Mike ever told you about Claudia's childhood?" I say.

"What about it?"

I enlighten her.

"Good grief. That explains rather a lot. Not that I'm about to excuse her." She pauses. "Interesting, though, that he chose to confide all this in you, don't you think?"

"Not really. Claudia and I had a fight and he wanted to set the record straight."

"Or maybe he wanted to unburden himself and thought you might be a good listener. I always get the impression that Mike's rather lonely. He works hard, has a lot of work friends. There have been women in the past. But these days I'm not sure he has much by way of female company. . . ."

"Hang on — what are you suggesting?"

"Me? I'm not suggesting anything. . . . Another cup of tea?"

All the way home, Sam can't stop talking about Mason and Tyler. "They're really good fighters — way better than anybody at my school." In a matter of hours, they've become his heroes.

He's still going on about them over dinner. "So how come Mason and Tyler get to wear their soccer shirts at home and I'm only allowed to wear it when I'm actually playing?"

"It's because the lower orders treat football shirts as leisure wear," Mum says.

"Estelle says it's terribly vulgar."

The words "can" and "worms" immediately come to mind.

"What's lower orders and vulgar?" Rosie says.

I glare at my mother. "Great. Now look what you've started."

"What have I started? All I'm saying is that it's common to wear football kit in the street."

The conversation is going over Rosie's head and she's lost interest — unlike her brother. "So, are Mason and Tyler common?"

"Of course they're not," I tell him.

"I think they probably are. The streets around where they live aren't very nice and they say shit and fuck a lot."

My mother waves a forkful of meatball at Sam and tells him to go and wash his mouth out with soap. "Where on earth did you learn filth like that?"

"I'm sorry," Sam says, "but I'm only trying to explain to Rosie."

"No, you're not," I say to him. "You're looking for an excuse to say swearwords. You've heard Mason and Tyler use them and you think it's clever. Now stop it."

"And these are the kinds of youngsters you're letting my great-grandchildren play with? Very nice."

I promise everybody ice cream for dessert if we can change the subject. Mum says she doesn't fancy it and Sam still wants to know if Mason and Tyler are common.

"Common is a horrible word," I say, taking a tub of Phish Food out of the freezer and leaving it on the counter to thaw. "People who use it are snobs who think they're superior to other human beings. There's nothing wrong with Mason and Tyler wearing their football kit to knock about in."

"So, does that mean that from now on I can wear mine at weekends and when we go out?"

"Absolutely." Please don't let him have picked up on the hesitation in my voice. "Now finish your meatballs."

After dinner we Skype with Abby and Tom.

"You've been away weeks and weeks and weeks," Rosie says. "Aren't all the sick people getting better yet?"

"They are," Abby says, "but it takes time to wipe out diseases like cholera and typhoid. People are still getting ill."

"How much time?" Sam says.

"It's hard to say. But I'm really hoping we'll be back by the beginning of May. And it's already March."

"That means you're going to miss my chess tournament."

"I know, darling," Abby says. "I'm sorry."

"That's OK." Sam is close to tears.

"And when you get back we can go to Disneyland like you promised?" Rosie pipes up.

"You bet."

"Good."

Once we've finished on Skype, I give Sam a hug. "Don't worry about the chess tournament. It'll be all right. You'll have me and Nana supporting you and cheering you on. You're going to be fine."

"I know. It's just that all the other kids will have their mums and dads."

"And your mum and dad will be there in spirit."

Rosie wants to know what "in spirit" means. After I've explained, the kids head upstairs for baths, and I put the kettle on for coffee while Mum scrapes plates into the trash can.

"By the way," Mum says, "I've decided not to go to the wedding."

"But you have to go. You've promised Estelle. She really wants you there."

"I know. But when I explain, she'll understand. It's going to be a long day, and I'm

274

not up to it. I don't have the energy. And what with my irritable bowel syndrome —"

"Hold on. Since when did you have IBS?"

"Since I Googled my symptoms. I've got the cramps, wind and diarrhea. I've had it for a while. I just didn't want to worry you."

"But after your physical the doctor said you were fine."

"Ach, what does he know?"

"OK . . . tell me honestly: Has this got anything to do with Estelle dating this Max guy?"

Mum pauses in midscrape. "What are you talking about? You keep bringing this up. Why would it have anything to do with Estelle?"

"Is she planning on bringing Big Max to the wedding?"

"I don't know. She thinks it might be too early to introduce him to the family, but she's thinking about it."

"And how do you feel about that?"

"I don't care. She can do what she likes. Personally I think it's far too early. But it's her decision."

"I think you're jealous."

"Jealous? Of what?"

"Of Estelle. She's dating somebody and you're not."

"Are you serious? Why would I want to

start dating at my age? I'm almost dead."

"You're not — but all the more reason perhaps."

"You're crazy."

"Maybe."

Mum insists we drop the subject and announces she's got a chicken neck to stuff for tomorrow's dinner. I leave her with a cup of coffee and take mine into the living room. The phone is lying on the sofa arm. I pick it up and hit Tanya's number. She's full of apologies for leaving me out of the loop and not telling me she was going back to work. "I've just been so upset. I know you have been as well after your confrontation with Claudia. But I suspect you're stronger than me. I can't face people just now."

I do my best to convince her that going into hiding will do no good and might even fuel the gossip.

"Possibly. But to be honest, I don't care. I just need some space."

She promises to stay in touch and we make a tentative plan for her, Ginny and me to get together for a curry one night soon.

I am finishing my coffee while half watching the TV news and admiring my orange

276

tulips, which have reached that droopy, but arty pre-death phase, when I hear yelling and screaming from one of the bedrooms. As I charge up the stairs, there's a loud thump. Somebody has fallen or most likely been pushed off the bed. For the second time today I'm imagining broken heads.

Sam's bedroom door is wide-open. The pair of them — unbathed and still in school uniforms — are rolling on the floor punching and kicking, faces contorted, teeth bared, in a perfect imitation of Mason and Tyler.

"What on earth is going on in here? Stop it at once." I manage to get both my arms around Rosie's waist and lift her off her brother. She struggles against me, kicking and yelling. Then she lands a particularly powerful — but I assume accidental — blow on my shin.

"Rosie! For God's sake. That really hurt."

"I hate him. I hate him."

By now Mum has come to see what all the noise is about.

"Rosie, that's a terrible thing to say. Of course you don't hate Sam. You should be grateful you've got a brother. What I wouldn't give to have my brother back."

Rosie carries on, straining against me.

"Mum, please. Not now," I say.

277

Sam is on his feet. "She stole my iPad."

"I did not," Rosie screams, lurching forward, arms flailing. "You weren't using it. And it's not your iPad. It's to share."

"I was using it."

"No, you weren't. It was on the bed."

"I went to the loo. I was in the middle of *Skylanders Trap Team* and you stole it and ruined the game."

"I didn't. I didn't." Once again Rosie lurches forward in an attempt to break free.

Mum sees the iPad lying on the bed and picks it up. "Right, this is being confiscated."

"Why?" Sam bleats. "It's not my fault."

"I don't care whose fault it is," I tell him. "I've had enough of both of you. This fighting has to stop."

I send them to have baths and tell them we will reconvene downstairs to discuss their behavior as soon as they're done. They glare at each other, but there are no objections or attempts to resume hostilities.

Mum and I wait for them in the living room. Mum tells me I look done in.

"I feel it. I'm not sure how much more of this I can take."

"Do you think they were copying those boys you were telling me about?"

"Partly. But it's more than that. . . . Mum,

278

tell me honestly: do you think the kids are suffering from separation anxiety? Do you think they're playing up because they're missing Abby and Tom?"

"I don't think it's that. Of course they miss their parents. But I've got another theory."

"What's that?"

"Well, it's not my place to say anything, but if you ask me they're exhausted. I think they do too much. When did all this after-school nonsense start? Nobody did it when you were at school and you did all right."

All this time, my mother has been thinking the same as me. She sees more than I think. Old as she is, there are no flies on her.

"I'm glad you said that. I've been thinking the same thing. I tried talking to Abby before they went away. She and Tom aren't fools. They get it. But all the parents at Faraday House push their kids. There's so much competition. It's as if they're on this treadmill that they can't get off."

"It's not them that need to get off. It's the children."

Just then, Rosie and Sam appear in their pj's. They're both looking pretty sheepish. Rosie is clutching Denise, who's turned a bit limp and black again.

"Sorry for fighting," Sam says.

"I'm sorry, too."

"You know," Mum says, "your grandma isn't as young as she was. She gets tired. She can't cope with all these fights. It's too much for her. You'll wear her out. And if she gets ill, where will you be?"

"Mum, stop it. You're scaring them. I'm not that decrepit."

"I'm just saying, that's all."

Rosie and Sam look close to tears.

"OK," I say to them. "We need to talk."

I start by sitting them down and asking if they are aware that they're fighting more than usual. They both shrug.

"Well, take it from me, you are. And I think I know why. You're doing too much after school and as a result you're getting tired and bad-tempered."

"Is it why I'm finding it hard to get to sleep?" Rosie says.

"It might be."

"So, can we stop doing them?" Sam says.

"Do you want to?"

His face lights up. "Could we, really? You mean Mum and Dad wouldn't mind?"

"I think we should stop French," Rosie says. "It's really boring. And I hate Zumba."

Sam says the only thing he wants to keep up is his chess. "I've got the big tournament soon, and Mum and Dad will be disappointed if I give up."

"Sweetheart, you don't have to carry on with it just to please your mum and dad. If Bogdan is upsetting you with his yelling, it's fine to stop."

"No. I can manage. I want to carry on. And with football, too."

"What about computer club?"

"Boring." He pauses. "But Mum says we won't get into a decent university if we don't do loads of extra stuff outside school. She says we need a hinterland."

Rosie wants to know what a hinterland is.

"It means learning other stuff apart from what you learn in school," Sam says.

I tell them that I'll speak to Abby and Tom and that they should stop worrying. "It'll be fine. I promise."

"Good luck with that," Mum says under her breath. She heaves herself out of the armchair and goes back to stuffing her chicken neck.

CHAPTER ELEVEN

Sunday is snow cold, the sky a doom-laden gray. I'm all for spending the afternoon watching a movie and toasting marshmallows. Mum says we're out of marshmallows. The kids say they've seen everything.

"Since when did that bother you?"

Since they got bored with being stuck inside for most of the weekend because of bad weather.

"When I poked my head outside earlier," Mum says, "it was bitter. Talk about March winds. . . . Believe me, you're better off staying in."

The wind word is music to my grandchildren's ears. Yay. Let's go to the park and fly the kite. The crêpe man will be there in his van and we can warm ourselves up with pancakes and hot chocolate. I'm aware that the kids are going stir-crazy and need a run, so I give in. They rush to get their coats. I remind them that they're going to need extra sweaters as well as hats and gloves.

Mum says she's going to take a nap. I hear her plodding up the stairs, oomphing and sucking in her breath. Her knees are bad today. Even so, part of me envies her. I want an excuse to be horizontal, eyes shut, for an hour or so.

The events of the last few weeks are catching up with me. Last night after I went to bed, I lay staring at the ceiling, fretting about the kids' behavior and what to do about it. What if my diagnosis, not to mention my mother's, was wrong? Suppose Sam and Rosie gave up a load of after-school activities and nothing changed? Moreover, if Sam really was determined to carry on seeing Bogdan — who returned after I berated him, just as my mother had predicted, and was being only slightly less horrible — I couldn't see his behavior improving anytime soon. The pressure on Sam would be just the same.

Then it occurred to me that I could be overreacting. Maybe it would be more sensible to find strategies to help the kids deal with their stress rather than remove it altogether. Hadn't Tanya mentioned some amazing yoga teacher who worked with kids? Was it really necessary for them to abandon the after-school activities that their parents believed were so important? This led me to another thought: I was interfering. I had to remind myself — not for the first time — that it was none of my business how Abby and Tom chose to raise their children.

On the other hand, when I suggested to the kids that they give up some of their commitments, they couldn't wait. More to the point, I pretty much promised to make it happen. I couldn't go back on that. I didn't know what to do — or say — for the best. I didn't want to put more pressure on Abby and Tom. It was the reason I was putting off Skyping them.

We're not the only people who have decided to fly kites. Despite the cold and gray, the park is full of mums, dads and overexcited kids and dogs shouting and barking and getting caught up in kite strings.

It's Sam who notices Seb. He's sitting on a patch of half-frozen mud, rubbing his knees and looking sorry for himself. Above him, a giant magenta-and-emerald butterfly with ribbons floating from each wing is about to career into the branches of an oak tree.

I'm guessing he was running with the kite,

lost his balance and tripped. Sam rushes over to see if he can help. I jog after him, with Rosie several paces behind, whining that she wants to get on with flying our kite, not help Sebastian. We reach Seb at the same time as his grandfather.

"Lord. What's he done now? All I did was nip to the loo. First it was the drone. . . ." Mike turns to Sebastian and asks what happened.

"I wasn't looking where I was going. Then, as I fell, I let go of the kite." He points to the oak tree. By now the butterfly is lodged high in the naked branches. "I'll never get it back now."

Mike helps him up and the boy starts brushing mud off the arms of his fleece.

"Your knees OK?" Mike asks. Apparently they're fine.

"Don't worry," Sam says. "You can help us fly our kite."

"Cool. Thanks."

But Rosie isn't having it. "No, he can't. If the boys are in charge I won't ever get a turn."

"Yes, you will," Mike says, lowering his body to Rosie's height. "Because I'll be watching. I'll make sure you get a go."

Rosie tilts her head to one side. "Are you a grandpa?"

"I am. I'm Seb's grandpa."

"I used to have two grandpas. Then one died, so now I only have one."

"That's very sad."

"It's OK. Grandpa Brian's in heaven. Mummy says it's nice there. I wish I could go and visit him, but you can't. How old are you?"

"I'm sixty."

"That's really old. But not as old as Nana Frieda. She lives with us and she'll probably die soon because her guts hurt all the time and give her acid. So then I'll have two people in heaven."

"Well, I'm sure your nana won't be going for a long time."

"Actually she's going very soon. She keeps on saying it. She says the Nazis didn't get her, but her guts will."

Mike starts laughing. I inform him that my mother is a bit of a character.

"She sounds it."

The three children run off to join the kite flyers at the top of the hill.

"And don't go where I can't see you!" Mike and I chime in unison.

"Ha. Once a parent . . . ," Mike says to me.

"Isn't that the truth? . . . So, no Hero?"

It turns out that Hero wanted to stay at

286

home with her dad and watch *Frozen.*

"Oh dear. Poor dad."

"I know. Bloody film. It's not even funny. At least *Shrek* had jokes for adults."

"I couldn't agree more. That said, I did notice one adult joke in *Frozen.*" I tell him about the bit where Anna and Kristoff are arguing about how well she knows Hans. He asks her if she knows Hans's foot size and she says that it's not foot size that matters. "So there you go . . . *Frozen* has a penis joke."

"Huh — I never noticed that."

"You know, my mother would accuse me of being a hussy if she knew I'd said the word 'penis' in front of a man I hardly knew. In fact, my mother would probably call me a hussy if I said it in front of a man I did know."

That makes him laugh. "OK, if it makes you feel better, I'll strike it from the record."

"That would be good."

We wander over to an empty bench. Above us, kites swoop and soar. There are red-and-gold Chinese dragons with fangs and long multiarched tails. There are ladybirds and bumblebees and giant rainbow box kites. Then there's ours — the Rhombus Eezie Whiz. It's made of thin, eminently tearable canary yellow plastic. Tom got it for a fiver on Amazon.

We sit blowing into our gloved hands while we watch the kids. Seb, being the oldest, appears to have taken charge. He's running alongside Rosie, doing his best to help her to launch the kite. But she lacks speed and inches. The kite drifts to the ground and she hands it back to the boys.

Mike decides we need coffee to warm us up. While he joins the queue at the crêpe van, I don't take my eyes off the kids. I'm on the lookout for fights.

The coffee is extra hot and makes an excellent hand warmer. "So," Mike says, "with your having spotted the only adult joke in *Frozen,* I'm guessing you like comedy."

"Love it." I take a tiny sip of coffee. "When we were young, Brian and I were always going to comedy gigs. We saw Billy Connolly do the butt crack routine years before he was famous."

Mike looks nonplussed. I remind him: Bloke buries his dead wife outside his house, with her butt exposed. Punch line: "I needed somewhere to park m' bike."

Mike roars with laughter. "I've never heard that before."

"OK," I say, "so what do you reckon is the funniest comic line ever?"

"Easy. *When Harry Met Sally,* 'I'll have what she's having.' "

"You think? . . . It's not as funny as that line in the Woody Allen moose routine." I explain the setup: that Allen finds himself at a Jewish fancy dress party with a dead moose. "Then he casually drops in the line 'The moose mingles.' Like the moose is a person. What's more, the moose understands party etiquette."

"It's not as good as 'I'll have what she's having.' It's the way the old lady says it. Cracks me up every time."

"How can you say that? The idea of a moose socializing at a Jewish party is way funnier. It's the absurd juxtaposition of ideas."

"I disagree."

"How can you disagree?"

"What do you mean 'how'? It's easy. I just disagree."

"Well, I think you're wrong."

"I'm not wrong. If you polled a load of people and asked them which line they thought was funnier, they'd all choose the *When Harry Met Sally* line."

"How can you possibly know that?"

"Call it an educated guess."

"An educated guess is meaningless."

"Not for the purposes of friendly argument."

"Yes, for the purposes of friendly argument."

He takes a beat. "We're getting on rather well, aren't we?"

"You think?"

"Absolutely."

Laughter bursts out of me. It feels good.

Despite their best efforts, neither of the boys can get the kite in the air. They're both frustrated, but not half as frustrated as Rosie, who has come running over to complain that it's been ages since she had a turn.

Mike takes her hand. They trot off together, me following. "Come on," he calls out to the boys. "Let an old man show you how it's done."

Sam hands over the kite and Mike rewinds the string, leaving perhaps thirty or forty feet to play with. Then he starts running downhill into the wind. The kite shudders and dips a few times until finally it billows and soars.

"He's done it!"

Fast as he can, Mike lets go of more and more string. The Rhombus Eezie Whiz rises high above the trees. Mike calls to Rosie. She runs toward him and somehow he manages to keep hold of the kite string and maneuver her onto his shoulders.

"Wheeee!" she yells. "Let me hold it. Let me hold it."

Everybody gets a turn. Even me. As I take control, I'm struck by how bright the yellow kite is against the slate sky.

When everybody's exhausted, we adjourn to the crêpe van for pancakes and hot chocolate. The kids, apparently unaware of the cold, eat theirs on the roundabout in the empty play area. Mike and I stroll back to our bench.

As we sit down, Mike notices the dedication carved into the back. "In memory of Minnie and Arnold Goldsworthy, who spent many happy hours here, enjoying the sunshine." He notices the couple's dates. "Look, they both died in their nineties, within months of each other."

"It's funny — Brian and I used to fantasize about living until we were ancient and then dying together."

"I'm sorry. That was thoughtless of me. I didn't mean to upset you."

"It's OK. You didn't. It just triggered a memory, that's all. It happens a lot. You get used to it."

"Believe it or not, it was the same after my wife left me."

"That doesn't surprise me. Sometimes I think grieving can be worse if the person is still alive. No matter how much you fight against it, there's this vestige of hope that remains to torment you."

"That's exactly how it was."

"Well, at least I didn't have that."

"I suppose not." He rearranges his scarf, which is coming loose, and asks me how I've been since my contretemps with Claudia.

"I've calmed down. Thank you for telling me about her problems. It helps to understand."

"I'm not sure it makes it any easier, though. I try to distance myself from Claudia's disputes, but I get to hear about them from Laurence. He says he can talk to me because I understand her. So I end up as his agony aunt. It gets pretty tedious."

"I can imagine."

He rests his plastic fork on his plate. "Judy, can I ask you something? . . . I was wondering . . . Would you like to meet for a drink one evening? I know you're busy with the children and you probably don't get much spare time, but . . ."

I find myself reaching out and touching the back of his hand. "Thank you. It's a kind thought. But I'm not ready. I can't go on a date while I'm still hanging on to Brian's clothes. It's been eighteen months and I still can't part with them. Can you believe that?"

"I do. Eighteen months is nothing. . . . Tell you what. Suppose we agreed it wasn't an actual date . . . ?"

"Even so. But I want you to know I'm flattered."

"Well, I guess that's something."

"Thank you for understanding."

We go back to our crêpes, which are now stone cold.

"And anyway," I hear myself say, "there's another reason I couldn't go out with you."

"What's that?"

"Claudia."

"What on earth has it got to do with her?"

"Let's put it this way: After what happened between us, I'm sure she'd have a view on me dating her dad."

"I'm sure she would. But why would I tell her? It's none of her business. Anyway, it's all moot because you won't come out with me."

"I'm sorry."

His face breaks into a warm smile. "Come on, let's go and gather up our kids."

Mum and I are watching *Antiques Road-*

show. It's her Sunday night ritual. If I'm around I'll join her. She loves the stately home settings, the eccentric gentlemen appraisers in their stripy blazers. But most of all she loves to laugh at the English. She is particularly amused by their feigned lack of interest in money, the way they pretend it's beneath them to be even remotely interested in what an item is worth. She's lived here for over seventy years, but even now there's something of the amused foreign spectator about my mother. I admire it in a way. It shows that her parents left her with a sense of cultural identity. It was their legacy to her. All her life she has clung to it for grim death.

"Look at her," Mum says, unzipping a banana. "She thought that brooch was Fabergé and it's junk and she's all po-faced and saying it doesn't matter because it's all about the sentimental value, not the money. What is it with these people?" She bites off a chunk of banana.

"Mum, what would you say if I told you a man asked me out this afternoon?"

"What?" She hits the pause button. "You're telling me some stranger walked up to you and asked you out?"

"Don't be daft. I know him vaguely. He's one of the granddads at the school."

"Single?"

"Yes."

"Solvent?"

"I have no idea. I presume so."

She swallows the mouthful of banana. "Perfect. Go out with him."

"I said no."

"Of course you did. So why did you even bother to tell me?"

Good question. Why am I telling her? "I don't know. Maybe I wanted to let you know that men still find me attractive."

"You're a good-looking woman. Why wouldn't they?"

"I also told you because I need to hear you say I did the right thing. Only that's stupid because I know you won't."

"Damn right. I won't."

"The thing is, it would feel as if I was cheating on Brian."

"Oh, for crying out loud — the man asked you out, not to give him a blow job." As if to emphasize her point, she takes another bite of banana.

"What did you say?" I'm astounded, but I'm also laughing.

"Don't look so surprised. I watched *Sex and the City*. Hussies, the lot of them. But that Samantha, she was the worst. Who behaves like that?"

"Like what?"

"Put it this way . . . If I'm going to put a penis in my mouth, it has to belong to somebody I know."

My mother seems to be implying that she is familiar with fellatio. That must mean she went down on my dad. There's an image to keep me awake all night.

"I get so frustrated with you," she continues. "A nice man asks you out and you turn him down. Why would you do that? So what does he look like?"

"Does it matter? I'm not going out with him."

"I like to get a picture."

"He's attractive . . . tall, slim, trendy haircut, nice glasses. Lovely smile . . ."

"Do you fancy him?"

"I haven't thought about it."

"Well, think about it now."

"Mum, you have to stop bulldozing me. I wish I hadn't said anything now."

"What else do you like about him?"

"He made me laugh."

"Ha! A good-looking man who can laugh you into bed. What more do you want? Why don't you call him and tell him you've changed your mind?"

"I haven't changed my mind. And anyway, I don't have his number."

My mother lets out a long sigh. "Judy . . . don't you want the chance of some happiness?"

"Yes. When I'm ready."

"The way you're going, you'll never be ready. Before you know it, you'll turn around and you'll be an old woman. . . . Now let me get back to my program." She hits the remote.

I know she's probably right, but I can't help the way I feel. Brian was my husband. Nobody could take his place. I tell her I'm going upstairs to check on the children.

Sam is sound asleep. Rosie is still reading.

"Sweetheart, it's late. Come on, put your book down and close those eyes."

"I've tried, but they won't stay shut. Denise says she can't sleep either, so I've been reading to her."

This can't go on. She's got school in the morning. I can't let her have another day off. "What am I going to do with you?"

"Grandma, can I sleep in your bed again? I think if we could snuggle up, my eyes would stay shut."

It's not a habit I want her to get into, but how can I say no? "OK, you run and get in. I'll be there in a bit. There's something I need to do first."

She trots off, clutching Denise. Meanwhile

I head downstairs to Brian's study and try Skyping Abby. She's bound to be working. I don't expect her to answer. But after a few rings, she appears, albeit severely pixilated. But the sound quality is good, which makes a change. She says that she and Tom are still working ridiculous hours. The cholera and typhoid outbreak isn't even close to being under control. "But we're OK. We've got showers now and the food's not too bad. It's mostly the heat that gets us down." She pauses. "So I had a nice chat with Nana earlier."

"Nana? You Skyped with Nana?"

"Yes. I called you and she answered. She said you were at the park flying the kite."

"Goodness, I had no idea she knew how to do that."

"It's not hard, and I guess she's seen you do it enough times. . . . So she told me you're both worried about the kids fighting and that you think they're exhausted."

"She told you that?" Mum has blabbed — no doubt with the best of intentions — but now Abby's going to be cross with me. Fabulous.

"Yes. She also said that the two of you have discussed it and you both think they're doing too much after school."

"Look, I could be wrong," I say, already

backtracking. "Kids fight. It's par for the course. You and Tom think these activities are important. I don't want to interfere."

"You're not. Honestly. After I spoke to Nana, Tom and I sat down and discussed it. We don't want to put more pressure on the kids. It's bad enough us being away. So if you think they need to drop some of their after-school activities, go for it. Do what you think best. We can review things when we get home. It seems the most sensible thing to do."

"So you and Tom aren't angry?"

"Why on earth would we be angry?"

"I thought you might think I was letting you down. I know how important you think it is for the kids to have a hinterland."

"I still think that. But right now it feels as if something's got to give. And FYI, you're not remotely letting us down. Have you any idea how much we appreciate what you're doing? You're amazing."

I don't have time to tell her how much I appreciate the compliment, because she has to go. Another ambulance has arrived.

Downstairs Mum has fallen asleep in front of the TV. I kiss her on the forehead and she stirs.

"I just spoke to Abby," I say.

"Ah. . . . So, are you annoyed with me for

spilling the beans? I was only trying to help. I knew you were putting off talking to them."

"I was at first. But they've decided to let me do what I think is best. So thank you. For once I appreciate you interfering."

"You're welcome. Now pick up the phone to that chap of yours and tell him you'll go out with him."

"Will you stop it? He's not my chap. And like I said, I don't have his number."

"I'm sure you could find it if you wanted to."

Chapter Twelve

Ginny is in mourning. She's just been for her regular NHS pap smear and been informed that it will be her last. Statistics show that women over sixty-five are unlikely to get cervical cancer. She's sixty-two. The test is every five years. So that's it. She's done.

"I just feel so past it."

"What, because you're unlikely to get cervical cancer?"

"No. I just want to be of an age where I could."

I suppose that sort of makes sense.

"It's not for sissies," she says.

"What isn't?"

"This getting-old lark." She looks weary and a bit sad.

"OK — tell me honestly. Is that what's really getting you down? Or is it Emma and the boys?"

"Let's put it this way — worrying about

Emma and the boys doesn't help."

Ginny is looking after Mason and Tyler again and we're all having tea together. When she invited us, I suggested she and the boys come to me. I thought Mason and Tyler might behave better on foreign turf. I'd also like Mum to meet Ginny. But Ginny had to be home for a delivery, so we agreed to come to hers.

"I wish Ivo were here," she says. "I worry about that situation, too. It breaks my heart that his mother refuses to let him have anything to do with his cousins. Mason and Tyler are no angels, but we're family. The woman is a terrible snob. If Mason and Tyler were at private school, she'd be making excuses for them left, right and center. In fact, she'd probably be offering to pay for them to see a therapist. This is all about Emma and the boys not being good enough."

I ask if she's tried talking to Ivo's dad. "My son is just as bad as his wife. But in a way I suppose I can't blame them. They're frightened that Mason and Tyler might be a bad influence on Ivo. But to allow no contact at all — it's so cruel."

I agree that it is indeed cruel.

"Still, I'm buggered if I'm going to let the blighters get me down."

I decide not to remind her that they already are.

The children are playing in the garden. It's still coat weather, but the biting wind has dropped. I keep getting up and going to the window to check on them. Rosie is on the trampoline. I still worry about it not being surrounded by a safety net. But so far she hasn't even come close to falling off. The boys are playing soccer. Sam and Tyler are taking it in turns to score goals against Mason, who is guarding the miniature net.

"All quiet on the western front?" Ginny says.

"So far so good."

We start chatting about the school fair. Ginny says everything's all under control. "The volunteers are going great guns. Parents have been donating raffle prizes left right and center."

"So, I bumped into Mike on Sunday. He was in the park with Seb."

"He's a lovely man. Don't you think?"

"He asked me out."

"No! So what did you say?"

"I said no."

"What? But Mike's gorgeous. How could you possibly have said no?"

"Come on, Ginny, you know why. I'm not ready."

"You'll never be ready."

"That's what my mum said."

"Well, she's right. For heaven's sake, woman, what's the harm in going out for a drink?"

"Apart from what I've just said . . . he's Claudia's father. That's the harm."

"Bugger Claudia. What's she going to do?"

"Make my life miserable."

"I'd like to see her try. Mike would be down on her like a ton of bricks."

"You reckon?"

"I'm certain."

Ginny begs me to reconsider. "Come on. It'll be fun. You need to start enjoying yourself."

In the end — purely to shut her up — I agree to think about it.

"Good girl. You won't regret it."

I find myself steering the conversation round to my mother. I explain about her being jealous of Estelle Silverfish. "On the one hand, Mum thinks she's too old and ill to start dating. On the other hand, I think she'd really like to. It's so strange. In all these years she's never shown an interest in men."

"I guess it's never too late." Ginny looks thoughtful. "I know your mother drives you round the bend, but you're so lucky to have her. I'm not ashamed to say I'm rather jealous."

"Do you ever think about looking for your mum?"

"I don't need to look for her. My brother, William, sees her all the time. She lives a couple of miles down the road."

"You're kidding. But don't you worry about bumping into her?"

"I used to. But William says she's getting frail, so she doesn't go out much anymore. She has somebody in to clean and do her shopping."

"Have you ever thought about going to see her?"

"Why should I? She could pick up the phone. She never has. Not when Emma and Ben were born and not when Mason and Tyler came along. The woman's got a heart of stone. She made her position plain, years ago. I was never to darken her door, and I won't."

"But she's old now. She's not the same person. People mellow."

"You sound like my brother. He says she's too proud to admit it, but he's convinced she'd like to see me."

"So there you go."

"No, I don't. It's just wishful thinking on William's part. He's always been a glass-half-full type."

"On the other hand, he could be right. She might be aching to see you. She knows she did a bad thing all those years ago. I'm guessing she's lived to regret it."

"That's her lookout."

"Now who's being hard?"

Ginny is making a fresh pot of tea when the doorbell rings. I tell her I'll get it. It rings again. And again.

"All right. I'm coming."

An elderly woman, who manages in her panic to tell me that her name is Joyce and that she's Ginny's next-door neighbor, is standing on the step in her carpet slippers. She's holding a weeping Rosie by the hand.

"Good Lord. What on earth's happened? I thought you were in the garden. Are you all right? Where are the boys?"

"I got scared" — sob — "and I ran away."

"Scared of who?"

Joyce pitches in. "Her and her brother got mixed up with a bunch of bloody tearaways — that's what happened." She's pointing to the grassy verge, a few yards down the street. "I can't believe you haven't heard the noise. Somebody's going to get killed."

I can't see anything from the front step, so I move onto the garden path. Mason, Tyler and Sam are standing in the middle of the road with an older boy I don't recognize. The boy throws something to the ground. There's a loud bang, followed by a bright yellow flash. He's setting off fireworks.

"What did I tell you?"

"Oh my God." I tear down the path, yelling as I go. Joyce hangs on to Rosie. There are more flashes and smoke. A firework with an effervescing purple-and-silver tail whooshes twenty feet into the air. These are small domestic fireworks, but no less dangerous for that. The younger boys are waving lit sparklers, laughing. There's another loud crack as the boy lets off another banger. A Catherine wheel is spinning out of control and heading toward Sam's feet. I'm running, but my feet are like lead. All the time I'm still shouting at them to stop, to come away. In my mind I can see dead, fingerless children with charred faces. The older boy has seen me. He drops whatever it is he's holding, grabs a large box of fireworks, which is lying on the ground, and legs it. The other boys drop their sparklers, which fizzle out as they hit the ground. Then Ginny appears from nowhere. She lumbers past me in pursuit of the boy. I can hear her huffing and puffing. She doesn't stand a chance of catching him.

Meanwhile I get hold of Sam and start

shaking him by the shoulders. I'm so angry that I want to wallop him. "What the hell do you think you're doing? You could have killed yourself."

Sam looks at me silent and blinking. He's never seen me so worked up and it's clearly scaring the living daylights out of him. "But that boy said it would be OK. And so did Mason."

I look at Mason. He's holding something called a Devil Banger in one hand and a cigarette lighter in the other.

"Drop those right now." There is steel in my voice. He doesn't argue.

"It wasn't our fault," Tyler bleats. "It was that big boy. He said it would be a laugh. I think he stole the fireworks."

"I don't care what he said. Have you any idea how dangerous these things are?"

Sam looks like he might burst into tears.

"They weren't dangerous," Mason says. "They were small ones. They weren't like proper big fireworks."

"I don't care how big they were. Children get killed playing with fireworks. How could you be so stupid?"

Sam is crying. I can't bring myself to comfort him. Ginny appears, red-faced and panting. "Little sod got away. I've got no idea who he is."

Mason and Tyler say they don't know either. I can't tell if they're telling the truth or protecting him.

Now it's Ginny's turn to yell. "How many times have I told you not to leave the garden? And to think you took little Rosie with you on the street. I swear I'm going to fill that side entrance with barbed wire."

Mason and Tyler are looking at the ground.

"Right. Inside. All of you. Now."

Rosie is still standing on the doorstep with Joyce. Ginny and I thank her profusely for all her help. "If you hadn't knocked on the door when you did," Ginny says, "I dread to think what might have happened."

Joyce looks grumpy. "Take my advice: You need to rein those two in before they get out of control. By all accounts, they're already getting a reputation."

"Thank you," Ginny says, making it clear — to me at least — that she's perfectly aware of the situation and doesn't require anybody else's input.

Joyce says she has to go. She's missing the snooker.

"Bye-bye, Rosie. At least you had the sense to run away from these stupid boys."

"I didn't like all the bangs," Rosie says to me as Joyce makes her way down the path.

"I know, darling. I know. They are silly boys. But it's all over now."

While I cuddle Rosie on my lap, Ginny sits the boys down, stands over them and barks a lecture. She tells them how appalled and horrified she is by their behavior. "Do you have any idea the damage you could have caused — not just to yourselves, but to other people? It's a wonder Joyce didn't call the police and let me tell you — if the police had shown up, you would all be in very serious trouble."

Mason and Tyler are smirking.

"I don't believe this. Do you seriously think this is funny?"

Sam says he's going to throw up and runs to the bathroom. Rosie is tooting her horn, telling me what a good girl she was by running away. Meanwhile I'm blaming everybody: the anonymous boy, Ginny's hooligan grandchildren, Ginny and Emma for not being able to control them, me for not keeping a closer eye on Sam and Rosie.

After a couple of minutes, Sam reappears. I ask him if he threw up.

"Just a bit . . . Grandma — I'm sorry. I didn't think. I just thought it would be exciting."

Of course he didn't think. He's nine. But that doesn't stop me being furious.

310

"We're going home," I tell him. "Get your things."

Ginny can't stop apologizing. "I feel terrible. I need to have a serious talk with Emma about their behavior. They will be punished, I promise you."

I want to tell her not to worry, that boys will be boys and it's OK. But I can't. It's not OK. The outcome could have been so different.

The atmosphere is uncomfortable to say the least. Ginny knows I blame Mason and Tyler. But we manage to say our good-byes and promise to speak tomorrow.

I barely say anything on the drive home. I'm still too het up. As soon as we get in, Sam bursts into tears. "Please don't be angry with me. I hate it when people are angry. You have to forgive me."

For the first time, I feel able to give him a hug. "It's all right, darling. It was my fault. I should have been watching you more carefully."

"So, do you forgive me?"

"Of course I forgive you. But you have to promise me you will never, ever do anything like that again. You mustn't let older boys tell you to do things you're not sure about. You need to check with an adult."

"Are you going to punish me?"

311

I look at him. He's still white with shock. There's a long vein of sick down his front.

"No. I think you've been punished enough."

"And are you going to tell Mum and Dad?"

"They've got enough to worry about at the moment. I don't think they need to be told right away. But they will need to know eventually."

"But I'm not very good at secrets," Rosie says. "What if I tell them by accident? What if the words come out whoosh, like sick, and I can't stop them?"

"Rosie, I hope you're not planning on getting Sam into trouble on purpose."

"Of course not."

"I bet she is," Sam says.

"Because that would be a very unkind thing to do."

"I know and I'm not going to. I promise. But what if it did just come out by accident?"

"Then I would deal with it. OK?"

"OK."

Of course Mum wants to know what's going on. "Sam was naughty," Rosie says. "Him, Mason and Tyler set off fireworks. And there was this other boy. He was big. I didn't like him. But I was a good girl. . . ."

Mum looks at me. "Is this true?"

I nod.

"But where were you? How could you let this happen? Sam could have been killed. Who are these ruffians you've been letting the children hang around with?"

"Mum, please don't. I'm already beating myself up. I don't need you to make it worse. What can I say? I took my eye off the ball."

She can see I'm close to tears. "It's all right," she says, her tone softening. "You made a mistake. But nobody was hurt, thank God. Let's just forget about it."

But Sam can't forget about it. Over dinner, he says he doesn't want to play with Mason and Tyler anymore because they hang around with bad boys and it's scary.

"That's fine. You don't have to see them again."

What else could I say? He has every right to want to keep away from these kids. I'm not sure that I want him hanging around with them either. The problem is, how do I explain all this to Ginny?

Later that evening, Tanya calls to say that Ginny is in pieces. "She feels terrible. She's yelled at Emma and accused her of being a useless mother. So they're not speaking. It's such a mess. Mason and Tyler aren't bad boys. They just need some discipline. I love Emma, but she's so focused on her business that she neglects the boys."

I tell her I'll talk to Ginny. "Which isn't going to be easy, since Sam wants nothing more to do with Mason and Tyler."

"Why would he? But Ginny's going to be so hurt. Her horrible daughter-in-law already keeps Ivo away."

"I know. But what can I do?"

"I don't know. . . . But changing the subject, I do have one bit of advice."

"What's that?"

"Go out with Mike. He seems like a lovely chap."

"Bloody hell . . . is there anybody who doesn't know he asked me out?"

Tanya laughs. "Just do yourself a favor and go out with him."

CHAPTER THIRTEEN

The following day, thanks to a broken-down delivery truck on the main road, we get to school just as the bell is being rung. I can't help thinking it's a blessing in disguise. With Claudia away, Mike might be dropping off Hero and Sebastian and I'd rather not bump into him. What if he asks me out again? I don't care what everybody else thinks — I'm not ready. But Tanya's right: he is a lovely chap and because of that I don't want to upset him by refusing a second time.

In order to avoid him, I drop Sam and Rosie at the main gate and watch from the car as they run up the path and into school. It's only as I'm pulling away that I notice Rosie's reading folder lying on the front passenger seat. Miss Carter was due to hear her read today, and I imagine Rosie's already fretting.

As I head toward the school building, the

women who have hung around for natter and a gossip are leaving. As they pass me, I nod and smile or offer the occasional hello. A woman I don't know stops to congratulate me for confronting Claudia. She says it's been a long time coming. Others seem to be making a point of ignoring me. For the first time, it occurs to me that nearly everybody in the school knows who I am: that woman, the one who had the bust-up with Claudia. I am both famous and infamous. Infamy doesn't bother me — so long as it doesn't affect Sam or Rosie. I'm not sure what I would do if people stopped inviting them on playdates because of what I did.

I make my way to Rosie's classroom and hand the reading folder to Miss Carter. As I head back to the main door, I can hear footsteps quickening behind me.

"Judy, wait up." It's Mike. Of course it is. Bumping into him when I've been trying to avoid him seems like such a cheesy twist of fate. I can't help feeling we're starring in a bad rom-com.

"Hi, Mike. . . ."

"Listen . . . I'm glad I bumped into you. . . . I want to apologize."

"Apologize? What on earth for?"

He holds the door open and lets me through. "I think I may have upset you the

316

other day by asking you out. I probably stirred up a lot of emotions — muddied the waters as it were — and I just want to say that I'm sorry."

I tell him he has nothing to apologize for, that I'm fine. But if I'm honest, seeing him again is unsettling me. I don't know . . . Maybe I would like to go out with him. I think he senses I'm torn, but he dares not push it. So he changes the subject. As we walk to the school gate we discuss the weather. We agree that it feels as if spring might be just around the corner.

"So, Ginny tells me everything's in good shape for the school fair," he says.

"Yes, she told me the same."

I'm done. I'm out of small talk. I have no idea what to say next. And nor, it seems, has he. We continue in silence. Inside my head, it's anything but silent. "Do yourself a favor. Go out with him."

". . . He's not asking you to give him a blow job."

I hear myself saying the thing I had no intention of saying: "Mike, I've been thinking. I would like to go out with you . . . That's assuming the invitation is still on."

He stops in his tracks and so do I.

"Of course it is. But why the change of heart?"

"First of all, I like you. And deep down I know it's time."

"Well, if you're sure . . ." He's managing to look more anxious than pleased. "I would love to take you to dinner."

"I'd like that."

"Excellent." His face relaxes and breaks into a smile.

Once we reach my car, we exchange phone numbers and he says he'll call me to make a date.

When I get home, Mum has already left for the old folks' day center. She goes three times a week — not as a participant, you understand. She *works* there. Oh yes. So does Estelle Silverfish. They call themselves volunteer helpers, and the staff who runs the center are happy to indulge them — partly because they do an excellent job. Along with the paid helpers, Mum and Estelle Silverfish help the cooks prepare lunch. They lay the tables, serve and clear up. Whereas Estelle Silverfish will tell you how much she enjoys working at the day center, Mum says it half kills her and she's not sure how much longer she can carry on. That doesn't stop her coming home afterward and insisting on cooking dinner for the kids and me. Despite her complaining I've never met an old person as determined to fight the dying of the light as my mother — except of course when it comes to finding some male company.

Mum has loaded the breakfast things into the dishwasher and tidied the kitchen. So I go upstairs to make beds, gather up dirty laundry and clean bathrooms. (Not Mum's. She keeps hers immaculate). It occurs to me — as it often has — that I have cleaned a toilet or toilets almost every day of my married (and widowed) life. Brian was happy to vacuum, cook, do his share of child care, but he never offered to clean the toilet. He said just thinking about it made him gag. Not long ago I calculated how many times I've done it. Allowing days off for illness and vacations, I worked out that I've cleaned the toilet thirteen thousand times — give or take. Allowing three minutes to do a decent job, that's thirty-nine thousand minutes or twenty-seven days. I've spent nearly a month of my life scrubbing skid marks off a toilet bowl. Without gagging once.

Back downstairs, I load the washer and select the forty-degree program. As water fills the drum I find myself staring, yet again, at the black plastic sacks full of Brian's socks and underwear. After what just happened between Mike and me, I have an urgent need to connect with my husband. I open one of the sacks and take out a pair of his GoldToe socks. I stand there, pincering bits of lint off them. "OK . . . I'll come straight to the point. Somebody — and by that, I mean a man — has asked me out on a date and I've said yes. I know you're not cross with me. You were adamant that after you died I should get on with my life and be happy. I know I have your blessing. But I need you to understand that no matter what happens in the future, I will never ever stop loving you." I put the GoldToes to my lips and kiss them. "I adore you."

Brian adored me, too. I know he still does — wherever he is. That's not to say our marriage was perfect. It wasn't.

We met when we were nineteen. He was this well-built, fair-haired, blue-eyed rugby player who was studying law. I was in the second year of my nursing degree.

My friends — particularly the Jewish ones who knew my mother's story — used to tease me because I had a penchant for Aryan men. When I reminded them that my mother had married a blond Englishman — so it ran in the family — they decided that her choice was even more bizarre.

"People think I'm only with you," I told

Brian, "because I'm acting out some weird SS storm trooper fantasy."

"Well, you're definitely my Jewish princess."

"You mean I'm a brat?"

"What? No. Of course not. I'm referring to your dazzling biblical beauty."

I remember attempting a coquettish smile. I may even have tossed my hair. "That's all right, then."

I was gobsmacked when he told me I was the first girl he'd slept with. "But you're so good-looking . . . and you're so — you know — skilled."

He joked about how he'd been saving himself for the right girl. Years later he confessed that when he was a teenager, sex had petrified him. "Then you came along and I wasn't scared anymore. And lo and behold, I turned out to be rather good at it."

I seem to remember telling him not to get above himself.

We married at twenty-one. In those days nobody batted an eyelid at us tying the knot so young. With help from Brian's parents, we managed to buy a small garden apartment. Abby arrived almost a year to the day after the wedding. I gave up nursing and didn't go back — and only then part-time

— until Abby started preschool. Since I'd taken such a long break so early on in my career, I had a lot of catching up to do. So I was working hard and studying for exams while taking care of Abby and running a home. Even so, I thought our life was damn near perfect.

Then out of this clear blue sky, it came crashing down. Brian was having an affair. She was a teacher at school. I'd worked out what was going on. It wasn't hard. He was buying new clothes he couldn't afford, working late, losing interest in sex — at least with me.

When I confronted him he denied it. He told me I was crazy, that I needed my head examined. But I wasn't having it. I'd read enough agony columns to know that's what cheats did — how they projected their guilt onto the innocent party.

"Hey, J.R., this is me you're talking to, not Sue Ellen. If you don't tell me what's been going on, I'm leaving right now and taking Abby with me."

The moment he confessed I became so angry, so frenzied and out of control that I scared myself. I went for him with my fists. I threw stuff — pieces of fruit and Abby's toys mainly. I remember sitting on the sofa, tugging my hair and howling.

I lost count of the number of times he said that he was sorry, that he didn't mean to hurt me, that the affair was over and all he wanted was to be with me.

I said I would only stay if we went for couples' therapy. By now I'd decided that the affair had to be my fault. I was working too hard. I was always exhausted. I'd been neglecting him.

But that wasn't it. He sat in the therapist's office, looking down at his hands.

"I had the affair because I needed to prove to myself that I was a real man."

"I don't understand. What are you saying?"

"I'm saying that until a few months ago, you were the only woman I'd ever slept with and it affected my self-esteem."

"So sleeping with me makes you feel bad about yourself?"

"Don't be ridiculous. Of course not. I'm trying to explain that because I never slept around or had loads of girlfriends, I never felt like one of the lads. I needed to do this in order to feel like more of a man."

"And do you feel like a man knowing how much you've hurt me?"

"I hate myself for what I've done to you, but at the same time . . . yes, I feel more like a man."

"Well, bully for you. But I hope you don't feel like a decent man, because decent men don't do what you did."

But I knew they did. Even decent men were only human.

I got it. I understood. But years later I was still angry. I would lose my temper with him for no apparent reason. I was still in pain. I felt that I couldn't trust him. Brian did his best to reassure me. "I will never, ever hurt you again. You have to believe me."

After couples' therapy, we tried for another baby. We thought a second child was the cement our relationship needed. After a year, I still wasn't pregnant. We went for tests. Nothing showed up. I often wondered if my emotions had played a part and that perhaps I wanted to punish him by not giving him another child. These days I prefer to think it was a combination of genes and bad luck. My mother struggled and failed to produce a second child. I was the same.

Eventually I stopped obsessing about whether Brian was cheating on me. I must have been in my mid-forties. I was in charge of a surgical ward at a London teaching hospital. I was more confident and at ease with myself. I knew that if Brian did cheat on me again, I wouldn't fall apart. I would cope. Gradually I stopped fretting about the past and allowed myself to be happy. Brian picked up on that and, schmaltzy as it sounds, I told him I forgave him and we sort of fell in love all over again.

My face is wet with tears as I knot the black sacks and carry them into the hallway. I've left the pair of GoldToe socks on top of the washer. I can't part with them. I'm going to put them in my dresser drawer alongside Brian's watch.

Ten minutes later I'm heaving the sacks into the giant recycling bin in the supermarket car park. When it's done, I take my shopping list from my bag and head into the supermarket. I don't look back.

Mike rings me that evening and suggests dinner at a new French bistro that's just opened in Soho. Apparently everybody's raving about it. I tell him it sounds great and we make a date for the following evening.

When I tell my mother that I've changed my mind and agreed to go out with Mike, she manages to be both ecstatic and maudlin. "Mazel tov. Finally you've done it. From now on there will be no stopping you. Nobody should grow old on their own. It's no life. People need companionship."

I know she's referring to herself. "Mum,

you're not alone. You've got me and the kids."

"I know, but it's not the same as snuggling up to a warm body in bed and waking up in the morning with him next to you. I miss that."

I put an arm around my mother and give her a squeeze. "Of course you do. We both do. But if it matters to you that much, then do what Estelle did and register with an online dating site."

"No, my boat's long gone. Please God, I'll enjoy seeing you find some happiness."

"OK — now you're just being a martyr."

By half past seven the children are in bed reading. I've told them I'm going out to dinner with a friend. If I tell them I'm seeing Sebastian's granddad, they will want to know if he's my boyfriend. Even if I say no, it will be round the school in no time.

Mum can't stop fussing over what I should wear. She forbids me to wear black. "It'll look like you're still in mourning and he'll think you haven't got over Brian."

"But I haven't got over Brian. He knows that."

I tell her she's talking nonsense about me not wearing black. It suits me. She accuses me of being difficult. In the end I choose a charcoal wrap dress, which she's fine about once I've teamed it with some chunky rust-colored crystal earrings and a matching bracelet.

I would rather Mum didn't meet Mike — at least not yet. I still have memories from when I was a teenager, of her interrogating my boyfriends about their prospects. But my wish isn't to be granted. He arrives a few minutes early, while I'm in the bathroom finishing my makeup.

Even from the bathroom I can hear Mum greeting him. She's using her posh telephone voice. She ushers him into the living room. When I join them, they're happily comparing proton pump inhibitors and discussing whether it's best to take them with food or on an empty stomach.

"I like your mum," he says once we're outside. "It's hard to imagine what she went through during the war."

"I can't believe she managed to tell you about the war and her ailments — all in five minutes."

"Let's put it this way: Your mother isn't one for lengthy pauses."

As we set off, a text pings. I apologize and am about to ignore it and switch off my phone, but he insists I take it.

Lovely chap. Good teeth. Wake me when
you get home.

"It's from Mum. She likes you, too. Says
you've got good teeth."
"Oh boy. I am so in there."

The restaurant is an homage to fin de siècle
Paree. Everywhere you look there are gilt
mirrors, giant crystal chandeliers and wait-
ers in black uniforms with long white
aprons. You half expect to see Proust and
Oscar Wilde leering through their monocles
at all the young men.
The food is as classical as the décor. We
eat onion soup, excellent boeuf bourgui-
gnon, followed by crème caramel. Mike
orders a bottle of the house red.
"I was so worried you'd be a wine snob,"
I tell him. "Most men our age are. If they're
not boring about wine, it's bloody golf."
"Actually I play quite a lot of golf."
My heart sinks as my face reddens. "Oh
God. Sorry. No. I didn't mean . . ."
He's laughing. "I'm teasing. I've never
been on a golf course in my life. It would
bore the pants off me."
"Really? You're not just saying that to
make me feel better?"
He assures me he isn't. "Music is my

thing. I'm a bit of an old rocker. I'm really into Led Zepplin."

"But their music is such a horrible tuneless racket."

"Er, excuse me . . . That tuneless racket was produced by one of the most important and innovative rock groups in history. Their music was influenced by people like Muddy Waters and Skip James and —"

"Who?"

He rolls his eyes, but not without humor. "My wife hated them, too."

"I'm not surprised. Women like tunes . . . Simon and Garfunkel, Leonard Cohen, ABBA. And please don't knock ABBA, because I love them. And you can't deny they've stood the test of time."

"They certainly have that."

He thinks I'm shallow.

"I hated the *Mamma Mia* movie, though," I say in an effort to redeem myself. "Utter drivel. I gave up after ten minutes."

He smiles and nods. I have no idea if I've gone up in his estimation or have sunk, irreparably, to the bottom.

It gets worse. I don't know how I manage it, but somehow I let slip that I read the *Daily Mail.*

"You surprise me." He looks crestfallen.

"I know it's a nasty right-wing tabloid rag.

But I think that in order to have an informed view of what's going on in the world, you need to know what the right is thinking. I read the *Guardian,* too, but there's no showbiz gossip."

He's looking at his watch. I've dug myself in deeper with my talk of showbiz gossip. He can't wait to get away.

"Sorry if my tastes are disappointing you."

"Disappointing me? Why on earth would you think that?"

"You're looking at your watch."

"What? No. Oh, crap. I've done it again. It's my Apple watch." He reaches across the table to show me the fancy timepiece. "It vibrates every time I get an e-mail and I automatically take a look. It's such bad manners. I'm really sorry."

I tell him he's forgiven. "So you don't object to my choice of newspaper?"

"Not at all. I read the *Mail* most days."

"You do? But when I mentioned it, you looked so disappointed."

"I wasn't remotely disappointed. Just surprised. People are usually so sniffy about the *Mail.* I used to work there many moons ago. Good bunch mostly. Pretty down-to-earth. Not like those grand self-important types you get on the *Guardian.*"

He tells me a bit about his career in

journalism — how his first assignment, for a local paper in Yorkshire, was to collate the results of the Leeds Annual Flower Show.

"I was careless and got a load of them wrong. There were so many complaints the editor threatened to fire me." He puts down his wineglass. For a moment he seems lost in thought. "I met my wife while I was working up north. Seems like a lifetime ago."

"And after she left, you never remarried?"

"Uh-uh. I've had a couple of long-term relationships, but I haven't lived with anybody since Catherine. Even though she abandoned Claudia, I couldn't stop loving her."

"And what about now? Do you still love her?"

He swirls wine around the bottom of his glass. "These days I don't feel anything. I don't know when it happened. It was very gradual. Days would go by and I realized I hadn't thought about her. Then it was weeks. Now months go by and I hardly give her a thought."

After dinner we go for a stroll through Soho and find ourselves reminiscing. We're old enough to remember the greasy pavements, the neon-lit strip joints and seedy jazz clubs. Now it's buzzing with trendy bars and restaurants and hipsters selling artisanal cheeses at eleven o'clock at night.

We both recollect a folk club called Lovin' Spoonful. I can't remember where it was, but Mike thinks he can — somewhere off Charing Cross Road. It's only a five-minute walk.

"It was along here somewhere," Mike says as we turn into a side street. In the end he admits he's confused. He can't make up his mind if Lovin' Spoonful is now a tattoo parlor or a branch of Banana Republic.

"I know it's a cliché," he says. "But time really does fly."

"Tell me about it. Can you believe I once wore an afghan coat?"

"I bet you looked amazing."

"They didn't half smell, though. Mine was particularly goaty."

"I wouldn't have minded," he says.

On the drive home he asks me what music I'd like to listen to.

"ABBA," I say, just to wind him up.

A moment later "Super Trooper" is blasting out of the speakers.

"Hang on . . . I thought you hated ABBA."

"Seb and Hero love it," he said.

I'm laughing. "I believe you. Thousands wouldn't."

As we sing along to ABBA's greatest hits, I tease him. "So, how come if you hate ABBA, you know all the words?"

"I dunno. I guess playing the songs for the kids, I just picked them up."

"Yeah, right."

Try as he might, he can't keep a straight face. I turn up the volume and we join in: "The Winner Takes It All."

We're still laughing and singing as we pull up outside my house.

"I've had a wonderful time," I tell him.

"Then that makes two of us." He hesitates. "I'd really like to do it again."

"Me, too."

"I was hoping you'd say that."

He makes no attempt to move in for a good night kiss. But I'm worried he might and I don't know how I would handle it. I decide to take the initiative by planting a kiss on his cheek. "Good night and thank you again for a lovely evening."

"I'll call you," he says.

I'm waving him off when the front door opens. Mum is in her dressing gown and slippers beckoning me. "Come inside. You'll catch your death. I've made cocoa."

CHAPTER FOURTEEN

"So, if I did decide to start Twittering," Mum says, "who do you think I should follow? I think it should be important people like the Pope and Barbra Streisand."

"That's certainly one way to go," Tanya says.

"Mum, before you go on to Twitter, wouldn't it be a good idea to get the hang of Facebook?" She signs off all her comments: Love and kisses . . . Frieda.

"What do you mean? I'm great at Facebook. Oh, I know! I could follow that Mark Zuckerberg."

"Well, if you do," Ginny says, "you can tell him from me that if I find another ad on my sidebar for a walk-in bath, I'm going to leave. I may have just had my last pap smear, but I'm not quite in my dotage."

"I get those ads, too," Mum says. "The thing is that at my age, you need to start worrying about becoming infirm."

Here we go.

"Mum, stop it. You're nowhere near becoming infirm."

"That's what you think." She gets up to put the kettle on.

It's Saturday afternoon. I haven't seen Tanya in a while. Plus I wanted to get things back on an even keel with Ginny, so I suggested they come to tea. Mum has also been nagging me about meeting them. She says she hates not being able to put faces to names. I think she feels excluded if she hasn't met — and approved or not approved of — all my friends.

When I asked Ginny if she would be bringing Mason and Tyler, she said that she and Emma still weren't speaking and she hadn't seen the boys since the fireworks incident. It was rotten that they were still at loggerheads and she wasn't seeing the boys, but at least I didn't have to tell her that Sam didn't want to be friends with them anymore.

Ginny and Tanya want to know how my date went.

"He took her to this very nice French place," Mum says from the other side of the kitchen. "They haven't kissed yet. But they're seeing each other again."

"Thanks, Mum."

"So, do you like him?" Ginny says.

"I do. But you know . . . I've still got some issues."

"Of course you have. But now isn't the time to turn back. Onward and upward, that's my motto."

It's not lost on me that my mother and Ginny are happy to dish out dating advice while refusing to act on it themselves.

Suddenly Rosie and Cybil appear. They would like a snack. My mother comes over and places a cake stand full of homemade delights on the table. "So, what would you like? There's chocolate cake, honey cake, a nice piece of strudel maybe?"

"Please may I have a bit of all of them?" Cybil says.

"Of course you can, my darling. Good choice."

"Me, too," Rosie says.

"These two won't need any rocking tonight," Tanya says, laughing. "They'll both be in diabetic comas."

"Oh, come on," Mum says. "A bit of what you fancy does you good."

I get up to finish making the tea. Mum joins me. She needs more plates. "Do you mind telling me what that girl has done to her hair? What does she think she looks like?" She is of course referring to Tanya's dreads. "I've no idea how she keeps it clean. Wouldn't surprise me if she's got things nesting in it."

I pray to God that the noise of the water boiling and the tinkling of china are masking my mother's stage whisper. I hiss at her to shut up. "I'm only saying." She helps herself to plates and returns to the table. While Mum arranges slices of cake, Ginny is reading a text on her phone.

"Oh my God."

"What?" Tanya says.

"I knew this would happen. I knew it."

I put the tea tray down on the table. "What is it?"

Ginny jerks her head toward the girls. She wants to wait until they have gone back upstairs before she reveals what's in the text. Mum hands Cybil one plate. Rosie gets two. The extra one is for Sam, who is alone in his room playing chess.

"OK . . . I've just got a text from one of the mothers I'm friendly with at school. Did I know it's all round the school that Sam and my grandsons were caught letting off fireworks and the police were called?"

"You didn't tell me the police were involved," Mum says.

"Me neither," says Tanya.

I make it clear that the police weren't

involved. "Somebody's gilded the lily because it makes for better gossip." I finish handing round mugs of tea. "But how did it get out? None of us told anybody."

"It'll be Rosie," Mum says. "You can't expect a child her age to keep a secret."

"She's managed not to tell her parents," I say.

Mum says that's different. "It wouldn't occur to her that she could get Sam into trouble by telling her friends."

"She'll have told Cybil," Ginny says, "and Bob's your father's brother."

"Bugger."

"Short of locking her up," Tanya says to me, "there was nothing you could have done to stop her. She was bound to tell the kids at school."

"Right . . . so now I have a grandson who not only takes assault rifles into school, he lets off fireworks. Nobody's going to want their kids anywhere near him. Oh . . . and I'm forgetting Rosie teaching everybody to say motherfucker."

"Yes," Tanya says, "but that was Cybil's doing."

"Nobody will remember that. I'm bound to get a call from the head. Sam could be expelled for this."

Ginny tells me not to be so daft. "Of

course he won't get expelled. It didn't happen on school property. It's a private matter."

"Jeez . . . Claudia is going to love this."

"Sod Claudia," Ginny says. "Who cares what she thinks?"

"Only the entire bloody school."

Tanya says there's nothing to be done. I simply have to wait — like she's doing — until it blows over. Meanwhile Ginny's shaking her head.

"This is all my fault. I don't know what's going to become of Mason and Tyler. They'll be shoplifting next. I've been having nightmares about them ending up in court."

Tanya takes Ginny's hand, tells her it isn't that bad. But I'm with Ginny on this. Mason and Tyler need discipline. Without it, one day not very long from now they might well end up in court.

"In other news," Ginny says, "my brother, William, called this morning to say that my mother has had a heart attack."

"Bloody hell," Tanya says. "You kept that quiet."

"It was very mild and she's back home. The upshot is that William thinks I should go and see her."

"This is the mother who threw you out and told you never to darken her door again?" Tanya says.

Ginny manages a smile. "The same."

I ask her what she wants to do.

Ginny shrugs. "Want and ought are different things. What I want is to leave her to stew. She hasn't asked to see me. Why should I risk going there and have her tell me to get lost again?"

"You could live to regret it," Tanya says.

I tell Ginny that I'm with Tanya. "It won't be easy. But your mother's not well. Even though the heart attack wasn't serious, she's old and you don't know how much time she has left."

"When I last saw her, she made her position very plain. I was never to darken her door again. I was her only daughter. Have you any idea how that felt? What sort of mother rejects a child like that?"

"I'm not making excuses," Tanya says. "She did a terrible thing. . . ."

"It was more than that. It was unforgivable."

"Maybe. Maybe not," I say. "That's for you to decide."

Ginny rubs her hand over her chin. "Going to see her would be such a risk."

"So would not seeing her."

On Monday morning after I've dropped

Sam and Rosie at school, I finally decide that I need to see Mrs. S.J. I've thought about taking Tanya's advice to do nothing and let the gossip about Sam and the fireworks blow over. But I'm worried that in the meantime mothers will forbid their children to play with Sam. I decide that the only way to limit the damage is to speak to the head and explain what happened. Once she knows my side of the story, she might be able to spread the word.

I'm with her secretary, arranging an appointment, when Mrs. S.J. appears from the adjoining office. Since I am now infamous, she recognizes me at once.

"It's Mrs. Devlin, isn't it? Sam and Rosie's grandmother?" She makes no allusion to my run-in with Claudia.

I explain that I was making an appointment to see her. She turns to her secretary, asks her to tell her nine thirty that she's running a bit late and ushers me into her office. She sits me down, offers me coffee (which I politely decline) and looks at me with real concern. "Mrs. Devlin, I'm glad you popped in. I was actually going to give you a call."

"Look . . . if it's about Sam letting off fireworks, that's why I'm here. I wanted to explain what actually happened."

"I hear the police were involved."

"No, they weren't. That's nothing more than wicked gossip."

I tell her about Sam and Ginny's grandsons getting involved with an older boy.

"But surely somebody was supervising them?"

"There was. . . . What can I say? I fell down on the job."

Mrs. S.J.'s pitying smile reminds me of one of Claudia's. "Are you sure you're coping?" she says. "It can't be easy looking after two boisterous children when you're a woman of . . . a certain age."

How dare she? She's a damn sight more of a certain age than I am. I'd say she's five or six years more, and she runs an entire bloody school.

"I get tired — *as I'm sure you do.* But I think I'm doing OK."

"So you wouldn't say that the children's behavior has taken a turn for the worse since their parents went away?"

"I admit there have been a couple of unfortunate incidents, but they have been completely blown out of proportion by Claudia Connell."

"I heard about your contretemps with Dr. Connell. So unfortunate." Mrs. S.J. steeples her hands on her desk. "Please don't take

342

this the wrong way, but is it possible you overreacted? From what I've heard, all she was trying to do was offer you some advice. And she is an expert."

"I don't know what you've heard, but I don't think I overreacted. Look, I haven't come here to defend myself against Dr. Connell. I know you have great respect for her and it's not my place to get in the way of that. Right now my only concern is Sam's reputation and that he doesn't get ostracized because he was led astray by some older boys. Sam's a good kid. And he's learned his lesson. So if anybody raises the issue with you, I would be immensely grateful if you could set the record straight."

"I will certainly do my best. But as a quid pro quo, maybe you could think about making your peace with Dr. Connell. She's back from her book tour, so maybe the two of you could meet for coffee and talk things over. People tell me she can be a tad overbearing — not that I've seen any evidence of it — but she knows her stuff. Don't be too swift to judge her. If you ever feel that you're struggling with Sam and Rosie, I know she would set her differences with you aside in a heartbeat and be only too willing to help."

Mrs. S.J. has been blinded by Claudia's

apparent brilliance. Nothing I can say will change that. But as for having coffee with the woman: I would sooner chew razors.

I'm on my way home when Mike calls to check that we're still on for dinner tonight. "Of course."

He says I don't sound too enthusiastic.

"I'm sorry. Forgive me. I'm tired, that's all. I think everything is starting to catch up with me."

"Then let's stay in. Come over to my place and I'll cook dinner."

"At your place . . . ?"

"OK — I know what you're thinking. But there's no agenda, honestly. I promise to behave like the perfect gentleman."

"In which case, that sounds great."

The moment I arrive Mike hands me a large glass of wine. "Get this down you. It'll do you good."

His apartment is in a brand-new block. He bought the show flat because it came furnished and there was nothing for him to do except move in. I insist on a tour. There's a kitchen that I would give an arm and a leg and several bits of offal for. Ditto the bathroom. The place has oak floors, masses of closet space and natural light galore, but it isn't what you'd call homey. It's a bit cold and blokey: light gray walls, matching Venetians, black leather sofas with stainless steel legs. There isn't a scatter cushion, throw or knickknack in sight. Instead the walls are covered in photographs — mostly black-and-white cityscapes and street scenes.

"Wow, these are seriously good. Did you take them?"

"I did."

"You're very talented," I say as I move in on a color portrait of an old Arab woman with piercing blue eyes and a burnished face like a car tire.

"I took it on my old Leica. I prefer film. I'm not crazy about digital cameras. The result is too perfect."

"That's strange for a man whose job is all about new technology."

"Possibly, but there are plenty of good things about old tech."

He shows me a photograph of Brooklyn Bridge at dusk. I congratulate him on how well he's captured the fading light. "I took that on the Leica, too. See how grainy it is? You don't get that effect with a digital camera."

"OK . . . and grainy is good because . . . ?"

"You get a much grittier, more raw image,

which is great for urban scenes."

I take a step back from the photograph and take a moment to consider. "I guess I can see that." But I'm not sure I can.

We take our drinks to the sofa. Only then do I notice the mass of tech stuff lying around. I count three sets of speakers. One pair looks like red lollipops on sticks of steel. Then there are the tall black shiny ones that have more than a passing resemblance to Darth Vader. There are several sets of headphones lying on the desk, along with a couple of GPS systems. A 3-D printer sits on the floor next to the broken drone that he and Seb were flying the other day.

"Sorry about all the clutter," he says. "Occupational hazard, I'm afraid. Stuff arrives. I review it, send it back to the company and then more turns up. It's never-ending."

I realize that sitting between us is a black plastic helmet. Attached to it is what looks a viewfinder.

"So what does this do?"

"Aha . . . I'll show you. It's a virtual reality headset. You'll love it."

Before I can protest, he takes my glass and puts it on the coffee table. Then he starts arranging the helmet on my head and making adjustments to the viewfinder thingy. It's pretty heavy and clunking, but he says that's because it's only a prototype. The real thing will be much lighter.

One moment I'm staring at a blank screen. The next I'm flying. I'm soaring and swooping over mountains, lakes, fjords and fields. I can look up and down, even behind me. It's only when I start diving, hurtling toward the water, that I start to feel sick and — quite irrationally — scared. "Mike, stop! Get it off me. Quick! It's making me feel weird."

He does as I ask, but he thinks it's hysterical that I'm such a wimp. "Come on . . . it's great. You really feel as if you're there."

My head is swimming. I'm struggling to regain my balance. "It isn't great. It's horrible."

He laughs and says he'll put some music on.

I'm expecting Led Zeppelin, but once again he surprises me — this time with Frank Sinatra. He hands me back my wine. "Don't worry. I'll get you into Led Zeppelin one day."

We sit on the sofa listening to "Summer Wind" while delicious meaty smells waft in from the kitchen. "I've done beef in Guinness. It's the first time I've made it, so I apologize in advance." I tell him I'm sure it will be perfect. And it is — tender chunks of beef in rich dark gravy with cheesy, mustardy croutons.

"This is gorgeous. I always think there's something rather sexy about a man who can cook." The words are out of my mouth before I can stop them. It's the wine.

"You think?" He grins at me across the table and tops up my glass.

"Hey — I thought you were going to behave."

"What have I done? It's you who started going on about men who cook being sexy."

"I know. But only because you've got me tipsy."

For dessert, we eat fancy, albeit shop-bought, Italian ice cream — my contribution to dinner.

"So . . . I hear Claudia's back from her book tour."

"She is. But do we have to talk about my daughter?" He looks positively pained.

"If you can bear it, I think we should — just for a minute. We can't kid ourselves that she isn't going to find out that we're seeing each other. Are you absolutely sure it isn't going to put a strain on your relationship?"

He takes a sip of wine. "OK . . . the way I see it, you and I are just getting to know each other. I think that for the time being we should carry on as we are and try to forget about Claudia. I've said it before — it's none of her business who I'm seeing. We'll cross the bridge of Claudia when we come to it. If things do get sticky I can usually rely on Laurence to make her see sense. He's a lovely chap. I told him that if he married Claudia he would always have his hands full. But he doesn't seem to mind. He understands her. If anybody can reach her, Laurence can."

"That's all well and good, but if we carry on dating, I still think we should have a plan."

"I agree and we will. I just don't want to spoil things by thinking about it right now. OK?"

"OK."

He makes coffee, which we drink back on the sofa. He suggests watching a movie. We plump for *The Shawshank Redemption*. We've both seen it a dozen times, but we're agreed that it never loses its appeal.

Despite two cups of coffee, I fall asleep. I wake up, just as the credits are rolling, my head resting against Mike's arm. He's stroking my hair. I stay still, eyes closed, focusing on his touch. It's a while before I let him know I'm awake: "Um, that's nice."

As I sit up, he turns his body toward me. My eyes are open now, locked on his. He starts by brushing my lips with his . . . planting small kisses. I make no attempt to pull away. I do the opposite. My mouth opens before his. I'm the one taking the lead, urgently probing, wanting, needing. It's Mike who pulls away, tells me it's too soon, that I'm not ready.

He's right. Of course I'm not ready. But I've shocked myself. Grief killed off my libido. I thought I would struggle to resurrect it. Now Mike has done just that. He wants to drive me home, but I can see he's tired. Plus he's had several glasses of wine. "Please just call a cab. I'll be fine." He says that putting me in a taxi isn't very gallant. I tell him that crashing the car when you're knackered and pissed isn't very gallant either. He takes the point.

That night, in the bed I shared with Brian, I relive the kiss I had just shared with another man and choose not to feel guilty.

CHAPTER FIFTEEN

I'm drinking coffee in the garden. For the first time this year, there's real warmth in the sun. The flowers have opened on the magnolia tree. In the street, cherry blossom is falling like confetti. The TV weathermen are busy telling us spring has arrived. "What do they know?" Mum keeps saying. Like a lot of people, she hasn't trusted TV weather forecasters since they failed to predict the 1987 hurricane. "A bit windy, my tush." She's predicting the weather will get worse before it gets better.

But I haven't come into the garden to enjoy the sunshine. I'm here because I can't bear to watch what is going on in the house — or to be more accurate, what's going on in my bedroom. I escaped to the garden when the undertakers came to collect Brian. As they zipped him into a body bag, I pruned the roses. Today is less gruesome, but still distressing. Ginny and Tanya are clearing the rest of Brian's clothes.

Before they arrived I went to his dresser and took out his favorite sweater — the one I have decided to keep. It's pale blue cashmere. I bought it for him years ago in the Harrods sale. They had thirty percent off cashmere and I grabbed the last one in his size. The elbows are thin with wear and there's an ancient curry stain down the front that has always refused to come out no matter how much Shout I use.

Until a few weeks ago, I wasn't sure that I would ever be strong enough to part with the rest of Brian's stuff. I wanted to be able to touch his clothes and smell them, to imagine that I was touching and smelling him. Then I told Ginny I'd kissed Mike, how much I'd enjoyed it and that I didn't feel guilty afterward. She looked me in the eye and told me she would brook no argument. It was time to pack up Brian's clothes. How many times had Abby said this and how many times had I put up a fight? This time I didn't.

Ginny and Tanya offered to help. So did Mum. But I wanted to do it on my own. It was something far too intimate to share.

Despite my newfound determination, it still took me a couple of weeks to pluck up the courage. I knew it needed to be done fast. Pull the clothes off the hangers. Shove them in sacks. Keep going. Don't allow myself to think or reminisce.

I pulled everything off the hangers, but I made the mistake of piling it on the bed before attempting to put it in bags. I couldn't resist sitting beside the mound of jackets, shirts and pants, stroking the fabric. Then I started remembering. He wore that suit to so-and-so's wedding — that jacket the night we celebrated our thirtieth wedding anniversary. It wasn't just his clothes I was about to bag up. It was his life. Our life. My throat ached as I tried to fight back the tears. I was so overcome with pain that I had to run downstairs and switch on the TV to soothe me. The following day I called Ginny. I'd thought about taking Mum up on her offer of help, but she would have got as upset as me. Ginny told me to stop fretting. I should leave it to her and Tanya.

It was Tanya who suggested the memory box. It was such an excellent and obvious idea, but for some reason it hadn't occurred to me. The first thing I did this morning when I woke up was to go rummaging in the basement for a suitable container. It had occurred to me to buy something fancy, but Brian didn't do fancy. He wouldn't have approved. Instead I used the box that our most recent microwave had come in. Brian was a firm believer in keeping packaging in case an item had to be returned.

Once I'd wiped off the dust with a damp cloth, it was fine. The sweater went in first, but not until I'd held it to my face and tried to find Brian's smell. But it was long gone. The sweater smelled of nothing in particular. His watch went in next. It was a vintage Rolex he treated himself to when he turned forty. For somebody who had no interest in cars or expensive hi-fi and bought his clothes in Marks & Spencer, the Rolex was a strange thing to covet. But he fell in love with it. He spotted it in an antique watch shop in the Burlington Arcade. The oblong case, brown leather strap and art deco face reminded him of the watch his dad wore. He had no idea what make it had been — only that it would have been cheap. When the old man died, Brian's brother inherited it. Brian got his signet ring. We couldn't really afford the Rolex, but I could see how much it meant to him, so I insisted we dip into our savings. It cost two thousand pounds. He wore it every day. Years later he was still saying how much pleasure it gave him. Even when he was so ill and wearing it felt uncomfortable, he kept it beside him on the nightstand.

After the watch came the GoldToe socks. Then the photograph album from our wedding. It's bound in white imitation leather, now yellow and torn. I can't bear to look inside — come face-to-face with all the soft-focus photographs of us — two babes in the woods gazing into each other's eyes, full of plans and hopes. We always laughed at those photographs — especially at Brian's mullet. We called them soppy and cheesy. But we kind of adored them.

Last into the microwave box was a large padded envelope. It contained all the birthday cards Brian had ever sent me. He'd drawn inside each of them — ham-fisted cartoons of stickmen with crazy hair — recording the ups and downs of my previous year. They were funny, sometimes sad — and better than a diary could ever be.

So while I sit in the garden, focusing on the weather and the magnolia tree, Ginny and Tanya are loading black plastic sacks. When they're done, they will drop them off at a charity shop. I made them promise not to choose the Oxfam shop in the high street. I imagined being out shopping and suddenly coming face-to-face with one of Brian's suits in the window.

I know I'm ready to sleep with Mike. I

knew from that first kiss. But Mike is insisting I need to slow down and give it more thought. One night after a date, while we were in his car making out like teenagers, I accused him of not wanting to go to bed with me. That upset him.

"Of course I do. I'm just scared, that's all."

"Scared? Why?" Then it dawned on me that there might be mechanical issues. "OK, if the problem is what I think it is, it's nothing to be ashamed of. I mean, you are a man of a certain age. . . ."

"Everything is fine in that department, thank you very much. . . . I'm just scared that you'll feel guilty afterward — that you'll have some kind of emotional meltdown and won't want to see me anymore."

"That won't happen."

"You don't know that."

I could feel myself grinning. "So you really like me, then?"

"You know I do."

"I like you, too. And it's not just because you refuse to play golf and don't get snotty about wine."

"I know. It's because you think I'm really hot."

"I guess you're OK . . . for an old bloke."

"Only OK? I've kept my hair. Your mother

thinks I've got good teeth. You can tell her from me that they're all mine."

"I'll make sure to do that."

"Well, you are beautiful," he said.

"For an old biddy." I've never been good at accepting compliments. I drove Brian potty with it.

"Behave. You are a very attractive woman."

"Thank you. You're very kind."

"Kindness has got nothing to do with it. It's true."

He leaned in, cupped my face in his hands and kissed me. After a moment or two, I pulled away. "Come on. Let's drive back to your place and go to bed."

"Not tonight. See how you feel after you've got rid of the clothes."

Despite my protests, I know that Mike is right to insist we take things slowly. He is giving me time to arrange my emotions so that I can make room for him, without forcing Brian out. I've asked Mike if he's jealous of my feelings for Brian.

"A bit maybe. I'm only human. But they're precious. I wouldn't dream of getting in the way of them. If things get serious between us, I am going to have to learn to live alongside all that."

His kindness and generosity are just two

of the reasons I'm falling for this man. He's also a very good listener. I can't stand those older men who proffer loud opinions about the state of the world and how to fix it. Brian's dad was like that. He seriously wondered how the planet would carry on spinning when he was gone. In many ways Mike is like Brian. But I try not to compare or contrast them. Mike is who he is. I don't want him to think he's competing with a dead man.

We see each other once, maybe twice a week. Mostly we go out to dinner — occasionally to a movie. But movies get in the way of talking and we talk a great deal. If Mike's free during the day we might take a drive and have a pub lunch by the river. It's all very comfortable and middle-aged. And I love it. That said — I didn't love it the other night when Mike sat me down and made me listen to Led Zeppelin. My thoughts hadn't changed since the seventies. "It's just a racket," I told him.

"Come on — 'Stairway to Heaven' isn't a racket."

"No, it's a monotonous dirge. And the guitar solo is just showy and affected."

He shook his head, called me a philistine and acknowledged he was never going to change me. So far we've discovered only two things that we disagree on: Led Zeppelin and the merits of chocolate-coated orange peel. I'm a fan, whereas he considers all candied fruit to be the work of Satan.

It's not just my growing friendship with Mike that dares me to think my life could be looking up. In other news, Rosie and Sam are getting along much better and Rosie is sleeping properly. Without the pressure of so many after-school activities, they're starting to relax. Sam is still seeing Bogdan, which to my mind is far from ideal. The man still yells, but not so often or as loud. The chess competition is in a couple of weeks. Sam is nervous, but he's holding up. The gossip about him setting off fireworks has yet to die down. A couple of mothers have canceled playdates. But Sam is so taken up with preparing for the tournament that he hasn't noticed.

Ginny and Tanya also seem to have turned a corner. Tanya has stopped being a focus of school gossip — which gives me hope that soon Sam will do the same. She's working from home again and back at the school gates.

Ginny's big news is that she's speaking to Emma. They made up because Ginny got stomach flu on the day of the spring fair.

She called me first thing to say she was throwing up every few minutes and that she was scared because she kept feeling faint. I offered to come over, but she wouldn't hear of it. Tanya and I were her deputies — which was news to me and, I suspect, to Tanya — and were needed to help set up stalls and generally direct operations and rally the troops. "I'll call Emma and ask her to come and sit with me."

Even though Ginny was at the fair in spirit only, it couldn't have gone better. We raised ten thousand pounds for the school fund and Mum won a goldfish, which she named Topol. But Topol wasn't long for this world. A week later, poor Topol was no more and Mum had flushed him down the loo. She thought it was OK to overfeed goldfish the way she overfeeds people.

Everybody attributed the fair's success to Ginny's exceptional organizational skills. I couldn't argue with that. On the day, thanks to her printed instructions, everything slotted into place. Afterward, she received a large thank-you-slash-get-well bouquet from the PTA.

Most important of all, Abby and Tom think they might be back in a few weeks. The typhoid and cholera epidemic is pretty much under control. I couldn't be happier.

Each time we Skype, they look and sound exhausted. They're ready to come home.

On the downside, the kids have nits. Abby recommended an organic lotion. If that didn't work, I was to buy chemicals. She was quick to remind me not to mention the infestation to any of the mums. The unofficial line is that children at private school don't get nits.

Mum has also fallen out with Estelle Silverfish. As I feared, she dug in her heels and refused to change her mind about going to Estelle's granddaughter's wedding. Despite her protestations about not being up to such a long day, I'm convinced that she couldn't face it because Estelle Silverfish had decided to take Big Max. But whatever the truth, they're not speaking.

Ditto Claudia and me. At the moment we're happily avoiding each other. She has no idea I'm dating her father. I still think he should tell her on the grounds that she'll be even more furious if she finds out by accident. Mike says what he always says, that it's none of her business. But I think he's playing a waiting game — betting that I will eventually cave in and call Claudia to initiate peace talks, just like Mrs. S.J. suggested. I am ashamed to admit that I have considered it. Loath as I am to countenance it, I could see a situation in which I might be forced to swallow my pride in order to protect my relationship with Mike.

"Ginny to Judy. Come in, Judy." Ginny is waving at me from the back door.

"Sorry, hon. I was miles away."

"Just to say that we're done. Everything's been bagged up and loaded into my car. Now, are you sure you don't want to take a final look?"

I make my way across the lawn. "I'm absolutely sure."

"Oh, and FYI," Tanya says, appearing beside Ginny, "I've dusted the dresser drawers and the bottom of the closet. So there's nothing for you to do."

As I step inside, I call for a group hug. "Thank you so much. I don't know what I would have done without you two." I hand them each a box of posh chocs. Tanya says I shouldn't have.

"Yes, she bloody should," Ginny laughs. "I can't remember the last time I tasted chocolate that wasn't a Snickers or a Kit Kat."

After Ginny and Tanya leave, I make a point of not going upstairs to look at the row of empty hangers and cry. Instead I get ready to go out. Mum's day center is having its annual open day — the mayor is coming — and I promised I'd drop in as soon as I could get away. Since Rosie and Sam are still on spring break, she's taken them along to show them off. They seemed happy enough to go. Unlike me, Mum doesn't believe in bribing children, so I can only assume that she persuaded them to go by playing her "Do it for your old Nana, who's not long for this world" card.

When I arrive, most of the old folk and their families are in the lounge. An amateur choir is performing songs from the shows. The upright, pee-proof armchairs have been arranged in rows and everybody's singing along to "Second Hand Rose." I look for Mum, but she's not there. It's odd because when she's in the mood she enjoys a good singsong. Maybe she and her friends are teaching the kids how to play rummy in the games room.

I should go and look for her, but I don't. It's not the third-rate singers that keep me rooted. It's the audience. I know I'm staring, but I can't help it. Lately I've developed a morbid fascination with advanced old age. There's plenty of it here: shuffling men in baggy track suit bottoms and pee-spattered Velcro trainers. Whiskery old ladies hunched over their walking frames. Twenty-five years from now, that could be me. Mum has told Abby more than once that she wants to be put down if she gets like that. Abby assures her she'll die in her sleep after making a roast chicken dinner for the entire family and changes the subject.

I can't believe I'm getting old. OK — older. I know I shouldn't complain. I've made it this far. Brian didn't. I'm lucky. Even so, aging has taken me by surprise. I find it hard to believe that I was once this right-on student who could quote long passages from *The Female Eunuch*. I wore tie-dyed T-shirts and knew all the words to "Suzanne" and the Monty Python parrot sketch. Hell, I even owned a Pet Rock. (When I told Mike about the Pet Rock, he said he'd had one, too. He decided to buy me one as a memento. Turned out people were selling them on eBay with the original carrying cases for nine dollars. It's now sitting on top of the cistern in the downstairs loo. The kids call it Dave — after the mailman).

I think about dying a lot. It's a new thing. After Brian died I was too busy mourning him to consider my own demise. It's the aches and pains that get me going. When I wake up in the morning, my body feels stiff. If I walk too far, my back aches and my hips feel sore. Sometimes my thumbs hurt for no reason. I haven't told Mum because it would turn into a competition, which she would have to win. But I'm aware that my bones and joints are starting to wear out. Whenever I think about dying, I'm reminded of when I was a kid and I used to lie awake at night, trying to imagine infinity. It caused pandemonium and panic in my brain and I'd call out to Mum. The same happens now — minus the mum bit — when I think about ceasing to be. What's more, for an atheist, it sucks not being able to look forward to the afterlife. Oblivion doesn't have quite the same allure as eternal bliss and resurrection. I've told Mike I'm considering downgrading to agnostic. He called me a wuss. I said I didn't care.

Eventually I wander into the games room, which is quieter. A few men are playing chess. They're not as old as the ones in the lounge. They're wearing flannels and pastel-colored sweaters and they've taken the trouble to shave. One of them is playing Sam. There's a small group gathered round watching and discussing Sam's technique. "See how he plays for king attacks? Now he's moved his bishop at f-one to c-four. Perfect setup. Unless of course he's left his queen exposed — which he hasn't."

Every time Sam makes a move the old men cheer. "Great move. Face it, Bernie, you don't stand a chance against young Kasparov here. The kid has you licked." Sam is beaming, lapping it up.

I decide to leave him to his game. By now I've spotted Rosie. She's chatting to a particularly frail-looking old lady who is sitting alone at a card table playing patience. Her veined, knotty hands are shaking so much she can barely hold the cards.

"So, if you were a fruit or a vegetable, which one would you want to be? I'd want to be a potato because they have eyes . . . geddit? My teacher told us that joke. . . . So, you know you're going to die soon, right? Well, my nana Frieda says that in the olden days people used to be buried with a bell to let people know in case they were still alive. I think you should ask for a bell and a phone. Then you could text people to tell them you were alive. Also I've got nits. Do you want to see? My head is really itchy. I asked Grandma if I could have one as a pet, but she said no."

Luckily the old lady appears to be deaf.

I'm about to tell Rosie to leave the poor soul in peace when I spot Mum. She's sitting on one of the sofas at the far end of the room, surrounded by half a dozen of her friends, who have pulled up chairs in a semicircle in front of her. More to the point, she's weeping into her handkerchief.

"What on earth . . ."

I feel a hand on my arm. It's Pam. She runs the center. Mum always refers to her as "Pam, the head one." "If I were you," she whispers, "I'd leave her."

"But she's upset. What's going on?"

"Don't laugh. They're having an intervention."

"Excuse me?"

Pam sits me down and explains in the most diplomatic terms she can muster that Mum's friends are fed up with her.

"I'm not surprised. She never stops moaning about her health. She must drive them crazy."

"No, it's not that. They don't mind Frieda complaining. They're used to it and they love the fact that she's happy to Google all their symptoms. They're upset because of the way she treated Mrs. Silverfish. She's so hurt that your mother didn't go to her granddaughter's wedding. The feeling is that your mum's jealous of Mrs. Silverfish because she's got a gentleman friend. I think Frieda would love a companion, but she's convinced she's too old."

"Tell me about it. I keep telling her to join Estelle's dating site. But she won't."

"And it's this stubbornness that's driving her friends mad. So they've decided to call her on it. I'm keeping an eye on things. They're being very gentle with her. She's got a bit emotional, that's all."

"I'm not surprised."

I find a place to sit where Mum can't see me, and Pam fetches me a cup of tea from the kitchen.

"But how long has this been going on? I can't stand seeing her so upset."

Pam says only about twenty minutes and that if I can bear to, I should give it a bit longer. "I've got a feeling they might be getting somewhere with her."

I tell her I'm doubtful, but I agree to keep out of the way.

"Your grandson seems to be in his element over there," Pam says. "When he was younger, Bernie had quite a reputation on the chess circuit. He won dozens of tournaments."

"Really? But his friends seem to think he doesn't stand a chance against Sam."

Pam laughs. "I think you'll find that was for Sam's benefit." She taps the side of her nose. Then she makes her excuses and leaves me. The mayor is due any minute and she needs to be in the lobby to greet him. Once she's gone, I go back to watching the kids. Rosie has produced a Kinder Egg from her pocket and is unwrapping it for her old lady. Sam has just beaten Bernie, but he's not pleased. "Why did you do that? I wasn't controlling the center of the board. You know I wasn't. You could have taken advantage, but you didn't. You let me win."

"I did no such thing," Bernie says, doing his best to sound indignant.

"Yes, you did. Now we have to play again and you've got to promise to play properly."

"OK, young man. You want a fight? You got one."

They start setting up the chessboard. Meanwhile, on the other side of the room, Mum is blowing her nose. Afterward Estelle Silverfish gives her a hug. Her friends are queuing up to give more hugs.

I'm torn. I don't know whether to let her know I'm here and that I know what's been going on or to disappear, give her a few minutes to compose herself and then show up as if nothing's happened. I decide to make a quick exit and leave her with her dignity.

On the way home Mum goes on about how mediocre the singers were. "Off-key, the lot of them. But it was a good turnout. The mayor came with the mayoress. Would it have been too much effort for her to get her roots done for the occasion? But Sam and Rosie had a good time. Everybody went crazy for them."

"Ladies kept pinching my cheek," Rosie said. "And it hurt. And one of them said I was shiny."

"She didn't call you shiny," Mum says, laughing. "She called you a *shaineh maidel*. It's Yiddish for 'pretty girl.' "

"I enjoyed playing chess with Bernie," Sam pipes up. "He's a great player. He beat me. Then afterward he showed me where I went wrong. It was good fun. Can I play him again?"

Strange as it may seem, this is the first time I have ever heard Sam refer to playing chess as fun.

"Seriously?" Mum says. "You want to play chess with an old man? Wouldn't you rather play with kids of your own age?"

"Uh-uh. Bernie's an amazing player."

"OK. If you're serious, I'll ask him."

I put off looking at Brian's closet until bedtime. I open the double doors and stare into the emptiness. It's done. The clothes are gone. But I haven't destroyed his mem-

370

ory. Brian will be with me for as long as I live. I know that now.

I surprise myself by how well I sleep.

The following morning, I'm having a lie-in with coffee and the newspaper when my phone rings. It's Mike. He wants to know how I'm feeling now that Brian's clothes have gone.

"Surprisingly OK."

"You sure?"

"Positive. I know I needed help doing it. But it was the right time."

"OK . . . so would it be too soon to ask if you'd like to come to my place one night . . . I mean, for a sleepover?"

"Finally. I thought you'd never ask."

It's only after I've come off the phone that I realize a sleepover would mean leaving the kids with Mum. I can hear her pottering around downstairs. I reach for my dressing gown, which is lying beside me on the bed.

Mum is clearing away the kids' breakfast things. They're in the living room watching TV.

"Mum, Mike's asked me to spend the night at his. How do you feel about that?"

"And good morning to you, too," she says without looking up from the countertop she's wiping.

"Sorry, but I wanted to ask you quickly,

before the kids come barging in."

"Fine. Go. You're hardly likely to get pregnant."

"No. I don't mean how do you feel about it morally. I mean, would you be up for looking after the kids?"

"No problem. But you should tell them if I suddenly drop down dead from a heart attack they should run to a neighbor or call the ambulance."

"You are such a ray of sunshine."

"I'm just being practical." She pauses. "Oh . . . and while we're on the subject of men, I've had a change of heart."

"How do you mean?"

"I'm going to take a look at that dating site of Estelle's."

"Really? That's amazing. It'll be fun. It'll take you out of yourself."

"And Estelle and I have made up, by the way. I apologized for letting her down over the wedding. I was being selfish."

"I'm glad. You shouldn't fall out with your best friend. So how come you changed your mind about dating?"

"Well . . . I was lying in bed the other night and I had this sudden epiphany. Suppose after you die, there's no afterlife? What if it's just nothing? You can't waste your life and hope for better things on the other side.

You need to grab happiness where you can."

"Amen to that," I say.

She changes the subject and says that if it's all right with me she's taking Sam to meet Bernie. It turns out she's spoken to him on the phone and he's invited Sam along to one of the coffee shops in the high street to play a few games. "Usually he meets up with his chess buddies. But today they can't make it. So he's got nobody to play with. He said I was more than welcome to bring Sam along."

"You sure he wasn't saying that just to be polite?"

"No. He likes Sam and he thinks he's a really talented kid."

"So, how well do you know Bernie?"

"He's only been coming to the center for a month or two. To be honest, I've hardly spoken to him." She pauses. "Are you asking me if Sam will be safe with him?"

"I guess I am."

She says not to worry. She will hang around and read a book while they play. "I won't let Sam out of my sight."

Since Rosie has a playdate and I was planning on doing some grocery shopping in the high street, I tell her I'll join them for a few minutes. I'd like to meet Bernie, get the measure of him, as well as to thank him for inviting Sam along to play.

The moment we walk in, Bernie gets up from his seat to greet us. He has to be six-four or -five. He's wearing tailored slacks and a navy sports jacket. His appearance isn't lost on my mother, who is giving him the once-over.

"Wow, for an old man, he's really tall," Sam whispers. "I've only ever seen him sitting down."

I tell him not to be so rude.

"It's fine," Bernie says. "And do you know what? I haven't lost an inch with age. Not a single inch. In fact, I'm the same height and weight now as I was when I beat Razor Robinson in 1948."

"Was he a famous chess player? I've never heard of him."

Bernie chuckles and explains that before he took up chess he was an amateur boxer.

"I was pretty good, too." He takes off his jacket, flexes his right biceps and invites Sam to feel it.

"Wow."

"Yep. Still rock hard. I lift weights at the gym three times a week. I make some of these young guys look like weaklings, I can tell you. The secret to healthy aging is to keep fit."

Mum says she had no idea he was a boxer.

"Only for a few years when I was young. After Razor Robinson broke my nose, my mother threatened to have a stroke. So I never turned professional. Instead I became an accountant and took up chess as a hobby." He turns to Sam: "Guess how many chess trophies I've won. Go on. Guess. OK, I'll tell you . . . twenty-four."

"That's a lot," Sam says.

"It is a lot."

But Sam's more interested in Bernie's boxing career. He wants to know if he knocked Razor Robinson out.

"You bet. Clean out in the third round. I got him with a sucker punch. But not before he did this." He taps his lumpy, splayed broken nose and turns sideways. "It's given me a great profile, don't you think?"

"That is so cool," Sam says.

"No, it isn't," Mum snaps. "It's horrible. Boxing is nothing to be proud of. If you ask me, it should be banned. What sort of civilized society allows people into a ring with the sole aim of beating each other senseless?"

"Women don't get it," Bernie says, giving Sam a conspiratorial wink.

"What's that supposed to mean?" Mum says.

"It means that men have a basic primal urge to fight and dominate and achieve personal glory. Women will never understand that."

Sam is looking up at Bernie, wide-eyed and in awe. Mum tells him to take no notice of Bernie's primal urges — the mention of which has made her turn quite pink. Boxing is obscene, she says. Sam ignores her.

"So, would you teach me some boxing moves?" he says.

Bernie puts up his fists and starts bouncing on his feet, bobbing and weaving. I get the feeling he's showing off to Mum. If he is, it's not working. She's looking at me, rolling her eyes.

"Sure. No problem," he says.

"You will not," Mum says.

I feel it's time for me to step in. "Thanks for the offer, Bernie, but I'm not sure Sam's mum and dad would approve. Might be best if you stick to chess."

"But they let me have the rifle. I know they wouldn't mind."

"Well, I think you need to check with them first."

Bernie nudges Sam. "While we're playing I'll also give you a few tips on how to get round women." He pauses. "So, Sam, what can I get you to drink? A Coke maybe?"

"I'm not allowed soda."

Bernie turns to Mum and makes a sad clown mouth.

"Don't look at me. I don't make the rules."

"Come on," he says, offering me the same beseeching face. "Once can't hurt."

I feel myself smiling and caving. "OK, just this once."

"Yay."

"See?" Bernie whispers to Sam. "I told you I was good at getting round women."

Then he insists on treating Mum and me to coffee and Danish.

Bernie's cocky and full of himself, but I've warmed to him. He's funny, he has an old-fashioned twinkle in his eye and I like the way he is with Sam. After we've had coffee, I take my leave and head to the super-market.

Sam and Mum don't get home until after lunch. Sam is full of the new techniques Bernie has taught him. "He taught me to castle early and get my king behind my wing pawns. Bogdan never taught me that."

I have no idea what he is talking about, but I tell him it sounds great. Mum, on the other hand, isn't in the best of moods.

"If I have to listen to one more minute of that man talking about himself . . ."

"But he tells really cool stories," Sam says. "I loved the one about boxers putting starch on their bandages to make their punches harder."

"Well, I don't approve of the way he's filling your head with all this aggression."

"Bernie says you need a bit of aggression when you play chess. He taught me this opening called the Sicilian Dragon. That's quite aggressive. I wish Bernie was my chess coach instead of Bogdan."

"No, you don't," Mum says. "The man's got an ego the size of a planet. And your parents wouldn't approve."

"Awwww."

She hands Sam a plate on which she has placed a large slice of chocolate cake and shoos him out of the kitchen.

"So, did I detect just a smidgen of sexual tension between you and Bernie?"

"What? Weren't you listening to a word I just said? The man's cocky and arrogant. For your information, I do not find that sexy."

"Maybe. But for his age he's very well preserved."

"I wish they would preserve him — preferably in aspic."

"No, you don't. I think you quite like him."

"I do not. And anyway, he's seeing some-body. A woman from the day center called Pearl."

"Really? That's a pity."

"You don't know what you're talking about," she says. Then she heads to the larder and takes out a packet of split peas. If there are enough carrots and onions, she's going to make pea soup. We haven't had it in ages.

CHAPTER SIXTEEN

The early-morning sun is casting shadows on the white bed linen. Mike kisses the length of my neck and moves on to my breasts and stomach. "So, what do you fancy for breakfast?"

"You."

"That goes without saying," he says, stroking the insides of my thighs. "But what would you like apart from me?" Smiling, I reach down, take hold of him and start pumping slowly.

"It's not going to happen unless I take another tablet. We might as well eat while we wait."

Middle-age sex.

Last night, on the sofa while he had his hand inside my skirt, I was still under the impression that he didn't need performance-enhancing drugs. But when I suggested moving things to the bedroom, he said maybe give it a few more minutes.

Of course I asked why. He looked a bit sheepish, took his hand away, said he'd only just taken his tablet and that it took a while to kick in. "Please don't be cross with me. I know I should have come clean when you asked me the other day, but I was too embarrassed. . . . Erectile dysfunction is hardly a turn-on."

"But I told you I wasn't bothered."

"Even so . . ."

To make him feel better I told him I had a confession, too. I reached into my bag and produced my post-menopause must-have — my trusty tube of FemGlide. "Sandpaper sex isn't much of a turn-on either. So maybe I should go to the bathroom now and . . ."

He took it from me. "Don't you dare. You leave that to me."

"Seriously? You find that sexy?"

"You bet. Don't you?"

Since he'd mentioned it, I guess I did.

Our mutual age-related deficiencies turned out to be liberating. In my twenties I worried about new boyfriends seeing me naked. I tortured myself about my figure, which was gorgeous — my weight, which was perfect. Last night as I let Mike undress me and get busy with the FemGlide, I didn't give a damn about my thick waist, my thicket bush, my breasts, which swayed and swung. And nor, it seemed, did he. I lost count of the times he told me how beautiful I was.

It was all so easy. The fact that we'd taken time to know each other helped. We relaxed, let go. We had fun. Neither of us had anything to prove. It was slow and tender and when I came I cried. Of course Mike panicked and thought my tears were his fault — that he'd done something wrong.

"It was perfect. You did nothing wrong."

"What, then?"

"It's been so long," I said, wiping my eyes with the back of my hand, "that I'd almost forgotten what an orgasm felt like. I didn't know if I could still do it. But I did and it was wonderful. Thank you."

I didn't tell him that I had also been worried about whether I could come with a man who wasn't Brian. I thought the guilt might kick in. But it didn't. The truth was, I hadn't felt so turned on in I don't know how long — decades probably. Brian and I had been married forever. Even before he got ill, sex wasn't as high on the agenda as it had once been. It had given way to affection and comfortable companionability.

"The pleasure was all mine," Mike said.

"Really?"

"Like you need to ask." He took my hand,

placed it on his erection and we did it again. We would have gone for the hat trick, but his tablet was starting to wear off. So we drank Scotch and lay in each other's arms, watching *Louie* reruns until we fell asleep.

Mike takes another tablet and makes bacon sandwiches. We eat them in bed while we wait for him to get a hard-on. Every so often I reach out and start fiddling with his penis. "Just checking."

He says that despite his excellent multitasking skills, he can't get an erection and eat bacon at the same time.

"Bet you can." I'm laughing and stroking his balls. He's practically choking on his sandwich.

We're still eating and fooling around when my phone rings. The caller display says Ginny. I decide to let it go to voice mail. Then it occurs to me that if she's calling at eight in the morning it could be urgent. Mike peers under the covers. "I'll be a while yet. Take it."

"Hi, Ginny. You OK?"

"Fine. I didn't realize it was so early. I didn't wake you, did I?"

"No, we're up."

"We? Oh God. You're at Mike's, aren't you? I'll go."

"No, don't. It's fine — really."

"So you slept over."

"I did."

"Wow. . . . So how was it?"

"Maybe we could hook up later for a chat?"

"Roger that. You can't talk."

"Not really. . . . So, were you calling about something in particular?"

"I was. I've been up all night thinking about it. I've decided to go and see my mother. You're right. She's ill. I don't know how much time she has left. I could live to regret it."

"Good for you. I know you're doing the right thing."

"The thing is, I was wondering if you'd come with me for moral support. I can't believe I'm asking you. You know how gung ho I am. It takes a lot to scare me, but I'm absolutely petrified. I don't want you to come in with me. But if you could wait outside in the car . . ."

"I can do that. When were you thinking of going?"

"I think it might be best to strike while the iron's hot. Maybe this morning? She doesn't go out, so any time will do."

"OK. I could pick you up, say, around eleven?"

I look a question at Mike. He says that's fine by him. He's got a piece to write.

"Perfect," Ginny says. "Thank you so much. I don't know what I'd do without you."

While Ginny says she'll treat me to lunch afterward, Mike is lifting the sheet and pointing. "Sorry, Ginny. Got to go. Something's just come up."

Ginny's mother, Edith, lives in a dark Victorian Gothic villa facing Hampstead Heath. The green-and-cream paint is bubbling and curling. The asphalt driveway is cracked and full of weeds. It's the kind of place the Addams family might have taken as a vacation rental.

To calm Ginny's nerves, I made sure we spent most of the journey discussing Mike and me. Ginny is delighted that we finally did the "deed." "It would be wonderful if you two made a go of it. Shame about that bloody daughter of his. When she finds out she isn't going to be best pleased."

"Tell me about it."

I park the car on the street. Ginny picks up the bouquet of red tulips that's been lying on the backseat and stares out of the window, gathering her thoughts. "I haven't set foot in this house for over thirty years. It feels so weird."

"You'll be fine. Remember — slow, deep breaths."

She opens the door. "Into the valley of death rode the six hundred . . ."

"Come on. It won't be that bad."

"You don't know my mother. Wish me luck."

I lean over and give her a hug and a kiss.

Once she's out of the car, she pauses to inhale. Then, shoulders back, she marches up the driveway. Before she knocks on the door, she turns to glance at me. I nod and give her the thumbs-up. She picks up the brass knocker and brings it down once and then again. She gives the old lady time to answer, but after half a minute or so there's no sign of Edith. She knocks again. Still nothing. I watch her crouch down and open the letter box. The next moment she drops the bouquet and comes charging down the drive. I unwind the car window. "What is it?"

"She's lying on the hall floor. She must have had another stroke."

We dash back up the drive, me on the phone to the emergency services. Ginny is ahead of me, shouting through the letter-box.

"Mum. It's Ginny. Can you hear me? Lift

your hand if you can hear me." She looks at me and shakes her head. "I think she's gone."

"You don't know that. She's probably just unconscious."

Ginny picks up a large piece of stone from the neglected rockery and smashes a pane of glass in the front door. While I yell at her to watch out for broken glass, she reaches inside and releases the lock.

Lying in the dark-paneled hallway on a worn cherry red carpet is a gaunt figure with long gray hair that looks like it could do with a wash. Ditto her faded silk dressing gown. Judging by the way her limbs are splayed and twisted, she's taken a bad fall.

Ginny is on her knees, feeling for a pulse in the old lady's wrist. I'm looking at her face, which is corrugated and pale and caved in at the mouth, for want of her false teeth.

"Nothing. I think she's gone." I get down beside Ginny and put an arm around her shoulders. But she doesn't need comfort. There's not a glimmer of emotion. Ginny hasn't had a relationship with her mother in three decades. To her, this could be any sad, unfortunate old lady lying dead on the floor.

There's a knock on the door. Two women paramedics come striding in and ask if we wouldn't mind moving back.

Ginny and I hover by the stairs. One of the paramedics is checking for a pulse in Edith's neck.

"Why are they bothering?" Ginny says. "They can see she's gone."

"I've got a weak pulse here," the paramedic says. Her colleague arranges an oxygen mask over Edith's face.

"Good God. She's alive?"

"Just about."

Ginny says she'll go with Edith in the ambulance. I offer to follow, but by now she's texted her brother and arranged to meet him at the hospital. "You go home. We'll be fine. And, Judy . . . thank you for everything."

"No problem. Go. And keep me posted."

When I get home, Rosie asks if I had a nice time at my friend's house.

"I had a very nice time. Thank you."

"When Cybil comes for sleepovers she sleeps in my bed, and sometimes we watch movies on the iPad. Did you sleep in the same bed with your friend?"

"Actually we did."

"Did you watch stuff?"

"Not so much."

"That sounds really boring."

Mum, who is sitting reading the newspaper, doesn't look up. Rosie says she's going to her room. She's got a playdate this afternoon and she wants to get together some games to take with her. I check that she's all the way upstairs before telling Mum about finding Edith collapsed on the floor.

"Good God. What a shock for Ginny . . . and for you. I'll put the kettle on. What you need is a nice cup of sweet tea."

"Mum, I'm fine, honestly." But she's filling the kettle anyway. "It's Ginny I'm worried about."

"Of course you are. Such a lovely woman. From what you've told me the mother sounds like a piece of work, though. . . . I don't care if she is on her last legs."

As we sit drinking tea, the conversation gets back to my "sleepover" with Mike.

"So, are you two going steady now?"

The phrase makes me smile. I haven't heard it in years. "We haven't sat down and discussed it. But I guess we are." I remind her not to say anything to the kids. "I don't want it getting back to Claudia. Mike still hasn't told her we're seeing each other."

"Is that wise? Somebody could see you in the street and start gossiping."

"I agree and I've told him. But he's

prepared to take the risk."

"That's daft. Take it from me: There will be hell to pay if she finds out by accident."

"I know. But thinking about it, there will be hell to pay if Mike tells her. It's pretty much a lose-lose situation."

"Unless of course you make peace with her."

"That's not going to happen." That's my official line, but if there's no other option — if push really does come to shove — I can't rule it out.

Mum shrugs. "Well, don't say I didn't warn you. So, I have news: Estelle came round last night, and we signed me up to SeniorsConnect dot com."

"Wow. Good for you. So, did you message anybody?"

"You have to be kidding. You want to see some of the things they put in their profiles?"

She tells me about Jerry007, whose main interest is the economy. There's another guy who wants a woman who wears high heels and is able to appreciate his accomplishments. There are a couple anxious to point out that they can still drive at night.

Fading night vision? That's a thing as you get old? My mother says it is. Fabulous. Something else for me to look forward to.

"They're hardly going to sweep a girl off her feet," Mum says.

"Is that what you want? To be swept off your feet?"

"Why not? I've come this far. I've paid. Why shouldn't I get my money's worth?"

"So you'll keep on looking?"

"For a while. I guess you have to click on a lot of frogs before you find your prince."

The phone rings. Mum gets it.

"Oh, hi, Bernie." She covers up the mouthpiece and whispers: "Talking of frogs."

I tell her that's a horrible thing to say.

"What do you mean you've suddenly got an outie belly button? You're not overweight. I can't see why that would happen. Does it hurt? . . . It does?"

The doorbell rings. Bogdan. Since the start of the school holidays, he's been tutoring Sam during the day. I leave Mum to her call and answer the door.

I can't help noticing that Bogdan is wearing different trousers. He usually wears brown ones. These are gray. The legs still stop at his ankles, though.

"So — how is my star pupil doing?" Ever since Mum told him that I would cut off his balls, Bogdan has been superpolite to me and softer on Sam.

"He's fine."

Sam must have heard the bell, because he's on his way downstairs.

"Excellent to see you, Sam. I hope you have been practicing. Today I hev very special moves to teach you. Today you will learn Dresden Trap."

I leave them at the dining room table and take myself into Brian's study. Despite his improved behavior, I still don't trust Bogdan not to shout and I can hear everything from there.

A few minutes later Ginny calls to say her mother is in intensive care.

"They've got her hooked up to all sorts of wires and whatnot. She's hanging in there. There's not much of her, but she's a tough old bird — a bit like me. And apparently it was a heart attack, not a stroke. So if she does pull through there won't be any paralysis. I guess that's something."

Ginny says she's going to stay overnight at the hospital. "My brother wanted to stay, too, but I sent him home. No point us both being there."

I ask if she'd like me to come to the hospital tomorrow and bring her a change of clothes.

"If you don't mind, that would be wonderful." She says Emma would do it, but it's difficult because she doesn't have a car. I should ask her for the front door key.

I can hear yelling coming from the dining room. I tell Ginny that Bogdan is on the rampage and that I have to go.

He's banging the table, demanding to know where Sam learned about the Sicilian Dragon.

"My friend Bernie taught me."

Bogdan is up in arms. How dare Sam see other chess coaches behind his back?

"He's not my coach. He's my friend."

"But he has no right to teach you new moves without my permission. This is an outrage."

I decide to go in and intervene. "Bogdan, I will not have you bullying Sam like this. Bernie is a family friend. He played a few games with Sam, that's all."

"It has to stop. It puts Sam off his stride. I have carefully structured syllabus. This confuses him and ruins everything."

"Seriously?" The truth is that Bogdan is feeling threatened.

"Yes, seriously."

"Grandma, can you go away please? Bogdan's right. Maybe I am getting a bit confused."

My grandson is desperate to keep the peace. He'll do anything not to upset Bogdan and, in turn, his parents. I can't help admiring him.

"You sure?"

"Positive."

As I retreat, Bogdan offers me a victorious smirk.

When the session is over, Sam — apparently untroubled — heads to the kitchen to get a snack. Bogdan goes back to being conciliatory.

"I'm sorry to yell," he says. "I already apologized to Sam. I get frustration because I don't want this new person poking in his nose and upsetting applecart."

"He just played a few games with Sam, that's all."

"I know. But it can be harmful. I want Sam to be the best."

"But shouldn't he have some fun, too?"

Bogdan looks appalled. "But becoming champion is serious business. What is the point of fun? Fun is for stupid people."

"Well, I happen to think fun is important. Especially when you're nine."

Back in the kitchen, Mum is still on the phone to Bernie.

"OK. I just Googled it, and it's as I thought. It's almost definitely an umbilical hernia. You need to get it checked out. . . ."

394

I've got a great gastroenterologist. He's known me for years. I could come with you if you like."

Once she's off the phone I make the point that she's showing great concern for this man she dislikes so much.

"He just seemed so pathetic, that's all. Men always act so big and butch until they get ill. Then they fall apart. And his girl-friend doesn't want to know. She's one of these people who never gets sick. She doesn't do illness."

"So are you going with him?"

She shakes her head. He'd rather go alone.

"Well, I think you like him."

"No, I don't. I hate self-centered men."

"But you have to admit that despite his broken nose — or maybe because of it — he's rather good-looking."

She shrugs. "Maybe."

Mike and I arrange to meet at Conte's, the pizza place a few blocks from his apartment. When I arrive, he's already bagged a table by the window. As I watch him, I can't help finding something sexy about the way he munches on a bread stick while he turns the pages of the evening paper. The moment he sees me his face lights up. I quicken my step. I've missed him. I want to tell him about my day and find out about his.

"I spent my day typing," he says. "I didn't get dressed until after lunch."

He says that's the thing with being a freelancer. You get to the end of the week and realize you've spent most of it in your dressing gown.

I update him about Ginny's mum. Afterward I find myself telling him about Bogdan.

"It's none of my business, but if you ask me he sounds like a complete nut job. Why on earth haven't you got rid of him?"

"I wanted to. But Abby insists he's the best there is. She says I shouldn't take him too seriously — that he yells because that's what Russians do and we should allow for cultural differences."

"Well, I think he could be causing Sam real emotional damage. What possible good can come from constantly humiliating and undermining the poor kid?"

"To give Sam his due, he does seem to be coping. For a while I was really worried about his behavior, but since he's given up a lot of other after-school activities he seems much better."

"Maybe, but you won't convince me. The man's a martinet."

"You're right. But I'm caught between the

devil and the deep blue sea. Abby and Tom are by no means the pushiest of parents, but they want Sam to do well in this competition. And Sam doesn't want to let them down."

"Well, like I say, it's none of my business, but they could be storing up trouble for themselves."

"I agree. But what can I do — other than to keep on listening outside the door?"

He reaches across the table and takes my hand. "Come back to my place again. That'll cheer you up."

"I'd like that. But it means leaving Mum with the kids again. I don't like taking advantage. And I worry about something happening to her when I'm not there."

"OK . . . no problem. You have to do what you feel is right."

"On the other hand, I could give her a call — see if she'd mind."

Mum doesn't mind at all. The kids are asleep. She's about to go to bed. Why would it be a problem? I tell her I'll be back first thing. She tells me there's no rush.

We're lying entwined on the sofa, listening to Leonard Cohen on some fancy wireless speakers Mike has just been sent to review. "Wow — listen to that. It's as if he's right here in the room."

"I agree," I say. "They're amazing. I like the smooth horizontal sound pattern and flat response."

"You do? Wow, that is so sexy."

"What is?"

"A woman who knows something about sound systems."

"You'd be surprised what I know," I tell him in my best come-hither voice. I start unbuttoning his shirt.

In fact, I know nothing about sound systems. The line about horizontal sound patterns and flat responses is something I picked up years ago from a sales assistant who was trying to sell Brian and me some la-di-da hi-fi, which we couldn't begin to afford.

Leonard is about to take Manhattan and Berlin when Mike takes me — right there on the sofa. I tremble as he touches me. I breathe in his smell, move my body with his. Again it's slow and tender, but no less wanton for that.

Afterward as we lie there, him stroking my breast, he says he has something to tell me.

"I think I'm falling in love with you. No, scrub that. I know I'm falling in love with you."

"You are?" I feel my body tense. I suspect

he does, too.

"Oh dear. I shouldn't have said anything. It's too soon."

"No . . . I am glad you did." Glad and panicking. "But I don't understand. You're the one who wanted to take things slowly."

"I know." Now he's the one panicking. "I'm an idiot. I've said too much. You're not ready. I'm sorry — I didn't mean to upset you."

I kiss his cheek. "You don't have to apologize for telling me you love me. And you haven't upset me. You've taken me by surprise, that's all. But it's a wonderful surprise."

"I don't want to push it, but now that I've come this far . . . have you thought . . . you know . . . about how you might possibly feel about me?"

I kiss him again. "Just give me some time."

"Take as much as you need."

We decide to have an early night. Mike has got to be in the City by nine. Apple is launching the iPhone 7.

We start off spooning, him with his arms around my waist. A few minutes later he rolls over to his side of the bed and starts snoring. Outside, it's blowing a gale and rain is hitting the window like nails. The snoring and the weather aren't the only things keeping me awake. A man who isn't Brian has just told me he loves me and he wants to know how I feel about him. That's the reason I can't sleep.

When we're together, Mike's touch takes my breath away. He listens and cares and makes me laugh. We have chemistry — in and out of bed. I miss him when he's not around. Lately when I have news, he's the first person I think about telling. If that's not love, what is? This would all be good, if I weren't still in love with a dead man.

The next day while I'm chatting on the phone to Ginny, she reminds me of what I said a while back, about finding room for both of them.

"I know. But Brian was my husband. He was the one. I can't seem to get beyond that."

"You'll work it out. Just give it time. Don't let Mike rush you."

"I won't. I promise."

Once I'm off the phone, I can hear Mum clattering around, making dinner. I call out with an offer of help, but she says she's fine. So I leave her to it and go upstairs to help Sam with his packing.

Tomorrow is the start of the summer term, but Sam's class isn't returning to school. Nor is the one above him. Instead both years will be spending the week at an outward-bound center in Dorset, hiking, canoeing and climbing rocks. The idea is to build the kids' confidence and independence. Mum thinks the whole thing is foolhardy and crazy.

"You'd never get this at a Jewish school. Jews don't let their children climb rocks."

"What are you talking about? Of course they do."

"They don't. And you know why?"

"OK . . . why?"

"The Holocaust."

"Of course."

"Why are you laughing? The Holocaust amuses you?"

"Of course it doesn't. It's just that somehow everything with you comes back to Hitler."

"Quite right. Hitler taught us a very important lesson — that calamity can come out of a clear blue sky. We don't take risks. That's why you don't see Jews climbing rocks."

"That's nonsense."

"Fine. Have it your way. Don't say I didn't warn you."

I open the door to find Sam pulling clothes out of his dresser drawers by the armful and dumping them on the bed.

"Darling, you don't need all that. You're going for five days, not a month. Why don't we try and sort out what you actually need?"

" 'K." He sits himself on the bed and lets me sort through his clothes.

"Grandma, do I really have to go? Couldn't we say I'm ill or something? Then I could stay at home and practice my chess. I wouldn't be any trouble — honest."

It's not the activities Sam objects to. My mother hasn't got to him. His problem is he doesn't want to go away on his own.

All the mums I've spoken to say their children can't wait to go on the trip. That's probably not true. I'm guessing quite a few are scared of getting homesick but don't want to admit it for fear of being called chicken. Sam, on the other hand, is quite open about not wanting to go. He's convinced he won't cope on his own. It came to a head a few nights ago when I was putting him to bed.

"While Mum and Dad have been away I've had you and Nana to look after me and it's been fine. Even though you're not Mum, you're like her. You're a sort of deputy mum. That's what grandmas are. But I've missed Mum and Dad and I've still felt a tiny bit lonely. But when I go away, I'm going to feel even more lonelier. What if I get really upset?"

"If that happens, you tell one of your teachers and I will drive down and get you. You don't have to be miserable. Do you understand?"

"OK. And you absolutely promise you'll come and get me?"

"I absolutely promise. Now try to stop worrying. If I know you, you'll surprise yourself and everything will be fine."

Sam has also been telling his parents he doesn't want to go on the trip. Whenever Abby and Tom Skype, they make a point of trying to gee him up by emphasizing how much he's going to love all the activities. But Abby in particular is worried about how he'll cope.

"First Tom and I abandon him for all these weeks and now he's got to go away and leave the stability you've created. Plus he's got this chess tournament coming up. I'm worried the stress is all too much for him."

I keep telling Abby what I've told Sam, that at the first sign of trouble I will bring him home. She says that's all well and good, but then his friends will tease him for being a wimp and he'll never live it down.

"Tell you what," I'm saying to Sam now. "Would it make a difference if we spoke on the phone each day?"

"The teachers have said we can't call home because it'll make us homesick and upset."

"Well, I think they might make an exception for you."

"Really?"

"Leave it to me."

As I arrive at school with Sam and Rosie, the bus is pulling up at the gates. As Sam runs off to join his friends, Rosie heads into school, pausing to offer him only the briefest of good-byes. I suspect she's secretly jealous that her big brother is getting to go on a school trip and she isn't. Once she's disappeared, I go in search of Sam's teacher, Mrs. Gilbert. She has her head down, studying her clipboard. As her index finger moves over the page, she's muttering to herself about still being short of three permission slips.

"Sorry. Can't stop," she says as I approach. "Bit of a crisis . . ."

"Just a quick question." I make my case as briefly as I can.

"Fine, no problem. Sam can call home, so long as he doesn't tell the other children he's getting special privileges."

As I turn to go, I see that a queue has

formed behind me. Half a dozen or more mothers are waiting to speak to an already flustered Mrs. Gilbert. Some are waiting to hand over medication and asthma inhalers. The woman directly behind me is on a more important mission. "Mrs. Gilbert, can you confirm that the chicken you will be feeding the children is corn-fed? Olivia refuses to eat anything else. . . ."

I make my way back to the school gates, where the children going on the school trip have congregated along with their parents. Claudia is a few yards away, dispensing largesse to a couple of her acolytes. Laurence is with her. Quite a few dads have turned up to see their kids off. Since Laurence is an investment banker, I was imagining a tall, entitled WASP in a bespoke suit. Instead he looks like my uncle Norman: short, dark, bald, could do with losing forty pounds. Even in flats, Claudia dwarfs him.

"You're not the first person to notice they look odd together. The 'long and the short of it,' I call them."

The voice belongs to Tanya. She's standing next to me, grinning. "I wonder what attracted her to a multimillionaire banker."

"You are evil."

"I know, but I'm right."

"Not necessarily," I say. "The impression

I get from Mike is that Laurence is one of the few people who understands Claudia. That's why she fell for him. It wasn't his money."

"I bet the money helped, though . . . or maybe he's exceptionally gifted in bed. They say bald men often are. They have an excess of testosterone apparently." She pauses. "Talking of testosterone, I hear from Ginny that you and Mike are . . ."

"We are."

She laughs and offers me a wink. "Good for you."

Our conversation is cut short. A child in a Breton T-shirt is having a loud tantrum. His mother has given him bread sticks as a snack for the journey, but she's failed to provide hummus.

"Don't worry," her friend says. "He can share Raphael's baba ghanoush."

While the kids tear around in a frenzy of overexcitement, the parents swap angst about the trip.

"I'm furious that they're not allowing the kids to bring iPads. I mean, what harm could it do? Felix would only be bringing his spare one."

"I agree. Mind you, Izzy shouldn't even be going on this trip. She's far too tired after our spring break. She gets dreadful jet lag, even coming back from Europe."

"Well, I've put my foot down and said that on no account is Anastasia allowed to eat next to Flora. I won't have my daughter eating near fat children."

"And I've told Mrs. Gilbert that Maisie Armitage should be made to say her bedtime prayers to Jesus in private. Ours is a strict atheist home and I won't have it corrupted."

It's time for the children to board the bus. Sam hugs me tight and says he already feels carsick. I remind him that I've put a sick bag in his backpack. "And don't worry. Remember you can phone me. If it all goes pear-shaped, I will come and get you. I promise."

" 'K."

"Now off you go. And have a wonderful time."

"I love you, Gran'ma."

"Love you, too, darling."

I give him one final kiss and he joins the line of children waiting to get onto the coach. Mrs. Gilbert is at the foot of the steps, her eyes going from child to clipboard as she ticks off their names. So far she has confiscated at least three iPads. "This trip is not about you staring into your iPad and they will get broken. I don't care if your dad says it's insured along with the house contents. . . ."

Some of the mums are in tears as they wave off their offspring. Even a couple of dads are wiping their eyes. I'm crying, too, and it isn't just because I'm worried about Sam having a rotten time. It's because, as the bus pulls away, I catch sight of him throwing up into his sick bag.

CHAPTER SEVENTEEN

Edith has rallied. For a few days it looked as if the heart attack was going to carry her off, but Ginny called last night to say that she was off the danger list. "The doctors think that you and I getting to her when we did probably saved her life."

"So what's the prognosis?"

"They're not sure about her long-term prospects. They're still doing tests. But for now she's on the mend. So it looks like the pair of us has been given another chance."

"That's such wonderful news. I'm so pleased — for both of you."

She asked if I would mind bringing her another change of clothes. "My brother says I'm bonkers staying, but knowing my luck, the moment I leave her, she'll have another bloody attack and pop her clogs."

Until now, each time I've been to the hospital, Edith has been unconscious and I haven't been allowed into the room. So

Ginny and I would chat in the corridor while I handed over clothes and books and chocolatey treats. The day before yesterday I brought her a bottle of Scotch. She called me an angel and said she might ask the doctors if she could be given it intravenously. Instead she kept it hidden. She wasn't sure if it was against the rules to bring booze into hospital — even if you were only visiting.

This morning when I arrive, Edith is awake, but no less frail than when we found her collapsed on the floor. She's pale as veal. Her sinewy neck and tiny head are supported by a mountain of pillows. Her nightgown is gaping at the neck, revealing the top of her bony rib cage and the electronic pads that are attached to the heart monitor above the bed. But her teeth are in and judging by her clean fingernails and grease-free hair, now brushed off her face and held in place by a velvet headband, she's had a decent sponge-down.

Edith's body may be feeble, but her brain — not to mention her voice — is anything but. She's up in arms about something. Having just walked in, I can't make out what. All I know is that "it" won't do and that she's very cross about "it" not doing. Since she's in midrant and I fear that if I interrupt she might turn on me, I don't. Instead I hover just inside the door with my bunch of pink tulips and a holdall containing Ginny's change of clothes.

"It's unbearable. Can't you get them to do something?" Ginny, who is perched on the edge of the bed, fanning her mother with a copy of the *Times,* says she's already tried. All the electric fans are being used. "I can only imagine the money they must be wasting keeping the place at blood heat. The windows don't open because God forbid they might let in germs."

"Tell you what, why don't I pop out and buy a fan?"

"Would you? That would be wonderful. For now, though . . . if you could just move the newspaper a notch to the left . . . Ah, that's better."

"Knock, knock. Only me."

Ginny stops waving the *Times* and swings round. "Judy! Come in. I didn't see you there. . . . Mummy — this is Judy." It has always struck me as odd how grown women — posh ones at least — happily infantilize themselves by referring to their parents as "mummy" and "daddy."

Edith looks me up and down. "Good grief. Another strange face. How many more new nurses am I expected to endure? But since you're here, you should know that the heat is worse than the Black Hole of Calcutta. What's more, the hospital tea is undrinkable. Please fetch me some Earl Grey with lemon. Oh, and the blind needs pulling down. I can hardly see in this sun. And when you've done that you can help me off with my bed jacket. I'm perspiring like a coolie in all this heat."

"Mummy . . . Judy's not a nurse. Look, she's not wearing a uniform." Ginny gets off the bed and pulls down the blind. "She's a very good friend of mine. She was with me when I found you, and she's stopped by to see how you're doing." Ginny starts helping her mother off with her bed jacket. That done, she comes across to relieve me of my bag and the bunch of flowers.

"Look, Mummy, Judy's brought you tulips. Aren't they lovely? I'll go in search of a vase later."

"How thoughtful," she says, barely glancing at the tulips. Instead she focuses on me. "Judy — short for Judith, I presume. Are your people Jews?"

Ginny looks like she doesn't know where to put herself. "Mummy — for heaven's sake . . . please."

"My mother is Jewish, yes."

"I have a lot of time for the Jews."

"You do?" Ginny says, looking both re-lieved and puzzled. "Since when?"

"Since always. The Jews have clung to life through thick and thin — mostly thin. I admire that."

"Thank you."

"Crafty lot, mind you, the Jews. Very clever. You wouldn't want to do business with them."

Before I have a chance to say anything, Ginny tells her mother she needs to speak to me in private and bundles me out of the room.

"I can only apologize. I would love to tell you it's her medication speaking, but I'm afraid it isn't. If it makes you feel any bet-ter, she hates most racial groups — even the Scots and the Irish. Always has. But now that she's old, her inhibition has deserted her, and she says precisely what's on her mind. I'm so sorry."

"Stop it. You don't have to apologize. It's water off a duck's back. She's old and a bit dotty. You're not going to change her. Just keep her away from my mother, that's all."

"Good Lord. Can you imagine?"

"It wouldn't be a pretty sight. . . . So, how have you and Edith been getting on? She doesn't appear to have thrown you out yet."

"I'll walk out before she gets a chance.

413

Lord, she's a demanding, cantankerous old cow. Mind you, she always was. But it's got worse with age. And yes, before you say anything, I know she appears to have me wrapped around her little finger. But she's old and ill. I haven't seen her in decades. . . ."

"I get that. But you need to watch her. If you're not careful she'll run you ragged and you'll be the one in hospital."

"Thank you and duly noted. The thing is, her unpleasantness aside, we've actually been getting on rather well — which isn't at all what I was expecting."

"Have you talked about her kicking you out?"

"I brought it up this morning. I know I should have left it until she's stronger, but I couldn't wait. I don't know when she's going to have another heart attack. But I didn't get anywhere. She refuses to discuss it. All she's prepared to say is that she made a regrettable decision. I suspect that's as close as she'll come to apologizing. She says what's done is done and we should put it behind us . . . stiff upper lip and all that."

"I suppose that's better than nothing."

"I guess. Anyway, it's all I'm going to get, so I will have to make do. By the way, she wants to meet Emma and the boys."

"That's wonderful."

"That's not the half of it. . . . She wants the lot of us to move in with her."

"Seriously? But you've only been back in her life two minutes."

"I know, but she says she wants to make up for lost time. The thing is, I'm not sure if I could put up with her unpleasantness. I can see her turning me into some kind of unpaid skivvy. On top of that, the house is so run-down and dingy. I can't see Emma and the boys wanting to move in."

She perks up when I remind her that the house is in an excellent school catchment area. "Good Lord. You're not wrong. I hadn't thought of that. A decent school would do the boys no end of good. It's just what they need." She pauses. "But even then I'm not sure I'd be doing the right thing. I've hated her for all these years. It's far too soon. We'd come to blows in no time."

"So what did you tell her?"

"I said I'd think about it and talk it over with Emma."

I insist she come to me for dinner this evening. "It'll cheer you up. Tanya's got yoga, but Mike will be there. Mum's doing roast chicken . . . Oh, and FYI, I haven't said anything to her about Mike being in love with me. She'll only start auditioning caterers."

"Roger that," Ginny says, tapping the side of her nose.

I'm laying the table while Mum fries onions for the chopped liver hors d'oeuvres. "Mum, stick the extractor on! You're stinking out the entire house!"

"What?"

"I said, would you stick . . ."

I'm wasting my breath. She can't hear me. It's easier to do it myself.

I abandon the table laying, head into the kitchen and flick the switch on the cooker hood. I'm pincering a piece of fried onion from the pan when my mobile rings. Mum manages to slap my wrist, yell at me about first-degree burns and hand me a cloth — all at the same time.

It's Sam.

"Hi, darling. How's it all going?"

"Great. We did canoeing this morning and we learned how to capsize and get back up again. Some people couldn't do it, but I could. It was easy. I wasn't a bit scared."

"Sam, that's wonderful. I'm so proud of you. And I know Mum and Dad will be, too."

My mother is waving her spatula. "Tell

him Nana says to be careful and to keep out of danger."

"Will you be quiet?" I hiss. "No, not you, darling. It was Nana interrupting."

"OK . . . so later on we went into the woods and the teachers pretended to abandon us and we had to find our way out, using a map and a compass. Our group was the second back to base and we won a silver medal. It's not real silver — just plastic painted silver. . . ."

"That's fantastic. So you're not missing home?"

"A bit. But I'm OK."

"Sure?"

"Yeah. The Cake twins are being bullies as usual."

"The Cake twins? Who are they when they're at home?"

"Hugo and Orlando. They're in the year above me. They're just idiots. They keep starting fights and calling this girl Flora fat. She is a bit fat, but they didn't need to make fun of her and make her cry. Mrs. Gilbert says Flora's just got glands and she made them apologize and they had to miss canoeing."

"Messrs. Cake sound like delightful young men. If they start picking on you, promise you'll tell me."

"They never do at school. I always keep out of their way. . . . So, the best thing about being here is that nobody makes you have a bath. The boys are having a competition to see who smells the most by the end of the week."

"Great stuff. I look forward to smelling you when you get back."

"Yeah, I'm going to be really stinky."

"Let's hope so. Well, I'm glad you're enjoying yourself."

"I really am. So, Grandma, would you be upset if I stopped calling? It doesn't mean I don't miss you."

"Good Lord, of course not. I'll leave it up to you. Call if you need me. Otherwise I'll see you on Friday."

"So he's having a good time?" Mum says.

"He's having a great time. So if you don't mind, there will be no more doom-mongering."

"I don't doom-monger. I am on the lookout for pitfalls, that's all."

"Well, I'd prefer it if you could stop being on the lookout. Just for a few days. Please?"

While the onions sizzle, my mother washes the liver and slices off the odd gall bladder.

Mike arrives with posh chocs for me and flowers for Mum. She coos and clucks over them, says yellow roses are her favorite (I happen to know she prefers pink) and asks if he would possibly mind helping her in the kitchen. Ginny has already offered to help but was politely turned down.

"Mum, don't ask Mike. He's a guest. I can help."

"Oh, he doesn't mind, do you, Mike? Judy — you stay and talk to Ginny. Why don't you open that lovely prosecco she brought? Pour me a glass while you're at it." She bundles him away.

"Only too happy to oblige," Mike says, turning to grin at me and mouth, "She loves me."

"Do you think she's going to ask him what his intentions are?" Ginny says.

"I wouldn't put it past her."

We both do our best to eavesdrop. But Mum has closed the door. While Ginny pours the wine, I excuse myself and go upstairs and check on Rosie.

She appears to have fallen asleep in the middle of one of her unboxing games. An object I can't identify is wrapped in several layers of loo paper held together with bits of Scotch tape. I put it on the nightstand. Then I pull up the duvet and kiss her newly washed hair. Heaven only knows what her brother's smells like by now.

On the way down I hear Mum speaking

to Mike: "You know, if anybody deserves some sugar in her bowl, Judy does. Please don't hurt her."

"I would never, ever do that. You have my word."

Back in the living room, I tell Ginny what I overheard.

"You are so very loved," she says, handing me a glass of prosecco. "You know that, don't you?"

"I do. I'm a very lucky girl."

When it comes to offal, Ginny is a zealot. Kidneys, heart, sweetbreads; she does it all. "You can't call yourself a meat eater," she said when I asked her if she "did" liver, "and then wimp out when somebody sticks a slice of brain in front of you." She demolishes Mum's starter. Mike does the same, but it's an act of supreme valor, since I know he struggles with liver. When Mum offers him seconds he manages to decline while praising her culinary skills to the skies. Mum kvells.

"The secret's in the onions," she says. "They make it sweet. You need to fry them very slowly until they caramelize."

Mike and Ginny are also full of admiration for her stuffed neck.

"Onions and chicken fat."

But the star is her roast chicken, which is as moist and succulent as ever. "Everybody overcooks chicken because they're scared of salmonella. But it's all about timing. There's a sweet spot when it's just done and still juicy. I've spent years perfecting it. And of course I stick a lemon in the cavity. And . . . an onion."

Then she tells the story about how when onions were rationed during the war, Mrs. Lewin, who took her in after she arrived in London, would make them last by refrying them. "It wasn't until the end of the week that we actually got to eat them. Of course by then, they were done to a crisp. On a Friday night, everybody got a pile of burned onion on their plate. People today — they don't know they're born."

"I'll drink to that," Ginny says, raising her glass.

Mike asks Ginny how her mother's doing.

"She's on medication. For the time being, she's not too bad. . . ." She pauses and says that perhaps she shouldn't say any more over dinner because it will spoil the atmosphere. I tell her she won't be spoiling anything. "Come on. What's happened?"

She puts down her glass. "OK . . . I had a meeting with her doctor this afternoon. He confirmed what I suspected, that she doesn't have much time left. Her heart is weak. The arteries are blocked. But there's no question of surgery. She wouldn't survive. When I asked him how long she might have, he wouldn't commit himself. But he didn't contradict me when I suggested it was months rather than years."

I ask if this means she's made up her mind about moving in with Edith. "I'm still torn. Part of me says I should move in. But she's such a difficult, vinegary old woman. I am still very angry with her. . . ."

"Of course you are," Mum says. "She threw you out of the house. You have every right to be angry. If you want my advice, move in and let her see that you're angry. Where is it written you have to be all sweetness and light?"

"But she's dying," Ginny and I say, practically in unison.

"It doesn't matter," Mum says, jabbing her knife in front of her. "Honesty is what matters. Just because she can't face what she did to you and wants to sweep it under the carpet, it doesn't mean you have to. Keep confronting her. It doesn't have to be in a hostile way. Believe me, it's the only way you stand a chance of a proper reconciliation — one that really means something. She's banking on you feeling sorry for her and that you will walk on eggshells around her. Don't do it."

"It all sounds a bit hard-hearted," Mike says.

Ginny says she's not sure she's got the stomach for it.

"It is hard-hearted and you will need to be strong, but I've seen it work."

I look a question at my mother.

"Estelle," she says.

Of course.

She explains that Estelle Silverfish and her older brother were raised by their impoverished widowed mother. "They didn't have a pot to piss in — if you'll excuse my French. Anyway, all her life poor Estelle played second fiddle to the brother. As far as her mother was concerned, the boy could do no wrong. What money she had, she spent on him. The sun shone out of his backside. Meanwhile Estelle was virtually ignored. So, when her mother was dying, Estelle confronted her. She demanded to know why she had loved her brother more. At first the old lady denied she had a favorite. She told Estelle she was imagining it. But Estelle refused to back down. She kept on at her mother, insisting on an explanation. Finally, a few weeks before her mother died, she got what she'd been waiting for. It turned out that she thought a boy was more likely to be successful in life than a girl. Bear in mind that this woman was dirt-poor and feared for her old age. She thought her son, not her daughter, was the one who would be in a better financial position to look after her when the time came. The irony was that the son died in a car crash in the eighties, and it was Estelle who looked after her mother when she got old. But the point I'm trying to make is that with honesty came forgiveness. Estelle says those last weeks with her mother were the happiest of her life. But peace only broke out because Estelle forced the issue."

"Goodness," Ginny says. "Well, that's certainly food for thought."

"Right . . . speaking of food," I say, eager to lift the mood. "Who's for dessert? Mum made cheesecake."

Mum is serving seconds of her cheesecake ("you have to use curd cheese. Philadelphia won't do") when my mobile starts ringing on the coffee table. I want to ignore it, but Mum says it could be Sam. I assure her he's fine and that it won't be him, but she insists that something might have happened. "Quick, answer it."

"Seb's on the same trip," Mike says. "I thought they weren't allowed to call home."

As I head over to the coffee table, I explain about Sam's special dispensation.

"You're being too slow," Mum says. "He'll ring off."

I grab the phone. It is Sam. I nod at my mother.

"What did I tell you? Is he all right?"

"Hello, darling. You're calling late. Everything OK?"

"Grandma, you have to believe me: I didn't do what they're saying I did. They're all lying. . . ."

"Whoa, Sam. Hold on. Just take a breath and calm down. . . ."

"Something's happened. What did I say? Nobody listens to me. What is it? Is he in hospital?"

"Mum, be quiet." I lower myself onto the sofa. "OK, start again and tell me slowly what's been going on."

He's close to tears, spewing out facts in no particular order. I keep having to stop him and make him repeat himself. But from what I can gather, Sam has been accused of stealing.

Ben Wilkinson, who is in Sam's class and in a dorm a few doors from Sam's, has had his iPad stolen (somehow he managed to sneak it past Mrs. Gilbert's gimlet eye). It appears that Sam was seen sneaking out of

Ben's room after lunch. Then, this evening, before bed, one of Sam's roommates was sitting on Sam's bunk and found the iPad under the duvet. "But I didn't steal it. I didn't. You have to believe me."

"Of course I believe you. Somebody's out to cause mischief. Do you know the name of the person who says he saw you sneaking out of Ben's room?"

"Seb. He says I was holding it. But he's lying. He's lying."

"Seb saw you?"

"Yes. He thought I was just borrowing it. That's why he didn't tell any of the teachers."

I look across the room at Mike, who's starting to look troubled. "What is it? What's going on?"

I hold my palm out at him.

I ask Sam where he is and where the teachers are. He's in the office, on the landline he used to call home. The teachers are having dinner. "Let me speak to Mrs. Gilbert."

"But she wasn't going to call you until tomorrow."

"I don't care. I'd like to speak to her now. Please go and fetch her."

He tells me to hang on.

"So?" my mother says.

"Sam's been accused of stealing an iPad."

"What? Oh, for heaven's sake, that's ridiculous. Don't worry. It'll turn out to be something of nothing — just kids getting up to mischief. It'll sort itself out. You'll see." She gets up and begins gathering and scraping plates. Ginny says she'll start loading pots into the dishwasher.

Meanwhile Mike is asking me how Seb was involved in all this.

"Apparently he saw Sam come out of this kid's room, carrying his iPad. At the time he thought Sam was borrowing it."

Mrs. Gilbert is on the line. I am determined not to get het up. I agree with my mother. There has to be some mistake.

"Sam isn't a thief. I've never known him to steal anything. Are you sure there hasn't been a mistake?"

"Sebastian is adamant that he saw Sam walking away from Ben's dorm with the iPad."

"I'm finding this so hard to understand. There has to be more to it. Sam doesn't lie, and I'm sure Sebastian doesn't."

By now Mike is hovering in front of me, asking if he should speak to her.

I shush him and shake my head.

"OK," he says, "but at least put your phone on speaker."

427

I hit the speaker icon.

"Mrs. Devlin — has Sam told you about his sister's Star of David necklace?"

"The Star of David? What about it?"

"When Sam arrived, he was wearing it. He said it was for good luck. I made him take it off in case he lost it. But he's been showing it to all his friends. . . . Apparently it's very old and has an interesting history. From what I gather he's made no secret of the fact that he stole it from his sister."

"Sam stole Rosie's Star of David necklace? But he knows how precious it is to her. Why would he do that?"

"Like I say, he's been using it as a good-luck charm. And in case you're worried, I've made sure he's put it away and that it's safe." She pauses. "Mrs. Devlin, please don't take this the wrong way. . . ."

"I'll do my best."

"The thing is . . . Sam is under a lot of stress just now. His parents have been away a long time. He's got this big chess tournament coming up. If we look back at his recent behavior . . . first there was the gun incident. Then you caught him setting off fireworks. And now this. I am inclined to agree with Dr. Connell. I think Sam is unhappy and crying out for attention."

"Do you?"

"I do."

"Well, please don't take this the wrong way, but that's bollocks."

"Look, I know there isn't any love lost between you and Sebastian's mother and that this is hard to come to terms with. But I do think you should keep an open mind."

I am fighting to stay calm. "Sam is not a thief."

"But he admits stealing from his sister. He's been bragging about it."

"That's different. He would never steal from anybody else."

"You can't be sure of that."

"Yes, I can."

"I think that under the circumstances it would be best if you came and collected Sam. And you should let his parents know that the school takes stealing very seriously. There will be a meeting with Mrs. S.J. We might well decide to suspend him for a while."

"That's absurd. How can you suspend him on the word of one child? Suppose Seb has accused Sam because he has an ax to grind."

"Sebastian has no ax to grind. Even though they're in different years, the boys are friends. The poor lad was sobbing when he told me about Sam stealing the iPad.

And afterward he actually threw up. That's how upset and traumatized he is. It's taken us longer to calm him down than Sam."

"You still can't be sure you've got the full story. What if somebody put Seb up to it?"

"I asked him that. Nobody put him up to it. And what reason would he have to hurt his friend? All the evidence points to Sam being the guilty party. I really do think you should come and get him."

"Fine, I'll be there in the morning. But I will not have Sam found guilty and sentenced by some ridiculous kangaroo court. You haven't heard the end of this."

I put down the phone and sit shaking my head, insisting to Mike that there has to be some explanation.

"Of course there is. They're both good kids. Your mum's right. It'll sort itself out. Just give it a few days."

CHAPTER EIGHTEEN

Sam dozes — head lolling on his shoulder — most of the way back to London. He didn't sleep much last night and he's white and puffy-eyed with upset and exhaustion. He's also pretty grubby, but that's the least of his — or my — worries.

He wakes up just as we're coming off the motorway.

"Are we nearly home?" he says, rubbing his neck, which has gone stiff from all the lolling.

"Not far now. Hungry?"

"Bit. We couldn't stop for McDonald's, could we? I haven't eaten anything since yesterday. I've been too upset."

We each demolish a Big Mac and large fries. Sam has Coke. I have black coffee. I've been up since six, and I need more caffeine than a Coke can offer.

"As soon as we get home, it's a bath and bed for you. We'll talk later."

He dips a couple of fries into a puddle of ketchup. "No, I want to talk now. You have to believe me. I didn't steal Ben's iPad. I swear it."

"Maybe not. But you stole Rosie's Star of David. That was a wicked thing to do."

"Does she know?"

"Not yet. She thinks it's still in her drawer."

"Does she have to find out? I could put it back. She would never know I took it. That way she won't hate me. You can still punish me."

"And punish you I will, don't you worry. But why did you do it?"

"I was jealous."

"Of Rosie? Why?"

"Because Nana Frieda gave her a precious thing and not me. And also because I was worried about going on the trip and I wanted something to bring me good luck. Rosie said the star was for good luck."

Thinking about it, I guess it would have been more even-handed if Mum had found something to give Sam as well. But that didn't give him an excuse to steal.

"Nana gave the star to Rosie to help her. She didn't do it to upset you. Remember how frightened Rosie was when she thought there were Hitlers under her bed? Nana adores you, Sam. You know that. She didn't set out to exclude you."

"I know. I just thought that having the star might make me less homesick."

"That's still no excuse. You know what upsets me even more? The fact that you were bragging to your friends about stealing it. Where did you get the idea that stealing is cool?"

He shrugs like a truculent teenager. "Dunno."

"So, were your mates impressed?"

"Not really."

"That's because they've got more sense."

"Fine. Perhaps they have. But I didn't steal the iPad. Seb is lying. I don't know why he is, but he is. We're meant to be friends. After I let him fly my kite that time on the Heath, he said that even though he was in the year above me, we could be friends. Now he's done this." Sam's eyes are watering up. "I hate him and I want to kill him." There's real fury and venom in his voice. I watch him as he rubs his eyes with the heel of his palm. This child isn't lying.

"It's all right, my darling. I believe you. We'll get to the bottom of it. Don't worry."

It's me, not Sam, who sneaks into Rosie's

room and puts the Star of David back in her drawer. She will never be any the wiser. I know I've done the wrong thing. Sam doesn't deserve to be protected from his sister's wrath. He needs to understand that actions have consequences. But just now Sam's got more important things to worry about and I'd rather we focused on them. Meanwhile I confiscated his computer and his chess set. He wasn't bothered about losing the computer. The chess set was another matter. "You can't take it away. I need to practice for the tournament."

I told him he should have thought about that before stealing from his sister.

Of course Mum thinks it's all her fault that Sam stole the Star of David. "I should have given him something. It was so stupid of me. How could I leave him out like that? He must have felt I didn't love him. But at the time, I was so worried about Rosie."

"That's what I told him. Stop feeling guilty. He knows you love him."

But she can't help feeling that she did a bad thing and she's overcompensating by giving Sam extra hugs, pinching his cheek so that he cries out and telling him not to worry and that we are going to sort this iPad thing out. "We're David and the school's Goliath," she says. "And we're going to win

— just like Erin Brockovich."

"Who's he?" asks Sam.

"Your grandmother will explain."

Mum has been asking me if I'm going to tell Abby and Tom what's happened. She insists they have a right to know. Of course they do. But I don't want to worry them unnecessarily. I want to wait a few days until I know a bit more. I have a plan. I'm going to speak to Seb. Since Claudia would never agree to me speaking to him, I'm going to ask Mike if he can arrange it. Mum says he'll never go for it because his first loyalty is to Claudia. But I think that if I suggest we speak to Seb together, he might.

I haven't spoken to Tanya in a while, so I call her first to tell her what's been happening and to ask what she thinks of my plan. She's all for it. She even offers to seek Seb out in the playground next week and interrogate him herself. She thinks it would look less obvious and it wouldn't involve Mike. I thank her, but I don't want to go behind Mike's back.

"Judy, I'm so sorry this has happened. It's crap. You don't deserve it. More to the point, Sam doesn't deserve it. He's a good kid."

"He is. But so is Seb and that's the problem."

"I wouldn't be so sure. Seb could well have problems. Claudia sets herself up as the perfect mother. But you never know what goes on behind closed doors."

"I agree. You don't. On the other hand, Seb and Hero seem like lovely kids."

When I call Ginny, she's also in favor of speaking to Seb. But being Ginny, she can't resist saying what's on her mind.

"Judy, please don't take this the wrong way, but have you considered the possibility that Sam did steal the iPad? Kids do bad stuff. It doesn't mean they will become bad people."

"I know. But he swears he didn't do it."

"I'm sure he does. He's your grandson and of course you believe him. All I'm saying is keep your wits about you. Sam might not be innocent. And another thing . . . don't let your loathing for Claudia cloud your judgment."

"I'm not."

"You sure?"

"Positive."

I'm still on the phone to Ginny when the doorbell rings. Mum goes to answer it.

I can hear a woman's voice. "Hello. I'm Sebastian's mother. Is Judy home?"

436

"My God. Talk of the devil. You'll never believe who's at the door."

"Claudia? You're kidding. What on earth can she want? I mean, it's not as if it's Sam who's accused Seb of stealing."

"Well, it looks like I'm about to find out. I'll let you know."

"OK. Good luck. And whatever she says, keep calm."

"I'll do my best."

Mum comes back into the kitchen, wide-eyed and whispering, "It's her. Seb's mum. She wants to see you. I've shown her into the living room. She doesn't look too pleased. I'll be here if you need me."

"Where are the kids?"

"In their rooms."

"OK — whatever you do, don't let them come downstairs. This could turn ugly."

Claudia is standing in the middle of the room, dominating it with her height. She's wearing a gray cashmere poncho. On me it would look comical. On her it looks chic and elegant.

"We need to talk," she says by way of greeting.

"What about?" I direct her to an armchair and sit myself on the sofa opposite. The arrangement couldn't be more confrontational.

"You know what I want to talk about."

"I'm assuming it's about Sam and Seb. . . ."

"That's the second topic on my agenda. Let's start with my father."

"Your father?" It sounds daft, but with everything that's going on, it hasn't occurred to me that she's here to talk about my relationship with Mike.

"You're sleeping with him."

"I wouldn't put it quite so crudely. Other activities are involved."

"You seduced my father to get back at me."

"Oh, for heaven's sake . . . I did nothing of the sort. And there's no way your father told you that."

"He didn't need to. It's obvious. You offered yourself as bait and then just reeled him in."

"And I did this to make you jealous. To get my revenge. Seriously?" I hear myself laughing.

"You'll be laughing out the other side of your face when you find out the truth. The fact is he's using you just like you're using him. He only wants you for sex. Don't think for a minute that he sees anything else in you."

"And he told you that?"

"No. But why else would he be interested in you?"

I want to slap her. "I think you had better leave."

"I'm going nowhere." She folds her arms. Dr. Connell, therapist and bestselling author, has morphed into a petulant, jealous child.

"Fine. So let me ask you a question. How did you find out about your father and me?"

"It's none of your damn business."

"So let me guess. . . . You were discussing your son and my grandson and the issue of the stolen iPad and your father accidentally gave the game away. Am I right?"

She doesn't say anything.

"I'll take that as a yes."

"And while we're talking about Sam," she says, unfolding her arms, "you need to know once and for all that he is an angry little boy, desperate for attention. I was afraid he might end up doing something like this. And now he has. Seb is not lying. Sam is. And you and I both know that none of this would have happened if you'd taken notice of his cries for help."

"OK — I think we're done here. . . ." I'm already on my feet.

"Stay away from my father," Claudia says, getting up. "Stop using him as a pawn in your pathetic battle with me. I'm warning you: it's a battle you will never win."

"Oh, get a grip, you stupid woman. You sound like you've stepped out of a Jackie Collins novel. Your father isn't a pawn. He's a highly intelligent man who is perfectly capable of making his own decisions."

"You can't bear it, can you," she says, "that I've been proved right about Sam?"

"You need to go." I'm aware that my hand has formed a tight fist.

"I'm going. I've said what I came to say."

I have three missed calls and a couple of texts on my phone. They're all from Mike. The first text reads: Claudia knows about us. On warpath. Call me.

I call. "You're too late. She just paid me a visit. It wasn't pleasant."

He asks me if I'm OK.

"I wasn't. But Mum sat me down and made me a cup of sweet tea. I'm better now."

"Christ, I've made such a mess of everything. I called round to discuss this whole Sam and Seb situation and I let the cat out of the bag. She didn't take it well."

"You think?"

He invites me over to his place for dinner. "Let's discuss everything over a bottle of wine and a pizza."

Mum says I should ignore Claudia. "She thought she had her father to herself, and now her nose has been put out of joint. She's probably like this with all her father's girlfriends. She'll come round."

"I doubt it."

"Well, if she doesn't, it's her loss."

"What makes you think that Mike would choose me over her? She's his daughter."

"She's also crazy."

"Makes no difference. When it comes to it, she's his blood. I'm not."

I don't leave until the children are asleep. Mum was anxious for me to get them down because Estelle is coming over. She's bringing strudel ("Of course it's not a patch on mine"). The plan is to sit, drink coffee, force down Estelle's second-rate strudel and go window-shopping for possible suitors for my mother.

But come bedtime, both kids played up. Sam said he was too upset to sleep. Rosie — who has come out in sympathy for her brother — said the same. Earlier, when Sam told her why he had been sent home early from the Dorset trip, she set sibling rivalry aside and sprang to his defense. "Sometimes I don't like you because you hit me or you make fun of me, but I know you would

441

never steal. Only bad people steal, and you're not a bad person. You should beat Seb up for being a big fat liar."

Sam couldn't bring himself to look his sister in the eye.

"I should tell her the truth," he whispered when I finally got him to bed.

"OK, but not now. I'm not sure you could handle Rosie being angry with you as well. Leave it until all this other stuff has blown over."

When I arrive at Mike's, he hands me a glass of wine and tells me again that he's sorry. "I should have told her weeks ago. You were right. I was burying my head in the sand. I fucked up."

"I agree that it wasn't ideal, but to be honest, I'm not sure she would have reacted differently however you handled it. We always said it wasn't going to be easy."

"So you're not angry?"

"Not with you. But you should know that Claudia accused me of using you as a pawn in my battle with her. She also said that you only wanted me for sex and warned me to keep away from you."

"She really said that?" His lips are tight with fury. "Right, where's my phone? I'm not having this."

I grab his arm and beg him not to confront

her until he's calmed down. "You'll end up yelling, and it won't achieve anything."

"But how dare she march into your house and say those things to you? It's outrageous."

"It is. But I coped. No real harm was done. You should have a night's sleep and call her tomorrow. Better still, go and see her."

Mike starts pacing. "She's only behaving like this because you stood up to her. She feels threatened by anybody she can't dominate, and it's about bloody time she got over it."

We eat our pizza without much enthusiasm. Neither of us is very hungry. We manage a couple of slices each and then we're done. Afterward we sit on the sofa finishing the wine.

"So, how's Sam doing?"

"Not great." Because I'm tired and a bit drunk, what I say next leaves my mouth uncensored by my brain. "He simply can't understand why Seb lied. He thought they were friends."

"So you're calling Seb a liar?"

"I don't think he makes a habit of lying. But I think he's lying now and we need to find out why."

Mike puts his wineglass down on the coffee table and moves down the sofa. In a second, the intimacy between us is gone. The atmosphere has become confrontational.

He says he thinks we need to get one thing straight. "I am the first to admit that my daughter has her issues. But she's a good mother. And Laurence is a great dad."

"I'm not accusing her or Laurence. Good parents have children who lie."

"I agree. So Abby and Tom could have a child who is lying."

"Sam isn't lying."

"Neither is Seb. Claudia has spoken to him. . . ."

"I don't doubt it. And of course she's going to defend him. She's defending her reputation. Who's going to take advice from a child expert whose kid lies and accuses an innocent boy of theft?"

"This isn't about Claudia's reputation. It's about Seb. I've spoken to him, too. We had a brief chat on the phone, and I can tell you that he's distraught about telling on Sam — so much so that he's been throwing up. But he felt it was the honest thing to do. This isn't a child who's lying."

"Let me speak to him. Let me see what I can find out."

"No. I'm not having you interrogating him."

"I don't want to interrogate him. I just want to ask him a few questions."

"Fine," Mike says. "Then you have to let me ask Sam a few questions."

"Why are you being like this? Sam is the victim here, not Seb. All I'm doing is defending my grandson."

"No, you're not. You're being obstinate and pigheaded. Despite everything, Claudia happens to be a damn good shrink, and to be frank, she makes a perfectly good case for Sam having problems. He stole his sister's necklace. The boy has demonstrated he is capable of theft. I think you're in denial."

This echoes what Ginny was saying. But it feels a hundred times worse coming from Mike. I feel betrayed. "Where has this come from? Whenever we've discussed Sam's bad behavior, you've always agreed with me that it's been about him being stressed from too many after-school activities. And the thing with the fireworks wasn't his fault."

"Well, I've changed my mind. I'm not saying Sam's a bad kid. He isn't. But his parents have been away for God knows how long and he's probably pissed off. And who could blame him? To be honest I don't think

445

Sam is the only one with the problem. You have a problem, too, because you refuse to see what's going on."

"Your daughter really does have you wrapped around her little finger, doesn't she?"

"That's not true and you know it. But I will support her if I think she's right. And she happens to be right about this."

"Bollocks she is."

I'm on my feet, gathering up my bag and coat.

"Where are you going?"

"Home. Claudia wanted me to stay away from you, and after this outburst, I don't think that's going to be a problem."

"Don't be so ridiculous. Can't we have a simple disagreement? This is about kids."

"No, it's not. It's about your relationship with your spoiled, arrogant daughter."

"How can you say that when five minutes ago I wanted to read her the riot act for the way she treated you?"

"Yes, but when the chips are down, when it really matters, you will always choose her over me."

"I haven't chosen her, you daft woman. I've agreed with her. Are you saying I'm not allowed to agree with my own daughter, who happens to have a doctorate in child psychology?"

"What you've done is side with a jealous crazy woman, who by your own admission feels threatened by me. You can call it agreeing. I call it choosing. Now I'm leaving."

When I get home, it's gone ten. The lights are out, which means Mum is in bed. I'm grateful. I can't face having to tell her why my eyes are puffy and my face is streaked in mascara.

As I reach the landing, I hear voices coming from Rosie's room.

"It's OK, Sam. I get why you did it. You wanted the star for luck because you were feeling scared, just like I was scared of the Hitlers. But if you'd asked, I would have let you borrow it."

"Grandma and Nana wouldn't have. They'd have been scared about me losing it. So you're not angry with me?"

"A teensy bit maybe."

"I can give you compensation."

"What's that?"

"It's when a person hurts another person and they pay them money to say sorry."

"I don't want money."

"What, then?"

"I want four Kinder Eggs."

"Three."

447

"No. Three wouldn't feel like a proper sorry. I want four."

"And then you won't be angry anymore?"

"Correct."

"OK. It's a deal. Right, I'm going back to bed. Grandma will be cross if she finds us up this late."

Grandma, who just about managed to stop blubbing by the time she got home, has started all over again.

Chapter Nineteen

Mike calls first thing. "Look, this is ridiculous. We both said things we didn't mean. . . ."

"So you've changed your mind. You think Claudia's wrong about Sam. You don't think I'm part of the problem. . . ."

"It's not as simple as that."

"Yes, it is. If you haven't changed your mind, there's no point in us talking."

"Of course there is. It's daft, us falling out over our grandchildren."

"Mike, I told you last night. This isn't a simple falling-out over grandchildren. It goes deeper than that and you know it."

"But I don't want to lose you. I love you. The other evening I promised your mother I would never hurt you, and now I have and I don't know how to put it right."

I want to feel sorry for him, but I'm still too angry and upset. "I'm afraid I can't help you with that. I've got too much on my plate just now. I need to get to the bottom of this thing. . . ."

"I can't help thinking you're obsessing. Hasn't the time come to accept that Sam stole the iPad?"

And I lose it. "No, it bloody hasn't! Sam did not steal the iPad. Now, go away and leave me to help my grandson." With that, I cut him off.

Mum can't believe how she misjudged Mike. She says all the irritation has made her IBS worse. She decides to clean the oven.

While Mum gets busy with Mr. Muscle, I arrange to meet Ginny and Tanya in the coffee shop around the corner from school.

When I arrive they're already there, drinking lattes and talking about Edith.

"Well, I think you're being very brave," Tanya's saying to Ginny.

I pull out a chair. "So you've decided to move in?"

"Yep, and Emma's coming, too. She said she'll do anything to get the boys into a decent school — even if it means living with an old woman she's never met and is supposed to hate, in that horrible old house. She's already made an appointment to see the head."

"You really don't hang about in your family."

"What's the point? It all makes logical sense."

Tanya raises her coffee cup. "Well, here's to it all working out. Good luck to all of you."

"We're going to need it. I can't help thinking we've bitten off a great deal more than we can chew. But as Emma says, it won't be forever."

"You'll be fine," I say, patting Ginny's hand.

"Just keep telling me," she says.

I get myself a cappuccino and treat us all to chocolate brioche. "I don't want to comfort-eat alone."

"And why are we comfort-eating?" Ginny says.

I bring them up to speed.

"He's an idiot," Tanya says. "Siding with bloody Claudia over you."

Ginny puts down her cup. "At the risk of making myself unpopular, I think Mike may have a point."

"What point?" Tanya shoots back. "Claudia is an evil bitch. He has no point. I can't believe you're saying that."

"I told Judy and I'm telling you . . . don't let your hatred of Claudia cloud your judgment about all this." Ginny looks at me. "Judy, you are my friend. You've taken care of me while my mother's been in hospital, and I don't know what I would have done without you. I would do anything for you. But can you really be sure that Sam didn't steal this boy's iPad? Surely it's a case of Occam's razor: the obvious answer is usually the right one."

"What can I say? I know my grandson."

"We think we know people. But the uncomfortable truth is that sometimes we don't. You have to at least consider the possibility that Sam did this."

I explain how I overheard Sam confessing to Rosie about stealing her Star of David. "If that's not an honest kid, I don't know what is."

"I agree that it would seem that way. But even so, you can't be a hundred percent certain he didn't do it. If there's any doubt at all in your mind . . ."

"There isn't."

Tanya lets out a long breath. "Judy, you know I'm totally on your side . . ."

"Oh God . . . I sense there's a 'but' coming."

"Not exactly. All I'm saying is that maybe Ginny's got a point. Perhaps you should press Sam a bit harder."

I feel browbeaten and weary, like the whole world has turned against me.

I get home to find a voice mail message from Mrs. S.J. It's a courtesy call to let me know that on Monday — during lunch break — she intends to question Sam and Seb about the theft. She thinks it would be appropriate if Claudia and I attended the meeting. Mrs. Gilbert will not be there, since she has already spoken to the boys and formed an opinion.

Sam says there's no way Mrs. S.J. is going to believe him. "Mrs. Gilbert didn't, so why should she? I hate Mrs. Gilbert and I hate the school. I want to leave."

Rosie says that if Sam wants to go to another school, that's fine, but she wants to stay because Cybil is her best friend and she doesn't want to leave her. I tell them that nobody is going anywhere, and we have to wait and see what happens on Monday.

Sam spends the weekend lolling in front of the TV or in his room playing chess. After his confession to Rosie, I felt I should return his chess set. Mum keeps telling him he needs to go out and get some fresh air. She suggests a walk on the Heath. But he's not interested, and I decide not to push it.

On Sunday night, while he's getting ready for bed, he breaks down and throws a pair of trainers at the bedroom door. "I hate Seb. I hate him. When I see him tomorrow, I'm going to punch him." He sits on the bed head down, arms folded, dragging his foot back and forth across the carpet.

"You will do no such thing. I know this is hard, but there is to be no lashing out. You will keep calm and answer Mrs. S.J.'s questions truthfully. Do you understand?"

He doesn't say anything. Instead he kicks a book across the floor.

"I said, do you understand?"

"S'pose."

I sit next to him and put an arm around him. "It feels dreadful when people don't believe you. It's one of the worst feelings in the world. And tomorrow won't be easy. It's probably the hardest thing you've ever had to do, but I will be with you. Never forget that I love you. We all love you."

Then he hugs me. "I love you, too, Grandma."

I meet Sam as he is coming out of the school dining hall. "Did you eat?"

He shakes his head. "Not much. I'm too nervous."

"I know, sweetheart. It'll be over soon. But try to remember what I said. No matter what happens, there is to be no punching."

"What if I can't help it?"

"You have to help it. If you lash out at Seb, it will make you look like a thug."

"No, it won't. It'll make me look angry and innocent."

I do my best to explain that's not how it works.

We're the first to arrive. Mrs. S.J. is polite but cool and directs us to a row of chairs arranged in front of her desk. We make pleasantries — agree that the weather is much improved. She asks if I would like her to open the window. A cup of tea maybe? I decline both offers.

There's a knock on the door. Seb comes into the room first, looking pretty sheepish. Claudia is behind him, all smiles and ostentatious greeting for Mrs. S.J. "A little bird told me that you didn't get your signed copy of my book. I can only apologize. I can't think what happened." She places a hardback copy of *How to Parent* on Mrs. S.J.'s desk.

I'm thinking all is lost and await Mrs. S.J.'s simpering genuflection. But to my surprise it doesn't come. Mrs. S.J. barely breaks a smile. "Thank you, Dr. Connell. That's very kind of you. Now, if you and Seb would like to take a seat . . ."

"Yes . . . of course." The ebullience has

vanished. Mrs. S.J.'s reserve has thrown Claudia off balance. I'm aware that Sam may not come out of this meeting the victor, but he will get a fair hearing.

Claudia and I exchange the briefest of glances. The boys don't make eye contact.

"I hope you don't mind," Claudia says to Mrs. S.J., "but my husband is away, and so I've brought my father along for moral support. He'll be here any moment. He's just popped to the loo."

"Of course. He's most welcome."

Claudia looks at me, her face full of smug, infantile satisfaction. The message is clear. She is the one with the power. She controls her father, not me. He loves her the best. So there. If she had a pigtail, she would flick it.

In walks Mike, full of apologies for being late. The man who swore he would never hurt me has just declared war. I sense him glancing in my direction. If he's looking for forgiveness, he can forget it. I stare straight ahead and take Sam's hand. I am unaware that I am gripping it so hard until he pulls away with a grimace and starts rubbing it.

Mrs. S.J. fetches an extra chair for Mike. "Right, I know this is difficult for everybody, but what I would like to do is hear from each of the boys without any interruption from the adults. . . . Sebastian, if you would start."

He shrugs and says there isn't much to tell. "It was lunchtime. I'd gone upstairs to get a sweater, and I saw Sam coming out of Ben's room with the iPad. That's all." I am aware that he's looking down, refusing to make eye contact with Mrs. S.J.

"Sebastian . . . look at me. Are you sure there's nothing else you'd like to say?"

He looks up. "I'm sure."

"He's lying," Sam yells. "He's lying. He won't even look at her. That proves he's lying."

"Sam, please," I whisper-shout. "What did I tell you?"

Mrs. S.J. suggests Sam take a breath and tell his side of the story.

"I wasn't even upstairs when Seb says I was. I was in the toilet. I'd finished lunch, and I had spaghetti sauce down my T-shirt. I went to clean it off."

"Did you ask permission to leave the table?"

"No."

"Did anybody see you leave?"

"I don't think so."

"Was there anybody else in the loo?"

"No, people were still having lunch."

"I see." She pauses and takes off her

457

glasses. "The thing is, Sam, much as I want to believe you, I have a problem. It's not just Sebastian who saw you. Somebody else did, too."

"Who?" I bark.

It's a boy called Felix. He's in Sam's year, but I've never heard of him.

"Felix was fetching something from his room, just like Sebastian."

I want to know why this Felix has waited until now to say anything.

"Like Sebastian, he didn't want to get Sam into trouble. Apparently he's been fretting ever since it happened."

"Right, I think we're done," Claudia says, picking her bag up from the floor. "Sam stole the iPad. There's nothing else to say."

I catch Mike giving me a beseeching look. All I can do is shake my head at him.

"But I didn't. I didn't. Seb is lying. Everybody's lying."

Claudia, who is already out of her seat, places a hand on Sam's head. "Sweetheart, none of this is your fault. You are unhappy and angry. People do bad things when they're upset. There are special people who can help you —"

"Shut up and take your hand off my grandson!"

She does as I say. "It's not too late to fix

458

this, Judy," she says by way of a parting shot. "Please. I beg you. Just get him the help he needs."

I'm biting my lip in an effort to stop myself from crying.

She and Seb turn to go. Mike hangs back and touches my arm. "I'm so sorry," he says.

I ignore him, stare out of the window and keep biting.

The door closes. Mrs. S.J. steeples her hands. "I'm so sorry, Mrs. Devlin. I know this has been an ordeal, but I do think the evidence is overwhelming."

"But they're lying." Sam is in tears. "I didn't do it."

"Well, I think you did. I think you did a very wicked thing, and what's worse is that you are refusing to take responsibility for it."

Sam's heard enough. "You can expel me if you want. I don't care. . . . Right now I'm going back to my class." He gets up and leaves the room, slamming the door behind him.

"Your grandson is a very willful young man."

"I'm not sure it's willfulness. He just knows he's innocent. Mrs. S.J., has it occurred to you that Sam is being set up?"

"It has. But we're talking about nine- and

459

ten-year-olds. I'm not sure they're capable of being that manipulative. And Sebastian and Felix are good kids."

"So is Sam."

"I agree. And for that reason I won't be asking his parents to remove him from the school. There is, however, one proviso. I must insist that they take Dr. Connell's advice and make an appointment for him with a child psychotherapist. I am in no doubt that Sam has some underlying issues that he needs to work through. I am also aware that he stole his sister's necklace and took it to Dorset with him. We need to understand what's going on."

I see no point in telling her that Sam has apologized to his sister about stealing the Star of David. She won't be interested. "And if his parents refuse to send him to a therapist?"

"In that case, I would have no choice. Sam would have to leave. I can't have pupils stealing. I have other children — not to mention their parents — to think about."

"Fine. I'll let you know what they decide."

"Tell them not to leave it too long."

"But what if Sam did steal the iPad?" I hear myself saying to my mother. "What if I've been wrong all along? Now that this Felix

460

kid has come out of the woodwork to support Seb's story, the evidence is overwhelming."

I'm slumped over the kitchen table — sad, angry and defeated. But mostly I feel doubt. I am the defense lawyer who has reached a cul-de-sac. Having believed in her client and advocated for him with such passion, she has reached a point where she is starting to believe the prosecution has a case. All she can do is recommend that her client accept a plea bargain and do his time.

"How can you say that about your own grandchild? Of course he didn't do it."

"But a second kid saw him."

"He could be lying."

"Why would he lie? It's taken him days to come forward."

"I don't know. Kids lie for all sorts of reasons."

I'm shaking my head. "But Sam stole the Star of David."

"That was different."

"Maybe, but it shows he's capable of stealing."

"Judy, stop it. You mustn't lose faith in him."

"I'm trying not to, but I don't know what to do for the best. . . . Maybe I should speak to him again."

461

"Why?"

"I need to give him one last chance to own up."

"Don't do that. I beg you. He needs you on his side. Who else has he got?"

"I am on his side."

"I'm not sure he'll see it like that."

Sam is on the sofa, staring at the TV. Some high-octane, flashbang cartoon is blaring, but I'm not sure he's taking any of it in. On the way home he told me that today was the worst day of his life. After he went back to his class, some of the kids started calling him a thief. A couple of boys even attacked him during afternoon recess. A teacher had to drag them off. He's come home with bruises on his arms and chest. How can I let him go back to school?

"Darling, I need to speak to you. Can we turn the TV off?"

He hits the remote but doesn't bother looking at me. "Am I in more trouble?"

"Of course not." I make him budge up on the sofa so that I can sit down. "Sam, are you absolutely certain there's nothing you want to tell me?"

"Oh, great. Now you don't believe me. Now the only person I have left on my side is Nana."

"I am on your side. But Felix says he saw

you, too."

His eyes are wide with rage. "Read my lips: I. Did. Not. Take. It."

"Are you sure? Because if you did, it's best you tell me now. We can talk about it. I will understand and so will your mum and dad. Sometimes good people do bad things. It happens all the time, particularly if they're under stress. Is it possible you've been unhappy while Mum and Dad have been away and you haven't felt able to tell me because you don't want to upset me?"

"No."

"No what?"

"No, that isn't possible."

"So why do you think Felix accused you?"

"I don't know. Maybe because Seb said he'd bash him up if he didn't."

"Seb doesn't bash people up. You know that."

"Fine — so you believe him and Felix over me?"

"No . . . I believe you."

"No, you don't. If you believed me you wouldn't be asking me all this stuff about being unhappy. You think I did it." Tears are tumbling down his cheeks.

"I don't. I just want to be sure."

"I'm going upstairs."

"Sam, please don't walk away. Let's talk."

"I don't want to talk. Everybody hates me and thinks I'm a thief."

"Darling, nobody hates you."

"Seb does. The teachers and Mrs. S.J. do. My friends do. And now you do."

He disappears upstairs.

A moment or two later, Mum brings me some tea. "Here, drink this."

I take the cup from her.

"That went well," she says.

Sam refuses to come out of his room for dinner. When I go to his room he's on the bed, lying on his stomach.

"Sam, please. Let's talk."

He throws a pillow at me. "I hate you. Go away. I hate you."

He's not ready to be placated. I leave. Later on, Mum takes him meat loaf on a tray.

"Sam didn't do it," Rosie says as we eat. "I know he didn't. By not believing him, you've upset him."

"I know. But I need to be sure."

"Well, I'm sure — even though he stole my Star of David. But I know that he wouldn't steal from his friends."

"Sweetheart, it's wonderful that you're so loyal, but you can't be sure."

"What's loyal?"

I explain.

"You should be loyal, too. You're his grandma. Grandmas should stick up for grandchildren."

"I am sticking up for him."

"No, you're not."

"I'm doing my best." I'm close to tears.

Mum tells Rosie that's enough and to finish her meat loaf. "It's nearly time for bed."

When I go to check on Sam, he's asleep. He hasn't touched his dinner or changed into his pajamas. I can't see the point in waking him, so I pull up his duvet and kiss him on the forehead. "I'm sorry, darling. I love you so much. Let's talk in the morning."

Only I don't get a chance to talk to him. At seven thirty, when I poke my head around his door to tell him breakfast is ready, his bed is empty. At first I don't panic. I assume he's in the bathroom or one of the other bedrooms. Then I see the note on the nightstand: *It's horrible when nobody beleavs you. I am running away because you all think I am a thief and I'm not and I don't know how to proov it.*

Even though there's no point, I tear round checking the bathrooms and bedrooms. Mum hears me thundering and yelling out Sam's name. She calls up the stairs, demanding to know what's going on.

"Sam's run off."

"What do you mean 'run off'?"

"He's left a note. He's gone."

I charge downstairs, shoving the note into her hand as I pass and run into the street. Nothing. Mum is standing in the doorway, in her lavender fleece dressing gown, reading the note. She slaps her hand to her chest. "My God."

"What have I done? This is all my fault." I'm trembling and crying and I don't know what to do. "I'm going to take the car and look for him."

"No, you're not."

"But I have to. I can't just sit here."

"We don't know when he left. He could be miles away by now."

Mum pulls me back inside and says she's going to call the police.

CHAPTER TWENTY

In less than an hour, the police have helicopters searching the area. There are officers scouring neighbors' gardens, garages and sheds. Others are checking out parks, open spaces and waste ground.

The first question they asked was whether Sam had a reason for running away. I showed them the note, told them the tale of the stolen iPad.

"And then I stopped believing in him."

The two male officers who responded to the 999 call — both fathers — said they understood what I was going through, but I shouldn't blame myself.

I want to know who else I should blame.

A family liaison officer called Lisa is keeping us plied with tea and optimism. She insists that because Sam has run away rather than been abducted, they will find him pretty quickly.

"Sam is young. He isn't streetwise. He'll

soon get tired and hungry and come home with his tail between his legs."

I'm not so sure. He's taken thirty pounds from my purse. That could keep him in Big Macs for days.

"People don't have tails," Rosie says, looking up from her coloring book. She's not worried about Sam running off. She seems to think that he's gone on some great adventure, which will somehow prove his innocence. Her big brother is a hero.

Constable Lisa explains the tail-between-the-legs expression to Rosie. Then she wants to know if Sam said anything to her about his plan to run away.

"Uh-uh." She picks up a purple glitter pen.

"You're absolutely sure?"

"Cross my heart. But Sam will be OK. He's big."

The police want a recent photograph. Sam's latest school portrait is sitting on the bookcase in its cardboard frame. I keep meaning to get a proper one. It's not lost on me that those photographs of missing — usually found murdered — kids you see on TV and in the papers are more often than not school portraits.

They want to know if there's anywhere Sam might have gone — favorite haunts, hangouts. There's nowhere. He's allowed to run the odd errand to the minimart on the corner, but that's as far as he ever ventures alone.

"What if he's had an accident? Or somebody has hurt him? . . . What if some pedophile has got hold of him?"

Constable Lisa says they can't rule anything out.

"I always thought," Mum says, "that the worst thing in my life had already happened. And now this."

"Mum, please. Just for once can we have a crisis in this family without you comparing it to the Holocaust?"

I want to join in the search, but the police won't let me. They would rather I was at home in case Sam comes back. They want a copy of the class contact list.

I can't settle. Instead I pace and tidy magazines and rearrange apples in the fruit bowl. Finally I get round to calling Ginny and Tanya. They both want to come over, but I'm not sure what good it will do and I think I'd rather there weren't too many people around. Tanya suggests it might be better for Rosie if she stayed with her.

"She might be OK now, but all the anxiety and stress are going to get to her. She needs a bit of normality. Rick and I will take the

469

girls out for pizza tonight. They can even have Coke. Rosie will love that."

I agree it might be for the best. Tanya says she'll be over in twenty minutes.

Rosie doesn't want to go. She says it's fun talking to the policemen about how they catch baddies. Plus Cybil's at school and she'll be on her own for the rest of the day.

"She'll be back in a few hours. Then later on Tanya and Rick are going to take you both out for pizza."

That swings it.

Tanya arrives with hugs for Rosie, promises of fun and a chocolate bar that I'm not supposed to see. Once I've checked that Rosie has everything she needs, Tanya goes out to the car and puts Rosie's bag in the trunk. Rosie and I walk a few paces behind. She's holding my hand.

"The police will find Sam, won't they?" she says. The anxiety has finally set in.

"Of course they will, darling. I promise."

" 'K. . . . Did you pack Denise?"

"Like I would forget."

"But I don't want her."

"Why on earth not? You love Denise. You never go to bed without her."

"Cybil doesn't know about her. She'll laugh and think I'm a baby."

"Cybil's your best friend. Of course she

won't laugh."

"She will. And anyway, I've got my Star of David now."

She puts her hand down the neck of her T-shirt and pulls out the necklace. "I don't need Denise anymore. The star will look after me."

I want to say, "Like it looked after Sam," but I don't. "All right, darling. If you're sure, I'll get her out of your bag."

"I am sure."

Tanya is already in the car. I get her to release the trunk lid. Then, while Rosie looks on, I hunt around in Rosie's backpack for Denise. "I think your end has come," I tell the carrot as I take her out of Rosie's toilet bag.

Rosie wants to hold her one last time. "Good-bye, Denise. Sorry, but it's time for you to die. I've got my star now. Hope you don't mind."

With that she shoves the carrot into my jacket pocket. "You can eat her if you want," she says as she climbs into the car. After I've strapped Rosie into the car seat, I move round to say good-bye to Tanya.

"Why would she choose now of all times to give up Denise?" I whisper through the open window.

"Her carrot comforter? Who knows? Kids

are weird." She stretches her arm through the window and takes my hand. "Don't worry about Rosie. Rick and I will take good care of her. Let me know if there's any news."

After I've waved them off, I head back to the house. On the way I drop Denise into the recycling container. I also send up a prayer — to God, to Brian, to all the dead relatives I can think of: "Please let me keep my promise to Rosie."

I decide to text Mike. Ashamed as I am to admit it, I do it because I want him to feel as guilty as I do: Sam ran away last night because nobody believes him. Police searching for him. Still think he did it?

The hands appear to have stopped on the kitchen clock. That's because I'm checking the time every thirty seconds. I need to contact Abby and Tom, but I keep telling myself that Sam will be back any minute. Why worry them?

Mum can't settle either. She's turning out kitchen cupboards and attacking them with Lysol and a scouring pad.

A detective arrives. He looks about nineteen. He wants to know if Sam could have been speaking to strangers online.

"He's nine. He has no interest in social media."

The detective — "Call me Jason" — wants to examine Sam's computer anyway.

"So, are there people who visit the house? For example — does Sam have a tutor?"

"Only Bogdan, his chess coach. He's a bit weird. But I don't think Sam is with him. He doesn't even like him much. Plus he has no idea where he lives." I also tell him about Bernie.

The detective takes both men's contact details. A couple of officers will pay them a visit. Was there anybody else I could think of? There isn't.

Six p.m. It's getting dark. I stand at the living room window, eyes welling up as I imagine Sam alone, lost, cold. Constable Lisa says she'll stay the night in case there are any developments. I take this to mean that she's trained to offer support if the worst happens. Mum insists on making her eggs and chips. It gives her something to do.

By now I've left voice messages and e-mailed Tom and Abby, asking them to call urgently.

Ten o'clock comes and goes. I can't stop shaking. Lisa says it's because I haven't eaten and my blood sugar is low. But I can't face food. Instead I pour myself a large Scotch. I stop shaking, but alcohol on an empty stomach has made me feel sick. When the doorbell rings I run to answer it. "Sam!"

Mike is standing on the doorstep, his face crumpled with anxiety. He sees the disappointment on my face. "Sorry. It's only me. I just saw your text."

"Really? I sent it hours ago." I can't find it in me to be cordial.

"I've been in meetings. I had my phone on silent. So, is there any news?"

"Nothing. I hope you and your daughter are pleased with yourselves. Now go home. I don't want you here."

"But I want to be here."

"Why? Because you're feeling guilty? Because you realized you backed the wrong horse?"

"I didn't back the wrong horse."

"My God, even now with Sam gone, you can't admit you were wrong. What sort of person are you?"

"One who has come to realize that you were right and this situation is probably more complicated than I thought. I'm here because I want to be with you and because I want us both to get to the bottom of this. Please let me help."

He's standing on the doorstep, beseeching

me. I should let him in, forgive him, but I can't.

"I don't want your help. When you turned up at that meeting with Claudia, you made it perfectly clear where your loyalties lay. You sat there while she gloated and patronized me. You made your choice."

"I came to that meeting to support Seb."

"That's not the whole story and you know it. You told me you loved me, but it's meaningless if you're going to turn against me the moment Claudia snaps her fingers. I couldn't be in a relationship with you on those terms."

"It wasn't like that. Claudia doesn't tell me what to do. I've shown you that I am perfectly capable of standing up to her."

"When it suits you, maybe."

"That's not fair." He looks wounded, but I still refuse to take pity on him. "So, when it turned out that this Felix kid had accused Sam as well . . . what was I supposed to think? Be honest, Judy. What did you think?"

And there he has me. But I'm not prepared to confess to my crime — at least not to him.

"Go away, Mike. Just go away."

"You really mean that?"

"I do."

He turns, heads down the garden path and

doesn't look back.

I pour myself some more Scotch. At some stage, I fall asleep. I wake several times in the night. In the black, I'm overcome with fear and guilt. I cry myself back to sleep.

At seven o'clock Mum brings me a cup of tea. "Guess who just called . . . Bernie. He was in such a state. He offered to come and sit with me. I said no. So instead he's in his car driving around the neighborhood, looking for Sam."

"Wow, what a thing to do. I hope you thanked him. You know, I think you've misjudged Bernie."

"You could be right. Meanwhile that Bogdan hasn't even picked up the phone. Can you believe that?"

"He's probably pissed off at being questioned by the police."

"Jerk . . . So, could you manage a slice of toast?"

I shake my head. I still can't face food. I'm more concerned about why Abby and Tom haven't called.

Constable Lisa says the police are trying to find out what the problem is. "They've been onto MediGlobal and apparently there's been another minor quake in Nicaragua. It's nothing serious, but communications are down where Abby and Tom are."

"But I need to get a message to them."

"You will. I promise. They're sorting it out."

We wait. Another day to be measured in teaspoons. I take a shower and force down half a banana. Constable Lisa looks as if she's ready to drop. "Don't you ever go off duty?"

"The other family liaison officer I work with is off sick. I'll stay a few more hours, if that's OK."

"Of course it's OK. Apart from anything else you're wonderful at keeping my mother occupied."

As if on cue, Mum gets out her photograph album. Constable Lisa joins her on the sofa.

"That's me with my mother and father in Berlin, just before the war. I was a pretty little thing — even if I do say so myself."

Just after midday, Constable Lisa has news. Abby and Tom are in Costa Rica. They decided to take a couple of days' break. They're somewhere in the wilds of the rain forest.

"But why didn't they tell me? It's so un-like them."

"Apparently it was a spur-of-the-moment

thing. They're flying back to Nicaragua today."

"I can't face them. They left Sam and Rosie in my safekeeping. They trusted me. Look what I've done."

Constable Lisa says it isn't my fault.

"I doubted him. Whose fault is it?"

I keep on pacing — from the living room to the street — with occasional detours to the loo. Mum tells me to sit down. A watched pot never boils. I go upstairs and put on an extra sweater. I can't get warm. Mum says I need to eat.

"I can't eat. . . . Where is he, Mum? Where is he?"

She wraps me in her arms. "I wish I knew, my darling. I wish I knew."

In the afternoon Bernie calls again to say he's had no luck, but he'll go out again after he's had something to eat. Mum says he must be exhausted and begs him not to. But he insists.

"He's a good man, a mensch," Mum says before she goes upstairs for a snooze. The only other person she has ever referred to as a mensch is my dad.

Constable Lisa suggests I get some air.

"I shouldn't leave the house."

"Go for a walk. It'll do you good. You've

got your mobile. If anything happens I'll call."

So I go. The sun is warm on my face. I take off my coat. A few men are in shorts, showing off winter white legs. I head for the Heath. I feel separate from the world. I am stranded on my island of grief, just like I was when Brian was dying. Anguish is so isolating. I remember popping out to pick up groceries and being reminded that a world existed outside Brian's sickroom. I would watch people going about their business, leading their normal lives, and feel jealous. I judged them. What did they know about suffering, these people who fretted about the deli running out of quince jelly for their manchego?

I change my mind about going to the Heath. Instead I take a detour and head to Edith's house. It occurs to me that she's out of hospital and that Ginny has probably moved in.

Ginny answers the door in yellow rubber gloves. When she sees me, alarm shoots across her face. "Judy, what on earth are you doing here? What's happened?"

"Nothing. I just needed a break."

"Oh, sweetheart. Of course you do. I should have called to ask you over. Come in. Come in. Emma and Tanya are here."

As she leads me down the dark hall into the kitchen, she confirms that she's pretty much moved in and that she'll probably let her place go.

Tanya wraps me in a hug. Emma hesitates because she doesn't know me that well and then gives me a bear hug, too.

"I'm so sorry about Sam. He's such a great kid."

"Oh, and before you ask," Tanya says, "Rosie's fine. She wanted to go to school today. Rick's working from home, so he's picking them up in a bit and they're going to the movies."

I want to know if she's fretting about Sam.

"From time to time, but being with Cybil is keeping her spirits up." She says they're happy to have her for as long as necessary.

Ginny wants to know who's for a cuppa.

"Not for me, thanks," I say. "I don't think I can manage another drop. I've been drinking tea by the gallon."

"Still no news, I take it," Tanya says.

I shake my head.

"They'll find him. You'll see."

"Of course they will," Ginny says in that hearty, chin-up, chest-out voice of hers.

Emma says that a boy in Mason's class ran off a while back. "The police found him in the cinema, curled up on a seat. He'd slept through three showings of *Fifty Shades of Grey*. Heaven knows how he got in."

We all laugh. Then the atmosphere gets awkward. Nobody dares to say the unsayable: that Sam could be dead.

"So . . . we thought we'd give the house a bit of a spring clean," Ginny says, making jazz hands in her rubber gloves. "It's amazing what can be achieved with a bit of elbow grease. My mother is supposed to have a cleaner, but Lord only knows what she does. Rearranges the dirt by the look of it. I've already let her go."

"It needs more than elbow grease," Emma says. "If you ask me this place needs a flamethrower."

Emma and Tanya make odd-looking cleaning ladies. They're both in full makeup, Tanya with her dreads and Emma in a flared tea dress and frilly pinny, looking like she's stepped out of a Tide commercial circa 1959.

"I have no idea why Edith is still living here," Tanya says. "It's vast and dark and cold. It would give me the willies."

"Tell me about it," Emma says. "But the boys love it. They've decided it's haunted. At night they turn off all the lights and go around hunting for ghosts. But mostly they love the garden." Emma nods toward the kitchen window. I peer out through the film of grime.

The garden is wild and scruffy. Bits of fence are falling down. But it must be half an acre — almost unheard-of in London. The boys have found a load of old wood and appear to be building a den. "And not a thug or ruffian in sight," Emma says. "The house is grotty and my grandmother may be a pain in the backside, but being here with the boys, I feel like I've won the lottery."

Ginny is beaming. "You'll feel even better when we get the place shipshape."

"Don't hold your breath," Tanya says, pulling a face and getting busy with a palette knife. She's attempting to scrape a layer of thick yellow viscosity off the cooker hood.

Ginny shows me the fridge. It's filthy and sprouting mold. There are soggy black salad leaves and unidentifiable ends of meals wrapped in plastic. The yogurt is growing green fur.

"And the oven and stove look like they haven't been cleaned since before the Blitz."

"Right," I say, taking off my jacket. "What can I do?"

Nothing. Ginny says I'm not to lift a finger. "You just sit down and take it easy."

"But that's all I've been doing. I'd rather be busy. It'll take my mind off things. The police will call if there's any news."

Ginny relents. If I really want something to do, I can take her mother a cup of tea.

"So, I take it that you'd rather not?"

"You take it correctly."

I ask her how things are going with Edith.

"She's very weak physically. But she's still ruling the roost. She loves the boys, though. I would never have predicted that. She says their noise has brought some life back into the house. And she talks to Emma about the fashion business. I think she's trying to make a connection with her that she missed with me."

"And have the two of you talked?"

"No, and I'm not sure we will. I'm not expecting my story to end the way your mum's friend Estelle's did. I can't see my mother's stiff upper lip starting to tremble anytime soon."

"All you can do is keep trying."

Edith is sitting in a high-backed velvet armchair that has seen better days. At her feet is an ancient electric bar fire. A knitted patchwork blanket has been placed over her knees. Her head has slumped forward so that her chin rests on her chest. For a second I think she's dead. But as I approach, she lifts her head and squints up at me.

"I know you. . . . You're Ginny's Jewish friend. It's Julie, isn't it?"

"Judy."

"Ah. I knew it began with a *J.* "

I place the cup and saucer on the walnut occasional table beside her.

"No. No. Use a coaster. Use a coaster."

I slip a mat under the saucer. I can't think why she's so insistent. The tabletop is covered in rings and stains.

"I was so sorry to hear about your young grandson. Have they found him?"

"I'm afraid not."

"He'll turn up. He'll soon get bored. Mind you, from what I hear he's a spirited lad — stands up for himself. That's what you want in a boy. He'll go far. Mark my words."

"I think girls should stand up for themselves, too. Don't you?"

She doesn't reply immediately. I wonder if she thinks I'm goading her — harking back to when Ginny stood up to her. Maybe I am.

"Girls are different," she says after a few moments.

"In what way?"

"Even in this day and age, you have to

484

protect them. Men prey on them. I don't know what Ginny has told you about our estrangement, but I was only looking out for her. And I was right. That excuse for a husband abandoned her and the child and left her without a bean."

"But you wanted her to have an abortion."

"Quite right. It was the only sensible option. Ginny thinks I was worried about what my friends would have said and I admit that was partly true. It was shallow and small-minded of me. But it wasn't just that. I wanted her to have a future. I wanted her to make the most of herself, to have a career . . . to be somebody. I wanted her to have the things I didn't have."

"But then there would have been no Emma . . . no Mason and Tyler."

"Why are they called Mason and Tyler?" she says, sidestepping my remark. "Such nasty, common names. Lovely boys, though. Very robust. Full of life."

"That they are."

Edith picks up her cup and saucer with a knotty blue-veined hand. "Lovely girl, Emma. Good brain. Very focused on her business. And boy, she puts in the hours. I admire that. I've never been one for fashion, but I can see she looks very stylish. I have high hopes for her."

I slide a dining chair out from under the table and sit myself down opposite Edith. "Look, I know it's none of my business and feel free to tell me to shut up, but you need to talk to Ginny. Tell her what you've told me."

She plays for time by replacing her cup and saucer on the table and fiddling with the coaster to make sure it's in the correct position. She hasn't so much as sipped the tea. "There's nothing to talk about. The past should stay in the past. Neither of us can change it. All we can do is move on and make the most of whatever time I have left. I suppose Ginny has told you I'm dying. She thinks I don't know, but I've spoken to the doctors. I know the score . . . a year at best."

"Isn't that all the more reason to have a conversation about what happened between you — to tell her you're sorry?"

"She knows that. When I was in hospital, I told her it wasn't my proudest moment. What more does she want?"

I take a deep here-goes-nothing breath. "Edith, do you love your daughter?"

She bridles. "What sort of question is that? Of course I do."

"Then tell her."

"I've left her the house and all my money.

486

Isn't that enough?"

"Does she know that's what you've done?"

"She'll find out as soon as I'm gone — as soon as she sees the will. I didn't even split it with her brother. Not because I don't like him, you understand. It's because he's wealthy and doesn't need it. Meanwhile I'll thank you not to tell her what I've done."

"I won't. But you should. Just let her know you love her and that you've provided for her."

"You know the problem with the world today? Feelings. I blame Princess Diana. Nobody in this country had feelings before she died. Now people are hugging and emoting all over the place. Even footballers do it. In my day we didn't have to tell people we loved them. They knew it."

"Well, Ginny doesn't know it. Far from it. Speak to her. Please. I beg you. For both your sakes."

Edith hands me her cup and saucer and informs me that her tea is lukewarm. "It's your fault it's gone cold. Forcing me to listen to all this nonsense."

"I didn't force you. If you'd asked me to leave, I would have gone. That makes me think that deep down you don't think what I'm saying is really nonsense."

"If it's not too much trouble I would like

another cup of tea. Maybe Emma could bring it to me this time. She's much more agreeable."

"I'll ask her."

"Very good."

As I turn to go, Edith calls after me, "Your grandson will come home. Don't give up hope." She offers me the glimmer of a smile. The old lady appears to do feelings after all.

Back in the kitchen Ginny asks what took so long. "Has my mother been lecturing you about the country going to the dogs because there are too many immigrants?"

"Actually we talked about Sam and she told me not to give up hope."

"For once I agree with her. Please don't despair."

I realize I don't have the energy to start helping with the cleaning. I know it would take my mind off things, but since Sam disappeared I've been sleeping in fits and starts. I'm all in. Ginny says she can see the exhaustion in my face. She tells me to go home to rest. She wants to get me a taxi, but I'm determined to walk. I don't want to rush back to the confinement and fear — the sodding cups of tea.

I'm a few yards from my front gate when I see him. At least I think it's a him. It's getting dark, so I can't quite tell. The person is sitting on the garden wall, short legs swinging, sneakers hitting the brickwork. For a second I think it's Sam and my heart jolts. I start running toward him. Then I notice his posture, the shape of his head. "Seb? Is that you?"

He jumps down from the wall, looks at me, but doesn't say anything.

"Sweetheart, what are you doing sitting out here in the cold?"

"Is it true that Sam's run away?"

"I'm afraid it is."

"It's all my fault. I lied. I'm so sorry. I should have owned up. I didn't mean for this to happen. Sam will be all right, won't he?"

"Whoa, Seb, calm down. What's going on? Are you saying that you stole the iPad?"

"No."

"Then who did?"

CHAPTER TWENTY-ONE

I make Seb hot chocolate and we sit at the kitchen table while he says — in fits and starts that I sometimes strain to hear — what he's come to say. Mum and Constable Lisa are in the living room, watching one of the soaps. When he's finished, he begs me not to call his mother.

"Let me tell Granddad first. He'll understand better and then he can help me tell Mum."

"But your mum doesn't know where you are. She'll be worried."

"No, she won't. I told her I was going around the corner to Granddad's. She lets me go on my own 'cos it's so near."

I phone Mike, and ten minutes later, he's ringing the doorbell.

"It's only Mike," I call out to Mum.

"What does he want? After what he did, I don't know how he's got the cheek to show his face here."

I poke my head around the living room door and tell her she doesn't have to say hello.

"Too right I'm not saying hello."

I leave her to the TV.

"You were quick," I say to Mike.

"What's going on? What has Seb told you?"

"I think you should hear it from him."

Seb is staring into what remains of his hot chocolate. He's too embarrassed to look at his grandfather. Mike pulls out a chair and sits down next to him.

"Come on, Seb. Whatever it is, you can tell me. Now, then . . . what's all this about?"

Seb carries on staring into his mug. "Sam didn't steal the iPad. I lied. It was the Cakes."

"The who?"

"School Mafia," I volunteer. "Orlando and Hugo Cake. They're twins. Dear little chaps by all accounts, who — inter alia — go around the school demanding money and threatening to hurt kids who don't pay up."

Mike is almost laughing. "Oh, come on . . . they're ten. I'd get it if this was some deprived inner-city school, but —"

"Granddad, you have to believe me. It's been going on for months. They're doing it to a few kids. I've been stealing money from

Mum's purse."

"What? How much?"

"I dunno. Sometimes they only want five pounds. Sometimes it's ten. If I don't give them what they want, they say their brother Alex will beat me up. He's in the senior school. He's fourteen. I've seen him a few times. He's huge."

Mike's lips are pursed. His right hand is a fist. "Bloody thug . . . if I get hold of him . . . So — what's the story with the iPad?"

"It's complicated."

Seb explains that the Cakes stole the iPad and hid it under Sam's bed for fun.

"For fun? Surely it would have been more fun to keep it, get their brother to sell it on eBay and cut them in on the deal."

"You don't know how much they hate me. It's because my mum's famous. They're jealous. They told me to lie to Mrs. Gilbert and accuse Sam of stealing the iPad because they knew how upset I would be. They said they wanted to watch me cry like a baby. After I told Mrs. Gilbert, I did cry and I threw up. I could hear the Cakes laughing. They thought it was hysterical. I know I shouldn't have lied, but they said if I didn't, their brother would get me. Later on, they said the same to Felix. Getting Sam into trouble was just a bonus. They've enjoyed every minute."

Mike looks at me. "It's so twisted. These Cakes are bloody psychopaths. I can hardly believe that at their age they managed to come up with something so despicable."

"I'm not sure they did," I say. "If you ask me, it was the older brother egging them on. This Alexander is the real psycho. He's the one getting his kicks. His little brothers are just pawns."

"So, has this brother ever hurt you?" Mike says.

"No. But the twins have. They've beaten me up twice when I've refused to give them money. Felix has been beaten up once. They pick on us because they think we're goody-goodies who won't fight back. I've tried fighting them, but it's two against one."

"But you must have been covered in bruises. How come your mother didn't see?"

"They were on my body, not on my face. I never showed her."

Mike is grimacing. "I don't understand. Why on earth didn't you report them when they started demanding money?"

"I was too scared. They said their brother would kill me. I thought about telling Mum, but you know what she's like. She would have made a huge fuss —"

"Too damn right she would."

"But that would have made it worse. Nobody wants their mum fighting their battles — and especially not my mum. She'd have written about it in the papers or wanted me and the Cakes to do something stupid like go on TV to talk about bullying. Then I really would be dead."

"And you're telling me," Mike says, "that the school knows nothing about this?"

"They know the Cakes are bullies, and they just tell us to keep away from them. Sometimes they get sent to S.J. And there's this counselor woman who comes to the school to talk to them about their behavior, but it hasn't done any good. And they never have enough teachers on duty during recess — especially at lunchtime. Me and Felix got beaten up in the toilets. The teachers never check in there."

"Christ Almighty. And for this your parents pay. How much are the fees at this bloody school? It's despicable. You could have ended up in hospital."

I touch Mike's arm. "Take it easy. I'm sure Claudia can handle the school."

Seb wants to know if his mother will be suing S.J. Mike says he wouldn't be at all surprised.

"Good. S.J. bloody deserves it for not getting rid of the Cakes."

Seb is trailing his finger through a drop of spilled hot chocolate, spreading it over the table. "Now everybody's going to be angry and hate me."

Mike puts an arm around him and says nobody is going to hate him. "I just wish you'd trusted an adult and spoken up. Then these boys and their brother would have been dealt with. We wouldn't have let anybody hurt you."

"You say that, but you don't know. Adults can't be there all the time. You have no idea how scared I was."

Mike calls Claudia while I relay the news to Constable Lisa and my mother. Mum calls the Cakes evil and sick — just like the Nazis. Constable Lisa barely raises an eyebrow. She says she could tell me stories that are far worse — and not all from deprived inner-city neighborhoods. "That bloke who wrote *Lord of the Flies* knew what he was talking about."

When Mike comes off the phone from Claudia, Mum makes no attempt to come and say hello to him.

"So, how did Claudia take the news?" I ask him.

"She didn't say much. I think she's in shock. She wants me to drop Seb home."

495

He turns to his grandson, who's putting on his coat. I bend down and give him a quick hug. "Seb, thank you for owning up. I know it was hard, but you don't know how important it is. You're a good kid and you've been very brave."

"No, I haven't. I'm a coward. I should never have lied. And now Sam's missing, and it's all my fault. What if something really bad happens to him?"

"Let's just hope it doesn't. Please don't be too hard on yourself. You were scared. Fear often makes us do the wrong thing."

Bernie calls first thing the next morning to find out how Mum's doing and to tell her he'll go out looking for Sam again today. This time Mum won't hear of it. "You need to rest. You've done enough. Leave it to the police now. They know what they're doing. Meanwhile I don't know how to thank you. You're a mensch, Bernie, a proper mensch."

Once again, he offers to come and keep her company, but she tells him she prefers to worry alone. He makes her promise to call if she needs anything.

Around eleven, Mike stops by. "Mind if I come in? I just wanted to give you an update."

Mum is in the kitchen, so I take him into

the living room. He sits on the sofa. For a second, I dither about where to sit. After last night I feel close to him again. Part of me wants to sit next to him, to kiss and make up. But I choose an armchair.

Mike says that according to Laurence, Claudia is roaming around the house stony-faced. She can't bring herself to speak to Seb.

"It's Laurence who's consoling him. . . . God forgive me for saying it, but I think her main concern is how all this is going to affect her career. What does it look like, a child expert whose kid allows himself to be bullied and beaten up because he can't confide in his mother? The way she sees it, she's been made to look a complete fool."

"Not a fool — just fallible, like the rest of us. It will do her good."

"I'm inclined to agree." He leans forward. "So in the end you and I were right about our boys. They're both good kids. I shouldn't have judged Sam the way I did. . . ."

"OK . . . before you go on . . . I need to tell you that it wasn't just you who judged him. I have a confession. Once Felix accused Sam, I found myself doubting him, too. When we got home after the meeting with Mrs. S.J., I practically accused him of stealing the iPad. It's the reason he ran away. Me losing faith in him was the final straw."

"But it was the logical thing to think. We all thought it. You can't blame yourself."

"But I do. I think I always will."

He looks at his watch and says he has an interview to do in town. "But I'm more than happy to cancel it if you'd like me to stay and keep you company."

I tell him it's probably best if he goes. "I'm afraid you're not in Mum's good books. If you stay, there'll be an atmosphere. I'm not sure I could cope."

"So long as I'm back in your good books."

"Let's talk . . . as soon as this is over."

"Sure," he says, clearly worried that I haven't quite forgiven him — which I probably haven't. But right now I can't give my relationship with Mike any more thought. My grandson is still missing. He could be dead. Sam is all I can think about.

Constable Lisa went home late last night to get a few hours' sleep. Now she's back, playing cards with Mum. I ask her if the police have been able to get a message to Abby and Tom.

"I don't know. The last I heard they were

still having technical problems. But they will."

"This is ridiculous," I snap. "What technical problems? The truth is, nobody cares. Nobody's putting themselves out."

"Come on, Judy. You know that's not true. We care. We've got officers out looking for him. Everybody cares. You're saying that because you're worn-out."

I take a breath. "I'm sorry. You're right. I am worn-out. The thing is, I just don't know what I'm going to tell his parents. I'm not sure I can face them."

"Maybe you should leave that to us."

I'm so beside myself with guilt and shame that I'm starting to think that I might have to.

The morning crawls by. Bernie calls again. We run out of tea bags. Mum pops to the shop on the corner. I put a wash load on, then mop the kitchen floor and clean the bathrooms. I discover a pile of ironing that will keep me occupied for another hour. Mum says she's going to bake a cake for when Sam gets home. I almost tell her not to bother.

After lunch — toast and more tea — Constable Lisa gets a call. Every time her phone rings or she gets a message on her radio, I assume Sam's bloated body has been found floating facedown in the river.

"OK, roger that. I'll pass on the news."

"What?"

"He's been found."

"Alive?"

"Very much so. He's exhausted, but fine."

Mum starts shaking and sobbing. Her hand goes to her mouth. "Thank God. Oh, thank God."

I want details. Where was he found? When? How?

Constable Lisa says he spent the entire time riding the tube. Somebody found him about an hour ago, asleep on a train at Tottenham Court Road, and reported it to the transport police.

I can't shout or jump for joy. All I feel is quiet relief. Mum and I sit together on the sofa, holding hands as we let the tears roll. Even PC Lisa starts crying. I'm guessing that in her job, it doesn't always end like this.

"But I don't understand," Mum says. "He's been on the underground all this time and nobody noticed? How does that happen? How could people not wonder about a nine-year-old child all on his own — particularly at night?"

"Maybe they didn't think he was alone," Constable Lisa says. "You know what people are like. They walk around, lost in their own thoughts. They don't pay attention."

Another call comes in to say that Sam has been taken to St. Thomas' Hospital. But only as a precaution. The police are sending a patrol car to collect me and take me to him. I ask Mum if she wants to come, but she says it would be too emotional. "You go. I'm going to call Bernie and ice that welcome-home cake."

As I climb into the police car, the lovely copper says: "How's about we have some fun and I blue-light you there?"

He turns on the siren, too. Then he hits the gas. I keep thinking how much Sam would love this. The way the traffic parts verges on the biblical. We careen across red lights, drive on the wrong side of the road, headlights flashing. I can't stop laughing. It's the thrill. More than that, it's sheer, joyous release.

The doctor who examined Sam says he's hungry and a bit dehydrated, but apart from that he's good to go. I should let him eat what he likes for the rest of the day and make sure he gets plenty of fluids.

Sam is waiting for me in a cubicle in the ER. A woman police officer is with him. He's sitting on the edge of the examination couch, legs swinging, and wolfing down a cheese and tomato sandwich. He's also messing around with a pair of police hand-cuffs. He looks up at me the moment I walk in. I take in the filthy hands and matted hair, the shamefaced expression.

"Hi, Grandma."

"Hi, you."

"I'll leave you to it," the police officer says. "Bye, Sam. Good luck." She relieves him of the handcuffs and offers him a smile and a wave. "And remember — no more running away when things get tough." She turns to me and says how glad she is that it all worked out. Then she pulls back the curtain and is gone.

I hold him so tight he says he can't breathe. I kiss him, tell him I love him, that it's all OK . . . that Seb has admitted he lied. I explain about the Cake twins.

"The Cakes are scary."

"Have they ever threatened you?"

"Uh-uh. They mostly pick on kids in their own year." He takes another bite of his sandwich. "I couldn't bear it when nobody believed me. Then when you doubted me, it felt like nobody cared about me."

"Oh, sweetheart, I'm so, so sorry. I don't know what came over me. I promise that I will never doubt you again. Not ever. But running away was such a stupid thing to do.

502

Anything could have happened. Have you any idea how worried we've been?"

"I'm sorry. But it seemed like it was the only way I could get you to believe me."

On the way home — in a taxi — Sam tells me about his time on the tube. "It was pretty boring really. I just kept going to the end of the line and back again."

"But didn't anybody speak to you? Didn't anybody want to know what you were doing?"

"Only this tramp. He got on late one night. He sleeps on the tube most nights because it's warm. His name was Colin. He stank of poo, and he was a bit drunk. We played I Spy, and he offered me some of his burger. But I said no because I thought it might have come out of a bin. He asked me if I had any money, and I gave him ten pounds so that he could buy some breakfast. Then he said he knew a place where I could stay — with his friends, under the highway —"

"Oh my God."

"But I said no because I was scared. Then I fell asleep. When I woke up, he was gone, and I realized he'd taken all my money."

"You mean my money — the money you stole from me."

"Yes. Sorry. I'll pay you back. With interest if you want."

"It's OK. I think we can forget about the money."

"So, anyway, then this lady found me and the police came. They were very nice. One of them gave me half of her Kit Kat."

When we get home Mum gets hold of Sam and practically squeezes the life out of him — just like I did. She only stops because a uniformed male officer is waiting to speak to Sam.

"Good afternoon, young man. Have you any idea the trouble you've caused?" He must be six-six. Sam is too petrified to speak. He just about manages to nod. The officer takes Sam into the living room, leaving Constable Lisa and me in the hall to eavesdrop.

"We had helicopters out looking for you. Have you any idea how much that costs?"

The officer starts lecturing Sam about cuts in police funding and penalties for wasting police time.

I'm not sure he's in a fit state for this, but Constable Lisa says it won't do him any harm to be read the riot act. "He needs to understand that actions have consequences and that running off isn't a way to deal with his problems."

I'm inclined to agree. "You know, I don't know what we would have done without you. You've been amazing."

"I was only doing my job."

"I know, but you do it brilliantly. Mum and I are so grateful."

"I'll beat your mother at pontoon one of these days."

"I heard that," Mum says, trotting out from the kitchen. "You can always try. . . . Meanwhile you deserve a promotion."

"Tell my commanding officer," she says, grinning.

"Don't think I won't," Mum informs her.

Constable Lisa says she'd best be off.

We thank her again and she's not offended when I say we're sad, but delighted to see her go.

"That's how it should be," she says.

After his lecture from the stern police officer, Sam is subdued and thoughtful. He says he had no idea that he had caused so much trouble, that there were all these policemen out looking for them. "Did you know they sent up helicopters to look for me?"

"I did."

"Wow. I thought they only did that for murderers."

Sheepish as he feels, I can tell that this is going to become his badge of honor.

While Sam is in the kitchen demolishing my mother's meat loaf, I call Ginny and Tanya to tell them the news. I call Mike last.

"Oh, thank God. . . . So, where did they find him?"

I tell the tale, including the bit about Colin the tramp. I've barely got to the end of the story when I hear the sound of breaking crockery coming from the kitchen. "Sorry, Mike. I've got to go. Mum appears to be smashing plates."

"Sure." Again I hear the disappointment in his voice. He wanted me to tell him he's forgiven. Instead I cut the conversation short. I couldn't spare him a few more seconds.

In the kitchen Mum is picking bits of china off the floor. She's broken a casserole dish. Sam wants to help. Mum is yelling at him to keep away because he has nothing on his feet. I'm yelling at her to mind her fingers. She says she is minding them. I had no idea that a domestic mishap could feel this good.

CHAPTER TWENTY-TWO

Over the weekend the four of us huddle together. Rosie won't let Sam out of her sight. I am in no doubt that while she was away her bravado gave way to desperate fear. I keep wondering if I made the right decision sending her to Tanya's. I can only imagine what was going through her mind when she was in bed at night, alone with her thoughts. But Mum says I'm overreacting and that at her age her imagination isn't sufficiently developed to picture the worst. I hope she's right.

I'm also worried about Sam. He's exhausted. I'm not sure he's up to competing in the chess tournament on Wednesday. But he's adamant that he wants to go ahead with it, and I don't feel inclined to argue.

Mrs. S.J. calls to say words cannot express how delighted she is that Sam has been found and that prayers were said for his safe homecoming in school assembly. "Mrs.

507

Gilbert and I made a bad call and it had a disastrous outcome. We can only be thankful that it ended the way it did." She wonders if Sam and I might feel up to coming into school on Monday so that she and Mrs. Gilbert can offer us their apologies in person. "I will of course be sending a formal letter of apology to Sam's parents."

"What about Seb and the Cake twins?"

"I shall be seeing the Cake family as well — including the older brother. You should also know that Dr. Connell and her husband have made a formal complaint against the school — as have Felix's parents."

"I see."

"I'm afraid I can't say any more until after the governors' meeting."

But I know as well as she does that by allowing the Cake twins to terrorize pupils, she has failed in her duty of care and that her job is in jeopardy.

Finally, on Sunday night after the children are in bed, Abby phones in a panic to say she's just received a message to call home urgently. But the line is hopeless. I could have shouted at her to redial. But I don't. I've never been so grateful for a bad line. Even though Sam is safe, my guilt hasn't lifted. I can't face telling my daughter what happened. I know I'm being a coward and that I can't put off the inevitable, but for now it's what I do.

The inevitable postponed, I manage, through the loud crunching on the line, to make her understand that everything is fine and that she shouldn't worry.

"You sure?" she yells.

"Positive. It's all sorted. I'll tell you everything when I see you. When are you coming home?"

"What?"

"When. Will. You. Be. Home?"

"Wednesday afternoon."

I do my best to explain that Wednesday is Sam's chess tournament and that they might just catch the end of it. I'm not sure if she hears.

The kids have spent the last three nights sleeping in Sam's bed. On Monday morning when I wake them with the news that their parents will be home in a few days, they start whooping and dancing and jumping on the bed. Usually I would nag them about breaking the springs, but not today. Rosie is counting on her fingers how many months her parents have been away. "January, March, April . . ."

"You forgot February. It's been over three months."

"That's a really long time for childrens to

be without a mummy and daddy. I think I've been very brave."

"I think you've both been brave."

"And now we get to go to Disneyland. Yay."

Rosie sings "If You're Happy and You Know It" all the way to school. At first Sam moans at her for singing a baby song. Then he joins in. And so do I.

When Sam and I arrive for our appointment with Mrs. S.J., Tanya is waiting to see her, too. Tanya's sister is getting married in Spain in a few weeks and she wants permission to take Cybil out of school for the wedding.

"Hi, Sam — how are you doing? That's quite an adventure you had."

"The police were looking for me with helicopters, you know."

"I do know."

"Usually they only do that for murderers and really bad people. It's a shame I didn't get to ride in one."

He wanders off and sits himself down on a chair near Mrs. S.J.'s door. Tanya says that S.J. has got the Cake family and Seb and his parents in with her. "I think we might have a long wait."

She's right. It's half an hour before

Mrs. S.J.'s door opens. The head of the senior school appears first. Grim-faced, he marches away, black gown billowing. Then come the Cake parents. She's pale with shock. He's grinding his teeth. I get the feeling he wants to punch somebody. The boys follow. Alexander, the psycho, looks so upstanding in his navy school blazer and striped tie. Then I hear his father telling him to wipe that bloody smirk off his face. The twins are giggling. I can't tell if it's nervous laughter or defiance. Then Mrs. Cake starts whisper-shouting at Mr. Cake. "I told you that counselor the school provided wasn't any good. I said the boys were running rings around her. But would you listen? No. Too busy fucking your blond intern. Now look what's happened. We'll never get them into another school and it's all your fault. . . ."

"Uh-oh — somebody's been expelled," Tanya says. "Bloody nut jobs, all three of them."

There's no sign of Claudia and Laurence. Tanya reckons that Mrs. S.J. is begging them to withdraw their complaint.

"I wish her luck with that," I say.

When they finally emerge, Laurence has his arm around Seb's shoulders. Claudia is a few steps behind, looking gray. She tells her husband to go on ahead. "I need a couple of minutes," she says, looking in my direction.

Laurence stops to introduce himself and tell me how glad he is that Sam has been found. "It must have been the most terrifying ordeal. I can't imagine what you must have gone through. But you must understand that Claudia was only trying to protect Seb. I do hope we can put this behind us."

"I hope so, too." He's her husband. Of course he's going to support her. What else is he going to do? I'm not prepared to offer him an analysis of his wife's character, especially not with his son standing there. Instead I turn to Seb and ask him how he's doing.

"Good. Mum and Dad wanted to send me to a new school, but I've managed to change their mind. I don't want to leave my friends. I'll be fine here now that the Cakes have gone."

"Good for you. I'm glad. That means you and Sam can still be buddies."

Laurence tells Seb they should be going. As they make their way to the door, Claudia steps forward. She vaguely looks in Tanya's direction but doesn't bother to acknowledge her.

"And hello to you, too," Tanya mutters.

"I'm so glad everything turned out well," Claudia says. Her tone is stiff, awkward. She'd rather be anywhere than facing me. But I can't help admiring her for doing the decent thing. "You must have been so frightened."

"We were."

"Of course, Laurence and I blame the school. None of this would have happened if the Cake twins had been dealt with properly. As you probably know, we submitted a complaint. But Laurence persuaded me to drop it. Seb loves it here. The Cakes are gone, and the governors have agreed to make sure more staff is around during recess. And since the school's current anti-bullying scheme clearly isn't working, Mrs. S.J. has agreed to put a new initiative in place. She has asked me to advise her."

"That's excellent news. But it's such a shame that Seb didn't feel able to come to you when he was being bullied. There he was, getting beaten up, and he couldn't confide in his own mother." I'm twisting the knife, hitting her when she's down, but only a saint could resist.

Claudia looks like she's been punched. For once she's lost for words. Meanwhile I've hit my stride and decide to carry on: "Isn't it time you accepted that despite your qualifications you don't have all the answers — that you're human like the rest of us? You get things wrong. You mess up."

"Yes, well, clearly I have some issues that I need to look at. . . ." Her sentence trails off.

"Apology accepted."

"It's unfortunate that Sam became involved. I hope he isn't too traumatized. If he needs counseling . . ." She stops herself. "Sorry . . . force of habit."

"He'll be fine. But thank you for the offer. I appreciate it."

"So, how are you doing?"

"Much better than I was."

"Good . . . Dad has been telling me how strong you've been. If it had been Seb, I think I would have gone to pieces."

"No, you wouldn't. I think that when we have to, we find the strength to cope."

"So" — she clears her throat — "Dad also mentioned that . . . that it might be serious between the two of you and . . . I . . . well, the thing is . . . I was wondering if perhaps the four of us could maybe go out for dinner. No pressure. I mean, if you'd rather not, I would understand. I just thought it might be a chance for you and me to get to know each other a bit better."

I'm laughing to myself. What was it she

said to me the other day? "Stay away from my father. . . . This is a battle you will not win."

"It's a lovely idea and thank you. The thing is, I'm not sure where your dad and I are at just now. Shall we say we had words?"

"About me?"

"Not entirely. But your name did crop up."

"I see. Well . . . let me know."

"Of course."

"Good. Right. Well, I'd best be off."

She offers me a thin, awkward smile and heads for the door. But Tanya gets out of her seat and calls after her.

"Yes?"

"Don't look down your nose at me," Tanya says as she approaches Claudia. "OK, while home truths are being handed out, I would just like you to know how much you hurt me and my husband with the gossip you started about us taking drugs. You decided that because we're in the music business and because I wear my hair in dreadlocks, we had to be on something. And people believed you. No doubt some still do. Well, for your information, we don't take drugs. Ever. It was wicked and evil, and I hope you are ashamed of yourself."

"Yes, well, we all make mistakes. . . . Now, if you'll excuse me, my husband is waiting for me." She heads out of the door.

"Did you see that?" Tanya says. "She was on the verge of tears. Wow. I just made Claudia Connell cry."

"I don't think it was just you."

"OK. But I've never seen her like that before. She looks like she's been poleaxed. Her entire world has collapsed around her."

"Indeed it has."

"Do you think I was too hard on her? She's had a lot to contend with."

"She has. On the other hand, you have to think about what she did to you. There was so much gossip, it was months before you were able to show your face at school."

"Funny how even now when she's so vulnerable, she can't find it in her to actually apologize. I reckon that's the best either of us is going to get."

"I'm inclined to agree."

Mrs. S.J. comes out of her office. "Mrs. Devlin . . . Sam. Good to see you. Do come in. Mrs. Gilbert is already here."

As Mrs. S.J. steps back into her office, Tanya looks at the time on her phone. "Sod it," she mutters. She can't be bothered to wait any longer to see Mrs. S.J. She'll take Cybil out of school without asking permission. Rick can call and say she's sick.

■ ■ ■ ■

The following morning, Mike calls to invite me for lunch.

"I've got smoked salmon and a bottle of Moët. I thought we should celebrate Sam's return."

"How can I refuse?" But that's not the reason I'm going. I'm going because last night I made a decision. I decided that I've held my grudge too long. It's time to make amends. I'll say one thing for catastrophe; it has a way of putting life into perspective.

I lean on the breakfast bar, sipping my champagne, while he finishes making smoked salmon sandwiches. "By the way, I bumped into Claudia yesterday. She looks totally done in."

"I know. This whole thing has knocked her sideways. Like I said, she's been forced to confront her imperfections as a mother. Imperfection doesn't sit well with my daughter. Laurence says she's already been on the phone to some PR company to discuss how to limit the damage if the press gets wind of what's happened."

"That sounds more like the Claudia I know. She's clearly got some fight left in her."

"Maybe. But I've made it clear to her that she needs to stop 'therapizing' other people and get some therapy of her own."

"Do you think she will?"

"Maybe not right away. But I fully intend to keep nagging her — as does Laurence. I still think that in the long run this fall from grace is going to do her a power of good."

"I hope you're right."

He cuts a sandwich into four elegant triangles. "Crusts on or off?" he says.

"On, of course. They're the best bit."

He slides a plate across the counter toward me and hands me a napkin. "So . . . where are we at — you and me? Are we good?"

"When you turned up at that meeting, I felt so betrayed."

"You're dodging the question."

"I know. But hear me out. I need you to understand how much it hurt — particularly as you'd said . . ."

"That I would never hurt you."

"Yes. And I suppose what worries me is that whenever I find myself at odds with Claudia, you will side with her against me."

"But I didn't side with her — not in the way you think. I merely thought she had a point, that's all. I thought Sam could be going off the rails and it did look as if he stole the iPad. And the main reason I came to that meeting was to support Seb. What would you have done in my position?"

"The same. I understand that now."

"But you need to understand something else. I can't be under your thumb any more than I can be under Claudia's. I try not to take sides, but when I do it is always based on a person's line of reasoning, not the person him- or herself."

"Fair enough."

"So, are we good?"

"We're good."

"I'm sorry for everything."

"Me, too."

He reaches across the breakfast bar and takes my hand. "I do love you, you know."

"This is excellent smoked salmon. Is it the wild Alaskan?"

"Stop it. I've just told you again that I love you."

"I know you do." I put down my half-eaten triangle and look at him. "And I love you."

"You do?"

I am as taken aback as he is. Before I left home, all I had planned was a reconciliation. Declarations of love weren't on my agenda.

"Wow. I wasn't expecting that," he says.

"I'm not sure I was either."

"But you're certain?"

I feel my face break into a smile. "To be honest, I think I've loved you for a while. But first Brian got in the way and then there was all this business with Sam and Seb. . . ."

"I want you to know that I will never try to part you from your feelings and memories. Brian must always have a place in your heart."

"Thank you."

He tops up our champagne glasses. "To the future. Whatever that might bring."

"To the future."

"So, do you have plans for this afternoon?"

"Not really. I've got to pick the kids up from school and then Bogdan's coming over to give Sam a final tutorial before the tournament tomorrow."

"The thing is, I've just put clean sheets on the bed."

"That's nice. Laundry day, is it?"

"Actually it isn't. I changed them especially. Plus I've already taken my pill. Seems a shame to waste it."

"I'm inclined to agree."

CHAPTER TWENTY-THREE

Over dessert, Mum makes the mistake of asking the kids what they think we should have for dinner tomorrow night when Abby and Tom get home. Sam wants to get McDonald's or pizza. Rosie thinks we should order Chinese. Mum is appalled that they could even think of celebrating their parents' return with junk food. Sam asks how Chinese can be junk food when the Chinese eat it every day. I agree, but Mum won't have it. Any food prepared outside her kitchen is junk food. She is going to serve up a proper home-cooked dinner and that's that.

"So we're decided," she says, "tomato soup, a nice piece of beef and strudel for dessert."

"No, that's what you've decided," Sam says.

"Don't you get huffy with me, young man. If you don't like my cooking, nobody is forcing you to eat it."

"Mum, take it easy. We all adore your cooking." I suggest to the kids that maybe we'll all go out for dinner on their parents' second night home. "And you guys can choose where we go. How does that sound?"

"Good."

"I can't believe they're finally coming home," Sam says. "I've missed them so much. I mean, it's been great living here with you and Nana . . ."

"So great that you ran away," Mum snorts while spooning another helping of apricot crumble onto his plate.

"Please, Nana, can we forget that now? So, anyway, apart from that, it's been really good. But I've still missed them."

"Me, too," Rosie says. "Your cuddles are nice, Grandma — and Nana's, too, even though she squeezes too hard — but I've really missed mummy and daddy cuddles."

"Of course you have, and all being well, in a few hours you'll be able to have all the mummy and daddy cuddles you want."

Then it hits me like a hammer how much I'm going to miss the children. Despite the hard work and traumas, looking after them has lifted my spirits, given my life meaning. They've been my reason for getting up in the morning. If it hadn't been for them, I wouldn't have got to know Ginny and

Tanya. And I wouldn't have met Mike.

"You have no idea how much I'm going to miss you two."

"Will you be lonely?" Rosie says. "Because if you are, you and Nana could always come and live at our house."

"I might be a bit lonely at first. But I've got Nana and my friends. I'll be fine. And I think it might be time for me to get back to work."

"Really?" Mum says. "That's the first time you've mentioned it."

"It's only just occurred to me."

"Don't make any sudden decisions — not until you're really sure."

"I won't. I'll give it some more thought. But I think I'm ready."

"Well, if you're sure . . ."

Mum looks crestfallen and I can't work out why. I get the impression there's something on her mind, which she doesn't want to talk about in front of the kids. I'll speak to her later.

Sam says he wishes his mum and dad could be there for the chess tournament. I tell him that depending on what the traffic is like coming home from the airport, they might just catch the end of it.

"So, how do you feel about the competition? Are you absolutely sure you're up to it? After everything that's happened, nobody would hold it against you if you pulled out."

"I'm fine. I really want to give it a go. It's just a shame it'll be over by the time Mum and Dad get back. I wish they could have got an earlier flight."

"I know, darling. But cheer up. Nana and I will be there."

"So, are you nervous?" Mum says.

"A bit. Bogdan says I'm too impulsive, that I don't take time to plan my moves. But when Bernie called earlier he told me to watch my back, do my best and have fun. He said winning isn't everything. I told him to try telling Bogdan that."

"That Bogdan's meshuggah."

"Grandma?" Rosie pipes up. "Do you have a boyfriend?"

"Excuse me?" I glance at Mum.

"Don't look at me." She shrugs. "I didn't say anything."

I ask Rosie what makes her think that I've got a boyfriend.

"Well, Cybil said that she heard her mum on the phone to Ginny and that they were talking about you going out with Seb's granddad. It's OK if you are. I like Seb's granddad. He put me on his shoulders that time when we flew the kite."

"Yeah, I don't mind either," Sam says,

"now that Seb and I are friends again. So if you got married to Seb's granddad, Seb and me would be related. That's so cool."

"Maybe you and Seb could be page boys," Mum says. "And Rosie could be a bridesmaid."

Once I told Mum that I had forgiven Mike and that our relationship was back on track, it didn't take her long to come round. She realizes that fantasizing about weddings is a far more agreeable pastime than holding grudges. Tanya and Ginny have warned me to keep her on a short leash, though. They're worried she's going to start putting pressure on me to turn her fantasies into reality.

"Er, excuse me, people . . . if I could get a word in edgeways here. . . . As it happens, I am going out with Seb's granddad. He's a lovely man. But it's still early days. Nobody's talking about getting married."

"Is that because you're still missing Grandpa Brian? Cybil said that her mum said that you're still struggling with your grief. What's grief?"

"It's when you get sad after a person dies. And yes, she's right. My grief has made things difficult."

"So, have you and Mike done mouth kissing?" Rosie says.

"Of course they have," Sam says.

"Really? Do old people do mouth kissing, then? That's yucky and weird."

"Did you know that when people kiss, up to a billion bacteria pass between them? It says so in my *Amazing Facts* book."

Rosie says that's even more disgusting.

The kids seem happy to leave the subject there and ask to get down from the table. I let Rosie go, but I ask Sam to come with me into his grandfather's study.

"What for?"

"You'll see."

He follows me across the hall. "I've got something for you," I say, closing the door. Brian's Death Valley snow globe — which Sam faithfully returned to me from show-and-tell — is sitting on his desk. I pick it up. "I think Granddad would have wanted you to have this."

"Wow. Are you serious?" He takes it from me. "This is for me? To keep?"

"It is. Promise you'll look after it."

"Of course I will. It's the most precious thing I've ever owned."

"I'm glad you like it."

"I love it. Thank you, Grandma." He reaches up and gives me a kiss.

"My pleasure, darling."

He rushes to show Rosie — me yelling at him not to drop it. "Now I've got something precious to bring me luck."

"Good. But you still haven't got me my Kinder Eggs. I want them."

"I know. Can you wait until Mum and Dad get back? I'll ask them for the money."

" 'K. But don't forget."

At bedtime, Sam puts the snow globe next to him on his nightstand.

"Good night, darling. Please don't stay awake worrying about tomorrow. You're going to be fine."

"I'm not worried. I've got the snow globe. Even though it's too precious to take with me, I know it's going to bring me luck."

"I'm sure it will."

I kiss him good night. When I check on him twenty minutes later, he's snoring.

Meanwhile Rosie can't sleep. She's too excited about her mummy and daddy coming home tomorrow and is trying to work out what present to get them. "I'm going to get flowers for Mummy and licorice for Daddy 'cos it's his favorite."

Downstairs, Mum is making cocoa. "You want a cup?"

"Sure. . . . Mum, are you OK? You seemed a bit upset before."

"I'm fine."

"No, you're not."

"I am. I got a bit emotional because I'm

so proud of how you've coped with the kids these past months."

"Proud of me? Why? Because I made such a great job of keeping Sam safe?"

"You are going to have to stop beating yourself up about this. Yes, you made a mistake, but you were at the end of your tether. Anybody would have done the same. The fact is that when Abby and Tom asked you to take care of the kids, you rose to the challenge. You have been a wonderful grandma. Do you remember how at the beginning you thought you wouldn't be able to cope?"

"I do. I thought I would have to ask Abby and Tom to come home."

"But you didn't. You found an inner strength. And not only that, something wonderful has come out of all this. The children and Mike have helped you get over your grief. Look at you. You're even talking about going back to work. You have no idea how happy I am for you. . . ."

"But?"

"There's no but. What makes you think there's a but?"

"Because I know you. Come on. There's something on your mind and I want to know what it is."

"It doesn't matter."

"Yes, it does and you're not going to bed until you tell me."

She puts two mugs of cocoa down on the kitchen table and sits opposite me. "OK . . . the thing is that looking after you and the children has given me a new lease on life, too. But now that you've got your life back on track, I suppose I will have to move back to my place. I know it's pathetic and I know I have lots of friends, but I worry that I'll be lonely. And I'm not in the best of health. . . ."

So that's it. She thinks I'm going to ask her to leave.

"Oh, Mum, for heaven's sake. I'm not going to throw you out. Nothing could be further from my mind."

"Really?"

"Of course really. I love having you here. We get on, don't we? We enjoy each other's company?"

"Most of the time."

"You like cooking. I like eating. It's a perfect match."

"What about Mike?"

"What about him?"

"What if you two moved in together? Or got married?"

"Mum, please. You really must stop talking about us getting married. It's way too early."

"But what if you did? And I know you will."

"No, you don't. But OK . . . if we did, we'd work something out. Mike really likes you — even though you were mean to him. Nobody's going to cast you into the wilderness. Please stop worrying."

She looks like the Red Sea has just parted in front of her.

Each year, the Southern Region Under-Twelve Chess Tournament is hosted by a different school. This year Faraday House has the honor — but not the junior school. The tournament has been assigned to the senior school because it has a hall big enough to accommodate the hundred or so contestants. This is of course good news for the three Faraday House children competing. They will be on their home turf.

Sam, Mum and I drop Rosie at the entrance to the lower school.

"Good luck, big brother."

"Thanks, little sister."

Rosie runs off and we walk the few hundred yards to the upper school. Part of me wishes that Mum hadn't insisted on coming. She's hitting the Rescue Remedy bottle every few minutes to calm her nerves and I can tell it's making Sam more anxious.

The lobby is a thicket of children — mainly boys — consuming high-energy drinks and huddling with their dads, who are handing out last-minute advice. In the alcove under the grand stone-and-iron staircase, Ginny is manning the refreshment table. There's a long queue and she appears to be on her own. I tell Mum I'd better see if she needs a hand.

"I'll come with you. I could do with a cuppa." She follows me. Sam follows her.

It turns out that the woman who agreed to be Ginny's helper has gone down with some bug. "Don't suppose you could help man the pumps?"

Ginny hands out tea, coffee, juice and doughnuts while I take the money. Mum slips behind the table and organizes her own cup of tea. I tell her there's a queue and she needs to get in line.

"But I thought I counted as friends and family."

Ginny says of course she does. Her tea is on the house. Mum sticks her nose in the air — purely for my benefit — and rejoins Sam on the other side of the table. Just then Bernie appears.

"You made it," Mum says.

531

"Of course I made it. I promised I would be here to wish Sam good luck and I never break a promise." He looks at Sam, "Hey, boy-chick, how's it going? Look at him. Tell me he doesn't already look like a grandmaster. You're gonna do great."

He's brought Sam provisions — two cream cheese bagels. Mum informs Bernie that Sam had a perfectly good breakfast, thank you very much, and he has a substantial packed lunch with him, which she prepared.

Bernie shrugs. Fine. So he'll eat the bagels. "Now remember what I told you," he says to Sam. "Be slow with your opening move. That psyches your opponent out, gets under his skin. . . . Get your pieces into the center early and don't charge around with your queen vacuuming up pawns."

"I know. You already told me a million times on the phone."

"It never hurts to hear it again. And bring out your knights before you develop your bishops . . . and bring your minor pieces out early on. . . ."

"OK, that's enough," Mum says. "The boy is nervous enough as it is. You need to let him be." Then she asks Sam if he'd like a doughnut to keep his energy up.

"But you said he'd only just had breakfast," Bernie says. "If he wants anything he can have a bagel."

"He doesn't want a bagel."

"What's wrong with a bagel?"

"Nothing's wrong with a bagel. I just think he'd prefer a doughnut."

Sam says he doesn't want either and says he's going for a pee.

At the same time I'm calculating the change from a twenty-pound bill, I watch Bernie lead my mother away from the refreshment table and out of earshot. He whispers something in her ear — confiding in her maybe.

I nudge Ginny. "I wonder what he's telling her. Maybe his hernia wasn't a hernia after all."

"I bet he's got an STD. I've read that these days they're rife among the elderly."

"Don't be daft. Why would he advertise the fact that he's got the clap? Plus Bernie's a nice man."

"That doesn't preclude him from thinking with his penis. . . . Now, will you please help me unpack this box of cups?"

Eventually the doors to the hall open and the children are asked to say good-bye to their parents. Mums and dads aren't allowed in because in previous years adults have been caught helping kids cheat. Sam has told me stories of parents trying to put off their child's opponent by laughing when he makes a move. He even saw one dad tapping his nostril to indicate to his son that he was making a bad move.

I'm fighting my way through the crowd to get to the doors and wish Sam good luck, but he's about to go in. Mum and Bernie are with him, pinching his cheeks and presumably telling him to give 'em hell. He catches my eye, waves and then makes a shooing motion. I suspect he doesn't want me there, making more fuss. I mouth, "Good luck," wave back and watch him stride into the hall. As a Faraday House kid, he won't be intimidated by its grandeur — the vaulted ceiling, oak paneling and Gothic stained glass windows. I suspect that the competitors from public schools are less comfortable. Sam sits down at a table in a long row of tables. A fair-haired girl about his age pulls out the chair opposite. The pair shake hands. To their side is a stop clock. When everybody is seated, the doors close. Inside, one of the organizers is welcoming them and going over the rules. "Right, if there are no questions, you may start your clocks."

Some parents wander off. I'm guessing they're the ones who are confident their kids won't be knocked out in the early rounds. Others — anxious to be there to wipe away the tears of defeat — kick around the lobby or take walks on the school grounds. Mum says that she and Bernie are going to pop to the day center for a couple of hours. They'll be back later. Since tea and coffee are still in demand, I decide to carry on helping Ginny man the refreshment counter. When we finally hit a lull, we sit ourselves down at the bottom of the staircase and drink tea.

"I can't tell you how glad I am that you and Mike have made up," she says. "Tanya and I were so upset when it looked like it had all gone pear-shaped."

"Not half as upset as I was."

"You are going to make each other very happy."

"I'd like to think so."

"You will. Mark my words." Then she gives me a nudge. "All shipshape in the bedroom department?"

"Excellent, thank you."

"Jolly good," she says with a wink. "Just checking. At our age, you never know."

"So . . . changing the subject, did you finish cleaning the house?"

"We most certainly did. And a thoroughly good job we made of it. I've even got somebody coming in to clean the carpets tomorrow." She takes a mouthful of tea. "Mum's left me the house, you know."

"Actually I did know. She mentioned it when I was there."

"And all her money."

"I knew that, too. So she told you. I'm glad. She wasn't planning on saying anything. And she made me promise to keep it a secret."

"Really? That doesn't surprise me. Why does she find it so much easier to open up to strangers? Anyway, she didn't exactly say anything to me. All she did was present me with a copy of her will."

"Oh, well . . . I suppose that's a gesture at least. Are you surprised she's left you everything?"

"I am. I always assumed she'd leave it to William . . . not that he needs it."

"That's what your mother said."

"It's funny . . . On one level, I'm overjoyed by what she's done. It's like winning the lottery. Lord only knows what that house must be worth — even though it's so rundown. Once I've sold it, I'll be able to help Emma get her business off the ground, buy her a house, me a flat . . . finally restore my bergère sofa. Gosh, I sound like I wish my mother dead, but you know what I mean."

"Of course I do . . . but you said you were

overjoyed only on one level."

"Yes, because the money doesn't make up for all the lost years. Given the choice, I would rather have had a mother who loved me."

"She did love you. She still does."

"How do you know?"

"Because she told me."

"Well, she hasn't told me."

"Then you'll have to take my word for it. She loves you very much."

"I wish she could tell me."

"Edith's not dead yet. She might open up."

"I doubt it."

"Then you have to accept that her way of telling you she loves you was to leave you all her money."

"Unless she's only done it to assuage her guilt."

"That's bound to be part of it. But it's not the whole story."

"Maybe you're right. I don't know. . . ."

"So, now that you've got all this money, I bet you start dating," I say.

"Excuse me. Where did that come from?"

"I don't know. It occurs to me that you might find yourself thinking differently about men now that you don't have to rely on one."

Ginny laughs and says she hasn't given it a moment's thought.

"I bet I'm right," I say.

"Who knows? If I've learned one thing lately, it's that life really is full of surprises."

I drain my teacup. "Ain't that the truth?"

Ginny's face brightens. "Oh, by the way, you'll love this. . . . So I told my son that Mum had left me all her money and five minutes later my snobby daughter-in-law is on the phone saying it's time Mason and Tyler got to know their cousin Ivo. Can you believe it? Now that I've moved up in the world, she wants us all to be friends. Suddenly we're socially acceptable. Ridiculous, pointless woman."

"What did you say?"

"What could I say? I want the cousins to know each other, too. And Ben has yet to meet his grandmother. So I was very gracious and said they should all come for tea. But part of me hopes that Mason and Tyler show Ivo how to set off fireworks."

"You are evil."

"I know."

This reminds me that Sam hasn't seen Mason and Tyler since the fireworks incident. I'm wondering if I can persuade him to warm to them again. I suggest to Ginny that we arrange another playdate.

"Judy, I know you mean well, but I don't think you should force it with Sam — and certainly not out of courtesy to me. I suspect he's still very angry with Mason and Tyler over the fireworks incident. Let Sam decide when he's ready. And who knows? After a few months at a new school my two might have turned over a new leaf."

So we agree that, for the time being, we won't upset the status quo.

After lunch, Mum reappears with Bernie. They want to know how Sam's doing. I tell them he's hanging in there. While Bernie nips to the loo and Ginny is refilling the tea urn with fresh water, I ask Mum if Bernie is OK.

"Of course he's OK. Why shouldn't he be?"

"It's just that I saw you two in a huddle earlier. I could be wrong, but I got the impression he was breaking bad news."

"He was breaking news. But it wasn't bad — at least not for him. He broke it off with Pearl."

"Why?"

"He realized she wasn't right for him. He said she was suffocating him. They'd only been going out a few weeks and already she was talking about getting married. . . . So he's asked me out on a date."

"Wow. That's wonderful. So, what did you say?"

"I said yes."

"So you admit you got him wrong."

"The man has his faults — don't we all? But the way he went out searching for Sam . . . the man's a prince and I told him so."

"He is. But it worries me that you'll always be disagreeing about this boxing issue."

"I also told him I'm never going to change my mind about it and that he can take it or leave it."

"And he said?"

"He said he'll take it. Says he doesn't like 'yes' women. He prefers a good sparring partner. He also said he was impressed how I diagnosed his umbilical hernia."

"Seriously? He found that sexy?"

"He likes the fact that I'm knowledgeable about health matters. He was even more impressed when the doctor confirmed my diagnosis. The doctor said it needs to be repaired, so he's booked him in for surgery. . . . So, it's a shame I wasted all that money on Estelle's dating site. But who cares? Bernie's taking me to a tea dance . . . at the Waldorf, would you believe? Apparently he's a great dancer. And you know what they say about men who can dance. . . ."

"I don't know. What do they say?"

My mother cackles and gives me a wink. "So I might start using my flat again after all. Just from time to time. So that Bernie and I can get a little privacy."

Sam makes it through to the last round but one. He comes in fourth in the tournament, which means no trophy. He's disappointed in himself — he brought his queen out too early in that final game. But he's glad it's over. Everybody is telling him that, bearing in mind what he's been through in the last few days, fourth place is a heck of an achievement. Bernie engages him in a bit of gentle bobbing and weaving and calls him champ.

"And by me, you're still a grand master," Mum says.

We're still congratulating him when Bogdan shows up. He says he's just finished tutoring a child a few streets away and thought he would drop by to see how Sam was doing.

"Now suddenly he's interested," Mum mutters. "He couldn't care less when Sam went missing. Didn't even pick up the phone."

"So you're Bogdan," Bernie says. "I've heard a lot about you. You'll be pleased to know that Sam came in fourth. Isn't that amazing?"

Bogdan's neck stiffens. His eyes widen. "Fourth? What are you telling me? How could he come in fourth?"

I tell Bogdan to ease up. "Please don't do this. You know what Sam's been through. He doesn't need more stress."

But Bogdan isn't listening. He's growling at Sam. "I thought you were a champion. Instead you blew it. So what went wrong?"

"I brought my queen out too early."

"Of course you did." Bogdan throws up his hands. "Why do you never listen? You are hopeless."

I get hold of Bogdan's arm. "OK. That's enough. I think you should leave."

He shakes me off. "You don't understand. I have reputation to think about. Now he ruins it. He should have won."

Sam is red with shame. I yell at Bogdan to get out. But he stays put, ranting about his ruined reputation.

Then it happens. Bernie with his broken nose from the night he beat Razor Robinson pulls himself up to his full six foot four and moves in on Bogdan. He towers over him.

"OK, sunshine. You've had your say. This is where it ends." The next second he has Bogdan in an armlock. Bogdan cries out with pain and starts swearing in Russian.

My mother swears back at him.

While parents and contestants watch, agog, Bernie manhandles a sniveling, protesting Bogdan toward the exit. My mother chases after them, waving her arms and still ranting in Russian. When they reach the door, Mum opens it and Bernie kicks Bogdan's backside, which has Sam in stitches.

Bernie rubs his hands and turns to Sam. "Take no notice of him. The man's a yutz."

"What's a yutz?"

"You don't want to know," Mum says, shooting Bernie a look. "It's a very bad word."

"Cool. I'll Google it when we get home."

By now Rosie has arrived. School is over and her teacher, Miss Carter, has escorted her to the upper school. I thank her, tell her that I was about to come and fetch Rosie, but she says she wanted to find out how Sam had done. But she barely gets a look-in congratulations-wise. Rosie's hero worship of her brother hasn't abated and she's hugging him and telling him to forget about the four Kinder Eggs he owes her.

Miss Carter says she's anxious to miss the

rush-hour traffic and should get going.

"Me, too," Bernie says. He's about to schlep out east to visit his daughter.

Rosie catches Mum planting a good-bye kiss on Bernie's lips and demands to know if he's her boyfriend.

"None of your beeswax, young lady," Mum says.

"He is. He is." Then she starts singing. "Nana's got a boyfriend. Nana's got a boyfriend."

After Bernie has gone, Sam looks thoughtful. He turns to Mum. "Nana, I've decided. No matter what you think, I want to ask Bernie to be my chess coach."

"I think it's a great idea," Mum says. "He thinks you're the cat's pajamas. Plus he's a born coach. He'd love it."

"But when I mentioned it before you said no."

"That was because I didn't know Bernie very well. I've changed my mind."

"Good. Because Bernie's great."

"Unlike that yutz Bogdan."

"Nana, you just said yutz."

"I know. I'm allowed. You're not."

I whisper to her that Abby and Tom might not approve of Sam being coached by Bernie. "I mean, he's hardly your conventional chess coach."

"Don't worry. You leave Abby and Tom to me."

Mum has hardly finished her sentence when Rosie starts squealing at the top of her lungs. "Mummee! Daddee!" Abby and Tom have just walked in. She charges toward them, followed by her brother. Their parents drop their rucksacks and open their arms. The children launch themselves with such gusto that Abby and Tom almost lose their balance. Mum and I watch the hugging, the hair ruffling, the swinging in the air.

Abby and Tom are frantically apologizing for missing the tournament. "We'd have been here an hour ago if it hadn't been for the damn traffic."

"Don't worry. It's OK," Sam says. "I came in fourth. I messed up in the last game 'cos I let my queen out too early. Are you disappointed?"

"Disappointed? How could we possibly be disappointed? Mum and I are really proud of you."

"Of course we are," Abby says. "Incredibly proud."

"But you're crying," Sam says, noticing the tears falling down his dad's face. "So's Mum."

Tom wipes his cheek. "Only because we're

so happy to see you guys."

"We've missed you so much," Abby says. "You've no idea."

"So we're still going to Disneyland Paris, right?" Rosie says. "Remember you signed an agreement."

"How could we possibly forget?"

Mum says Abby and Tom look thin and worn-out.

"So would you if you'd been through what they've been through." I take a breath. "Time for me to face the music, I guess. Do you think they'll forgive me for what happened to Sam?"

"Don't be daft. Of course they will. Anyway, once they hear the full story, they'll realize there's nothing much to forgive."

"I let him down. You never stopped believing in him."

"Oh, please. Enough already. You were worn-out. . . . I wasn't the one on the front line. Now stop fretting. Let's just go and say hello."

We approach gingerly, reluctant to disturb the family reunion. By now Abby is holding Rosie. Tom has Sam.

"Right," Abby is saying. "We want to hear all your news."

"There's loads and loads," Rosie says. "Sam and me have given up boring after-school clubs like French and Sam started firing a gun in class and he let off fireworks in the street. Then Seb said he stole an iPad but he didn't but then Sam ran away from home because he was so upset and the police came and they searched for him with helicopters and then they found him asleep on a train and he wants this man Bernie to be his chess coach 'cos he's more fun than Bogdan, who yells. Then Sam stole my Star of David and gave it back and Grandma has a boyfriend. It's Seb's granddad and they've been mouth-kissing, which is gross, and Nana has a boyfriend as well, and they've been mouth-kissing, too, which is even more gross. . . ."

ABOUT THE AUTHOR

Sue Margolis was a radio reporter for fifteen years before turning to novel writing. She is the author of *A Catered Affair, Coming Clean, Best Supporting Role,* and *Losing Me.* She lives in England with her husband and has three adult children and two grandchildren.

The employees of Thorndike Press hope you have enjoyed this Large Print book. All our Thorndike, Wheeler, and Kennebec Large Print titles are designed for easy reading, and all our books are made to last. Other Thorndike Press Large Print books are available at your library, through selected bookstores, or directly from us.

For information about titles, please call:
(800) 223-1244

or visit our website at:
gale.com/thorndike

To share your comments, please write:
Publisher
Thorndike Press
10 Water St., Suite 310
Waterville, ME 04901